Featured in *The Starry Rift*:

Stephen Baxter
Cory Doctorow
Greg Egan
Jeffrey Ford
Neil Gaiman
Kathleen Ann Goonan
Ann Halam
Margo Lanagan
Kelly Link
Paul McAuley
Ian McDonald
Garth Nix
Alastair Reynolds
Tricia Sullivan
Scott Westerfeld
Walter Jon Williams

ANTHOLOGIES BY JONATHAN STRAHAN

Best Short Novels: 2004
Best Short Novels: 2005
Science Fiction: The Very Best of 2005
Fantasy: The Very Best of 2005
Best Short Novels: 2006
The Best Science Fiction and Fantasy of the Year: Volume 1
Best Short Novels: 2007
Ascendancies: The Best of Bruce Sterling
Eclipse: New Science Fiction and Fantasy
The Best Science Fiction and Fantasy of the Year: Volume 2
Godlike Machines
The Starry Rift: Tales of New Tomorrows
Eclipse 2: New Science Fiction and Fantasy

WITH CHARLES N. BROWN

The Locus *Awards: Thirty Years of the Best in Fantasy and Science Fiction*

WITH JEREMY G. BYRNE

The Year's Best Australian Science Fiction and Fantasy: Volume 1
The Year's Best Australian Science Fiction and Fantasy: Volume 2
Eidolon 1

WITH TERRY DOWLING

The Jack Vance Treasury

WITH GARDNER DOZOIS

The New Space Opera

WITH KAREN HABER

Science Fiction: Best of 2003
Science Fiction: Best of 2004
Fantasy: Best of 2004

FIREBIRD

WHERE SCIENCE FICTION SOARS™

The City, Not Long After	Pat Murphy
The Ear, the Eye and the Arm	Nancy Farmer
Enchantress from the Stars	Sylvia Engdahl
Epic	Conor Kostick
Escape from Earth: New Adventures in Space	Jack Dann and Gardner Dozois, eds.
The Far Side of Evil	Sylvia Engdahl
Firebirds Rising: An Anthology of Original Science Fiction and Fantasy	Sharyn November, ed.
Firebirds Soaring: An Anthology of Original Speculative Fiction	Sharyn November, ed.
House of Stairs	William Sleator
Interstellar Pig	William Sleator
Journey Between Worlds	Sylvia Engdahl
Moon-Flash	Patricia A. McKillip
The Mount	Carol Emshwiller
Saga	Conor Kostick
Singing the Dogstar Blues	Alison Goodman

THE STARRY RIFT

TALES OF NEW TOMORROWS

AN ORIGINAL SCIENCE FICTION ANTHOLOGY

edited by

JONATHAN STRAHAN

FIREBIRD

AN IMPRINT OF PENGUIN GROUP (USA) INC.

FIREBIRD
Published by the Penguin Group
Penguin Group (USA) Inc., 345 Hudson Street, New York, New York 10014, U.S.A.
Penguin Group (Canada), 90 Eglinton Avenue East, Suite 700, Toronto, Ontario, Canada M4P 2Y3
(a division of Pearson Penguin Canada Inc.)
Penguin Books Ltd, 80 Strand, London WC2R 0RL, England
Penguin Ireland, 25 St Stephen's Green, Dublin 2, Ireland (a division of Penguin Books Ltd)
Penguin Group (Australia), 250 Camberwell Road, Camberwell, Victoria 3124, Australia
(a division of Pearson Australia Group Pty Ltd)
Penguin Books India Pvt Ltd, 11 Community Centre, Panchsheel Park, New Delhi - 110 017, India
Penguin Group (NZ), 67 Apollo Drive, Rosedale, North Shore 0632, New Zealand
(a division of Pearson New Zealand Ltd.)
Penguin Books (South Africa) (Pty) Ltd, 24 Sturdee Avenue, Rosebank, Johannesburg 2196, South Africa

Registered Offices: Penguin Books Ltd, 80 Strand, London WC2R 0RL, England

First published in the United States of America by Viking,
a member of Penguin Group (USA) Inc., 2008
Published by Firebird, an imprint of Penguin Group (USA) Inc., 2009

1 3 5 7 9 10 8 6 4 2

THE LIBRARY OF CONGRESS HAS CATALOGED THE VIKING EDITION AS FOLLOWS:
The starry rift: tales of new tomorrows: an anthology of original science fiction / edited by Jonathan Strahan.
p. cm.
Contents: Ass-hat magic spider / by Scott Westerfeld—Cheats / by Ann Halam—Orange / by Neil Gaiman—The surfer / by Kelly Link—Repair kit / by Stephen Baxter—The dismantled invention of fate / by Jeffrey Ford—Anda's game / by Cory Doctorow—Sundiver Day / by Kathleen Ann Goonan—The dust assassin / by Ian McDonald—The star surgeon's apprentice / by Alastair Reynolds—An honest day's work / by Margo Lanagan—Lost continent / by Greg Egan—Incomers / by Paul McAuley—Post-ironic stress syndrome / by Tricia Sullivan—Infestation / by Garth Nix—Pinocchio / by Walter Jon Williams
ISBN 978-0-670-06059-7 (hardcover)
1. Science fiction. 2. Children's stories. [1. Science fiction. 2. Short stories.] I. Strahan, Jonathan.
PZ5.S7965 2008 Fic—[dc22} 2007032152

ISBN 978-0-14-241438-5
Printed in the United States of America

For Marianne, Jessica, and Sophie,
who make every day a joy,
and
For Sharyn,
who understood the adventure that this book could be, and
gave me the chance to take it

THE STARRY RIFT

TALES OF NEW TOMORROWS

CONTENTS

INTRODUCTION

Jonathan Strahan

If anyone ever lived a science fictional life, it was the writer Jack Williamson. He was born in Bisbee, Arizona, in April 1908, almost exactly one hundred years ago, and died in Portales, New Mexico, in 2006. During his lifetime, the world changed unimaginably. As a young boy, he and his family traveled in a covered wagon from western Texas to their new homestead in New Mexico in 1915. It was just twelve years after the Wright Brothers first flew at Kitty Hawk; commercial radio broadcasts in the United States were still five years away (and television decades away); and women were still denied the right to vote. The twentieth century—sometimes called the "American Century" because of its love for technology, and because of America's growing economic and political dominance of the world's stage—had hardly begun, and yet in less than twenty years, Williamson would become an active participant in the evolution of modern science fiction. He and his contemporaries spun tales of interstellar adventure where galaxies collided, worlds exploded, brave heroes won out against incredible odds, and beautiful damsels were rescued from the clutches of terrible aliens—tales of pioneers and far frontiers from a man who had been a pioneer and traveled to at least one frontier himself. By the time his career was over, mankind would have split the atom, walked on the moon, ventured into outer space using robotic probes, invented devices smaller than the eye could see, slowed light itself to a standstill, and created a worldwide web of information and communications that reached into almost every household.

The story of Jack Williamson's life, his particularly *science fictional* life, is also the story of science fiction itself. Although people think that science fiction is about the future, it's not. Like all fiction, it's about its own time. It's about the world we live in—what we think and feel about it, and how we think or fear it might change in the coming years. The stories that Williamson and other writers like him (E. E. "Doc" Smith, A. E. van Vogt, Isaac Asimov, and L. Sprague de Camp) wrote before 1945 were published in cheap magazines[1] that were garish and brash but very much of their time.

Golden Age science fiction,[2] as it is known, reflected the attitudes of the first half of the American Century. It was forward-looking, confident, ultimately optimistic writing that put its faith in technology and the abilities of practical people to solve problems. It was also unlike other popular fiction of the time—particularly Westerns and adventure stories, both of which grew out of a similar pulp tradition—because it made heroes out of thinkers and scien-

---

1 Called "pulps," they were printed on cheap paper made from wood pulp.

2 The Golden Age of science fiction was the period from the late 1930s or early 1940s through the 1950s, when the science fiction genre first gained wide public attention and many classic science fiction stories were published. Many of today's most popular movies, from *Star Wars* to *I, Robot*, feature stories very much like those of the Golden Age.

tists. Traditionally, engineers and scientists have always been avid science fiction readers in their youth.

All this changed at the end of World War II. The *Enola Gay* dropped the first atomic bomb on Japan—the first atomic bomb ever used in warfare—thus ending the war and inaugurating what became known as the Cold War.[3] Technology and the people who created it became things to be feared, more likely to destroy our world than to save it.

People began to worry that progress might come at a high price. Nuclear power meant cheap electricity, but the threat of massive destruction always loomed. Computers could vastly increase our ability to learn and make decisions, but what if they decided to take over the world? New medical procedures could extend our lives, but what about overpopulation? Even everyday technologies like automobiles and manufacturing plants could provide jobs and prosperity but also lead to global warming.

By the mid-1960s, questions like these began to appear in darker, more pessimistic science fiction stories like John Brunner's *The Sheep Look Up,* Philip K. Dick's *The Man in the High Castle*, and J. G. Ballard's *The Drowned World.* And by the 1980s, when Margaret Thatcher had become the prime minister of England and Ronald Reagan was elected president of the United States, science fiction writers also seemed to have become much more aware that the political decisions we make today can radically affect our possible futures.

It was around this time that British writers like M. John Harrison

3 The Cold War was a period of conflict, tension, and competition between the United States and the Soviet Union and their allies that started in the mid-1940s and only ended in the early 1990s with the collapse of the Soviet Union. It reached its height in the late 1960s and early 1970s.

and Iain M. Banks began to rethink the whole genre, retaining its bright, shiny surface while adding depth, complexity, and more critical political and economic themes to the mix[4]. Books like Harrison's 1975 novel *The Centauri Device*, which was intended to "end space opera,"[5] and Banks's 1987 novel *Consider Phlebas*, which reinvigorated it, are prime examples. In the United States, writers like William Gibson, with his classic 1984 novel *Neuromancer*, and Bruce Sterling, with 1985's *Schismatrix* and his Shaper/Mechanist stories, were taking a different tack, exploring the dark, gritty world of cyberpunk, where technology was hijacked by the street and the first glimmerings of the Internet were imagined. Science fiction readers, who once showed up at conventions in skinny ties and sport jackets, were now more likely to be outfitted in black leather and mirrored shades.

Today science fiction continues to change. It is, after all, an ongoing conversation about what's happening in the world we live in and where we're going. It's often been said that we can choose *where* we live but not *when* we live—the future is where we're all going to end up together, and it's a future that we're creating right now, with every decision we make.

If that's true, then it's important that we hear the stories science fiction has to tell now. At a time when a major American city was only recently almost destroyed by an enormous hurricane, when international political and religious unrest seems to be spiraling ever more out of control, and when technology is getting stranger and

4 Science fiction has always dealt with political and economic themes—you need only look back to satires like Frederik Pohl and C. M. Kornbluth's *The Space Merchants* from 1953 to see that—but these themes seemed to become more prominent, more overtly discussed, in the 1970s and 1980s.

5 *Space opera* is a term used to describe the old-fashioned space adventure story.

more mysterious, we need to hear tales written today that ask serious questions about the world we are living in and the world we might face.

I turned to a handful of the best writers in the field, asking them to write stories that would offer today's readers the same kind of thrill enjoyed by the pulp readers of over fifty years ago. The futures we imagine today are not the same futures that your grandfather's generation imagined or could have imagined. But some things in science fiction remain the same: the sense of wonder, of adventure, and of fearlessly coming to grips with whatever tomorrow may bring. Some of the stories here are clearly the offspring of those grand old space adventure tales, but others imagine entirely new and unexpected ways of living in the future. *The Starry Rift* is not a collection of manifestos—but it is both entertainment and the sound of us talking to tomorrow.

Jonathan Strahan
Perth, Western Australia
November 2007

ASS-HAT MAGIC SPIDER

Scott Westerfeld

Four hours before takeoff I was in the gym. Two T-shirts to catch the sweat, a plastic slicker over that, and a hoodie on top of everything. I was the only person in that corner of the gym—the one with floor-to-ceiling windows—and the aircon was hardly denting the sunlight streaming in.

Of course, the sun wasn't hitting my skin, all covered up like that. Direct sunlight keeps you from sweating, which is why desert nomads wear long robes.

There on that stair-climber, I imagined myself a Bedouin crossing the Sahara, looking for somewhere to fill my canteen. But I guess there aren't too many stairs in the desert, and I bet Bedouins don't wear black hoodies, and I knew it was about a 100 percent certain I'd never see the Sahara.

Of course, Tau IV has its own deserts, and we can name them whatever we want. The New Sahara. The Ass-hat Desert. That Big Sandy Place Over There.

• • •

That morning I'd weighed myself, hoping that I'd mystically shed four and a half pounds while I'd slept. (Or, as I was supposed to start saying once we got to Tau IV, two kilos.) No such luck. Me and Charlotte were still seventeen hundred grams overweight.

Crap.

So I cursed the extra three inches I'd grown that year, then sat down to a hearty breakfast of one tablespoon (oops, eight grams) of peanut butter. For dessert I gargled with water. Sweet, sweet water. Source of life, and three-quarters of my horrible, unlosable weight.

(Here's a trick: If you gargle, your throat won't know you're dehydrated. Just make sure you spit the water out.)

Next, I put some sunscreen on my lips to keep them from cracking; if the colony-ship docs thought I'd been cutting too much weight before the launch, they'd hook me up to an IV and pump me back to hydration. Maybe add as much as half a kilo of water and sugar to my mass.

And that would mean leaving Charlotte behind.

Two hours before the weigh-in, I checked myself again. The scale at the gym was mega-sensitive, almost as precise as the machine I'd be facing at the weigh-in. It showed me still four hundred grams over, even after I'd stripped down to shorts. Of course, about a hundred grams of that was the sweaty shorts, but that was almost exactly what Charlotte weighed, so the two balanced out.

I was still screwed. The hair had to go.

Now, as you know from pictures, a lot of colonists were shaving their heads. (And shaving a lot more, which, at thirteen, thankfully wasn't an issue for me.) A few of them had even plucked their eyebrows so they could bring another gram of diamonds or private diary storage or hundred-year-old whiskey along. But those first few weeks on Tau were going to include a lot of hard physical labor, everyone knew, and evolution put those eyebrows up there to keep the sweat out of your eyes. Remove them at your own risk.

By that time I hated the sauna, for smelling like chlorine and desperation, and for curling up all my books as I read them for the last time. So I did the deed in the shower, clumsily chopping at my shoulder-length hair with scissors, then shaving the rest. From the mirror, a horrible fish-boy stared back at me, an appalled expression on his face. Blood oozed from a few spots, which grossed me out until I realized that blood must *weigh something*.

Clever me, bleeding.

And the whole time I was thinking about how my mom was going to *freak*. She'd made me promise not to do this. But what was she going to do, ground me? I was stuck inside a spaceship for the next two subjective years anyway, not to mention being a Popsicle.

After the hair massacre, on went fresh T-shirts and plastic pull-over and hoodie (the hood of which now rubbed freakily against my bare and sweating head), and I climbed more stairs until it was time for my appointment. The whole time my imagination ran rampant with feasts of potatoes and toast covered with jam, cheeseburgers and apple pie. Anything but peanut butter, plain lettuce, and salt-free pickles.

And for dessert, giant glasses of water, swallowed all the way down to the cracking desert at my core.

But on my last trip to the scale, I found I'd hit the target, and pulled Charlotte out of my bag for a little victory dance.

⁂

For those last weeks, I remembered this golden rule: every bite of food was actually massive amounts of rocket fuel.

Here's how it works: Every gram that goes to Tau requires five grams of fuel to get it up to light speed. This is one-fifth Isaac Newton's fault, and the rest is because of the inefficiency of the colony ship's engines.

But it doesn't end there. You see, the ship doesn't burn its fuel all at the beginning of the trip. So the fuel it's burning, say, halfway there has to be brought along. Which means the ship needs more fuel to push that fuel that far in the first place, see? On top of which, you need fuel to move the fuel that carries the fuel . . .

And then when finally you get halfway to Tau IV, you're going to need the same amount of fuel to slow you down, so you don't whip past your goal. So you have to count on all the extra fuel to get that fuel halfway there . . . and all the infrastructure to move all this fuel around, and spare parts and crew to fix all this infrastructure when it breaks, all of which need more fuel to push them all the way to Tau System.

Every gram of passenger or luggage turns into kilos and kilos of fission stuff, and that's why I was cutting weight.

When you see pictures of the *Santa Maria*, you'd think it would be so huge and luxurious inside. Guess what? It was one big fuel tank, with a tiny box attached full of short, skinny, hungry, hairless colonists.

After much debate, the weight limit was fixed per person: your body weight and any luggage combined, no matter what size you are. Everyone has the same number of genes, they said, and that's all that counts when it comes to long-term survivability. Tall and fat people need not apply.

So most of the colonists were short. My mom's really short, and I was too back when we took our emigration tests. Didn't count on growing three inches (seven point five centimeters, excuse me for living) in the year since then. And every centimeter I grew meant throwing away one more thing from my personal allowance: my Sennheiser earbuds, my pen and paper diary, even the old chemical photo of my (tall-gened) father, all of them cut.

All I had left was Charlotte.

I would have been sweating, if there'd been any H_2O left in me.

The guy looked like a wrestler, with no neck and a body that was *way* over the colonist limit. He must have hated us; at his size, he was never getting any closer to Tau IV than this shuttle pad.

He looked at me, naked and clutching Charlotte to my chest, and scowled.

"Damn, you're skinny."

I tried to shrug. "I grew a lot this year."

"Let me see your hand, kid."

I reached out, not quite sure what he was up to and trying to ignore the fact that my fingers were shaking. He gripped the webbing between my thumb and forefinger and pinched brutally.

"Ow!"

"Shut up." He peered at the webbing, which had turned a horrible pale color in the weigh-in room's bright lights. It took several long seconds to turn pink again.

"You're dehydrated," he pronounced.

"Am not!"

He snorted and pulled a plastic cup from the stand beside the scale. "You want to pee in this for me, kid?"

I swallowed. After a week of seriously cutting weight, you don't pee a lot. And when you do, it's yellow and nasty and burns like Tabasco coming out. "I just went. You know, didn't want to be over." I said this casually, like the whole weight thing had only occurred to me five minutes ago, though my bald and scabby head was kind of a giveaway.

He let out a long hiss through his teeth. "You colonists. Luckiest people on the planet, and still you got to steal."

"Steal? I'm not stealing anything."

"Think about it, kid. You're going to eat like a pig when you wake up. And that food is weight that had to be carried there, more fuel that us on Earth had to pay for."

"Yeah, well." I hadn't thought about it that way. Or rather, I had, but then my mom had explained why she was dieting to bring another few grams of diamonds. "Everyone's doing it. It's kind of, like, built into the formula."

He snorted. "If you weren't just a kid, I'd call the docs and have you hooked up." He gestured at Charlotte. "Then you'd have to leave that . . . what the hell is that, anyway?"

I didn't react, and he snapped his fingers. Slowly, and with a horrible feeling that he was going to get finger-grease all over Charlotte and make her slightly *heavier*, I handed her over.

He let out a laugh. "An old book?"

"Yeah," I said. "I used to have hundreds of them. That's the last one."

"Collector, huh?"

"Reader. Familiar with the concept?"

He laughed again. "Hey, don't get all tough on me, kid. I might get scared and have to snap your dehydrated little ass in half. Kind of like a pretzel stick. Or would you be all chewy inside, like beef jerky?" He rifled through the pages. "Come on, kid. You're all smart and stuff, passed all those tests. What do you think dehydrated guts would look like?"

"I think you're an ass-hat," I said.

He looked straight at me, a faint smirk on his face. I held his stare, which was pretty tricky, what with me being naked and hairless and trying to steal from humanity.

But I won the staring contest, and finally he let out a sigh, handing back Charlotte. "On the scale, kid."

He wasn't going to bust me. I swallowed, my parched throat crinkling like wrapping paper inside me, and stepped on. The red numbers spun in front of my eyes for a second, then steadied . . .

Fifteen grams over.

"*What?* But the scale at the gym said . . ."

He sighed. "Yeah. Been hearing that one all day."

"But that's not fair!"

"Hmm, I suppose not. But you know what? *This* scale is calibrated to the one that the universe uses. The one that will decide whether you lucky colonists will wake up on Tau or just float like Popsicles for eternity. So if I were you, I'd be *glad* this scale was a little better than the one in the gym."

"But what am I supposed to do?" I cried.

He handed me a plastic cup. "Spit. Or pee, I don't care. Fifteen grams ain't much."

I tried to spit, but my mouth was as dry as the Ass-hat Desert.

"You want me to make you cry, kid? Tears must weigh something."

I scowled at him, realizing that my eyes were in fact burning. But I was too dehydrated to turn my anger and shame into salt water. Salt traps water weight, and I hadn't eaten anything salty in a month.

"I can't spit."

He shrugged. "Why you need that book, anyway? It'll be in the ship's memory, even if it's porn."

"It's *not* porn. And it's not the same in memory."

He pulled it from me again and flipped through the pages. "Must be some book. What's it about, anyway?"

"A spider," I said. "And a pig."

"Sounds kinky," he chuckled. "And you're *sure* it's not porn?"

"No, I mean yes, I'm sure." I groaned. A few more minutes with this guy and I *was* going to cry. I wondered how many tears were fifteen grams.

"So, what's it about?"

I wondered if I was losing weight just standing here, my anger and frustration burning away the micrograms. "The pig is going to get eaten at Christmas, and the spider makes a web saying it's great."

"What's great? Getting eaten?"

"No, the pig. Like, the spider puts a message in the web saying, 'Terrific.' So nobody eats the pig."

"So the spider's magic?"

"No! The spider's not magic."

"So, how come it knows how to spell?"

I sighed. "Well, I guess it is *sort* of magic. But not in a major way. It just makes the web because it has to, otherwise the pig's going to get eaten."

"And the spider cares about this pig why?"

"Because they're friends," I said. My eyes were burning like chili peppers now, but still no tears came.

He leafed through the book some more. "Look, whatever, kid. I admit this thing's got a nice feel. Never read anything this way, myself. But you could pull the covers off, you know? That would cut some weight. All the words will still be there."

I clenched my fists. "No, I'm *not* pulling the covers off."

He fondled the dust jacket. "Hey, this paper wrapper comes off. That might help."

"*Put that back!* I'm not taking it without the dust jacket."

"And look, there's all these pages before the story starts, and a bunch of blank ones at the end. Man, they had trees to burn back then! You could tear those out."

"I'm not tearing *anything* out, okay? We've got to find a way to make *me* weigh less, not the book. What if I hold my breath?"

He laughed. "The air in your lungs doesn't hardly weigh anything, kid." He looked at his watch. "And I don't have all day. Got a shuttle to load."

I looked down at my fingernails, which were already cut down to the quick. I wished I had hair on my arms or my chest, so I could shave that off right now. I visualized myself running a few more dozen flights of stairs or eating one less tablespoon of peanut butter, hoping my brain could burn the calories with imaginary exercise.

"Listen, kid. The next time you wake up, you're going to be a hundred years of light-speed travel from the nearest other bunch of humans, on a planet that can barely support you. No hospitals, no police, no one to call for help. And *this* is the kind of book you want to bring? One about magic spiders?"

"That's *exactly* the book I want to bring," I said. And finally, I realized that I was going to have to tear Charlotte up and leave part of her behind. She was first edition, perfect except for the slightest foxing on the upper left of page eighty-six. And I felt a single hot tear float down my cheek. I started to reach for it.

"Don't, kid." He grabbed my wrist. "Your fingertips are so dry, they'll suck it back up." And he reached out and flicked the tear from my face with his thumb. Then he handed me the book. "Get on the scale again."

"Doesn't matter." I closed my eyes, wondering if ripping off just the back cover would be enough. "No tear is going to weigh fifteen grams."

"Quit wasting my time, kid. Get on the scale." He held out his hand and pulled me on.

My head was already dizzy from all the exercise that morning, from a week of dehydration and my nerves about the launch, and from the fact that my collection had gone from whole shelves full to just one book, and now that was going to be mutilated.

I didn't notice at first that he hadn't let go of my hand.

"Hey, look, kid. You're right on target."

I opened my eyes. The red numbers weren't quite steady, but they shimmered just under the allowance. My hand, resting in his, felt the slightest upward pressure. He clicked a foot switch, nailing the red numbers right where they belonged.

"Okay, kid. Get your butt on board."

I stepped off, then paused for a moment, wondering if this was really a good idea. "What about the universe? What about slowing down on the other side?"

He laughed. "Last few guys before you were under by a few grams. Most people are. Your mom's right. It is kind of worked into the formula, but we couldn't *tell* anybody that."

"Oh. But why did you . . . ? Why me?"

He laughed. "Because I'm an ass-hat magic spider, kid. And you are the saddest little pig I ever saw."

So, yeah, that's the other story I've been meaning to tell you. It's probably why I've read you this one novel so many times, even though your mom thinks it'll turn you into a vegetarian. And why you're called Wilbur, instead of some name you'd probably like a lot more. And it's also why you don't get to touch this book—*the* book, the only real one on this whole planet, I'll have you know—until you're old enough not to get finger-grease on it. Because it's a *perfect* book, except for the slight foxing on page eighty-six, and it's at exactly the right weight, right now.

SCOTT WESTERFELD was born in Texas in 1963. He studied at Vassar College and has worked as a software designer, a composer, and is now a full-time writer. His first novel, *Polymorph*, was published in 1997 and was followed by *Fine Prey*, *Evolution's Darling* (a *New York Times* Notable Book, shortlisted for the Philip K. Dick Award), and *The Risen Empire*. His novels for teenagers include the Midnighters Trilogy (*The Secret Hour*, *Touching Darkness*, and *Blue Noon*) as well as *So Yesterday*, *Peeps*, *The Last Days*, *Uglies, Pretties*, *Specials*, and *Extras*. Westerfeld has also contributed essays to *Book Forum*, *Nerve*, and the scientific journal *Nature*. He and fellow writer Justine Larbalestier divide their time between New York, Sydney, and Mexico.

Visit his Web site at www.scottwesterfeld.com.

AUTHOR'S NOTE

While I was traveling for a few months recently, a friend stayed in my apartment. Upon my return, I found he'd left a scale behind in the bathroom. I started stepping onto it during the day, watching my weight change as things came and went from my body. I was more variable than I'd thought, pounds arriving and departing like subway trains.

It occurred to me that in certain situations, like space travel, exact mass is very important—every *gram* must be accounted for. And every time you sweat, spit, cut your hair, or blow your nose, your mass changes. So I began to wonder what space-exploring colonists might go through to leave behind just a little more of themselves, if it meant they could bring along just a bit more cargo. Which brought up the question, "What possession would it be worth diminishing your own body to keep?"

This story is my answer to that question.

CHEATS

Ann Halam

My brother and I were not lost. We'd hired our kayak from the stand at the resort beach; the kayak man had taken our names and set down where we said we'd be going. Plus the kayaks had world-map locators, what did you think? He could nail us anytime he liked. If we were stationary too long without an explanation, or if we went crashing into the reeds of the bird reserve, we were liable to get a page asking if we were okay or yelling at us to get out of there.

So we weren't lost, but we were *pretending* to be lost. The reeds were double as tall as either of us would have been standing, the channels were an eerie maze, and they seemed to go on forever. There was nothing but blond, rustling walls of reeds, the dark, clear water, occasionally a bird silhouette crossing the sky, or a fish or a turtle plopping. We'd take a different channel when we came to one we liked the look of, totally at random. It was hypnotizing and slightly scary because the silence was so complete. There were *things* in those reeds. You'd glimpse something, out of the corner of your eye, and it would be gone. Once there was a sly, sinister rustling that kept pace with us for a long time: *something* in there tracking us, watching us. We talked about making camp and would we ever find our way out and what would we do if the mystery *thing* attacked—

"If it bleeds," said Dev, in his Arnie accent, "we can kill it."

I had wriggled out of my place; I was lying along the front end of the kayak shell (you're not supposed to do that, naturally), peering down into the water. I could see big freshwater mussels with their mouths open on the bottom, breathing bubbles. We could eat those, I thought. Then I saw a gray-green *snake*, swimming along under the kayak, and that gave me a shock. It was big, about two feet long, easily.

"Wow," I breathed. "Hey, do you want a turn up front?" I didn't tell my brother about the snake, because there was no way he'd see it before it was out of sight, and I know how annoying that is.

My brother said, quietly, "Get back in the boat, Syl."

I got back and retrieved my paddle. I was in time to see what Dev had seen. We had company. Another kayak, a single seater, had appeared ahead of us, about thirty, forty yards downstream. Whoever was riding in it had customized the shell; it was no longer the plain red, orange, yellow, or green it must have been when it left the stand. It was black, with a white pattern, and it was flying, or trailing, a little pennant off its tail. Skull and crossbones. The person paddling was wearing feathers in his or her hair, and a fringed buckskin shirt.

"How totally infantile."

"Sssh. It's the cheat."

"Are you sure?"

"I have the evidence of my own eyes," said my brother, solemnly.

We *hated* cheats. We hated them with the set-your-teeth-and-endure-it hatred you feel for the sneaky kind of classroom bully, the kind who never does anything to bring the system crashing on their heads (no flick knives, no guns), but who is always breaking rules that everyone else respects. It makes you mad because you could break the rules yourself, it's not hard, it's not smart; only you choose not to. The cheaters could *always* get a high score, *always* solve the puzzle, *always* make it through the maze, and what's the point in that? Cheating might not seem an issue in the kind of place where we liked to play. But it ruined the whole atmosphere, running into someone with that attitude. You're not supposed to pop into existence, you're supposed to paddle to the reserve from the channel by the beach stand. So we were vindictive. We wanted to *get* this clown in the Indian brave costume and the pirate shell. We wanted him or her thrown out of our little paradise.

We gave chase. We stayed far enough behind to be out of sight. The water wasn't fast running; it was easy to control our pace—close enough to follow the other kayak's wake. All the lonely mystery was wrecked, of course. There were no more monsters stalking us. We were just two very annoyed kids. We followed that cheating kayak, and we followed it, completely fixated. We came to a dark-water crossroads we must have seen before but didn't remember, and saw the reeds, the water, the air, go into a quivering shimmer. The cheat turned around. I caught a flash of a face; it looked like an adult, but you can't tell. We didn't hesitate. When the pirate kayak vanished, we shoved on our paddles and zoomed straight into the flaw—

So then we were in another part of the reedbeds.

"Stupid pointless, stupid pointless, stupid pointless—" muttered Dev, grinding his teeth. We couldn't see any wake, because some kind of backwash was disturbing the channel. We pushed on, the reeds opened, and we were facing a shining lip, kind of a natural weir. The water beyond it was much shallower: white water, clamoring over pebbles. We stood our paddles vertical to brake ourselves.

"What'll we do?" whispered my brother.

"I dunno, I dunno. Could we carry this and wade?"

"I've got a better idea! Let's *split* the kayak!"

I thought this was brilliant. Get out of our shell, swim to the weir, carry it, splosh along over those pebbles; obviously, we were never going to catch our prey that way.

"What if there isn't enough information?"

"There's got to be. Logically, this is a thing that keeps two kids afloat, right?"

We didn't think we were in danger of getting a page from the kayak stand for this trick, as we knew we were off the map. It didn't cross our minds that we were in *actual* danger, although we were. We could go into anaphylactic shock if we hit a real physical limit off-map, and that's like your lungs filling with water, no word of a lie.

I said, *"Excellent!"* and we got out into the channel, first me, then Dev. We hung there in the cool depth, holding on to our paddles, treading water: looked at the code and worked out how to make the kayak split in two. It made itself a waist and sort of budded, was what it looked like. Then we each wrestled into our single shells, scooped out as much water as we could, and went skimming over that lip, down the white water, which was shallow as all hell, until it became deeper but still clamorous, swooshing around rocks. Dev was yelling, *Whoooooeee! HereIgo!* etc. I was silent. When I get thrilled I don't shriek, I just grin and grin until my face nearly comes in half. I got into a flow state, I could do no wrong, it was just wonderful.

We never knew when we'd popped back onto the map. We

came flying out of the white water into a much broader, quieter, deeper channel, and the landscape was all different, but still related. I dipped my hand in the water and tasted salt.

"I know where we are," I said. "Those are the dunes at the end of the resort beach; this is the fish river they have there. We can follow it to the sea and kayak back along the shore." My brother turned around in a big circle in the midstream. There was no sign of the cheat, not a whisker. He looked up at the clear blue sky.

"You know what we just did, Syl?"

"What?"

"We did a cheat. We can't turn the pirate in; we're guilty ourselves."

"We were off the map," I said. "It doesn't count."

"Does."

I knew he was right, by our own private laws, so I said, "The shell was a pirate, stupid. The cheat-guy was an Indian brave."

We did our splitting trick in reverse, faster this time: got away with it, and let the current carry us.

So there we were, my brother and I, not lost at all, just paddling along the shore. It was harder work, plugging through the choppy little waves, but we were fine, we had life jackets, and nobody had *told* us the ocean was out of bounds.

"What the hell's that?" demanded Dev.

That was a helicopter, going *rackety rackety rackety* and *buzzing* us, so we could hardly see for the spray its downdraft was kicking up. Then we saw the rescue service logo on its side, and we were indignant. Safety was not being served!

"What are you *doing*?" I yelled, waving my paddle. "You're a danger to shipping! You'll capsize us! Go away!"

"Go and play with your stupid flying machine somewhere else!"

Next thing, we got a page. The pilot was talking to us, ton-of-bricks-style.

The rescue service was looking for *us*. We'd failed to return our kayak, and we were hours overdue. So that was us hauled out of the ocean, scolded, sent home. Mom and Dad yelling at us, whole anxious parent, we trusted you, how could you do that?—

We made the right faces, said the right things, and let it all go over us.

When my brother was a little kid I played baby games with him all the time, the ones I'd loved when I was a little kid myself. We were candy-colored happy little animals, jumping the platforms, finding the strawberries and the gold coins; we dodged the smiley asteroids in our little spaceships; we explored jungles finding magic butterflies; we raced our chocobos . . . I'm naturally patient, and I love make-believe; I didn't mind. My parents used to say, *You don't have to babysit, Sylvie*, but I never felt it was a burden, or hardly ever. I taught him things that would stand him in good stead, and I was proud of how quick he was at picking things up. Dev is not naturally patient, but he *sees* things in a flash. We drifted apart when he was five, six, seven. Then one day when he was eight and I was twelve, he came to my room with his Tablo—the games platform small boys *had to have* at that time—and said he wanted me to play with him again.

"Girls don't play boy games," I told him (I was feeling a bit depressed that day). "Boys don't play girl games. We can't go around together, and we won't like the same things. You just want to share my hub access, why not say so?"

"We *do* like the same things," he said. "I miss you. No one I know *gets carried away* in a game the way you do. Please. I want you to take me with you."

So we compromised. I did let him share my hub access (with our parents' approval), and I let him use it without me. It's true, boy games mostly bore me. Racking up kills in the war-torn desert city, team sports (bleegggh!), racing cars, fighter jets . . . Leaves me cold. I think it's *because* I have the ability to get into a game and feel that it's real. I can be a commando, I can kill. But there has to be a gripping story to it, or you might as well be playing tic-tac-toe as far as I'm concerned. Managing a football team in real life would be my idea of hell, so why would I want to play at it? I want to play at things I would love to do. The cockpit of a fighter jet or a formula car? No, thank you! I don't want to be strapped down. I want to run, swim, use my arms and legs.

He plays with his friends; I play alone. But we have our best times when we're together. Unlike most people who are good at handling code (I taught him that), we're not geeks. We don't think of it as taking a machine apart. The code is like our magic powers. Or our survival lore in the wilderness. Do you know how to make a fire without matches? I do. And it's *logic.* It's not a dumb secret word left lying around for me to find. It'll work with just about any game engine.

Our parents didn't ground us after the rescue helicopter incident. They just reproached us and were sad and played all the tricks parents play to make you feel guilty and get you back on the leash. But everyone seemed to take our word that we'd lost track of time, and for whatever reason the pages telling us we were overdue had not reached us. This told us something interesting. Our trip off the map *had not been logged* on the working record of the resort. The management and our parents were prepared to give us the benefit of the doubt over those missed pages, but if they'd known we'd disappeared off the face of the resort world-map, for two extra hours, that would have been a big deal.

We did a lot of thinking about those mystery missing hours. My brother came up with the idea that it was a time glitch, and when we'd been in that unmapped sector we'd been slowed down without realizing it—

He sat on the end of my bed, scrunching up his face. "Or speeded up," he added. "Whichever works."

I didn't tease him. Speeded up/slowed down is like "What time is it in Tokyo?"; it's hard to keep it straight in your head. "Except that we were in real time, bro. We weren't cruising around the Caribbean, were we? We were at *the resort*."

It's a basic venue, no frills. You go there and it's exactly like a day by the sea, with gentle "wilderness" areas like our reedbeds. You stay for exactly the time it feels like, which is the starter level, safest way to play total immersion games. The resort's meant for families with little kids. We just like it.

"Maybe we really did lose track of time," said Dev.

But I knew we hadn't. Something had happened when we went through that flaw, something sly and twisted. "No. There's something screwy going on."

These cheats who'd been annoying us were not normal cheats. Nothing like the legendary girl (supposed to be a girl, but who knows) called Kill Bill, who had wasted thousands of grunts in Amerika Kombat, and who never seemed to tire of her guaranteed headshots: when one server threw her out, she'd log on to another.

We'd seen our characters at combat venues, and they were cheating-good at racking up. But they weren't obsessed with high scores, of any kind. They mainly tended to turn up in our favorite freestyle adventure venues, *doing impossible things*. We thought there were three of them. Their fancy dress varied, but there were three costumes that seemed to be the default. We thought they were kids. Adults who spend as much time as my brother and I lying around playing computer games are usually very sad, and these people were not *sad*, they were smart. Just very, very irritating. We'd been talking for ages about getting them thrown out of the hub. But when we put our complaints together, and thought about paging the hub sysop, we knew it sounded futile. No adult would understand about a wrecked atmosphere or the sacredness of respecting the reality of a make-believe environment. It was a victimless crime.

"They put our lives at risk," suggested my brother. "Tempting us to go off the map like that. We could have got drowned and gone into shock."

Neither of us like the sound of that. It was whiny and stupid.

We felt we had to lie low, so we couldn't go back to the resort reedbeds to see if that flaw was still there and try going through it again. Dev wanted to do a massive search through every location where we'd spotted them, and keep tracking around and around until we nailed them again. But I said *wait*. Chances are they've spotted us, the same way we've spotted them. Don't draw attention, wait for an opportunity.

We were snowboarding in a place called Norwegian Blue. We were on a secret level, but not off the map: cross-trekking over tableland to reach the most incredible of the black slopes. Including one with a near vertical drop of a thousand feet into a fjord, and halfway down you hit the trees and you had to slalom like a deranged rattlesnake—an unbelievably wonderful experience.

It was night, blood-tingling cold under frosty stars. Everything was blue-tinged, otherworldly. We talked about deranged rattlesnakes, snowland bivvy building, triple flips, trapping for furs. New angles we might be able to wrangle with Norwegian Blue code; things we better not try. And, of course, the cheats.

"I'm beginning to wonder if we're getting stalked," I said as we scooted our boards one-footed up a long, shallow slope. "We keep running into these same people, lurking in our 'scapes? Maybe there's a reason. Maybe they're following us around. But why? It's starting to feel weird."

The tableland was a sea of great smooth frozen snow-waves. We reached a crest, rode on our bellies down the scarp, sailed far out into the hollow between two waves, and started another slow ascent. The air smelled of snow, crisp frost dusted our eyelashes, and my leg muscles pumped, easy and strong. I was annoyed with myself for raising the subject. The cheats were here even when they weren't here: stealing the beauty, making us feel watched.

"It's not us," said Dev. "It's hub access. You couldn't do the kind of cheats they do on general-public access levels. You need rich code. That's why we keep running into them. Kill Bill can go on getting chucked off forever, there's millions of servers—"

"Yeah."

There's no such thing as getting banned from all the general access servers. Not unless you're an actual criminal, a child molester or something.

"Our cheats haven't got many venues to choose from, if they

want to fool around the way they do. It's our bad luck they happen to be the same venues that we like."

I told you: Dev sees things. It was obvious, and I felt stupid. Also slightly creeped, wondering if we were ever going to be free of this nagging intrusion—

The black silhouette of another trekker appeared, off to our left, beyond the ice field that was the danger zone on this cross-trek, the place you had to avoid ending up. I knew it had to be one of them. I hissed at Dev, *"Look!"*

We dropped to the snow, and I pulled up our powerful binoculars.

"It's Nostromo," I breathed. "Take a look."

One of the three default costumes was white overalls, with grease stains, and a NOSTROMO baseball cap. That's what this guy was wearing, in the middle of the snowy Norwegian wilderness. Dev took a look, and we grinned at each other.

"We have a deserter from that space freighter in *Alien*."

We'd played Alien Trilogy Remastered, but maybe Dev had been too young, and the horror immersion effects too strong. Mom and Dad had put the *Dev wakes up screaming; we find this antisocial* veto on it, to my regret.

"Lost on this icy planet," agreed Dev. "Unknown to him, he is being watched!"

"If you can't beat 'em, join 'em," I whispered, meaning: we can't ignore them, but we *can* turn them into characters in our plot. We can hunt them down.

"If it bleeds, we can kill it," said Dev. "Do we have any weapons?"

"Soon can have," said I. "Let's arm ourselves."

I then tried to argue Dev out of the heavy hardware. I don't like guns. I prefer a knife or a garrote. "You can't cheat on the weight or you'll lose firepower."

"I *won't* slow us down. I'm very strong."

"Yes, you will, and anyway using guns at hub level is really bad for your brain. It wears out the violence inhibitors in your frontal lobes. They get fired up again and again, for no reason, and they don't understand."

"You talk about your brain as if it's a pet animal."

"At least my pet animal gets properly fed and looked after. *Yours* is starving in a dirty hutch with half a rotten carrot."

"*Your* brain is the brain of a sick, sick, blood-daubed commando."

"Yeah, well, I want to feel something when I kill someone. That's not sick, it's emotionally much more healthy than—"

We were having this charming conversation, pulling up our weapons of choice, cutting across to intersect with Nostromo's path, and still looking for one more beautiful belly-glide, all at the same time. If we'd been thinking, we'd have known that there had to be a flaw, and we were liable to run into it. If we'd been believing in the game, we would not have been scooting along side by side on an ice field. That's nuts. But we were distracted, and it just happened. A crevasse opened; we both fell into it, cursing like mad as the blue-white gleaming walls flew by. We pulled our ripcords, but the fall did not slow down. Instead, everything went black.

Black fade to gray, gray fade to blue. I sat up. I felt shaken and my head was ringing, but no bad bruises and no breakages. Health okay. Dev was beside me, doing the same check. Our snowboards lay near, looking supremely useless on a green, grassy field of boulders. The sky was more violet than blue, suggesting high altitude. The sun had an orangey tinge, and it felt hot, with the clear heat that you get in summer mountains. I had the feeling we were not in Norway anymore. The mountain peaks all around us, beautiful as any I'd ever seen, seemed far higher than that.

"Where are we?" gasped Dev. He was looking sick; the fall must have knocked more off his health than it had off mine. I thought I'd better pull up the first aid.

"South America," I guessed. "Up in the Andes. Or else a fantasy world."

"How are we going to get back?"

I thought that was a dumb question, and maybe he was stunned: then I realized I could not get at the first aid. I could not get at anything in my cache. I had the clothes I'd been wearing in Norwegian Blue, my knife, my garrote, and my vital signs patch. Nothing else—

"My God! They've wiped us!"

"Rebuild!" cried Dev, in a panic. "Rebuild! Quickly!"

But I couldn't rebuild. I couldn't get to the code. Nor could Dev. The world around us was solid, no glitches; nothing seemed to be wrong, but we were helpless.

We stared at each other, outraged. "This means war," I said through gritted teeth.

There wasn't a doubt in our minds that the cheats had done this. Nostromo had seen us chasing him, written that crevasse where we were bound to hit it, and wiped us down to zero. We got up and walked around, abandoning our useless boards. Dev threw rocks; I dug my hands into the crispy turf. It felt real the way only the best hub code feels: intense. The whole boulder field seemed to be live, none of it just decor.

"They're here somewhere," I said. "They have to be."

"They don't," said Dev, unhappily. "They could have dumped us here helpless and gone off laughing. Syl, *where are we*? I thought we knew all the hub venues, but I'm sure we've never been here before."

I wished I had the first aid. My brother wasn't looking good. I was afraid he would log out on me, and I knew I'd have to go home with him.

"C'mon, Dev. Get on the program. They lured us into this mountain world the way they lured us into the white water. Yeah, it's unfamiliar, but we didn't know there was white water in the resort reedbeds until we went through that flaw. These guys are good; they've found more secret levels than we have. But we're good too."

Something nagged at me, something bigger than I could believe, but I clung to my common sense. "This is a live area. There's probably stuff to do here, if we knew the game or if we had a guide. But there'll be ways out. We'll find one, figure out how to undo what they did to our cache, and get back on the bad guys' trail."

The orange sun moved toward its setting. We saw some weaselly sort of creatures, only with more legs, that watched us from a distance. We met huge golden-furred spiders, the size of a cat, who were shy but friendly. They'd come up to us and lay a palp—I mean, one of their front feet—on our hands, and look at us with big ruby eyes. They seemed to like being stroked and scratched behind their front eyes. We thought about eating the berries that grew on the crispy turf-stuff. We didn't find a flaw or a way out; we didn't stumble over any puzzles or hidden treasures, though we slapped and poked at hopeful-looking rocks until our hands were sore.

Finally we found the cheats. They were camped in a ravine on what I thought of as the southern end of the boulder field (in relation to that sunset). They had a little dome shelter, a hummocky thing thatched with the lichen—I couldn't see how it was held up. There was a fire in a circle of stones, a bucket on a flat rock by the stream that ran by their hideout. We were sick with envy. We didn't know how much real time had passed—the time counters on our vital signs patches had stopped when we fell in here—but it felt as if we'd been wandering, naked, clueless, unable to touch a line of code, for *hours.*

"Dev," I whispered, "you're going to go down there and tell them your sister is out on the hillside, health gone. Tell them you don't know what to do, because I'm refusing to log out, but I'm going into shock. White flag, surrender. Cry, if you can."

"That won't be hard."

"Okay, you bring one of them, and I'll be waiting in ambush."

"Pick them off one by one," he agreed. "Cool."

He was still looking sick, but he was back in the game. I remembered the flash of an adult face I'd seen in the reedbeds back at the resort, and I felt unsure. Had that been real or costume? *Usually* adults who play games obsessively are harmless losers, but there are the rare, supergeek predators, and they can use code; they don't have to wait until they can get you alone in the real world—

But we chose our ambush, and I felt better.

"Go on. Bring me back a fine fat cheat to choke."

The sun was darkening to blood color as it hit the horizon, and

I could feel the growing chill through my Norwegian Blue snowboarding clothes. I clung to the wire looped over my gloved hands, feeling weirdly that the garrote was part of me, a lifeline to the normal world, and if it vanished I would be trapped—

Dev came back up from the ravine, one of the cheats following close behind. It was the Native American one, now wearing a red-and-black blanket around his shoulders like a cloak. My brother looked very small and defenseless. Sometimes when I get to the point, it's hard to kill, but this time I had no trouble at all. I jumped, my wire snapped around the man's throat—but at the same moment somebody grabbed *me* from behind, by the forearms, and I had to let go or they'd have broken my bones. It was the Nostromo crewman. I screamed and I kicked and I yelled; it was useless. He held me off the ground and shook me like a rag doll, laughing.

They carried us down to their camp, tied us up, and sat looking at us, cross-legged, grinning in triumph. Their eyes glittered. Up close, I knew they *were* adults, and I was scared.

The pirate was a woman. She was about six feet tall. She had black hair that hung in wild locks from under her three-cornered hat, greenish brown eyes with kohl around them, and skin the color of cinnamon. She swept to her feet in one slick movement, grabbed my head, and stuck a slip of paper underneath my tongue.

"They're short of glucose," she announced. "Near to blacking out. What'll we do with them, Mister Parker? Qua'as?"

"I say we smoke a pipe of peace," said the Native American.

He didn't pull the pipe up. He fetched it from his pack, stuffed it from a pouch he wore at his waist, and lit it with a handful of the licheny stuff that he'd dipped in the flame of the brazier. My skin began to creep and my heart began to beat like thunder, and I didn't know why. "Mister Parker," the Nostromo crewman, cut our hands loose. The pipe went around and I drew in the "smoke." The sugar rush almost knocked me sideways, but I managed to keep a straight face.

"Oooh, that was restorative!" gasped the Nostromo crewman.

"Best drug in the universe," chuckled the pirate queen.

"Gonna be our *major* export one day—"

"Moron. The galaxy is full of sugars. My money's on Bach."

The three cheats laughed, high-fived each other, and kind of *sparkled*; and I understood why, because I desperately love and depend on glucose too. But the Native American looked at my brother and frowned. Dev was not looking restored.

We finished the pipe and the pirate queen put it aside.

"Now," she said, in a rich, wild, laughing voice. "I'm Bonny." She tossed back the lace at her cuff and tipped a lean brown hand to the man in the red-and-black blanket. "This is Qua'as, the Transformer. He's Canadian, but don't hold that against him, he's pretty cool; and Mister Parker, our engineer, you have met. So, who the devil are you, and why are you messing with us? Do tell."

"Get real," growled Mr. Parker, "if you'll pardon the expression. There are only, what is it? F-fourteen other people that you *could* be, assumin' you are not some kooky software dreamed up by Mission Control. So why the disguises? What the hell are you playing at? What was that with the *garrote*?"

"Did no one ever tell you, little sister," said Qua'as, "that only that which is dearest to your heart survives the drop back into normal space? What does that make you? A low-down disgusting violence perv? Eh? Eh?"

That was when I realized for the first time that I'd kept my weapons, but Dev's AK and ammo had gone when we were wiped to zero. I felt myself blush; I felt that Qua'as was right . . . I was so totally immersed in this game, so believing in it. I had the scariest feeling that I was *losing touch* with my physical self, back at home—

"Let us go!" cried Dev. "We're not afraid of you! We tracked you down! We'll turn you in to the sysop, the moment we log out!"

My brother's voice sounded thin and frail, a ghost's voice. But the cheats were glowing with life and strength and *richness.* They were richer than any game avatar I'd ever heard of. I could *feel* them teeming with complexity, buzzing with layers and layers of detail, deeper than my mind could reach. It was very, very weird—

"Oh no," said Bonny, staring at me, and I stared back at her, helpless, thinking she was looking straight through me, right back through the root server, back to the real world, into my head, or wherever "Sylvie" really lived—

"Oh, *no*!" groaned Qua'as. "You're real children, aren't you?"

"Y-yes?"

Mr. Parker smacked both his hands to his cap and held on, bug-eyed.

"*Oh, man*. We are so busted! GAME OVER!"

"What's wrong?" I quavered. "What is this place, er, game? Have we, did we, er, hack into a research level or something?"

I realized what was going on, with a rush of relief. They were test pilots. Dev and I had copped a sneak preview of a new, hyper-real immersion game in development. That explained the weirdness I had felt, the strange, super-convincing feel of this whole venue. So now our cheats were in trouble because the game was supposed to be dead secret until it was launched—

They looked at each other, tight-lipped.

"We thought you were colleagues of ours," said Qua'as the Transformer.

"Or the mind-police," growled Mr. Parker, with a wry grin. "We can insert ourselves into the hub games; we do it for light relief. We're not supposed to."

"You're test pilots. Game-development test pilots."

"Close," said Bonny, grimly. "But no cigar."

Qua'as heaved a sigh. "This is not a game, little girl. It's a planet. We are neuronauts. You are approximately five hundred and sixty light years from home."

My brother cried out, "Mom!" and fell over, legs still tied, curled into a ball.

Cold sweat broke out all over me, all over this body that wasn't real. I couldn't speak. I was too busy fighting, refusing to believe this insane story. I knew there were such people as neuronauts. I knew that they were making experiments in hyperspace: from a lab in Xi'an, in faraway China, and from another lab at a place called Kiowa Taime Springs, in the Black Hills. I'd seen it on the news. That just made me feel worse, like in a nightmare where someone says something you know is true, and the fear ramps up and up, because then you know you're not just lost for a night, the nightmare is *real*—

"I don't believe you."

"You'd better believe us, little girl," said Mr. Parker, dead straight. "Because this is not funny. You are handling this, but your friend isn't—"

"He's my brother."

"Okay, your brother. You have to accept what we're saying, and trust us to get you back, or your brother's going to die. Not die as in wake up at home. Plain dead."

"What are your names?" asked the pirate queen, more gently.

"I'm Sylvia Murphy-Weston, and my brother is Devan Murphy-Weston."

"You have hub access; are those names your hub access IDs?"

"Yes."

I could tell she was wondering how come we had such a level of access and whose children we were. But Qua'as put his hand on her arm. "That's all we need. Be calm, let's relax. We know the situation now. We're all friends . . . ?"

He raised his eyebrow at me, and I nodded.

"So we'll get onto it, Sylvie, and you and Devan will be fine."

They cut us loose and retired inside their shelter. I got Dev to sit up. I told him we would be all right. Mr. Parker came out again, bringing blankets, sugar water for us in a skin bottle, and a meal of jerky strips.

"Is this the friendly golden spiders?" asked Dev, unhappily.

"No, it's another animal, a kind of small eight-legged sheep."

"Is it *real*?"

"It's analog, if that's what you mean. And so are you. When you dropped into normal space, with us, our support code caused your digital avatars to draw the necessary chemicals out of this planet's information complex and made analog bodies for you. You became material. You can eat, you can die."

"So . . . so I have *two bodies* right now?" said Devan, hesitantly.

"Yeah. It's just about possible, but it's extremely dangerous."

We ate the jerky, and I didn't tell Dev that I suspected the "eight-legged sheep" was a little white lie. It was cold, but not as cold as a night camped out on the high range country, where I have never been in my body, only in an immersion game. We slept for a bit, hugging each other for warmth. Sometime in the middle of the night I woke up, when the pirate queen came out of the shelter and headed off down the ravine. Dev was awake too. We looked at each other and agreed without a word to follow.

Where was she going? To the secret lab? To the door in the air that would lead out of this game, back to the hub, back to normality? She climbed up onto a big fat boulder. We followed her up there, trying to be quiet, and found her lying on her back there, with her hand behind her head and her hat beside her, just gazing at the stars.

I don't know stars, but they looked different. They were very bright.

"Hi," I said.

"Hi," said the pirate queen, smiling at the great jeweled abyss.

"If it's so dangerous to have two bodies," I said, "where are yours?"

"Ah."

She sat up, and mugged a *you got me* face. "I was afraid you were going to ask me that. We don't have any bodies back home, Sylvie."

"Huh?" said Dev.

"Technically, er, physically, we are dead. And we don't know if we will ever die, which is quite a trip." She looked at me seriously. "That's the way it has to be. It'll change—we'll find a way around the problem. It's going to be possible for other people to fly to the stars, but so far, only 'nauts who can handle having no body left at home can survive this kind of travel. We're the forerunners."

"Nobody would do that," breathed Dev, after a moment. "Now

I *know* you're faking. You're cheating on us, telling us weird lies. This is a game. You're nothing but big *cheats*."

"Yeah?" said the pirate queen. "And what are you?" She was still looking at me, not at Dev, in a way that made my stomach turn over. "You've been messing with us, making the jumps we make, getting in deep, playing with the code as if it's your little Lego set. We thought you were two of our colleagues, psyching us out, because *you were cheating* the same way we can. It's rare. When it combines with someone who . . . well, someone who doesn't have much use for their physical body, that's when you get a neuronaut candidate."

"No," said Dev. "You're in a lab somewhere. Hooked up to life support."

She shook her head, slowly, sad and happy at the same time.

She was like an outlaw angel, breaking all the rules.

The crew—they were called the Kappa Tau Sigma Second Crew (KTS, for Kiowa Taime Springs)—had turned themselves in, for our sakes. You see, apparently it's okay on the Earth-type planets, where they're finding out what they can do with analog bodies, out there on alien soil, in the real no-kidding spaces between the stars. But it's hard on them (in some weird way), making the straight leaps from normal space to information space—the plane where everything exists in simultaneity, and a journey of 560 light years is pretty much instantaneous. The 'nauts get burnout, they get tired and irritated, so instead of doing it the hard way, they take shortcuts through the human datasphere, the code-rich hub games that are like playtime to them. They're not supposed to do it—it's supposed to be dangerous for our consensus reality or something, but they do. And the scientists *hate* them for it, and call them cheats, just the way we did.

Anyway, we got hauled back. Dev woke up on life support, in the hospital. I woke up in my bed at home. Then it was nightmare fugue for a while. We had the choice between angry, scared, tearful parents and psych tests, science questions, and medical procedures, when we were awake, or going to sleep and finding out what our sickeningly ripped-up neuronal mapping wanted to do to us next in the way of vile nightmares. Horrible, awful! When we talked to each other screen to screen, the conversation consisted mostly of me saying *Bad! Bad!* and Dev saying *Bad! Bad!* . . . We couldn't deal with sentences or anything.

But we got better. We came out good as new.

The morning after Dev came home from the hospital, I got into my wheelchair, which *I hate to do*, because it takes all my strength and reminds me that I keep on getting worse. Two years ago I could casually sling myself into the chair; now it's like climbing Mount Everest. I got my head in the support, I dehooked and rehooked all the tubes I needed, which is something else I *hate* to do, and I whizzed myself along to Dev's room. I hardly ever visit my family anymore. I prefer my bed. I used to fight like a tiger to keep myself going. There were years when I insisted on walking in a frame without motor assist, years when I insisted on getting up every day and going around in my chair. Now I love my bed. It's the only territory I'm still defending, the only place I have left to stand. Although, of course, I'm lying down.

My motor nerves are eating themselves. There's no gene therapy that will work for me; there's no cure. It's not fatal. I'm fourteen: I could live for decades . . . treating my brain like a pet animal and trying to ignore the sad sack that used to be my body. My mom and dad still desperately want that to happen. But I had talked to them (I'd recovered from our adventure much faster than my healthy, normal little brother). The Kiowa Taime Springs people had talked to them too. They were coming around.

I looked down at my little brother, my best friend, thinking about the day he came to me and insisted I had to start playing the games again, because he loved me. I thought of all the wonderful times we'd had, exploring and fighting, skimming over the snow, solving mysteries. I thought of paddling the channels in the reed-beds with him, and the way he'd yelled when he was shooting down the white water. I watched him breathe; his eyelashes fluttered on his cheeks. I knew what he was going to say when he woke. He opened his eyes, and blinked, and smiled. "Hi, Sylvie. What an honor!" But his smile faded. We both knew. We knew.

"Take me with you," whispered Dev, reaching out. "Please."

There was nothing I could say. I just sat there, holding his hand.

ANN HALAM was born in Manchester, England, went to convent schools, and then took an undergraduate degree in the History of Ideas at the University of Sussex, specializing in seventeenth-century Europe, a distant academic background that still resonates in her work. She first realized she wanted to be a writer when she was fourteen, when she won a local newspaper's story competition. She has written more than twenty novels for teenagers, starting with *Ally Ally Aster* and including *Taylor Five*, *Dr. Franklin's Island*, and most recently, *Siberia*. She has also written a number of highly regarded SF novels for adults as Gwyneth Jones, notably *White Queen*, *North Wind*, and *Phoenix Cafe*, and the near-future fantasy Bold as Love series. Her collection *Seven Tales and a Fable* won two World Fantasy Awards, and her critical writings and essays have appeared in *Nature*, *New Scientist*, *Foundation*, *The New York Review of Science Fiction*, and several online venues. She has been writing full-time since the early 1980s, occasionally teaching creative writing. Honors include the Arthur C. Clarke Award for *Bold as Love* and the Philip K. Dick Award for *Life*. She lives in Brighton with her husband, son, and two cats called Frank and Ginger; likes cooking, gardening, watching old movies, and playing with her Web sites (homepage.ntlworld.com/gwynethann and www.boldaslove.co.uk).

AUTHOR'S NOTE

The story "Cheats" was born when I first picked up the controller for a fantasy snowboarding game, and I swear I could feel the cold air; I could smell that crispy, frosty atmosphere you're in when you're lying facedown on a toboggan at the end of a downhill glide. Now I keep imagining a future with full-immersion games where your brain reacts to the virtual world exactly as if it's real . . . and why not? The real world we think we perceive all around us is really just built from a pattern of firing neurons. Plus, in the view of more and more scientists, the real universe is built from information, the same as the games are. I have a wild idea that young people who grow up as expert immersion gamers may come to see themselves as "made of information" in the real world, the way the games are "made of" computer code, and this gives me the wilder idea that there's a back door from virtual reality, where distance means nothing, into the spaces between the stars.

ORANGE

Neil Gaiman

(Third Subject's Responses to Investigator's Written Questionnaire.) *EYES ONLY.*

1. Jemima Glorfindel Petula Ramsey.

2. Seventeen on June the ninth.

3. The last five years. Before that we lived in Glasgow (Scotland). Before that, Cardiff (Wales).

4. I don't know. I think he's in magazine publishing now. He doesn't talk to us anymore. The divorce was pretty bad and Mum wound up paying him a lot of money. Which seems sort of wrong to me. But maybe it was worth it just to get shot of him.

5. An inventor and entrepreneur. She invented the Stuffed Muffin™, and started the Stuffed Muffin™ chain. I used to like them when I

was a kid, but you can get kind of sick of Stuffed Muffins™ for every meal, especially because Mum used us as guinea pigs. The Complete Turkey Christmas Dinner Stuffed Muffin™ was the worst. But she sold out her interest in the Stuffed Muffin™ chain about five years ago, to start work on My Mum's Colored Bubbles (not actually TM yet).

6. Two. My sister Nerys, who was just fifteen, and my brother Pryderi, twelve.

7. Several times a day.

8. No.

9. Through the Internet. Probably on eBay.

10. She's been buying colors and dyes from all over the world ever since she decided that the world was crying out for brightly colored Day-Glo bubbles. The kind you can blow, with bubble mixture.

11. It's not really a laboratory. I mean, she calls it that, but really it's just the garage. Only she took some of the Stuffed Muffins™ money and converted it, so it has sinks and bathtubs and Bunsen burners and things, and tiles on the walls and the floor to make it easier to clean.

12. I don't know. Nerys used to be pretty normal. When she turned thirteen, she started reading these magazines and putting pictures of these strange bimbo women up on her wall, like Britney Spears

and so on. Sorry if anyone reading this is a Britney fan ;) but I just don't get it. The whole orange thing didn't start until last year.

13. Artificial tanning creams. You couldn't go near her for hours after she put it on. And she'd never give it time to dry after she smeared it on her skin, so it would come off on her sheets and on the fridge door and in the shower, leaving smears of orange everywhere. Her friends would wear it too, but they never put it on like she did. I mean, she'd slather on the cream, with no attempt to look even human colored, and she thought she looked great. She did the tanning salon thing once, but I don't think she liked it, because she never went back.

14. Tangerine Girl. The Oompa-Loompa. Carrot-top. Go-Mango. Orangina.

15. Not very well. But she didn't seem to care, really. I mean, this is a girl who said that she couldn't see the point of science or math because she was going to be a pole dancer as soon as she left school. I said, nobody's going to pay to see you in the altogether, and she said how do you know? and I told her that I saw the little Quicktime films she'd made of herself dancing nuddy and left in the camera and she screamed and said give me that, and I told her I'd wiped them. But honestly, I don't think she was ever going to be the next Bettie Page or whoever. She's a sort of squarish shape, for a start.

16. German measles, mumps, and I think Pryderi had chicken pox when he was staying in Melbourne with the grandparents.

17. In a small pot. It looked a bit like a jam jar, I suppose.

18. I don't think so. Nothing that looked like a warning label anyway. Yes, there was a return address. It came from abroad, and the return address was in some kind of foreign lettering.

19. You have to understand that Mum had been buying colors and dyes from all over the world for five years. The thing with the Day-Glo bubbles is not that someone can blow glowing colored bubbles, it's that they don't pop and leave splashes of dye all over everything. Mum says that would be a lawsuit waiting to happen. So, no.

20. There was some kind of shouting match between Nerys and Mum to begin with, because Mum had come back from the shops and not bought anything from Nerys's shopping list except the shampoo. Mum said she couldn't find the tanning cream at the supermarket, but I think she just forgot. So Nerys stormed off and slammed the door and went into her bedroom and played something that was probably Britney Spears really loudly. I was out the back, feeding the three cats, the chinchilla, and a guinea pig named Roland who looks like a hairy cushion, and I missed it all.

21. On the kitchen table.

22. When I found the empty jam jar in the back garden the next morning. It was underneath Nerys's window. It didn't take Sherlock Holmes to figure it out.

23. Honestly, I couldn't be bothered. I figured it would just be more

yelling, you know? And Mum would work it out soon enough.

24. Yes, it was stupid. But it wasn't uniquely stupid, if you see what I mean. Which is to say, it was par-for-the-course-for-Nerys stupid.

25. That she was glowing.

26. A sort of pulsating orange.

27. When she started telling us that she was going to be worshipped like a god, as she was in the dawn times.

28. Pryderi said she was floating about an inch above the ground. But I didn't actually see this. I thought he was just playing along with her newfound weirdness.

29. She didn't answer to "Nerys" anymore. She described herself mostly as either My Immanence, or the Vehicle. ("It is time to feed the Vehicle.")

30. Dark chocolate. Which was weird because in the old days, I was the only one in the house who even sort of liked it. But Pryderi had to go out and buy her bars and bars of it.

31. No. Mum and me just thought it was more Nerys. Just a bit more imaginatively weirdo Nerys than usual.

32. That night, when it started to get dark. You could see the orange pulsing under the door. Like a glowworm or something. Or a light

show. The weirdest thing was that I could still see it with my eyes closed.

33. The next morning. All of us.

34. It was pretty obvious by this point. She didn't really even look like Nerys any longer. She looked sort of *smudged.* Like an after-image. I thought about it, and it's . . . Okay. Suppose you were staring at something really bright, that was a blue color. Then you close your eyes, and you'd see this glowing yellowy-orange afterimage in your eyes? That was what she looked like.

35. They didn't work either.

36. She let Pryderi leave to get her more chocolate. Mum and I weren't allowed to leave the house anymore.

37. Mostly I just sat in the back garden and read a book. There wasn't very much else I really could do. I started wearing dark glasses. So did Mum, because the orange light hurt our eyes. Other than that, nothing.

38. Only when we tried to leave or call anybody. There was food in the house, though. And Stuffed Muffins™ in the freezer.

39. "If you'd just stopped her wearing that stupid tanning cream a year ago, we wouldn't be in this mess!" But it was unfair, and I apologized afterward.

40. When Pryderi came back with the dark chocolate bars. He said he'd gone up to a traffic warden and told him that his sister had turned into a giant orange glow and was controlling our minds. He said the man was extremely rude to him.

41. I don't have a boyfriend. I did, but we broke up after he went to a Rolling Stones concert with the evil bottle-blond former friend whose name I do not mention. Also, I mean, the Rolling Stones? These little old goat-men hopping around the stage, pretending to be all rock and roll? Please. So, no.

42. I'd quite like to be a vet. But then I think about having to put animals down, and I don't know. I want to travel for a bit before I make any decisions.

43. The garden hose. We turned it on full, while she was eating her chocolate bars, and distracted, and we sprayed it at her.

44. Just orange steam, really. Mum said that she had solvents and things in the laboratory, if we could get in there, but by now Her Immanence was hissing mad (literally) and she sort of fixed us to the floor. I can't explain it. I mean, I wasn't stuck, but I couldn't leave or move my legs. I was just where she left me.

45. About half a meter above the carpet. She'd sink down a bit to go through doors so she didn't bump her head. And after the hose incident she didn't go back to her room, just stayed in the main room and floated about grumpily, the color of a luminous carrot.

46. Complete world domination.

47. I wrote it down on a piece of paper and gave it to Pryderi.

48. He had to carry it back. I don't think Her Immanence really understood money.

49. I don't know. It was Mum's idea more than mine. I think she hoped that the solvent might remove the orange. And at that point, it couldn't hurt. Nothing could have made things worse.

50. It didn't even upset her, like the hose-water did. I'm pretty sure she liked it. I think I saw her dipping her chocolate bars into it before she ate them, although I had to sort of squint up my eyes to see anything where she was. It was all a sort of great orange glow.

51. That we were all going to die. Mum told Pryderi that if the Great Oompa-Loompa let him out to buy chocolate again, he just shouldn't bother coming back. And I was getting really upset about the animals—I hadn't fed the chinchilla or Roland the guinea pig for two days, because I couldn't go into the back garden. I couldn't go anywhere. Except the loo, and then I had to ask.

52. I suppose because they thought the house was on fire. All the orange light. I mean, it was a natural mistake.

53. We were glad she hadn't done that to us. Mum said it proved that Nerys was still in there somewhere, because if she had the power to turn us into goo, like she did the firefighters, she would have done. I

said that maybe she just wasn't powerful enough to turn us into goo at the beginning and now she couldn't be bothered.

54. You couldn't even see a person in there anymore. It was a bright orange pulsing light, and sometimes it talked straight into your head.

55. When the spaceship landed.

56. I don't know. I mean, it was bigger than the whole block, but it didn't crush anything. It sort of materialized around us, so that our whole house was inside it. And the whole street was inside it too.

57. No. But what else could it have been?

58. A sort of pale blue. They didn't pulse either. They twinkled.

59. More than six, less than twenty. It's not that easy to tell if this is the same intelligent blue light you were just speaking to five minutes ago.

60. Three things. First of all, a promise that Nerys wouldn't be hurt or harmed. Second, that if they were ever able to return her to the way she was, they'd let us know, and bring her back. Thirdly, a recipe for fluorescent bubble mixture. (I can only assume they were reading Mum's mind, because she didn't say anything. It's possible that Her Immanence told them, though. She definitely had access to some of "the Vehicle's" memories.) Also, they gave Pryderi a thing like a glass skateboard.

61. A sort of a liquid sound. Then everything became transparent. I was crying, and so was Mum. And Pryderi said, “Cool beans,” and I started to giggle while crying, and then it was just our house again.

62. We went out into the back garden and looked up. There was something blinking blue and orange, very high, getting smaller and smaller, and we watched it until it was out of sight.

63. Because I didn’t want to.

64. I fed the remaining animals. Roland was in a state. The cats just seemed happy that someone was feeding them again. I don’t know how the chinchilla got out.

65. Sometimes. I mean, you have to bear in mind that she was the single most irritating person on the planet, even before the whole Her Immanence thing. But yes, I guess so. If I’m honest.

66. Sitting outside at night, staring up at the sky, wondering what she’s doing now.

67. He wants his glass skateboard back. He says that it’s his, and the government has no right to keep it. (You are the government, aren’t you?) Mum seems happy to share the patent for the colored bubble recipe with the government, though. The man said that it might be the basis of a whole new branch of molecular something or other. Nobody gave me anything, so I don’t have to worry.

68. Once, in the back garden, looking up at the night sky. I think

it was only an orangeyish star, actually. It could have been Mars; I know they call it the red planet. Although once in a while I think that maybe she's back to herself again, and dancing, up there, wherever she is, and all the aliens love her pole dancing because they just don't know any better, and they think it's a whole new art form, and they don't even mind that she's sort of square.

69. I don't know. Sitting in the back garden talking to the cats, maybe. Or blowing silly-colored bubbles.

70. Until the day that I die.

I attest that this is a true statement of events.

Signed:

Date:

NEIL GAIMAN was born in England in 1960 and worked as a freelance journalist before coediting *Ghastly Beyond Belief* (with Kim Newman) and writing *Don't Panic: The Official "Hitchhiker's Guide to the Galaxy" Companion*. He started writing graphic novels and comics with *Violent Cases* in 1987, and with seventy-five installments of the award-winning series *The Sandman*, established himself as one of the most important comics writers of his generation. His first novel, *Good Omens* (written with Terry Pratchett), appeared in 1991 and was followed by *Neverwhere*, *Stardust*, *American Gods*, and *Coraline*.

Gaiman's work has won the Hugo, World Fantasy, Bram Stoker, Locus, Geffen, International Horror Guild, Mythopoeic, and Will Eisner Comic Industry awards. His most recent books are *Anansi Boys*, *The Sandman: Endless Nights*, and a picture book, *The Wolves in the Walls* (with longtime collaborator Dave McKean). His short fiction has been collected in *Smoke and Mirrors*, *Fragile Things*, and *M Is for Magic*. Upcoming is a new novel, *The Graveyard Book*. Gaiman moved to the United States in 1992 with his wife and three children, and currently lives in Minneapolis.

Visit his Web site at www.neilgaiman.com.

AUTHOR'S NOTE

I was going to Australia, where editor Jonathan Strahan would look at me, I had no doubt, with enormous, hurt, puppy-dog eyes if I still didn't have a story for him. I was in Minneapolis Airport, waiting to get onto a plane to San Francisco, where I would change planes and fly to Sydney.

It occurred to me that it might be fun to write a story in which you only got answers and had to figure out what the questions were, and put the pieces together in your head yourself. I turned on the computer and started to write.

By the time I got to San Francisco, I had a first draft of this story almost done, and I sat in baggage claim and e-mailed it to Jonathan.

Very few stories write themselves. This one did. Just in time.

THE SURFER

Kelly Link

In the dream I was being kidnapped by aliens. I was dreaming, and then I woke up.

Where was I? Someplace I wasn't supposed to be, so I decided to stand up and take a look around, but there was no room and I couldn't stand up after all. My legs. And I was strapped in. I was holding on to something. A soccer ball. It slid out of my hands and into the narrow space in front of me, and it took two tries to hook it up again with my feet. The floor kept moving up and down, and my hands were floppy.

"One more pill, Dorn. Oops. Here. Have another one. Want some water?"

I had a sip of water. Swallowed. I was in a little seat. A plane? I was on a plane. And we were way up. The clouds were down. There was a woman who looked like my mother, except she wasn't. "Let me take that," she said. "I'll put it up above for you."

I didn't want to give it to her. Even if she did look like my mother.

"Come on, Dorn." My father again. Wasn't he supposed to be at the hospital today? I'd been at soccer practice. I was in my soccer clothes. Cleats and everything. "Dorn?" I ignored him. He said to the woman, "Sorry. He took some medication earlier. He's a bad flier."

"I'm not," I said. "A bad flier." I was having a hard time with my mouth. I tried to remember some things. My father had come by in his car. And I'd gone to see what he wanted. He was going to drive me home even though practice wasn't. Wasn't over. I drank something he gave me. Gatorade. That had been a mistake.

I said, "I'm not on a plane. This isn't a plane and you're not my mother." I didn't sound like me.

"Poor kid," the woman said. The floor bounced. If this was a plane, then she was a something. A flight attendant. "Wouldn't he be more comfortable if I stowed that up above for him?"

"I think he'll be fine." My father again. I kept my arms around my. My soccer ball. Keeping my shoulders forward. Hunched so nobody could take it. From me. Nobody ever got a soccer ball away from me.

"You gave me Gatorade," I said. The Gatorade had had something. In it. Everything I ought to know was broken up. Fast and liquid and too close up and then slow like an instant. Replay. My lips felt mushy and warm, and the flight attendant just looked at me like I was drooling. I think I was.

"Dorn," my father said. "It's going to be okay."

"Saturday," I said. Our first big match and I was missing practice. My head went forward and hit the soccer ball. I felt the flight attendant's fingers on my forehead.

"Poor kid," she said.

I lifted up my head. Tried as hard as I could. To make her understand me. "Where. This flight. Is it going."

"Costa Rica," the flight attendant said.

"You," I said to my father. "I. Will never. Forgive. You." The floor tilted and I went down.

When I woke up we were in Costa Rica, and I remembered exactly what my father had done to me. But it was too late to do anything about it. By then everything had changed because of a new flu scare. Costa Rica could have turned the plane around, but I guess by that point we couldn't have gotten back into the States. They'd shut down all the airports, everywhere. We went straight into quarantine. Me, my father, the flight attendant who didn't look anything like my mother, after all, and all the other people on the plane.

There were guards wearing N95 masks and carrying machine guns to make sure we all got on a bus. Once we were seated, a man who really needed a shave boarded and stood at the front. He wore an N95 mask with a shiny, tiny mike-pen clipped to it. He held up his gloved hands for silence. Sunlight melted his rubbery fingers into lozenges of pink taffy.

People put down their cells and their googlies. I'd checked my cell and discovered three missed calls, all from my coach, Sorken. I didn't check the messages. I didn't even want to know.

In the silence you could hear birds and not a lot else. No planes taking off. No planes landing. You could smell panic and antibacterial potions. Some people had been traveling with disposable masks, and they were wearing them now. My father always said that those didn't really do much.

The official waited a few more seconds. The skin under his eyes was grayish and pouched. He said, "It's too bad, these precautions that we must take, but it can't be helped. You will be our guests for a short period of observation. Without this precaution, there will be unnecessary sickness. Deaths that could be prevented. You will be given care if you become ill. Food and drink and beds. And in a few days, when all have been given a clean bill of health, we will let you continue with your business, your homecoming, your further travel arrangements. You have questions, but I have no time for them. Excuse me. Please do not attempt to leave this bus or to go away. The guards will shoot you if you cannot be sensible."

Then he said the whole speech all over again in Spanish. It was a longer speech this time. Nobody protested when he disembarked and our bus started off to wherever they were taking us.

"Did you understand any of that? The Spanish?" my father asked. And that was the first thing he said to me, except for what he'd said on the plane, when it landed. He'd said, "Dorn, wake up. Dorn, we're here." He'd been so excited that his voice broke when he said *here*.

"If I did," I said. "Why would I tell you?" But I hadn't. I was taking Japanese as my second language.

"Well," he said. "Don't worry. We'll be fine. And don't worry too much about the machine guns. They have the safeties on."

"What do you know about machine guns?" I said. "Never mind. You got us into this situation. You *kidnapped* me."

"What was I supposed to do, Dorn?" he said. "Leave you behind?"

"I have a very important match tomorrow," I said. "*Today*. In Glenside." I had my soccer ball wedged between my knees and the back of the seat in front of me. I was wearing my cleats and soccer clothes from the day before. For some reason that made me even more furious.

"Don't worry about the match," my father said. "Nobody is going to be playing soccer today. Or anytime soon."

"You knew about this, didn't you?" I said. I knew that doctors talked to each other.

"Keep your voice down," my father said. "Of course I didn't."

There was a girl across the aisle from us. She kept looking over, probably wondering if I had this new flu. She was about my height and at least twice my weight. A few years older. Bleached white hair and a round face. Cat's-eye glasses. Her skin was very tan, and she wasn't wearing a disposable mask. Her lips were pursed up and her eyebrows slanted down. I looked away from her and out the window.

Everything outside the bus was saturated with color. The asphalt deep purplish brown. The sky such a thick, wet blue you expected it to come off on the bus and the buildings. A lizard the size of my forearm, posed like a hood ornament on the top of a Dumpster, shining in the sun like it had been wrought of beaten silver, and its scales emeralds and topazes, gemstone parings. Off in the distance were bright feathery trees, some fancy skyscrapers, the kind you see on souvenir postcards, mountains on either side of us, cloud-colored, looking like special effects.

I couldn't tell if it was the drugs my father had given me, or if this was just what Costa Rica looked like. I looked around the bus at the other passengers in their livid tropical prints and their blank, white, disposable masks, at the red filaments of stubble on my father's face, pushing out of his skin like pinprick worms. So okay. It was the drugs. I felt like someone in one of my father's Philip K.

Dick paperback science fiction novels. Kidnapped? Check. In a strange environment and unable to trust the people that you ought to be able to rely on, say, your own father? Check. On some kind of hallucinogenic medication? Check. Any minute now I would realize that I was really a robot. Or God.

Our bus stopped and the driver got out to have a conversation with two woman soldiers holding machine guns. There was a series of hangar buildings a few hundred yards in front of us. One of the soldiers got onto the bus and looked us over. She lifted up her N95 mask and said, "Patience, patience." She smiled and shrugged. Then she sat down on the rail at the front of the bus with her mask on again. Everyone on the bus clicked on their cell phones again. It didn't seem as if we were going anywhere soon.

There was a clammy breeze, and it smelled like some place I'd never been to before, and where I didn't want to be. I wanted to lie down. I wanted a bathroom and a sink and a toothbrush. And I was hungry. I wanted a bowl of cereal. And a peanut-butter sandwich.

That girl was still looking at me.

I leaned across and said, "I'm not sick or anything, okay? My father gave me a roofie. I was at soccer practice, and he kidnapped me. I'm a goalie. I don't even speak Spanish." Even as I said it, I knew I wasn't making much sense.

The girl looked at my father. He said, "True, more or less. But, as usual, Adorno is oversimplifying things."

The girl said, "You're here for the aliens."

My father's eyebrows shot up.

The fat girl said, "Well, you don't look like UCR students. You don't look wealthy enough to be tourists. Besides, tourist visas are hard to come by unless you've got a lot of money, and no offense but

I don't think so. So either you're here because you work in the software industry or because of the aliens. And no offense, but you look more like the latter than the former."

I said, "So which are you? Aliens or software?"

"Software," she said, sounding a little annoyed. "Second year, full scholarship to UCR."

About three decades ago, a software zillionaire in Taiwan had died and left all his money to the University of Costa Rica to fund a progressive institute of technology. He left them his patents, his stocks, and controlling shares in the dozen or so companies that he'd owned. Why? They'd given him an honorary degree or something. All the techie kids at my school dreamed about getting into one of the UCR programs, or else just getting lucky in the visa lottery and coming out to Costa Rica after college to work for one of the new start-ups.

"I'm Dr. Yoder," my father said. "General practice. We're on our way out to join Hans Bliss's Star Friend community, as it happens. Their last doctor packed up and left two weeks ago. I've been in contact with Hans for a few years. We're here at his invitation."

Which was what he'd told me in the car when he picked me up at practice. After I'd drunk Gatorade.

"Amazing how easy it is for some rich lunatic like Bliss to get visas. I bet there are twenty people on this bus who are headed out to join Bliss's group," the girl said. "What I've never figured out is why everybody is so convinced that if the aliens come back, they're going to show up to see Bliss. No offense, but I've seen him online. I watched the movie. He's an idiot."

My father opened his mouth and shut it again. A woman in the seat behind us leaned forward and said, "Hans Bliss is a great man.

We heard him speak in Atlanta and we just knew we had to come out here. The aliens came to him because he's a great man. A *good* man."

I had gone with my father to see Hans Bliss talk at the Franklin Institute in Philadelphia last year. I had my own opinions.

The girl didn't even turn around. She said, "Hans Bliss is just some surfer who happened to be one of a dozen people stupid enough to be out on an isolated beach during a Category 3 hurricane. It was just dumb luck that he was the one the aliens scooped up. If he's so great, then why did they put him back down on the beach again and just take off? Why didn't they take him along if he's so amazing? In my opinion, you don't get points just for being the first human ever to talk with aliens. Especially if the conversation only lasts about forty-seven minutes by everyone else's count. I don't care how long he says he was out there. Furthermore, you *lose* points if the aliens go away after talking to you and don't ever come back again. How long has it been? Six years? Seven?"

Now the whole bus was listening, even the bus driver and the soldier with the gun. The woman behind us was probably twenty years older than my father; she had frizzy gray hair and impressive biceps. She said to the girl, "Can't you see that people like you are the reason that the aliens haven't come back yet? They told Bliss that they would return in the fullness of time."

"Sure," the girl said. You could tell she was enjoying herself. "Right after we make Bliss president of the whole wide world and learn to love each other and not feel ashamed of our bodies. When Bliss achieves world peace and we're all comfortable walking around in the nude, even the people who are fat, like me, the aliens will come back. And they'll squash us like bugs, or harvest us to make delicious people-burgers, or cure cancer, or bring us cool new toys. Or whatever Hans Bliss says that they're going to do. I love Hans Bliss, okay? I love the fact that he fell in love with some aliens who swooped down one stormy afternoon and scooped him up into the sky and less than an hour later dropped him off, naked, in front of about eighteen news crews, disaster-bloggers, and gawkers, and now he's going to wait for the rest of his life for them to come back, when clearly it was just some weird kind of one-night stand for them. It's just so sweet."

The woman said, "You ignorant little—"

People at the front of the bus were getting up. A man said something in Spanish, and the girl who didn't like Bliss said, "Time to go." She stood up.

My father said, "What's your name?"

The soldier with the machine gun was out on the asphalt, waving us off the bus. People around us grabbed carry-on bags. The angry woman's mouth was still working. A guy put his hand on her arm. "It's not worth it, Paula," he said. Neither of them were wearing face masks. He had the same frizzy hair, and a big nose, and those were his good features. You could see why he was hoping the aliens might come back. Nobody on Earth was ever going to fall in love with him.

"My name's Naomi," the girl said.

"Nice to meet you, Naomi," my father said. "You're clearly very smart and very opinionated. Maybe we can talk about this some more."

"Whatever," Naomi said. Then she seemed to decide that she had been rude enough. "Sure. I mean, we're going to be stuck with each other for a while, right?"

My father motioned for her to step out in front of us. He said, "Okay, Naomi, so once I tell the people in charge here that I'm a doctor, I'm going to be busy. I'd appreciate it if you and Adorno kept an eye on each other. Okay? Okay."

I didn't have the energy to protest my father's request to Naomi to babysit me. I could hardly stand up. Those drugs were still doing things to my balance. My eyes were raw, and my mouth was dry. I smelled bad, too. I stopped when we got out of the bus, just to look around, and there was the hangar in front of us and my father pushed me forward and we funneled into the hangar where there were more soldiers with guns, standing back as if they weren't really making us do anything. Go anywhere. As if the hangar was our decision. Sun came down through oily windows high above us, and somehow it was exactly the sort of sunlight that ought to fall on you on a movie set or in a commercial while you pretend to sit on a white, sandy beach. But the hangar was vast and empty. Someone had forgotten to truck in that white sand and the palm trees and the beautiful painted background. Nobody was saying much. We just came into the hangar and stood there, looking around. The walls were cinderblock, and a warm wind came in under the corrugated roof, rattling and popping it like a steel drum. The floor was whispery with grit.

There were stacks of lightweight cots folded up with plastic mattresses inside the frames. Foil blankets in tiny packets. So the next thing involved a lot of rushing around and grabbing, until it became clear that there were more than enough cots and blankets, and plenty of space to spread out in. My father and I carried two cots over toward the wall farthest away from the soldiers. Naomi stuck near us. She seemed suddenly shy. She set up her cot and then flopped down on her stomach and rolled over, turned away.

"Stay here," my father said. I watched him make his way over to a heap of old tires where people stood talking. An Asian woman with long twists of blue and blond hair took two tires, rolling them all the way back to her cot. She stacked them, and then she had a chair. She sat down in it, pulled out a tiny palmtop computer, and began to type, just like she was in an office somewhere. Other people started grabbing tires. There was some screaming and jumping around when some of the tires turned out to contain wildlife. Spiders and lizards. Kids started chasing lizards, stomping spiders.

My father came back with two tires. Then he went and got another two tires. I thought they were for me but instead he rolled them over to Naomi. He tapped her on the shoulder and she turned over, saw the tires, and made a funny little face, almost as if she were irritated with my father for trying to be nice. I knew how she felt. "Thanks," she said.

"I'm going to go find out where the bathroom is." I put the soccer ball down on my bed, thought about it, and picked it up again. Put it down.

"I'll come," my father said.

"Me too." Naomi. She bounced a little, like she really needed the toilet.

I put my soccer ball down on the gritty concrete. Began to guide it across the hangar with my feet and my knees. My balance wasn't great, but I still looked pretty good. Soccer is what I was made to do. Passengers in white masks, soldiers with guns turned their heads to watch me go by.

• • •

The October after I turned fourteen I became the first goalie for not one but two soccer teams: the club team that I'd belonged to for four years, and the state soccer team, which I had tried out for three days after my birthday. Only a few months later, and during state matches I was on the field more than I sat out. I had my own coach, Eduardo Sorken, a sour, bad-tempered man who was displeased when I played poorly and offered only grudging acknowledgment when I played well. Sorken had played in the World Cup for Bolivia, and when he was hard on me, I paid attention, telling myself that one day I would not only play in the World Cup but play for a winning team, which Sorken had not.

There was a smudgy black figure on the outside wall of the ranch house back in Philadelphia where I lived with my father. I'd stood up against the house and traced around my own outline with a piece of charcoal brick. I'd painted the outline in. When my father noticed, he wasn't angry. He never got angry. He just nodded and said, "When they dropped the atom bomb on Hiroshima, you could see the shapes of people who'd died against the buildings." Like that's what I'd been thinking about when I'd stood there and blackened my shape in. What I was thinking about was soccer.

When I kicked the ball, I aimed for that black silhouette of me as hard as I could. I liked the sound that the ball made against the house. If I'd knocked the house down, that would have been okay too.

I had two expectations regarding my future, both reasonable. The first, that I would one day be taller. The other, that I would be recruited by one of the top international professional leagues. I favored Italy or Japan. Which was why I was studying Japanese. Nothing made me happier than the idea of a future in which, like the present, I spent as much time as possible on a soccer field in front of a goal, doing my best to stop everything that came at me.

A pretty girl in a mask sat cross-legged on the floor of the hangar, tapping at her googly, earplugs plugged in. She stopped typing and watched me go by. I popped the ball up, let it ride up one shoulder, around my neck, and down the other arm. During flu season, up in the bleachers, during matches, everyone wore masks like hers, bumping them up to yell or knock back a drink. But our fans painted their masks with our team colors or wrote slogans on them. There were always girls who wrote DORN on the mask, and so I'd look up and see my name right there, over their mouths. It was kind of a turn-on.

Sometimes there was a scout up in the bleachers. I figured another year or two, another inch or two, and I'd slip right into that bright, deserved future. I *was* the future. You can't stop the future, right? Not unless you're a better goalie than me.

I went in a circle, came back around, making the ball spin in place. "Hey," I said.

She gave me a little wave. I couldn't tell whether or not she was smiling, because of the mask. But I bet you she was.

I was magic out on a field. In front of a goal. I stopped everything. I was always exactly where I needed to be. When I came forward, nobody ever got around me. I put out my hands and the ball came to me like I was yanking it through the air. I could jump straight up, so high it didn't matter how short I was. I had a certain arrangement with gravity. I didn't get in its way, and it didn't get in mine. When I was asleep I dreamed about the field, the goal, the ball sailing toward me. I didn't dream about anything else. This year, on the weekends, I'd been wearing that black silhouette away.

I stood a few feet away from the girl, letting her see how I could keep the ball up in the air, adjusting its position first with one knee, then the other, then my left foot, then my right foot, then catching it between my knees. Maybe she was a soccer fan, maybe not. But I knew I looked pretty good.

I was already a bit taller than that silhouette I'd painted. If you measure yourself in the morning, you're always a few centimeters taller. I'm named after my mother's father. (Italian, but you probably guessed that. Her mother was Japanese. My father, if you're curious, is African American.) I never met my grandfather, although one time I'd asked my mother how tall he was. He wasn't. I wish they'd named me after someone taller. My father is six foot three.

I circled back one more time, went wide around my father and Naomi. The little lizard-chasing, spider-stomping kids were still running around in the hangar. Some of them were now wearing the foil blankets like capes. I kicked the ball to a little girl and she sent it right back. Not too bad. I was feeling much better. Also angrier.

You could have gotten half a dozen soccer matches going all at once in the hangar. According to my watch it was less than two hours until the start of the match back in Glenside. Sorken, my coach, would be wondering what had happened to me. Or he would have been, except for the flu. Matches were always being canceled because of flu or civil unrest or terror alerts. Maybe I'd be home before anyone even realized what had happened to me.

Or maybe I'd get the flu and die like my mother and brother had. That would show my father.

Along the wall closest to the hangar doors where we'd come in were the soldiers who were still guarding us. Whenever people tried to approach them, the guards waved them back again with their machine guns. The N95 masks gave them a sinister look, but they didn't seem particularly annoyed. It was more like, *Yeah, yeah, leave us alone. Scram.*

The makeshift latrines were just outside the hangar. People went in and out of the hangar, got in line, or squatted on the tarmac to read their googlies.

"So you're pretty good with that thing," Naomi said. She got in line behind me.

"Want my autograph?" I said. "It will be worth something someday."

There was a half-wall of corrugated tin divided up with more tin sheets into four stalls. Black plastic hung up for doors. Holes in the ground, and you could tell that they had been dug recently. There was a line. There were covered plastic barrels of water and dippers and more black plastic curtains so that you could take a sponge bath in private.

I tucked my soccer ball under my arm, took a piss, then dunked my hands into a bucket of antiseptic wash.

Back inside the hangar, airline passengers sorted through cardboard boxes full of tissue packs, packets of surgical masks, bottled water, hotel soaps and shampoos, toothbrushes. A man with an enormous mustache came up to my father with a group of people and said, "Miike says you're a doctor?"

"Yes," my father said. "Carl Yoder. This is my son, Dorn. I'm a G.P., but I have some experience with flu. I'll need a translator, though. I've started learning Spanish recently, but I'm still not proficient."

"We can find a translator," the man said. "I'm Rafe Zuleta-Arango. Hotel management. You've already met Anya Miike"—the woman who'd made the chair out of old tires. "Tom Laudermilk. Works for a law firm in New New York. Simon Purdy, the pilot on the flight down." My father nodded at the others. "We've been talking about how we ought to handle this. Almost everyone has been able to make contact with their families, to let them know the situation."

My father said, "How bad is it? A real pandemic or just another political scare? Any reports of flu here? I couldn't get through to my hospital. Just got a pretty vague official statement on voice mail."

Zuleta-Arango shrugged. Miike said, "Rumors. Who knows? There are riots ongoing in the States. Calexico has shut down its borders. Potlatch Territories, too. Lots of religious nuts making the usual statements online about the will of God. According to some of the other passengers, there's already a rumor about a new vaccine, and not enough to go around. People have started laying siege to hospitals."

"Just like last time," my father said. Last time had been three years ago. "Has anybody talked to the guys with the guns? I thought Costa Rica didn't even have an army. So who are these guys?"

"Volunteers," Zuleta-Arango said. "Mostly teachers, believe it or not. There was a quarantine situation here four months ago. Small outbreak of blue plague. Lasted about a week, and it didn't turn into anything serious. But they know the drill. Simon and I went over and asked them a few questions. They don't anticipate keeping us here longer than a week. As soon as someone at the terminal has sorted through the luggage, they'll get it out here. They just need to check first for guns and contraband."

"My kit's in my luggage," my father said. "I'll set up a clinic when it shows. What about food?"

"We'll be getting breakfast soon," Purdy, the pilot, said. "I've gotten the flight crew together to set up a mess table over by the far wall. Looks like we've got two kerosene grills and basic staples. Hope you like beans. We'll make an announcement about the clinic when everyone sits down to eat."

I'd been caught in a quarantine once before, during a trip to the mall. Hadn't turned out to be anything serious, just a college student with a rash. During the really bad flu, three years ago, I'd stayed home and played video games. My father had been stuck over at the hospital, but our refrigerator is pretty well stocked with frozen pizzas. My father stays over at the hospital all the time. I can take care of myself. When I got the e-mail about my mother and my brother, I didn't even page him. It's not like he could have done anything anyway. I just waited until he got home and told him then.

Lots of people died from that flu. Famous actors and former presidents and seven teachers at my school. Two kids on my soccer team. A girl named Corinne with white-blond hair who used to say, "Hey, Dorn" to me whenever I saw her in the hall at school. She came to all my games.

Our first meal in the hangar, served from a series of the largest pots I'd ever seen: reconstituted eggs and fried potatoes and lots and lots of beans. That was our second meal, too, and every meal after that, as long as we were in the hangar. Be glad that you've never had to live in a hangar with eighty-four people eating beans for breakfast, lunch, and dinner. For variety, there were little fat yellow-green bananas and industrial-size jars of these rubbery, slippery cylinders that Naomi said were hearts of palm.

My father said a couple of things to me. I ignored him. So he started talking to Naomi instead, about aliens and Costa Rica.

After breakfast I went back and lay down on my cot and thought about how I was going to get home. I had made it as far as some weird place where everyone was running around, setting fire to these inflatable germ-proof houses, when I woke up, face and arms and legs stuck to the plastic mattress with sweat, confused and overheated and pissed off. I didn't know where I was or why and then, when I did, it didn't make me any happier. The girl Naomi was sitting on the floor beside her cot. She was reading a beat-up old paperback. I figured I knew who she'd borrowed it from.

"You missed the excitement," she said. "Some executive type got all worked up and tried to pick a fight with the guards. He said something about how they couldn't do this to him because he's a U.S. citizen and he has rights. I thought we gave up those years ago. Zuleta-Arango and some of the others held him down while your father stuck him with a muscle relaxant.

"Have you read this?" she said. "I haven't seen one of these in years. Me, reading a book. I feel so very historical. We got our luggage back, so that's one good thing, although they've taken our passports away. I've never even heard of Olaf Stapleton. He's pretty good. Your dad doesn't exactly travel light. He's got like a hundred more actual books in his luggage. And you snore."

"I do not. Where is he?"

"Over there. In the office he set up. Taking temperatures and talking to hypochondriacs."

"Look," I said. "Before he comes back, we need to get something straight. You're not my babysitter, okay?"

"Of course I'm not," she said. "Aren't you a little old for a babysitter? How old are you? Sixteen?"

"Fourteen," I said. "Okay, good. That's settled. The other thing we need to straighten out is Hans Bliss. I'm with you. He's a loser, and I don't want to be here. As soon as they lift quarantine, I'm calling my soccer coach back in Philadelphia so he can buy me a ticket and get me out of here."

"Sure," she said. "Good luck with that. It would be terrible if a global flu epidemic meant the end of your soccer career."

"Pandemic," I said. "If it's global, it's a pandemic. And they're working on a vaccine right now. Couple of days and a couple of jabs and things will go back to normal, more or less, and I'll go home."

"This *is* home," Naomi said. "For me."

While she read Stapleton, I went through the luggage to see what my father had packed. The things he hadn't: my trophies, my soccer magazines, the braided leather bracelet that a girl named Tanya gave me last year, when we were sort of going out. I liked that bracelet.

What he had packed bothered me even more than what he hadn't, because you could tell how much time he'd spent planning this. He'd brought maybe a third of his collection of paperback SF. And in my duffel bag were my World Cup T-shirts, my palmtop, my sleeping bag, my toothbrush, two more soccer balls. An envelope of photos of my mother and of my brother, Stephen. The little glass bottle with nothing inside it that my mother gave me the last time I saw her. I wonder what my father thought when he found that glass bottle in my dresser drawer. It was the first thing he ever gave my mother. She liked to tell me that story. It didn't work out between them, but they didn't hate each other after the divorce, the way some parents do. Whenever they talked on the phone they laughed and gossiped about people as if they were still friends. And she never threw away that bottle of nothing. So I couldn't, either.

My father collects books, mostly sci-fi, mostly paperbacks. Most people keep their books on a googly or a flex, but my father likes paper. I read one of his books every once in a while when I got bored. Sometimes my father had written in the margins and on the blank pages, making notes about whether these were hopeful portraits of the future, or realistic, or other stories he was reminded of. Sometimes he doodled pictures of blobby or feathery aliens or spaceships or women whose faces looked kind of like my mother's face, except with tentacles coming out of their heads or with insect eyes, standing on pointy rocks with their arms akimbo, or sitting and holding hands with men in space suits. My father read his paperbacks over and over again, and so sometimes I left my own comments for him to find. He'd packed two suitcases for himself, and one was mostly books. I pulled out Ray Bradbury's *R Is for Rocket* and wrote on the first page of the first story, down in the bottom margin, "I HATE YOU." Then I dated it and put it back in the suitcase.

One of the two small offices in the hangar became my father's clinic. He spent most of the day there—among the passengers on our flight there were seven diabetics, one weak heart, two pregnancies (eight months, and five months), a dozen asthmatics, a migraine sufferer, three methadone users, one prostate cancer, one guy on antipsychotic medication, and two children with dry coughs. My father set up cots in the second office for the children and their parents, reassuring them that this was only a precaution. In fact, they ought to think of it as a privilege. Everyone else was going to be camping out in the hangar.

He came back smelling of hand sanitizer and B.O. "Feeling better?" he said to me.

I'd changed T-shirts and put on some jeans, but I probably smelled just as bad. I said, "Better than what, exactly?"

"Dinner's at seven," Naomi said. "They divided us into meal groups while you were asleep, Dorn. Meal groups with cute names. The Two-toed Sloths—*Perezosos de dos Dedos*—and the *Mono Congos*, howler monkeys to you, and the *Tucancillos*. That's us. Us *Tucancillos* get dinner first tonight. We're rotating dinner slots and chores. We do the dishes tonight, too. The *Mono Congos* are on latrine duty. I am really not looking forward to that."

It was beans and rice and eggs again, along with some kind of pungent, fibrous sausage. Chorizo. I loaded so much food on my plate that Naomi called me a pig. But there was plenty of food for everybody. After dinner, Naomi and I went out to wash dishes in the area that had been rigged for bathing. After I'd rinsed several stacks of smeary plates and sprayed them with disinfectant, I poured a dipper of water over my own head.

I was washing dishes at a barrel next to the girl that I'd showed off for earlier. Not an accident, of course. Even with her mask on, she was better than pretty this close up. "American?" she said.

"Yeah," I said. "From Philadelphia. Liberty Bell, Declaration of Independence, AOL Cable Access Riots of 2012. Are you Costa Rican?"

"Tica," she said. "I'm a Tica. That's what you say here." She had long, shiny hair and these enormous baby-animal eyes, like a heroine in an anime. She was taller than me, but I was used to girls who were taller than me. I liked her accent, too. "*Me llamo Lara*."

"I'm Dorn," I told her. "This is Naomi. We met on the bus."

"Hola," Naomi said. "I'm at UCR. Dorn is here with his father because of Hans Bliss and the aliens. Because, you know, Hans Bliss said that the aliens are going to show up again real soon and this time he knows what he's talking about. Not like all those other times when he said the aliens were coming back."

Several *Tucancillos* stopped washing dishes.

"Hans Bliss is a big deal here," Lara said.

I glared at Naomi. "I'm not really interested in this guy Bliss. I'm just here because my father kidnapped me."

My father had got out of dish duty when Zuleta-Arango announced some kind of committee meeting. Figures. First he kidnapped me, and now I was stuck doing his dishes.

"Hans Bliss can kiss my fat ass," Naomi said. Now some of our fellow *Tucancillos* were beginning to seem really irritated. I recognized the woman from the bus, Paula, the one that Naomi had already gotten riled up. The younger guy who had grabbed Paula's arm, back on the bus, was—I saw now—wearing a SHARE THE BLISS, HANS BLISS FOR WORLD PRESIDENT T-shirt. He gave Naomi a meaningful look, the kind of look that said he felt sorry for her.

"Let's get out of here," I said.

"Cool," Naomi said. "*Porta a mi.* Wait a minute, look over there. Is that an alien? Does it want to say something to us?"

Everyone looked, of course, but it was just a huge, disgusting bug. "Whoops," Naomi said. "Just a roach. But I hear our friends the roaches love Hans Bliss, too. Just like everyone else."

The woman Paula said, "I'm going to punch her right in that smug little mouth! If she says one more word!"

"Paula," the big-nosed guy said. "She isn't worth it. Okay?"

Naomi turned around and said, loudly, "I am too worth it. You have no idea how worth it I am."

The guy just smiled. Naomi gave him the finger. Then we were out of there.

While we were walking back, Lara said, "*Tengala adentro*. Naomi, I am not saying that I am a big fan of Bliss, but do you think that he was lying about his encounter with these aliens? Because I have seen the footage and read the eyewitness accounts, and my mother knows a man who was there. I don't believe it can all be a hoax."

Naomi shrugged. Back in the hangar, people were sorting through their suitcases, talking on cell phones, tapping away furiously at their peeties and googlies. We ended up back at the wall where our cots were, and Lara and I sat on the floor. Naomi hunkered down on her tires.

"I believe there were aliens," she said. "I just resent the fact that the first credible recorded contact with an extraterrestrial species was made by an idiot like Bliss. People who decide to go surfing in a Category 3 hurricane ought to be up for the Darwin Award, not considered representative of the human race. Well, not considered representative of the best the human race has to offer. And we only have Bliss's story about what the aliens said to him. I just don't buy that an intelligent race, the first we've ever come into contact with, would casually drop by to tell us to be happy and naked and polyamorous and vegetarian and oh yeah, *destroy all nuclear stockpiles*. All of those are good things, don't get me wrong. But they're exactly the kind of things you expect a retro-hippie surfer like Bliss to say. And the result? What's left of the United States, not to mention Greater Korea, Indonesia, and most of the Stans are all stockpiling weapons faster than ever, because they've decided it's suspicious that aliens apparently want us to destroy all nuclear weapons. Which kind of puts this whole flu thing into perspective, you know? If Bliss's aliens come back, there are going to be a lot of missiles pointed right at them, a lot of fingers hovering on those special fingerprint-sensitive keypads."

"And a lot of naked people lined up on beaches everywhere, singing 'Kumbaya' and throwing flowers," I said.

"Including you?" Naomi asked. Lara giggled.

"No way," I said. "I've got better things to do."

"Like what?" Lara said. I started to think she was flirting with me. "What kind of things are you into, Dorn?"

"I'm a soccer player," I said. "A pretty good one. I'm not bragging or anything. I really am good. You saw me, right? I'm a goalie. And I'm kind of feeling like an idiot right now. I mean, if I'd known my father was planning to kidnap me and bring me down here, I would have at least learned to say some stuff in Spanish. Like, *This man is kidnapping me*. How do you say that? I don't know anything about Costa Rica except the usual stuff. Like there are a lot of beaches down here, right? And software. And iguana farms? I know a kid down the street whose father lost his job, and his father keeps saying he's going to raise iguanas in the basement under special lights and sell the meat online. Or else raise llamas in his backyard. He hasn't made up his mind. His kid said iguana tastes like chicken. More or less."

"I'm a vegetarian," Lara said. "It's okay that you don't know Spanish. You'll learn."

"I hope we're out of here soon," Naomi said, "because I have exams coming up. Is your phone working, Lara? My googlie keeps crashing when I try to get on. I just want to know if they've shut the university down."

Lara thumbed her phone. "My battery is almost dead," she said at last. "But I know the situation of the schools. They're closed for the indefinite future. My mother spoke to her cousin a few hours ago. Still no outbreak of this flu in San Jose or any other place in Costa Rica, but the government is asking people to stay at home except in situations of emergency. Just for a few days. All of the cruise ships are anchored offshore. My cousin runs a cruise-supply company, which is how she knows. The army is dropping food and supplies onto the decks of the boats. I've never been on a cruise. I wish I were on a boat instead of in here. On the talk shows, they are talking about the flu. How perhaps it was manufactured and then released accidentally or even on purpose."

"They say that every time," I said. "My father says sure, it's possible, but you'd have to be really stupid to do something like that. And anyway, all we have to do is sit here and wait. Wait and see if anyone here is sick. Wait and see if anyone out there comes up with a vaccine. Once they get a vaccine cultured, they get it distributed pretty quickly. The question is, what do we do for fun in the meantime?"

"No point in studying if we're doomed," Naomi said, sounding nonchalant. "Maybe I should wait and see how bad this flu really is."

"We're safer in here than almost anywhere else," I said. At dinner, my father had made some announcements. He'd said clinic hours would run every day from eight A.M. until four P.M., and that if anyone began to feel achy or as if they had an elevated temperature, they should come talk to him at once. He said the odds that someone in the hangar would have the flu were minimal. He'd already talked with everyone who'd been on the flight and there was no one coming from Calexico or from anywhere farther west than Cincinnati. Our plane had started out the previous morning in Costa Rica and there hadn't been any changes of crew, except a flight attendant who got on in Miami after spending her day off at home, with her daughter. He explained that if we got sick at all, it would probably be some kind of stomach bug or mild cold, the kind of stuff you usually got when you traveled. Anya Miike had stood next to him, translating everything he said into Spanish and then into Japanese for these two guys from Osaka.

People had set up card games in the hangar. They'd brought out duty-free gins or tequilas or marijuana or those little bottles of Bailey's. Kids were drawing with smart crayons right on the concrete floor of the hangar, or watching the anime *Brave Hortense*, which someone had loaded onto a googly with a fancy bubble screen. Big, fat tears were plopping out of Brave Hortense's eyes, faster and faster, and the evil kitten who had made her cry began to build a raft, looking worried. A few feet away from us, a man was streaming a Spanish-language news program. The newsfeed became a Spanish-language song set to a languid beat. Elsewhere you could still hear news coming from tinny or expensive little speakers. There was good news and there was bad news. Mostly flu news. Flu in North America, and also in London and Rome.

None in Costa Rica. The music made a nice change.

"I love this song," Naomi said. "It's on all the time, but I don't care. I could listen to it all day long."

"Lola Rollercoaster," Lara said. "She always sings about love."

"*¡Qué tuanis!* What else is there to sing about?" Naomi said.

I rolled my eyes.

People sprawled on their tires and talked in Spanish and English and Japanese and German and watched the guards who were watching them. A man and woman began dancing to the Lola Rollercoaster song; others joined them. Mostly older people. They danced close to each other without quite touching. I didn't see the point in that. If someone in here came down with the flu, dancing two inches apart wasn't going to be much of a prophylactic. Lara looked like she wanted to say something, and I wondered if she'd ask me to dance. But it turned out that her mother, a not-bad-looking woman in a pair of expensive cornsilk jeans, was waving her back over to where they'd set up cots.

"I'll see you later," Lara said. "*Buenas noches*, Naomi, Dorn."

"Buenas noches." And then, "I think she likes me," I said, when she got out of earshot. "Girls usually like me. I'm not bragging or anything. It's just a fact."

"Yeah, well, that's probably why her mother's calling her back over," Naomi said. "An American boy like you is no catch, even if you do have a wicked nice smile and nice green eyes."

"What do you mean?" I said.

"Everybody knows that American boyfriends and girlfriends only want one thing. Costa Rican citizenship. Look over there. See that *macha*, that blond girl? The one flirting with the cute Tico?"

I looked where Naomi was pointing. "Yeah," I said.

"She probably came down here on a tourist visa, hoping to meet guys just like him," Naomi said. "This is a real stroke of luck for her. We're going to be in here for at least five or six days. Lots of time for flirting. If I looked like her, I'd be trying to pull off the same thing while I'm at UCR. I'd rather cut off my legs than have to go back and live in the States. At least here they can grow you a new pair."

"It's not that bad," I said.

"Really?" Naomi said. "If girls seem to like you, Dorn, realize that it's probably not for your brains or your keen grasp of socio-political-economic issues. Tell me what you like best about our country. Is it the blatantly rigged elections, the lack of access to abortion, the shitty educational system? Is it the fact that most of the states where anyone would ever actually want to live would secede like Calexico and Potlatch, if they had someone like Canada or Mexico to back them up? Is it the health care, the most expensive and least effective health-care system in the world, the national debt so impressive it takes almost two whole pages of little tiny zeros to write it out? Tell me about your job prospects, Dorn. Who would you just kill to work for? Wal-Mart, McDisneyUniverse, or some prison franchise? Or were you going to join the army and go off to one of the Stans or Bads because you've always wanted to get gassed or shot at or dissolved into goo when your experimental weapon malfunctions?"

"Professional soccer," I said. "Preferably in Japan or Italy. Whoever offers the best money."

Naomi blinked, opened her mouth, and then closed it again. She pulled out a bar of chocolate and broke off a piece still in the wrapper and gave it to me. We pushed our masks up and chewed. "This is good," I said.

"Yeah," she said. "Even the chocolate is, like, ten times better down here. Oh boy. Look over there."

I turned around. It was that woman again. Paula. She was standing in a row of about two dozen other women and men and she was taking off all her clothes. Then she was standing there naked. They were all taking off their clothes. The homely guy who'd been wearing the HANS BLISS FOR WORLD PRESIDENT T-shirt turned out to have a full-color portrait of Hans Bliss—on his surfboard, on a towering wave, about to be lifted up by the aliens—tattooed across his chest. It was pretty well done. Lots of detail. But I didn't spend too much time looking at him. There were more interesting things to look at.

"These are the people that my dad wants to go hang out with?" I said. I thought about getting out my camera. There were other people with the same idea, holding out their cell phones, clicking pics.

"Look, a priest," Naomi said. "Of course there would be a priest. A Church-of-the-Second-Reformation priest, too, by the look of him. Try not to drool. Surely you've seen naked women before."

"Only on the Internet," I said. "This is better."

A guy in a black suit and a priest's collar was striding over toward the protestors, yelling some things in Spanish. A naked man, so hairy that he was hardly naked at all, really, stepped out of the line with his arms out wide. Hans Bliss's Star Friends believed in embracing all of mankind. Preferably in the nude. (Or as nude as you can get when you're still wearing your stupid little face mask.)

The priest had apparently had run-ins with Star Friends before. He picked up a tennis racket beside someone's suitcase and commenced swinging it ferociously.

"What's he saying?" I asked Naomi.

"Lots of stuff. Put on your clothes. Have you no shame. There are decent people here. Do you call that nothing a penis. I've seen bigger equipment on a housecat."

"Did he really say that?"

"No," Naomi said. "Just the stuff about decency. Et cetera. Now he's saying that he's going to beat the shit out of this guy if he doesn't put his clothes back on. We'll see who's tougher. God or the aliens. My money's on God. Does your father really buy into all this? The nudity? The peace, love, and Bliss *über alles*?"

"I don't think so," I said. "He just really wants to get a chance to see aliens. Up close."

"Not me," Naomi said. "Maybe I've just seen too many animes where the aliens turn out to be, you know, alien. Not like us. I am really, really tired of these Bliss people. Can I borrow another sci-fi book? Do women ever write this stuff? A story with some romance in it would be nice. Something with fewer annotations."

"Connie Willis is fun," I said. "Or there's this book *Snow Crash*. Or you could read some Tiptree or Joanna Russ or Octavia Butler. Something nice and grim."

The priest continued to shout at the naked Star Friends and make menacing, swatting motions with the tennis racket. Other passengers got involved, like this was a spectator sport, yelling things, or whistling, or shouting. My father and Zuleta-Arango and the rest of the committee were walking over. The guards watched from their station by the hangar entrance. Clearly they had no plan to get involved.

It was twilight. The sky through the windows was lilac and gold, like a special effect. There were strings of lights looped along the walls, and a few worklights that people had found in one of the offices and set up strategically around the hangar, which made it look even more like a movie set. You could see the blue-white glow of googly screens everywhere. And then there were the bats. I don't know who noticed the bats first, but they were hard to miss, once the yelling started.

The bats seemed almost as surprised as we were. They poured into the hangar, looking like blackish, dried-up, flappy leaves, making long, erratic passes back and forth, skimming low and then winking up and away. People ducked down, covered their heads with their hands. The Hans Bliss people put their clothes back on—score one for the bats—and yet the priest was swinging his tennis racket at the bats now, just as viciously as he had the nudists. A bat dipped down and I ducked. "Go away!"

It went.

"They have vampire bats down here," Naomi said. She didn't seem bothered at all. "In case you're wondering. They come into people's houses and make little incisions in the legs or toes and then drink your blood. Hence the name. But I don't think these are vampire bats. These look more like fruit bats. They probably live up in the roof where those folds in the steel are. Relax, Dorn. Bats are a good thing. They eat mosquitoes. They've never been a vector for flu. Rabies, maybe, but not flu. We love bats."

"Except for the ones who drink blood," I said. "Those are big bats. They look thirsty to me."

"Calm down," Naomi said. "They're fruit bats. Or something."

I don't know how many bats there were. It's hard to count bats when they're agitated. At least two hundred, probably a lot more than that. But as the people in the hangar got more and more upset, the bats seemed to get calmer. They really weren't that interested in us. One or two still went scissoring through the air every now and then, but the others were somewhere up in the roof now, hanging down above us, glaring down at us with their malevolent, fiery little eyes. I imagined them licking their pointy little fangs. The man with the music turned it off. No more sad love songs. No more dancing. The card parties and conversations broke up.

My father and Zuleta-Arango walked up and down the makeshift aisles of the hangar, talking to the other passengers. Probably explaining about bats. People turned off the worklights, lay down on their cots, pulling silver foil emergency blankets and makeshift covers over themselves: jackets, dresses, beach towels. Some began to make up beds under the cots, where they would be safe from bats if not the spiders, lizards, and cockroaches that were, of course, also sharing our temporary quarters.

Half a soccer field away, Lara sat on a cot leaning back against her mother as her mother brushed her hair. She'd taken off her mask. She was even better looking than I'd thought she'd be. Possibly even out of my league.

Naomi was looking, too. She said, "Your parents are divorced, right? That's why your father kidnapped you? Have you called your mom? Does she know where you are now?"

"She's dead," I said. "She and my brother lived out on a dude ranch in Colorado. They caught that flu three years ago when it jumped from horses."

"Oh," Naomi said. "Sorry."

"Why be sorry? You didn't know," I said. "I'm fine now." My father was headed our way. I took off my mask and lay down on my cot and pulled the foil blanket over my head. I didn't take off my clothes, not even my shoes. Just in case the bats turned out not to be fruit bats.

◉ ◉ ◉

All night long, people talked, listened to newsfeeds, got up to go to the bathroom, dreamed the kind of dreams that woke them up and other people, too. Children woke up crying. Naomi snored. I don't think that my father ever went to sleep at all. Whenever I looked over, he was lying on his cot, thumbing through a paperback. An Alfred Bester collection, I think.

We settled into certain routines quickly. Zuleta-Arango's committee set up a schedule for recharging googlies and palmtops and cell phones from the limited number of outlets in the hangar. After some discussion, the Hans Bliss people rigged up a kind of symbolic wall out of foil blankets and extra cot frames. That was the area where you went if you wanted to hang out in the nude and talk about aliens. Of course you could just wander by and get an eyeful and an earful, but after a while nude people just don't seem that interesting. Really.

My dad spent some of the day in the clinic and some of his time with Zuleta-Arango. He hung out with the Hans Bliss people, and he and Naomi sat around and argued about Hans Bliss and aliens. Somebody started an English/Spanish-language discussion group, and he got involved in that. He set up a lending library, passing out his sci-fi books, taking down the names of people who'd borrowed them. There were plenty of movies and digests that people were swapping around on their googlies, but the paperbacks had novelty appeal. Science fiction is always good for taking your mind off how bad things are.

I still wasn't speaking to my father, of course, unless it was absolutely necessary. He didn't really notice. He was too excited about having made it this far, impatient to get on with the next stage of his journey. He was afraid that while we were quarantined, the thing he'd been waiting for would arrive, and he'd be stuck in a hangar less than a hundred miles away. So close, and yet he couldn't get any closer until the quarantine period was over.

I figured it served him right.

Most of the passengers in quarantine were returning to Costa Rica. The foreign passengers were almost all in Costa Rica because of tech industry stuff or the aliens. Mostly aliens. Because of Hans Bliss. Some of them had waited years to get a visa. There were close to a thousand Star Friends in Costa Rica, citizens of almost every nation, true believers, currently living down along the Pacific coastline, right next to Manuel Antonio National Park; Lara had been to Manuel Antonio a few times on camping trips with friends. She said it was a lot nicer than camping in a hangar.

The first day, the Star Friends quarantined in the hangar got through, on their cell phones and on e-mail, to friends already out with Hans Bliss. My father even managed to speak to Hans Bliss himself for a few minutes, to explain that he had made it as far as San Jose. The Star Friends community was under quarantine as well, of course, and Hans Bliss was somewhat put out that his doctor was stuck at the airport. Preparations for the imminent return of the aliens were being hampered by the quarantine.

Like I said, I saw Hans Bliss speak in Philadelphia once. He was this tall, good-looking blond guy with a German accent. He was painfully sincere. So sincere he hardly ever blinked, which was kind of hypnotic. When he stood on the stage and described the feeling of understanding and joy and compassion that had descended upon him and lifted him up as he stood out on that beach, in the middle of that ferocious storm, I sat there gripping the sides of my chair, because I was afraid that otherwise I might get up and run toward the stage, toward the thing that he was promising. Other people in the audience did exactly that. When he talked about finding himself back on that beach again, abandoned and forsaken and confused and utterly alone, the man sitting next to me started to cry. Everyone was crying. I couldn't stand it. I looked up at my father and he was looking down at me, like what I thought mattered to him.

"What are we doing here?" I whispered. "Why are we here?"

He said, "I don't like this any better than you do, Dorn. But I have to believe. I have to believe at least some of what he's saying. I have to believe that they'll come back."

Then he stood up and asked the crying man to excuse us. "What were they like?" someone yelled at Bliss. "What did the aliens look like?"

Everybody knew what the aliens looked like. We'd all seen the footage hundreds of times. We'd heard Bliss describe the aliens on news shows and in documentaries and on online interviews and casts. But my father stopped in the aisle and turned back to the stage and so did I. You would have, too.

Hans Bliss held out his arms as if he was going to embrace the audience, all of us, all at once. As if he was going to heal us of a sickness we didn't even know that we had, as if rays of energy and light and power and love were suddenly going to shoot out of his chest. The usual agents and government types and media who followed Hans Bliss everywhere he went looked bored. They'd seen this show a hundred times before. "They were beautiful," Hans Bliss said. People said it along with him. It was the punch line to one of the most famous stories ever. There had even been a movie in which Hans Bliss played himself.

Beautiful.

My father started up the aisle again. We walked out and I thought that was that. He never said anything else about Hans Bliss or Costa Rica or the aliens until he picked me up at soccer practice.

I put on my running shoes. I stretched out on the concrete floor and ran laps around and around the hangar. There were other people doing the same thing. After breakfast, I went over to an area where no one had set up a bed and started messing around, kicking the ball and catching it on the rebound. Nice and high. Some people came over and we played keep-away. When there were enough players, we took two cots and made them goals. We picked teams. Little kids came and sat and watched and chased down the ball when it went out-of-bounds. Even Naomi came to watch. When I asked her if she was going to play, she just looked at me like I was an idiot. "I'm not into being athletic," she said. "I'm too competitive. The last time I played organized sports, I broke someone's nose. It was only kind of an accident."

Lara came up behind me and tapped me on the back of the head. "*¿Como está ci arroz?* What's up?"

"You ever play soccer?" I said.

She ended up on my team. I was pretty excited about that, even before I saw her play. She was super fast. She put up her hair in a ponytail, took off her mask, and zipped up and down the floor. Our team won the first match, 3–0. We swapped some players around, and my team won again, 7–0, this time.

At lunch, people came by the table where I was sitting and nodded to me. They said things in Spanish, gave me the thumbs-up. Lara translated. Apparently they could tell how good I was, even though I was being careful on the concrete. I didn't want to strain or smash anything. This was just for fun.

After dinner there was some excitement when the bats woke up. Apparently nobody had really been paying attention that first night, but this time we saw them go. They bled out into the twilight in a thin, black slick, off to do bat things. Eat bugs. Sharpen their fangs. Nobody was happy to see them come back, either, except some of the little kids, and Naomi, of course. This whole one corner of the hangar floor was totally covered in bat guano. My dad said it wasn't a health risk, but as a matter of fact, one of the joggers slipped on it the next day and sprained an ankle.

The next day: more of the same. Wake up, run, play soccer. Listen to Naomi rant about stuff. Listen to people talk about the flu. Flirt with Lara. Ignore my father. I still wasn't ready to check in with Sorken, or to check e-mail. I didn't want to know.

That afternoon we had our second invasion. Land crabs, this time, the size of silver-dollar pancakes, the color of old scabs, and they smelled like rotting garbage. There were hundreds of them, thousands of hairy, armored legs, all dragging and scratching and clicking. They went sideways, their pincers held up and forward. Everybody stood on their cots or tires and took pictures. When the crabs got to the far wall, they spread out until they found the little cracks and gaps where they could squeeze through. A boy used his shirt to catch three or four crabs; some of the kids had started a petting zoo.

"What was that about?" I said to Naomi.

"Land migration," she said. "They do that when they're mating. Or is it molting? That's why they're so stinky right now."

"How do you know so much about all this?" I said. "Bats and crabs and stuff?"

"I don't date much," she said. "I stay home and watch the nature feeds online."

By lunch that second day we knew about outbreaks of flu in New New York, Copenhagen, Houston, Berlin, plenty of other places. The World Health Organization had issued the report my father had been predicting, saying that this was a full-on pandemic, killing the young and the healthy, not just the very young and the very elderly. We knew there were hopeful indications in India and in Taiwan with a couple of modified vaccines. The mood in the hangar was pretty unhappy. People were getting calls and e-mails about family members or friends back in the States. Not good news. On the other hand, we appeared to be in good shape here. My father said that in another two or three days, Costa Rican health officials would probably send a doctor out to sign off that we were officially flu-free. The two children with the dry coughs turned out just to have allergies. Besides that, the most pressing health issues in the hangar were some cases of cabin fever, diarrhea, and the fact that we were going through our supply of toilet paper too fast.

On the third day in the hangar we built better goals. Not quite regulation, but you'd be surprised what you can do with some expensive fishing gear and the frames from a couple of cots. Then practice drills. I sat out the first quarter of the first game, and a Tico with muscle-y legs took the goal. We still won.

The hangar guards changed over every twelve hours or so. After a while they were kind of like the bats. You didn't even notice them most of the time. But I liked watching them watch us when we played soccer. They were into soccer. They took turns coming over to watch, and whistled through their teeth whenever I blocked a goal. They placed bets. On the third day a guard came over to me during a time-out, and pushed up his N95 mask. *"¡Que cache!"* He made enthusiastic hand gestures. *"¡Pura vida!"* I understood that. He was a young guy, athletic. He was talking fast, and Naomi and Lara weren't around to translate, but I thought I had a pretty good idea what he was saying. He was trying to give me some advice about keeping goal. I just nodded, like I understood what he was saying and appreciated it. Finally he clapped me on the shoulders and went back over to his wall like he'd finally remembered that he was a guard.

Naomi was working her way through Roger Zelazny and Kage Baker. She was a pretty fast reader. First a Baker novel, then Zelazny. Then Baker again. I kept catching her reading the endings first. "What's the point of doing that?" I said. "If you cheat and read the end of the book first, why even bother reading the rest?"

"I'm antsy," she said. "I need to know how certain things turn out." She turned over so she was facing the wall, and said something else in Spanish.

"Fine," I said. I wasn't really all that invested. I was rereading some Fritz Leiber.

About fifteen minutes later, Lara came over and sat down on the cot next to Naomi. She picked up the stack of books that Naomi had already read, commenting in Spanish on the covers. Naomi laughed every time she said something. It was annoying, but I smiled like I understood. Finally Lara said, in English, "All of these girls have the large breasts. I did not know science fiction was about the breasts. I like the real stories. Stories about real astronauts, or scientific books."

"My father doesn't really go in for nonfiction," I said. I didn't see what was so bad about breasts, really.

"It makes for depressing reading," Naomi said. "Look at the space program in the old disunited States. Millionaires signing up for outer space field trips. The occasional unmanned flight that conks out somewhere just past Venus. SETI enthusiasts running analysis programs on their personal computers, because some guys blew up the Very Large Array, and guess what, when the real aliens show up, some guy named Hans Bliss says something and they go away again. Poof."

"Our space program is state of the art," Lara said. "Not to brag, like Dorn is always saying. But we will be sending a manned flight to Mars in the next five years. Ten years tops. If I keep my grades up and if I am chosen, I will be on that flight. That is my personal goal. My dream."

"You want to go to Mars?" I said. I'm sure I looked surprised.

"Mars, to begin with," Lara said. "Then who knows? I'm in an accelerated science and physical education course at my school. Many of the graduates go into the program for astronauts."

"There are advanced classes at UCR doing some work with your space program," Naomi said. "I don't know much about it, except that it all sounds pretty cool."

"We sent a manned flight to the moon last year," Lara said. "I met one of the astronauts. She came and spoke at my school."

"Yeah, I remember that flight," I said. "We did that, like, last century." I was just joking, but Lara didn't get that.

"And what have you done since?" she asked me.

I shrugged. It wasn't really anything I was interested in. "What's the point?" I said. "I mean, the aliens showed up and then they left again. Not even Hans Bliss is saying that we ought to go around chasing after them. He says that they'll come back when the time is right. Costa Rica getting all involved in a space program, is, I don't know, it's like my father deciding to leave everything behind, our whole life, just to come down here, even though Hans Bliss is just some surfer who started a cult. I don't see the point."

"The point is to go to space," Lara said. She looked at Naomi, not at me, as if I were too stupid to understand. "To go to space. It was a good thing when the aliens came to Costa Rica. They made us think about the universe, about what might be out there. Not everybody wants to sit on a beach and wait with your Hans Bliss to see if the aliens will come back."

"Okay," I said. "But not everybody gets a chance to go to Mars on a spaceship, either. Maybe not even you."

I was just being reasonable, but Lara didn't see it that way. She made this noise of exasperation, then said, emphatically, like she was making a point except that she was saying it in Spanish and really fast, so it didn't really tell me anything: *"¡Turista estúpido! ¡Usted no es hermoso como usted piensa usted es!"*

"Sorry?" I said.

But she just got up and left.

"What? What did she say?" I asked Naomi.

Naomi put down her paperback, *The Doors of His Face, the Lamp of His Mouth*. She said, "You can be kind of a jerk, Dorn. Some advice? *Hazme caso*—pay attention. I've seen you play soccer and you're pretty good. Maybe you'll get back to the States and get discovered and maybe one day you'll save some goal for some team and it will turn out to be the block that wins the World Cup. I'll go out to a bar and get drunk to celebrate when that happens. But my money's on Lara. I bet you anything Lara gets her chance and goes to Mars. I don't know if you've noticed, but when she isn't playing soccer or hanging out with us, she's studying for her classes or talking with the pilots about what it's like to fly commercial jets. And she also knows how to get along with people, Dorn. Maybe you don't have to be a nice guy to do well in team sports, but does it hurt?"

"I am a nice guy," I said.

"Stupid me," Naomi said. "Here I was thinking that you were arrogant, and, um, stupid, and what was the other thing? Oh yeah, *short.*" And then she picked up the Zelazny again and ignored me.

Lara didn't speak to me for the rest of the day. She didn't come back when we played soccer in the afternoon, and even though it was the Tucancillos' turn to do the dishes, she didn't turn up.

We still had plenty of surgical masks, but by the fourth day hardly anybody was wearing them. Just the sticklers and the guards in their N95s. I think everybody else was using the remaining supply for toilet paper. I wore one like a headband during soccer. I kind of needed a haircut. I couldn't do anything about that, but I did have a bath on the fourth night, after dinner, in one of the makeshift bathing stalls. Some of the people on the flight didn't have a lot of clothes in their suitcase, and so some borrowing had been going on, and there were clothes and various species of underwear draped over tires. I leaned against the outside wall of the hangar, away from the latrines, and admired the sunset for a bit. Not that I was a huge fan of sunsets, but the ones here were bigger, or something. And it smelled better out here. Not that you noticed how bad it smelled in the hangar most of the time, but once you came outside you realized you didn't want to go back in, not immediately, at least.

And the guards didn't seem to mind. There wasn't really anywhere for us to go. Just asphalt and runways. Still no planes coming in. Nobody to watch the sunset with me, which was an odd thing to think, since I'm usually pretty comfortable being alone. Even out on the field, during the game, the goalie is alone more often than not. Lara wasn't talking to me. I wasn't talking to my dad. Naomi and I weren't talking to each other. The sun went down fast, regardless of how I felt about the whole thing, and yeah, I know that's a melodramatic way to think about a sunset, but so what? Universe 1, Dorn 0.

When I came back into the hangar, Lara was over in the petting zoo, just sitting there. A dog was curled up on her legs and she was thumping its belly, softly, like a drum.

The petting zoo was an ongoing project. There were the three smelly crabs and a skinny brownish snake in a plastic makeup case that the kids fed beetles to. Some girl had caught it when she went out to use the bathroom. There were lizards in recycled food containers and a smallish iguana one of the guards had donated. There were even two dogs who got spoiled rotten.

I wandered over, trying to come up with something interesting to say. "What's up?" was all I came up with.

She looked up at me, then down again. Petted the dog.

"Watching the iguana," she said.

"What's it doing?" I said.

"Not much."

I sat down next to her. We didn't say anything else for a while. Finally I said, "Naomi says I shouldn't be such a jerk. And also that I'm short."

"I like Naomi," Lara said. "She's pretty."

Really? I thought. (But I knew better than to say that out loud.)

"What about me?"

Lara said, "I like watching you play soccer. It's like watching the soccer on television."

"Naomi's pretty brutal, but she's honest," I said. "I may never get tall enough to be a world-class goalie."

"You'll be taller. Your father is tall. Sometimes I have a temper," she said. "I shouldn't have said what I said to you."

"What did you say exactly?" I asked.

"Learn Spanish," she said. "Then when I say the awful things to you, you'll understand." Then she said, "And I am going to go up one day."

"Up?" I said.

"To Mars."

She wasn't wearing her mask. She was smiling. I don't know if she was smiling at me or at the idea of Mars, but I didn't care all that much. Mars was far away. I was a lot closer.

My father was on his cell phone. "Yes," he said. "Okay. I'll talk to him." He hung up. He said, "Dorn, come sit down for a minute."

I didn't say anything to him. I just sat down on my cot.

I realized that I was looking around, as if something had happened. Naomi was over against the wall, talking to the HANS BLISS FOR WORLD PRESIDENT guy, the one with the big nose. He was a lot taller than Naomi. Did Naomi mind being short?

My father said, "Your coach. He wanted to talk to you."

"Sorken called?" I said. I felt kind of sick to my stomach already, even though I wasn't sure why. I should have listened to those messages.

"No," my father said. "I'm sorry, Dorn. It was Coach Turner. He was calling about Sorken."

And I understood the difference immediately. "Sorken's dead."

My father nodded.

"Is everybody else okay? On the team?"

"I really don't know," my father said. "Mr. Turner hasn't been able to reach everyone. A lot of people around Philadelphia came down with flu, just like everywhere else. If I'd had more time to plan, I don't think I would have booked that flight. You were right, you know. I got an e-mail from a colleague out in Potlatch who thought something was coming, and meanwhile I'd been in touch with Hans Bliss off and on, and the visas had just come, and it seemed like a minor risk, getting us onto the flight, getting us through the airport. I thought if we didn't leave right then, who knew when we'd get here?"

I didn't say anything. I was remembering how Sorken used to come down on me when I was being a showoff, or not paying enough attention to what was going on, on the field, during practice. Sorken wasn't like my dad. If you weren't paying attention to him or you were sulking, he'd throw a soccer ball at your head. Or one of his shoes. But I'd just left those messages from him on the phone. I didn't even know where my phone was right now.

I'd never really thought about Sorken getting the flu and dying, but it had always seemed like there was a good chance that my father would catch something. A lot of hospital workers died during the last pandemic.

My father said, "Dorn? Are you okay?"

I nodded.

"I'm sorry about Sorken," he said. "I never really sat down and talked to him."

"He didn't have much time for people who didn't play soccer," I said.

"It always looked like he was riding you pretty hard."

"I don't think he liked me," I said. "I didn't like him most of the time. But he was a good coach. He wasn't ever harder on me than he should have been."

"I told Coach Turner that you wouldn't be back for a while," my father said. "To be honest with you, I don't know what we'll do. If we'll be allowed to stay. There's been some talk in the hangar. Rumors that our government is responsible. That we were targeting Calexico. It doesn't seem likely to me, but we weren't going to be very popular down here, Dorn, even before people starting making up stories like that. And I'm not going to be much more popular back in Philadelphia. I checked in with my team. Dr. Willis yelled for about five minutes and then she just hung up. I skipped out even though I knew they were going to need me."

"Maybe you would have gotten sick if we'd stayed," I said. "Or maybe I would have gotten sick."

My father studied his hands. "Who knows? I was planning to tell you about the visas. Give you a choice. But then I just couldn't leave you. You know, in case." He stopped and swallowed. "I was talking to Paula and some of the other Hans Bliss people. As of this morning they haven't been able to get hold of anyone out that way. At the colony. They've been under quarantine, too, remember? And no doctor. Just two OB-GYNs and a chiropractor."

"Everything will be fine," I said. I was a regular cheerleader. But I couldn't help looking around again, and this time I could see all the things that I'd been trying not to see. All around us, other people were having, had been having, conversations just like this one. About people who had died. About what had been going on while we were trapped in here.

I said, "The aliens are coming back to see Hans Bliss, remember? So there's no way that Hans Bliss can just keel over dead from something like flu. Those aliens probably vaccinated him or something. Remember how he said he didn't ever get sick anymore?"

"Good point," my father said. "If you're gullible enough to buy all the things that Hans Bliss says."

"Hey, you two," Naomi said. She looked flushed and happy, as if she'd gotten the last word again with the Hans Bliss guy. She didn't seem to be annoyed with me. And I couldn't really be annoyed with her, either. Everything she'd said was true, more or less. I hadn't known her very long, but I already knew that that was the terrible thing about Naomi.

My father took the soccer ball out of my hands. I don't even know when I'd picked it up, but it felt right to let go of it. He put it down on the floor, sat down beside me on the cot, and patted my leg. "It will all be fine," he said, and I nodded.

My brother Stephen was older than me by four years. He didn't like me. According to my father, when I was a baby Stephen used to unfasten my seat belt and also the strap that held my baby seat in. When I was five, he pushed me down a flight of stairs. I broke my wrist. My mother saw him do it, and so once a week for the next two years Stephen went to see a counselor named Ms. Blair in downtown Philadelphia; I remember I was jealous.

When our parents got divorced, Stephen was ten and I was six, and they decided they would each take custody of one child. Stephen thought that this was a great idea. His goal had always been to become an only child.

My mother went back home to Dalton, Colorado, where she took over the bookkeeping at her family's fancy dude ranch and spa.

Whenever I flew out to visit, Stephen made sure I understood that it was all his. His house, his horses—all of them—his mom, his grandparents, his uncles, aunts, cousins. He came back east to stay with us once, and then he developed an inner-ear condition that made it impossible for him to fly. So he didn't ever have to come visit again. He didn't like my father much either.

The last time I saw my mom and Stephen, Stephen was applying to colleges. He didn't seem to loathe me as much as usual. He was practically an adult. I was just a kid. I was athletic, which he wasn't, but my grades were pitiful. I was small for my age. He could tell how annoyed I was that he was tall and I wasn't, and somehow it made things better. He had a girlfriend, a massage therapist at the spa, and he didn't even care that she made a point of being nice to me. I had a pretty good time on that trip. My mother and I rode out and went camping down in the canyons. Stephen's girlfriend cooked dinner for us when we got home. It was almost like we were a family. Stephen showed us a movie he'd made to send along with his college applications. When I said I liked it, he was pleased. We got into arguments the way we always did, but this time I realized something, that Stephen liked a good fight. Maybe he always had, or maybe he'd just grown up. If you stood up to him, it made him happy. I had never tried standing up to him before. He was applying for a visa so he could go study at a big-deal film school in Calexico.

A few months later, the horses at the dude ranch started dying. My mother e-mailed and said my uncle had brought the local vet in. They were putting the sick horses down. When we talked on the phone, she sounded terrible. My mother loved horses. Then people on the ranch started dying, too. Sometimes a flu will jump from one species to another. That's why a lot of people don't keep cats or birds as pets anymore.

I talked to my mother two more times the next day. Then things got worse, real fast. My father was staying over at the hospital, and lots of people were dying. My mother got the flu. She died. Stephen died. The girlfriend got sick, and then she got better again. She sent one e-mail before she got sick and one after she got better, which is how I found out what had happened. Her first e-mail said that Stephen had wanted her to tell us how much he loved us. But he probably died in quarantine. He probably felt like he was getting a cold, and then I bet his temperature shot up until he was delirious or completely unconscious and couldn't say anything to anyone. My dad said that their kind of flu was fast. So you didn't suffer or anything. I think the girlfriend was just making all that up, about Stephen and what he supposedly said. She was a nice person. I don't think he'd ever said anything to her about how much he disliked me. About how he used to try to kill me. You want the people you like to think that you get along with your family.

It was the hardest thing I ever had to do, telling my father when he finally came home. And we haven't talked about it much since then. I don't know why it's easier for some people to talk about aliens than to talk about death. Aliens only happen to some people. Death happens to everyone.

That night in the hangar, I dreamed about Sorken. He was standing in front of the goal, instead of me, and he was talking at me in Spanish, like the Costa Rican guard. I knew that if I could only understand what he was saying, he'd be satisfied, and then I could take the goal again. I wanted to say I was sorry that he was dead, and that I was sorry that I was in Costa Rica, and that I was sorry I hadn't ever called him back when he left all those messages, but he couldn't understand what I was saying because I couldn't speak Spanish. I kept hoping that Lara would show up.

Instead the aliens came. They came down just like Hans Bliss had said, in this wave of feeling: joy and love and perfect acceptance and knowingness, so that it didn't matter anymore that Sorken didn't remember how to speak English and I didn't know Spanish. For the first time we just understood each other. Then the aliens scooped up Sorken and took him away.

I grabbed on to the frame of the soccer goal and held on as hard as I could, because I was sure they were going to come back for me. I didn't want to go wherever it was, even though it was beautiful, so beautiful; they were even more beautiful than Hans Bliss had said. A wave of warm, alien ecstasy poured over me, and then I woke up because Naomi was hitting me on the shoulder. She had a plate of food with her. Breakfast.

"Stop moaning about how beautiful it is," she said. "Please? Whatever it is, it's really, really beautiful. I get that, totally. Oh shit, Dorn, were you having a wet dream? I am so very embarrassed. Oh yuck. Let me go somewhere far away now and not eat my breakfast."

I wanted to die. But instead I got changed under the foil blanket and then went and got my own breakfast and came back. Naomi had her nose in a book. I said, "I don't see what the big deal is. It's just something that happens to guys, okay?"

"It happens to girls, too," Naomi said. "Not that I want to be having some sex-education discussion with you. Although you probably need it, from what I hear about American schools nowadays."

"Like you had it so much better," I said. "And my dad's a doctor, remember? I know everything I need to know and lots of other stuff, too. And what were you doing last night? You woke me up when you came to bed. I don't even know when it was. It was late."

"My parents homeschooled me," Naomi said. "They wanted me to have every advantage." Her eyes were all red.

"What?" I said. "Are you sick? Is everything okay?"

"I think so," Naomi said. She scraped her nose with a sterile wipe. "I talked to my mom last night. She says that Vermont is still under martial law, so she can't get out to see my grandmother. She can't get her on the phone either. That's probably bad, right?"

"It might not be," I said.

Naomi didn't say anything.

"At least your mom and dad are all right," I said.

She nodded.

"Here," I said. "Let's get a book for you. Something cheerful. How about Naomi Novik?"

We sat and she read and I thought about stuff. Sorken. My father. My mother. My brother Stephen. I thought about how the kind of thing that Stephen thought was funny when he was alive wasn't really anything that I thought was funny. For example, when he pushed me down the stairs. I remember he was giggling. The last time I was out visiting my mother, it was different. He laughed at some of the things that I said, and not like it was because he thought I was an idiot. We got into one of those arguments about something really stupid, and then I said something and he just started laughing. I wish I could remember what I said, what we were arguing about.

Naomi looked up and saw me looking at her. "What?" she said.

"Nothing," I said.

"Hey," she said. "Do you surf?"

"No," I said. "Why?"

"Not much to do out there on the beach with Hans Bliss," she said. "Not a lot of soccer players. Everybody goes surfing. You know that Hans Bliss guy? Philip? The one with the tattoo and the mother. Paula." The one with the big nose. "He was telling me this story about a guy he knew, a surfer. One day this surfer guy was out in the water and he got knocked under by this really big wave. He went down and his board shot out from under him, really sliced him. But he didn't realize what had happened until he got out of the water, because the water was really cold, but when he got out of the water and pulled his suit down, it turned out that the fin on his board had cut his ball sac right open, and he hadn't felt it because the water was so cold. When he pulled his suit down, his testicle fell out and was just hanging there, way down on his leg on, like, this string. Like a yo-yo."

"So?" I said. "Are you trying to gross me out or something? My dad's a doctor, remember? I hear stories like this all the time."

Naomi looked nonplussed. "Just be careful," she said. "What's up? Bad news?"

I'd found my cell phone, and I was trying to decide whether or not to listen to Sorken's messages. But in the end I just deleted them. Then I went and got some people together to play soccer.

It was the fifth day, if you're counting, and nobody in the hangar had the flu, which was good news, but my father still had his hands full. There was the pregnant woman from Switzerland who had come over to join Hans Bliss. A couple of days in quarantine, and she decided that she'd had enough. She threw this major tantrum, said she was going into labor. The best part: she took off all her clothes before she threw the tantrum. So you had this angry, naked, pregnant woman yelling stuff in German and French and English and stomping her foot like Gojiro. It totally broke up the soccer game. We all stopped to watch.

My father went and sat on the floor next to her. I went and stood nearby, just in case she got dangerous. Someone needed to look out for my father. He said that he'd be happy to examine her, if she liked, but she probably wouldn't go into labor for another month, at least, and we weren't going to be stuck in here that long. And anyway, he'd delivered babies before. All you really needed was boiling water and lots of towels. I think he was kidding about that.

Just a few hours later, a Tico doctor showed up with a full mobile clinic. By that point we were just kind of kicking the ball around. I was showing off some for Lara. The doctor's name was Meñoz, and it was all pretty much like my father had said it was going to be. My father and Dr. Meñoz talked first, and then they looked at the clinic records my father had been keeping. I hung around for a bit, hoping that Dr. Meñoz would just go ahead and tell us that we were free to go, but it seemed like it was going to take a while. So Lara and I went around and got one last soccer match together. A lot of people came and watched.

That guard who'd talked to me a few times was, like, my biggest fan now. Whenever we were playing he yelled and clapped his hands, and he'd dance around when I stopped a goal. All the guards came over to watch this time, not just him, as if they knew that the rules didn't really matter now. So much for quarantine.

Before we started for real, something strange happened. My guard put down his gun. He talked to his friends, and they gave him a high five. Then he came out onto the field. He even took off his N95 mask. He smiled at me. "I play, too," he said. He seemed proud of having this much English. Well, it was more English than I had Spanish.

I shrugged. "Sure," I said. I waved at the other team, the one Lara was on. "Play for those guys. They need all the help they can get."

It was around three in the afternoon, and it was warm, but there was a breeze coming in through the vents up in the tin roof and through the big metal doors. Like always, there was music playing on someone's googly, and the little kids were having a conference over in the petting zoo, probably figuring out what to do with all of the freaky little animals they'd collected. I was almost enjoying being here. I was almost feeling nostalgic. It wasn't like I had a lot of friends in the hangar, but most people knew me well enough to say hi. When I wanted to get a match going, there were always enough people to play, and nobody got all that upset about the fact that my team won most of the time. Whatever happened next, I didn't think I'd be spending a lot of time playing soccer. Wherever we ended up, nobody was going to know much about me, about what I could do in a soccer game. I'd just be some American kid whose dad was a doctor who had wanted to see aliens.

Naomi, who had decided she enjoyed refereeing a match every once in a while, threw the ball in, and that hangar guard was on it immediately, before anyone else even thought about moving. He was amazing. He was better than amazing. He went up and down the concrete as if no one else was on the floor. And he put the ball past me every single time, no matter what I did. And every time, when I failed to stop him, he just grinned and said, "Good try. Good try."

The worst part is that he did it without even taking advantage of my height. He didn't go over me. He just went around. The way he did it was so good it was like a bad dream. Like science fiction. Like I was Superman and he was Kryptonite. He seemed to know what I was going to do before I did. He knew all about me, like he'd been taking notes during all those other games.

After a while both teams stopped playing and they just watched while he did all sorts of interesting stuff. If I came forward, he skimmed around and behind me. Score. If I hung back in front of the goal, it didn't matter. He put the ball where I wasn't. I didn't give up, though. I finally stopped a goal. I felt good about that, until I realized that he'd let me have the save. I hadn't really stopped anything.

And that was the last straw. There he was, grinning at me, like this had just been for fun. He wasn't even breathing hard. I made myself grin back. He didn't realize I knew he'd let me save that last goal. He didn't even think I was that smart. He clapped for me. I clapped for him. Everyone who had been watching was clapping and yelling. Even Lara. So I just walked away.

I didn't feel angry or upset or anything. I just felt as if I'd found out something important. I wasn't as good as I thought I was. I'd thought I was amazing, but I wasn't. Some guy who'd spent five days standing against a wall holding a gun could walk in and prove in about ten minutes that I wasn't anything special. So that was that. I know you'll think that I was being melodramatic, but I wasn't. I was being realistic. I gave up on soccer right then.

For some reason, I was thinking about the little empty glass bottle that my father gave my mother, that my mother gave me. I wondered what Sorken would think when I told him I was quitting soccer, and then I remembered Sorken was dead. So I didn't have to worry what he thought.

Something was going on with the Hans Bliss group. They'd disassembled their modesty wall. Actually, they'd just kicked it over. They were huddled together, looking really bad. Utterly hopeless. I could sympathize. My father and Zuleta-Arango and Dr. Meñoz were there too, so I went over. My father said, "Dr. Meñoz had some news about the Star Friends community."

"Not good news," I said.

"No," my father said. He didn't sound particularly upset, but that's my father. He doesn't ever seem particularly anything. "One of the last arrivals came in from Calexico, and he had the flu. They weren't being very careful in the community. Hans Bliss didn't believe they were in any real danger. Lots of physical contact. Communal eating. They didn't have good protocols in place. No doctor. They had no doctor."

"It might not have made any difference," Zuleta-Arango said. "There were deaths on one of the cruise ships, too. And in a few neighborhoods of San Jose, a few cities, they have set up additional quarantine zones. There are deaths. But the mobile units are being supplied with vaccines, which Dr. Meñoz says will do the trick. It isn't as bad as it's been in the States. We have been lucky here."

"Not all of us," my father said. "Hans Bliss is dead."

The pregnant woman began to wail. Lots of other people were crying. My father said, "The remaining community is in bad shape. As soon as quarantine is lifted here, I'll go out to see how I can help, if they'll let me."

Dr. Meñoz popped his cell phone closed and struck up a conversation in rapid Spanish with Zuleta-Arango, Miike, and Purdy. The

Hans Bliss people were still standing there. They looked like they'd been pithed. That guy Philip, the one with the surfer friend, the one that Naomi seemed to like, blew his nose hard. He said to my father, "We'll all go out. There will be things that they need us to do."

"What about me?" I asked.

"Yes," my father said. "What about you? I can't send you home."

Dr. Meñoz said, "As of right now, I'm authorized to lift quarantine here. This news is good, at least? There will be a bus outside the hangar within the hour. It will transport all of you into San Jose, to a center for displaced travelers. They are arranging for the necessary series of vaccinations there. Shall I make the announcement or would you prefer to do it?"

Zuleta-Arango made the announcement. There was something anticlimactic about it. Everyone already knew what he was about to say. And what he said wasn't really the thing that we needed to know. What we didn't know was what was going to happen next. Where we would be sent. What would happen in the next few weeks. When the flight ban would be lifted. Where the flu had come from. Whether or not the people that we loved would be okay. What we would find when we got home.

Naomi had already packed up her duffel bag. She said, "Lots of people have been coming by, bringing back your father's books. I finished the last Kim Stanley Robinson. I guess there are still a couple of short-story collections. I heard about Bliss. That really sucks. Now I feel bad about calling him an idiot."

"He was an idiot," I said. "That's why he's dead."

"I guess," Naomi said. "What's in that bottle?"

* * *

Like I said, the glass bottle with nothing inside it was the first present that my father ever gave my mother. He told her that there was a genie in the bottle. That he'd bought it at a magic shop. A *real* magic shop. He said that he'd already made two wishes. The first wish had been to meet a beautiful girl. That was my mother. The second wish was that she would fall in love with him, but not just because of the wish. That she would really fall in love with him. So already you can see the problem, right? You wouldn't fall for some guy who was telling you this. Because if you fall in love with someone because of a wish, how can it not be the wish that makes you fall in love? I said that to my mother one time and she said that I was being too literal minded. I said that actually, no, I was just saying that my father's made-up story was kind of stupid.

My mother always said that she'd never used that last wish. And I didn't understand that either. Why didn't she use it when they were getting divorced? Why didn't she use it to make Stephen like having a little brother better? I used to think that if I had the bottle I'd wish for Stephen not to hate me so much. For him to like me. Just a little. The way that older brothers are supposed to like younger brothers. There were other wishes. I mean, I've made lists and lists of all the wishes I could make, like being the best goalie there has ever been. Like getting taller by a few inches. Other stuff that's too embarrassing to talk about. I could come up with wishes all day long. That it wouldn't rain. That I'd suddenly be a genius at math. That my parents would get back together.

I hadn't ever made any of those wishes, not even the soccer wish, because I don't believe in wishes. Also because it would be like cheating, because when I was a famous goalie I'd always wonder if I were really the best soccer player in the world, or whether I'd just wished it true. I could wish that I were taller, but maybe one day I will be. Everyone says that I will be. I guess if I were Paula or one of the Star Friends, I'd wish that Hans Bliss had been smarter. That he hadn't died. Or I'd wish that the aliens would come back. I don't know which of those I'd wish for.

I gave the bottle to Lara when she came over to say good-bye. I didn't really mean anything by it.

She said, "Dorn, what is this?"

"It's a genie in a bottle," Naomi said. "Like a fairy tale. Dorn says that there's one wish left in there. I said that if he gave it to me, I'd wish for world peace, but he's giving it to you instead. Can you believe it?"

Lara shook the glass bottle.

"Don't do that," I said. "How would you like to be shaken if you were an invisible genie who's been trapped in a bottle for hundreds of years?"

"I don't believe in wishes," Lara said. "But it is very sweet of you, Dorn, to give it to me."

"It belonged to my mother," I said.

"His *dead* mother," Naomi said. "It's a precious family heirloom."

"Then I can't keep it," Lara said. She tried to give it back.

I put my hands behind me.

"Never mind then," Lara said. She looked a little annoyed, actually. As if I were being silly. I realized something: Lara wasn't particularly romantic. And maybe I am. She said, "I'll keep it safe for you, Dorn. But I have something important to tell you."

"I know," I said. "You were watching the guard walk all over me. During that last game. You want to tell me to pick a new career."

"No, Dorn," Lara said. Even more annoyed now. "Stop talking, okay? That guard isn't just a guard, you know? He was on the team for Costa Rica. The team that was supposed to go to the World Cup three years ago, before the last influenza."

"What?" I said.

"His name is Olivas," Lara said. "He got into a fight this summer and they kicked him off the team for a while. He sounds like you, Dorn, don't you think? Not very bright. But never mind. He says you are good. Talented."

"If I were any good, he wouldn't have been able to walk past me like that, over and over again," I said. But I started to feel a little better. He wasn't just a guard with a gun. He was a professional soccer player.

"No, Dorn," Lara said again. "You are *good*, but he is *very good*. There is a difference, you know?"

"Apparently," I said, "there is a difference. I just hadn't realized how big. I didn't know he was, like, a soccer superstar. I thought that maybe he was just average for Costa Rica. I was thinking that I ought to quit soccer and take up scuba diving or something."

"I hadn't realized that you were a quitter," Lara said. She still sounded very disapproving. Her eyebrows were knit together, and her lower lip stuck out. She looked even prettier, and it was because she was disappointed in me. Interesting.

"Maybe you ought to get to know him better," Naomi said, looking at me looking at Lara like she knew what I was thinking. "Dorn needs to pack. You two will have plenty of time to talk on the bus. It's not like you're never going to see each other again. At least, not yet. Lara, *pele el ojo*. Your mother is coming this way."

"Es un chingue," Lara said. *"¡Que tigra!"* She sighed and kissed

me right on the mouth. She had to dip her head down. Then she dashed off. Zip. When I thought about it, I wasn't looking forward to getting to know her mother, and her mother sure wasn't looking forward to getting to know me.

"So," Naomi said. She was grinning. "You know what Lara told me a few days ago? That she wasn't ever planning on having boyfriends. You can't get serious about boys if you want to go to Mars. So much for that. Not that you'll care, but you aren't the only one who got lucky."

"What?" I said. "Did that blond girl come over to show you her engagement ring or something?"

"No," Naomi said. She waggled her eyebrows like crazy. "*I* got lucky. Me. That cute guy, Philip? Remember him?"

"We're not thinking about the same guy," I said. "He's not cute. I know cute. I *am* cute."

"He's nice," Naomi said. "And he's funny. And smart."

I didn't know so much about nice. Or smart. I finished packing my suitcase, and started in on my father's. I wished I hadn't given away that little glass bottle. I could have given Lara a paperback instead. "You must have a lot to talk about."

"I suppose," Naomi said. "You know the best part?"

"What?" I said. I looked around for my father and finally spotted him. He was sitting on a cot beside the pregnant woman, who probably had a name but I'd never bothered to find out. She was sobbing against his shoulder, her mouth still open in that wail. Her face was all shiny with snot. I was betting that if her baby was a boy, she'd name him Hans. Maybe Bliss if it was a girl.

A girl walked by, dragging an iguana behind her on a homemade leash. Were they going to let her bring the iguana on the bus?

Naomi said, "The best part is he has dual citizenship. His father's from Costa Rica. And he likes smart, fat, big-mouthed chicks."

"Who doesn't?" I said.

"Don't be so sarcastic," Naomi said. "It's an unattractive quality in someone your size. Want a hand with the suitcases?"

"You take the one with all the books in it," I said.

People were still packing up their stuff. Some people were talking on their cell phones, transmitting good news, getting good news and bad news in return. Over by the big doors to the hangar, I ran into the guard. Olivas. I was beginning to think I recognized his name. He nodded and smiled and handed me a piece of paper with a number on it. He said something in Spanish.

Naomi said, "He says you ought to come see him practice next month, when he's back on his team again."

"Okay," I said. "*Gracias.* Thank you. *Bueno. Bueno.*" I smiled at Olivas and tucked his phone number into my shirt pocket. I was thinking, One day, I'll be better than you are. You won't get a thing past me. I'll know Spanish, too. So I'll know exactly what you're saying, and not just stand here looking like an idiot. I'll be six inches taller. And when I get scouted, let's say I'm still living down here, and let's say I end up on the same team as you, I won't get kicked off, not for fighting. Fighting is for idiots.

Naomi and I went out onto the cracked tarmac and sat on our luggage. Costa Rican sunlight felt even more luxurious when you were out of quarantine, I decided. I could get used to this kind of sunlight. Lara was over with her mother and some other women, all of them speaking a mile a minute. Lara looked over at me and then looked away again. Her eyebrows were doing that thing. I was pretty sure we weren't going to end up sitting next to each other on the bus. Off in the distance, you could see somewhere that might have been San Jose, where we were going. The sky was blue, and there were still no planes in it. They were all lined up along the runways. Our transportation wasn't in sight yet, and so I went to use the latrines one last time. That's where I was when the aliens came. I was pissing into a hole in the ground. And my father was still sitting inside the hangar, his arm around an inconsolable, enormously pregnant, somewhat gullible Swiss woman, hoping that she would eventually stop crying on his T-shirt.

It was kind of like the bats. They were there, and after a while you noticed them. Only it wasn't like the bats at all and I don't really mean to say that it was. The aliens' ships were lustrous and dark and flexible; something like sharks, if sharks were a hundred feet long and hung in the air, moving just a little, as if breathing. There were three of the ships, about 150 feet up. They were so very close. I yanked up my pants and pushed the latrine curtain aside, stumbled out. Naomi and that guy Philip were standing there on the tarmac, looking up, holding hands. The priest crossing himself. The kid with her iguana. Lara and her mother and the other passengers all looking up, silently. Nobody saying anything yet. When I turned toward San Jose, I could see more spacecraft, lots more. Of course, you already know all this. Everyone saw them. You saw them. You saw the aliens hovering over the melting ice floes of Antarctica, too, and over New New York and Paris and Mexico City, and Angkor Wat and all those other places. Unless you were blind or dead or the kind of person who always manages to miss seeing what everybody else sees. Like aliens showing up. What I want to know is did they come back because they knew that Hans Bliss was dead?

People still argue about that, too. Poor Hans Bliss. That's what I was thinking: Poor, stupid, lucky, unlucky Hans Bliss.

I ran inside the hangar, past Olivas and the other guards and Dr. Meñoz and Zuleta-Arango, and two kids spinning around in circles, making themselves dizzy on purpose.

"Dad," I said. "Dad! Everyone! The aliens! They're here. They're just outside! Lots of them!"

My father got up. The pregnant woman stopped crying. She stood up too. They were walking toward me and then they were running right past me.

Me, I couldn't make up my mind. It seemed as if I had a choice to make, which was stupid, I know. What choice? I wasn't sure. Outside the hangar were the aliens and the future. Inside the hangar it was just me, a couple hundred horrible bats sleeping up in the roof, the remains of a petting zoo, and all of the rest of the mess we were leaving behind. The cots. Our trash. All the squashed water bottles and crumpled foil blankets and the used surgical masks and no-longer-sterile wipes. The makeshift soccer field. I had this strange urge, like I ought to go over to the field and tidy it up. Stand in front of one of the cobbled-together goals. Guard it. Easier to guard it, of course, now that Olivas wasn't around. I know it sounds stupid, I know that you're wondering why aliens show up and I'm still in here, in the empty hangar, doing nothing. I can't explain it to you. Maybe you can explain it to me. But I stood there feeling empty and lost and ashamed and alone until I heard my father's voice. He was saying, "Dorn! Adorno, where are you? Adorno, get out here! They're beautiful, they're even more beautiful than that idiot said. Come on out, come and see!"

So I went to see.

KELLY LINK was born in Miami, Florida, and grew up on the East Coast. She attended Columbia University in New York and the University of North Carolina, Greensboro. She sold her first story, "Water Off a Black Dog's Back," just before attending Clarion in 1995. Her later stories have won or been nominated for the James Tiptree Jr., World Fantasy, Hugo, and Nebula awards.

Link's stories have been collected in *Stranger Things Happen* and *Magic for Beginners*. She has edited the anthology *Trampoline*; coedits *The Year's Best Fantasy and Horror* with her husband, Gavin J. Grant, and Ellen Datlow; and coedits the zine *Lady Churchill's Rosebud Wristlet* with Grant. She is currently assembling a new collection of short fiction for teenagers and adults, to be published by Viking.

Visit her Web site at www.kellylink.net.

AUTHOR'S NOTE

Like Dorn's father, when I travel I cram as many books as will fit into my suitcase. What follows is a very incomplete list of the science fiction and fantasy authors whose books I've lugged around with me over the years, and who I imagined Dorn would also be familiar with: Ursula K. Le Guin, Patricia McKillip, Alfred Bester, Kage Baker, M. T. Anderson, Octavia Butler, Ted Chiang, R. A. MacAvoy, Terry Pratchett, Sheri Tepper, Ray Bradbury, Fritz Leiber, and Margo Lanagan. Of course, since this story takes place in the future, Dorn and his father have read a number of excellent books that I've never heard of. Possibly some of them will be written by the readers of this anthology.

REPAIR KIT

Stephen Baxter

Paul Tielman, captain of the *Flying Pig*, stood rigidly at attention.

The face on the tridee screen was plump, sleek, and stern. "I suppose you're aware, Captain Tielman, of the importance of the successful operation of the new Prandtl Drive to Galactic Technologies, which happens to be your employer? Not to mention the expense of outfitting the *Flying Pig* with the prototype drive?"

"Of course, Chief Executive."

"And yet you are already ten days past your scheduled launch date."

"But, Chief Executive, we can't launch unless we're sure the drive is reliable. We're still missing one crucial component that—"

Tielman was silenced by an imperiously raised eyebrow. "Captain, overcaution is a failing. The ship will leave the yard in forty-eight hours' time, with or without you. Your choice."

"Very well, Chief Executive." The tridee blanked out. Tielman pushed his fingers through his thatch of stiff iron-gray hair. "I don't care if he is my boss, that man is a pompous, self-seeking, ambitious—"

Tielman's personal aide, John Burleigh, glanced across from his paper-cluttered desk on the other side of the captain's cabin. "Yes, sir," he said gently, his thickly freckled face creasing into a grin, "but, uh, don't you think he has a point? Galactic Tech's selling point is its innovative technologies. 'Tomorrow's Wonders Today!' But it's been a while since we had a significant breakthrough. The investors are getting twitchy."

Tielman growled, "Twitchy? *Twitchy?*"

Burleigh hurried on bravely, "We need the Prandtl Drive to work. If this test flight is muffed, Galactic will become a laughingstock—"

"And a sure way to muff it is to rush the *Pig* into space before she's ready. You know me, John, and you know my philosophy. The *Pig* is a test bed for new technology. We've flown a lot of missions, and the reason we've always made it home is because we follow my rules. What's rule number one?"

"Never fly without a backup for every single component," Burleigh intoned.

"Correct. We still don't have a backup for that quantum fuse, do we? No backup, no fly."

Burleigh said carefully, "But sir, don't you think you *are* being a little overcautious? After all, all that's involved is one single component—"

Tielman said solemnly, "There's no such thing as overcaution in space. Why, I remember once on a jaunt past the Trifid Nebula—"

"Yes, sir." Burleigh had heard all his anecdotes before. He leafed through the papers on his desk. "Incidentally, I had a memo from

Last Resort a couple of hours ago. . . . Here it is. I quote: 'Tell that button-pusher Tielman to get this ship into space and to forget the spare quantum fuse we haven't got. Tell him the All-Purpose Repair Kit I recently swindled from a Sirian will take care of everything—and that's a personal assurance. Jordan Stolz.'" Burleigh glanced up. "What do you think?"

"I think," Tielman said, "that the reason I call Stolz's one-man shop the Department of Last Resort is because that's what it is, and we aren't reduced to that just yet." But he felt trapped. "Oh, to no-space with it. Let's go down to Engineering and chew out Breen. If I have to suffer, so can the rest of the crew."

"That's the spirit, Captain," said Burleigh, standing.

Breen, chief engineer of the *Flying Pig,* was a tall, sparse man who had never been seen to grow angry. His calm, fatalistic nature was apparently immune to the vicissitudes of bureaucrats and balky machinery alike. He met Tielman and Burleigh in a large, instrument-encrusted room that had once been a part of the *Pig*'s rear hold and was now the central control room for the prototype Prandtl Drive.

On Tielman's request, Breen produced the ten-centimeter-long cylinder of gray metal that was the villain of the piece: the drive's quantum fuse. "It's just like an electrical fuse, in principle. It's basically a fail-safe device. If the drive begins to overload, this thing burns out and the drive closes down. Then we find the fault in the drive, repair it, install the spare fuse, and away we go."

"The trouble is we don't have a spare fuse."

"Quite," said Breen. "You need the superheavy metal cauchium to manufacture the fuses. Cauchium is very rare, and the stock of this shipyard has been used up. A fresh supply was on its way from the Fourth Sector, but the ship carrying it was waylaid by pirates on the other side of the Coal Sack Nebula. The pirates are demanding a ransom that the chief executive sees as too high, so . . ."

Burleigh tutted. "That's advanced technology for you."

Tielman said, "Then we can't fly."

Breen and Burleigh exchanged glances.

Breen said, "Look, Captain, all that's lacking is the spare for this one fuse. Right? And the fuse isn't part of the drive's actual operation. It's just a fail-safe."

Tielman snorted. "I have never before flown the *Pig* without the knowledge that she was free from all possible failure—no matter how 'harmless' or 'improbable' that failure may be. And I don't propose to start now. So unless you can devise a backup for that fuse, Breen—"

"Not without cauchium."

"Then the *Pig* doesn't fly, and that's that." And with that, he stalked from the room.

But as the hours passed, and the deadline drew closer, and the pirates beyond the Coal Sack gave no indication of a willingness to lower their price, the pressures on Tielman nibbled at his resolve, his orders conflicting with instincts built up over fifteen years in space.

At last he summoned Burleigh. They had been in similar situations before, and understood each other.

"Here we go again, sir," Burleigh said.

"Yes."

"Last resort time?"

"Last resort."

◉ ◉ ◉

When they entered his catastrophically untidy laboratory, Jordan Stolz lifted his head from an anonymous, ugly-looking tangle of metal and crystal. He creased his wrinkled face into a grin and shoved back his unruly, straggling blond hair. "Well, Captain Tielman," he said with heavy sarcasm, "this is an honor! And to what do I owe the pleasure of a visit by your illustrious self so early in the mission? Surely you can't have messed things up even before leaving the shipyard. . . ."

"Can it, Stolz," snapped Tielman. "You know the situation."

Burleigh explained, "The shipment of cauchium still hasn't got through. You sent a memo saying you had something to take care of our backup fuse problem."

"Ah, yes." Stolz scratched an unshaven cheek with a bony forefinger. "My All-Purpose Repair Kit! Now, where . . . ?" He rummaged through a pile of complicated junk in the corner of the laboratory. "I'm getting forgetful in my old age. I picked it up for a song on Sirius IV. Strange people, the Sirians . . . such great ancestry, and yet so decadent now, not to mention less than fragrant in their personal habits . . . ah!" Triumphantly, he picked a cubical device out of the heap. About half a meter to a side and made of some anonymous gray metal, it was featureless save for a cluster of buttons along one edge and two wide inlets, one in the upper face and one in a side of the cube. Stolz placed the device on a bench that he cleared of clutter with a brusque sweep of his arm. "Ingenious contraption. It took me a while to figure out the principles behind it. You see—"

Tielman interrupted, "Just tell us what it does."

Stolz blinked. "It's called a repair kit. What do you think it does? It repairs things. Anything small enough to fit into the inlet *here*, and to come out of the outlet *there*. I just need something that needs fixing—aha!" He grabbed a stylus from Burleigh's breast pocket and snapped it in two.

"Hey!" protested Burleigh.

"Don't worry," said Stolz, "the kit hasn't failed me yet." He dropped the two halves of the stylus into the kit's upper hopper and pressed the buttons along one edge of the cube. After a moment the kit began to emit a soft whine and seemed to flicker oddly, as if seen through a haze of swirling smoke. Then it returned to normal, and with a clatter an object tumbled from the outlet in its side to the bench.

Burleigh picked it up and examined it. It was his stylus. "Why," he said, "this is as good as new." He took a piece of paper from the bench and tested the stylus. "I'm impressed, Stolz."

"Don't encourage him," Tielman growled.

"Watch this." Stolz grabbed the paper from Burleigh's hands and, with a conjurer's flourish, tore it into a dozen pieces and dropped them into the All-Purpose Repair Kit. After a moment, out slid the piece of paper, whole and unblemished once more. Stolz said, "It's worked on everything I've tried. There's a size limitation, and it takes longer over objects that are more complicated or have greater mass, but that's not a serious problem."

In silence, Tielman examined the stylus and the flawless paper. "There has to be a catch."

Burleigh asked, "Why?"

"Because there always is." Especially, Tielman thought, if Jordan Stolz was involved.

Burleigh asked Stolz, "How does it work?"

"It's quite ingenious," said Stolz. "But simple in principle. As you know, every object in the universe extends in four dimensions.

There are the three spatial directions—up-down, front-back, left-right—and also the temporal direction—future-past."

Tielman said, "So an object exists in space and in time. So what?"

"So the repair kit has the ability to reach back along an object's temporal extension—*to reach into its past*—and to snip out a spatial cross-section, and bring it forward to the present." Burleigh looked as baffled as Tielman felt. Stolz said, "Look—you put a damaged object into the kit. The kit reaches into the past *and brings forward an earlier, undamaged copy of the object* in place of the present, damaged version. Actually, the repair kit doesn't really repair things. It replaces a damaged object with an undamaged copy of itself from the past."

Burleigh still looked confused. "But what happens to the original damaged copy?"

Stolz smiled. "It's put into the past, in the place of its earlier undamaged self. Conservation of mass and energy, you see. The present and past copies are neatly swapped."

"Hang on, there's something wrong with that." Burleigh looked dizzy. "Do you mean to say that somewhere in the past I was carrying about a damaged copy of that stylus?"

Stolz's smile broadened. "It is confusing, isn't it? You see, you're thinking in terms of naïve, old-fashioned causality, which doesn't really apply. For a short time the stylus in your pocket became broken—as the copy from the present appeared—and then, as the limit of the excised cross-section was reached, it became whole once more. Well, obviously it couldn't stay broken, since it was perfect before I snapped it in two, wasn't it?"

"Yes. I mean, no. It's impossible!" cried Burleigh, outraged.

"Impossible or not, it happened," replied Stolz, just as heatedly.

"Look," interposed Tielman, exasperated, "I don't particularly care how the thing works—as long as it does work. Stolz, can you guarantee me that that device will not fail?"

"Absolutely," replied Stolz with confidence. "I've made a thorough study of its workings. Those Sirian ancients were excellent engineers, even if their descendants do have personal hygiene problems. You see, you can forget the missing spare fuse. With the repair kit, we can fly without it. We can fix anything!"

Burleigh said, "Well, what do you think, Captain? Does the *Pig* fly?"

Tielman pressed his lips together. It was wholly against his nature to entrust himself to any machine whose workings he could not analyze and understand—which was why Stolz was Tielman's last resort, rather than his chief engineer. "We wait the full forty-eight hours the chief executive gave us. Then I'll make my decision."

As Tielman and Burleigh took their leave, the unkempt head of the sole member of the *Flying Pig*'s Department of Last Resort bent once more over his latest project, oblivious to the world.

The hours trickled away, and the hope that the vital cauchium might arrive in time to make up the spare quantum fuse dwindled. The pressure built up on the captain, a pressure made worse by knowing that Stolz had offered him an option. Tielman kept a place for Stolz onboard the *Pig*, and had relied on his gadgets in the past, but only as last-resort options when the *Pig* had got itself into trouble in deep space. He had never left Earth already reliant on Stolz's unreliable contraptions. And he had certainly never taken a ship into space without being sure he could bring it home.

But at last the deadline arrived, and Tielman realized he had no choice: if he didn't take the ship out, the chief executive would replace him with somebody who would, and he couldn't put his crew through that. So, with a heavy heart, he ordered the crew to their launch stations.

The *Flying Pig* eased her way out of the shipyard, and the Prandtl Drive powered her into space.

Tielman took his seat on the bridge of the *Pig*. The bridge was a large dome-shaped chamber centered on the main display tank, now glowing a uniform, comforting green. A dozen crewmen with control consoles clambered around the tank, endlessly checking on every aspect of the ship's performance.

"Well, no problems so far." Burleigh grinned up at his captain.

Tielman said nothing.

A display at his elbow warned him to prepare for the hop through no-space, for the speed of the *Pig* had risen to just below the velocity of light. You could travel slower or faster than light, but of course nothing could travel at lightspeed itself—so the *Pig* cheated. In a maneuver similar to electron tunneling, the ship stepped sideways through the other-universe of "no-space," and so avoided the light-speed barrier and surged on into greater "tachy-speeds," the realm of the tachyons, particles that traveled forever faster than light.

With a brief, disconcerting jolt, no-space was crossed, and the *Pig*'s speed rose instantaneously to just above lightspeed. Tielman watched the velocity indicator resume its steady upward motion. "Any problems over the hop?"

"None, sir." Burleigh consulted a readout. "Breen in Engineering reports the Prandtl Drive behaved better than the standard drive generally does. Uh—we've got another memo from Last Resort."

Tielman raised an eyebrow. "Well?"

"Tell that bus driver Tielman that he can kindly schedule his next hop so as not to coincide with my coffee break. I've spilled boiling liquid all over my—I think I'll skip the next part."

The other bridge crew chuckled. Tielman just brooded over the display tank, waiting for problems to arise, as they always did.

Burleigh said, "Oh, no—space it, Captain, I just can't understand you. What is there to worry about?"

"Something will go wrong. It always does. The only question is how much damage it will do."

"You aren't a barrel of laughs, sir."

"I'm not paid to be," Tielman said bleakly.

The ship surged on, far outrunning the light of Earth's sun.

It was a simple mission, designed to give the Prandtl Drive a thorough workout. The *Flying Pig*'s course was a straight line in toward the heart of the galaxy—though the plan was to turn back long before the Core would be reached.

The *Pig* would accelerate up to a predetermined maximum speed—a speed at which she would be the fastest-ever human ship, a speed at which it would take little more than four weeks to cross the galaxy from side to side—and then the Prandtl Drive would be shut down. As the ship coasted, the drive would be switched to deceleration mode and restarted, and the *Pig*'s speed would be whittled down to nothing. On the return journey the maneuverability and control of the drive would be tested.

Simple.

The first part of the voyage passed without any major problems. When the *Pig* crashed through the previous human speed record, Tielman allowed his crewmen to hold a small celebration, though he insisted that a full watch be maintained at all times. The maximum speed was reached without a hitch. The drive was shut down and checked over as the ship coasted before deceleration.

Then came the moment for the drive to be restarted.

Tielman resumed his seat on the bridge. The main display tank glowed a steady green. Crewmen busied themselves confidently over last-moment checks. “Any problems, Burleigh?”

“None, sir. All departments have checked in.”

A soft bell chimed. A crewman called out, “Ten seconds to restart. . . . Eight.”

Tielman sat and brooded.

“Six. Four. All lights green. Two. One. Restart . . .”

The ship convulsed like a wounded animal. The green glow of the main tank flickered and was drowned by virulent red.

I knew it, Tielman thought. His fist crashed onto a large scarlet button set into the arm of his chair, and a siren wailed throughout the ship. “Damage report!”

The bridge crew reacted to the situation as they had been trained. Each officer checked out the systems under his or her responsibility. A neutral white began to seep into the deep red areas in the display tank as the root of the damage was isolated, until eventually all that remained of the original mass of red was a small, stubborn crimson sphere.

Less than a minute after the beginning of the trouble, Burleigh was able to turn to his captain. “Sir, the trouble’s with the drive. The quantum fuse blew. There’s little damage, but the drive’s dead.”

Tielman pressed his lips together. So his ship was hurtling through the galaxy, faster than any ship had traveled before—and he had no way to slow it down, still less turn it around. "Terrific. Burleigh, come with me." He left the bridge.

In the drive control room, Breen and his assistants were running methodically through an elaborate checkout procedure. When Tielman and Burleigh entered the room, Breen rose, his face twisted. "Captain, what can I say, I—"

Tielman asked brusquely, "What happened?"

Running a hand through graying hair, Breen said, "The fault wasn't with the drive itself. It didn't overload! It's hard to believe, but the defective component was actually that quantum fuse—the one that—"

"I know which quantum fuse," Tielman said quietly.

"Why the thing didn't blow when we left the yard is a mystery to me. When I sent through the juice to restart the drive, a fault in the fuse's cauchium lining started a feedback loop. The drive began to spike, and the fuse itself blew out. But the fault was with the fuse itself. See?" Breen presented the culprit: the fuse, a metal-gray cylinder whose blankness was now marred by a black band around its center. "Well and truly blown."

"Then we can't restart the drive," Tielman said.

"No, sir."

Burleigh laughed. "And it's all because of the failure of the one component on the ship for which we don't have a backup. What are the odds?" But he shut up when Tielman glared at him.

Breen said, "Look, Captain, I'm sorry—"

"Save it. What options do we have? Is there any way to bypass that fuse?"

Breen looked doubtful. "We'll check, of course. But the quantum fuse is a pretty integral fail-safe. The drive isn't designed to run without it."

Burleigh, who had kept contact with the bridge, touched Tielman's arm. "Excuse me, Captain. Astrogation are asking to see you—urgent."

"What now?" Tielman turned to Breen. "Do what you can. Come on, Burleigh."

Burleigh hurried at Tielman's side as he strode toward Astrogation. "Captain, I don't see what the panic's about. All right, we're out of motive power, but we've plenty of supplies on board. All we have to do is wait, and—"

"'Wait'? Burleigh, at this moment the *Pig* is moving faster than any ship before her. How long do you think it would take to outfit another ship with a second Prandtl prototype? Six months? A year? Until then there is no ship in the galaxy that can catch the *Pig*. And meanwhile, in eight days we're going to be hurtling into the Galaxy Core." They turned into Astrogation. "Within a month—assuming we survive the Core—we'll be outside the galaxy altogether. Another month after that and our supplies will be running out. And so you see—"

A soft voice interposed: it was Gregg, the bald, plump, mustachioed head of Astrogation. "Actually I think you'll find we've less time than that, Captain, once I've made my own little contribution to the general hilarity."

"What do you mean?"

Gregg led them over to the centerpiece of the Astrogation Department. It was a chest-high cube containing a beautifully detailed three-dimensional image of the galaxy. "One of those things, I'm afraid," said Gregg. "Here's our course up to now—" A straight green thread appeared amid the disc of stars. "And here's an extrapolation of that course, now that we're plummeting along it helplessly." The thread lengthened toward the Core—then came to an abrupt end, well before it had reached the galactic center.

Tielman asked, "Why the termination?"

Gregg magnified the image of the end of the green thread. Stars exploded out of the image, and Tielman endured a brief, unforgettable sensation of enormous speed.

The thread ended in a red point.

Gregg said simply, "That's a red giant star. Somewhat bigger than Betelgeuse. If you want, I'll give you its catalog number."

Tielman knew where this was leading. "And it's in our way, isn't it?"

"In approximately two and one quarter days from now, we will hit the giant at a point about thirty degrees north of its equator." Gregg sighed. "The stars do get crowded as you approach the Core. Still, it's a big place, and you might expect to get through without running into anything."

"Oh, I wouldn't expect that at all," Tielman said.

"It's not our lucky day, is it?" Gregg said sadly.

Burleigh said, "I can guess what you're thinking, Captain. 'I told you so' doesn't even begin to cover it, does it?"

"For the first time since we left Earth you're absolutely right, Mr. Burleigh."

Half a fruitless, frustrating day passed. Then Tielman called a council of war in his cabin with Horne, head of Astrophysics, Gregg of Astrogation, Breen of Engineering, and Burleigh.

Horne of Astrophysics was a burly, blunt man. "But didn't anybody *notice* that our course was going to run through a star?"

"Of course we did, but it shouldn't have mattered," Gregg said bitterly. "We were supposed to turn back long before we reached the neighborhood of the giant."

Burleigh said, "I'm wondering what will happen when—if—we hit the star. It won't be a simple collision, will it?"

Horne replied, "No. You have to remember that the *Pig*'s moving at translight speeds. That means that when we go through the giant, the star's normal tardy-matter can't affect us, since it's impossible for any kind of energy to be transmitted faster than light from a tardy-object. So by the time, for instance, a quantum of heat has reached our position, we'll have left, if you see what I mean. Therefore we won't be crushed or burned by the star."

"Oh, goody," Tielman said menacingly.

Horne went on uncertainly, "But there's bound to be a high concentration of tachy-matter spread through the inner layers of the star—and that *will* hurt us. It will be as if, for instance, we were to run into the atmosphere of Jupiter at a quarter the speed of light."

Gregg of Astrogation said, "What's worrying me is what happens when we run into the deformed space around the star, which we'll hit long before the star itself."

Breen of Engineering said animatedly, "Yes, that's a point. At tachy-speeds our hull will be put under such stress that—"

Tielman held up his hands. "Gentlemen, this is all academic. Our intention is not to hit the star at all. What happens in detail if we fail isn't of much interest. Breen, have you made any progress with the drive?"

Breen shook his head. "There's no way I can repair the fuse, and we can't run the drive safely without it."

Gregg said, "Surely it's not so great a risk as a hundred percent certainty of smashing into a red giant."

Breen smiled. "Tell that to the Prandtl Drive computer."

Burleigh asked, "Is there no manual override?"

"Yes, but it's purely an emergency device designed to kill the drive, not to start it up."

"A dead man's switch," Tielman said. "How appropriate."

Breen said, "Look, Captain, we're working on it. I have a couple of men looking at ways to bypass the computer altogether, and fly manually. But even if we find a way, the chances are we'll wreck the drive altogether. It just isn't designed to be operated this way."

Tielman glanced at a wall chronometer. A little over one and a half days to impact. He looked around. "Anything else?"

Breen said nothing more. Horne folded his hands in silence. Gregg looked embarrassed.

Tielman stood. "All right. Keep working. We'll meet again in six hours, or earlier, if anything turns up."

They rose to leave—all save Burleigh, who quizzically caught his captain's eye. An unspoken conversation passed between them.

Last resort time, Captain?

Last resort time, Mr. Burleigh.

"Tell Jordan Stolz to report to the drive control room. *Now*—don't take any excuses. And tell him to bring that widget of his."

"Yes, sir."

The head and sole operative of the *Pig*'s Department of Last Resort arrived at the drive control center fully twenty minutes after his captain, Burleigh, and Breen. He brought with him a certain metal-gray, half-meter cube.

Breen grimaced. "And what is that unlovely contraption?"

"It's no-spaced heavy, that's what it is," cursed the red-faced and panting Jordan Stolz. He pushed back his unruly mass of gray-blond hair.

Burleigh hastily interposed, "This is Dr. Stolz's Sirian All-Purpose Repair Kit, which may be the answer to all our problems."

Breen looked dubious.

Tielman said, "Please bring us the faulty quantum fuse, Breen."

Breen, with a carefully neutral expression, crossed to a corner of the room, where four crewmen were quietly working. He returned with the fuse. "Now, if you will please explain what—"

"Later, later," said Stolz impatiently. "Hand over the fuse and let's get on with it."

Breen held on to the fuse and looked to Tielman for guidance.

"Just give him the fuse. He can't do it any more harm, can he? Explanations later."

Stolz bridled at Tielman's tone, but he wordlessly accepted the cylinder and rolled it into the intake of the repair kit. He pressed the buttons along the edge in careful order, then stepped back and waited.

The four men held their breath as the kit flickered and whined. The crewmen on the other side of the room glanced across curiously. The kit took longer over the fuse than it had over Burleigh's stylus. Stolz brusquely explained that this was due to the fuse's greater mass and complexity.

At last a gray cylinder rolled from the outlet and clanked to the floor. Breen picked it up and carefully examined it. He said, astonished, "Why, it's no longer burnt out. See? No black ring around the middle." He looked up at Stolz, openmouthed.

Jordan Stolz smiled triumphantly, like a successful amateur conjurer. He gave Breen the explanation he had previously given Tielman and Burleigh: that the kit had swapped the fuse for an earlier, unblemished copy of itself from the past.

Breen looked bemused, then startled, finally skeptical. But the evidence lay in his hands, in the shape of the restored fuse. "Well, I suppose I'll have to accept your explanation, fantastic as it seems . . . I'll check out the fuse. If it's as sound as it looks, there should be no problem, Captain."

Burleigh beamed and thumped Stolz on the back.

Tielman thought, *I don't believe it. It's too good to be true.*

Breen walked a few paces with the fuse in his hand. Then he paused. Then a few more paces, and a longer pause. The engineer's brow wrinkled up in thought.

I knew it, Tielman thought.

"I'm sorry, Captain," said Breen, striding back. "All this has hit me too fast. Even so my thinking must be muddled, or I would have realized immediately . . ."

Tielman said, "What's wrong?"

"If what you say is true, Stolz, then this is a copy of the fuse as it was before it was first installed."

"Yes."

Breen said heavily, "Then I can't put it into the drive! Don't you see, Captain? The fuse was badly flawed *before it was ever used*—it was badly manufactured—so this thing I hold will be flawed in just the same way. Stolz, your device has repaired the burnout, but it can do nothing about the original fault—the fault that caused the blowout in the first place."

Jordan Stolz looked startled, then thoughtfully amused. "I never thought of that! Of course—it's a flaw in the basic concept of the kit. The kit is useless when faced with a device that has *always* been faulty, because all past copies of itself are faulty too."

Tielman thought, *I knew there would be a catch.*

Stolz laughed. "No wonder I picked it up so cheaply—maybe that Sirian wasn't as stupid as he looked, or perhaps his stench addled my senses—"

Burleigh interrupted, "But the fuse, faulty or not, worked the first time around, otherwise we'd never have got out of the yard at all. Why shouldn't it work again?"

Breen said, "That the fuse didn't blow out on launch was a simple wild fluke. That fluke wouldn't happen again—I can guarantee it. Not with the drive chewed up the way it is now."

Burleigh puffed out his cheeks. "Well, that's that, then."

Tielman said, "I suggest you return to your studies, Mr. Breen. As for you, Stolz—you've got less than a day and a half to get that repair kit of yours to work."

Stolz cried, "Didn't you understand, Captain? It's a problem of principle! There's no way my repair kit can produce a usable version of that fuse—"

"You think so? Then I suggest you start looking for ways to prove yourself wrong."

Tielman would admit it to no one else, not even Burleigh, but he was deeply disappointed by Stolz's failure. Despite his innate pessimism, he had hoped that Stolz could pull off a miracle this time, as he had so often before. For the sake of morale he carefully kept from the crew all details of the Stolz fiasco. But he couldn't keep it from himself.

As the remaining time wore away, the furious tempo of work aboard the *Pig* increased, as ways to save the ship were dreamed up, tested, abandoned. Via the no-space communications links suggestions poured into the ship from all over the inhabited galaxy, including from the designers of the Prandtl Drive. But Breen reported no real progress. The only option was to start up the drive with the faulty fuse jammed in place and its controlling computer disabled—but as Breen estimated there was a 98 percent probability of the drive destroying itself altogether if they tried it, this was all but suicide. As time ground down, however, Tielman told Breen to be prepared to take just that chance, if there were no other option.

Then, with the *Flying Pig* only ten hours away from tachy-impact with the red giant—and one hour away from hitting the distorted space around the star—Burleigh came running to find Tielman. The aide looked excited. "Captain, it's Stolz. He says he's found a way to make his repair kit work."

This time Stolz was in drive control ahead of Tielman and Burleigh. He stood beside his apparently unchanged All-Purpose Repair Kit, hollow-eyed but beaming triumphantly. Breen was here, holding the faulty fuse, but with his arms folded and the stubborn, set expression of a man who has been fooled once and will not be fooled again.

Tielman said, "Well, Stolz?"

Stolz said smugly, "Save the congratulations for later, please, Captain. I fear there's not much time before—"

Perfectly on cue, a siren shrieked. The voice of one of the bridge crew rang through the ship. "All hands to stations. Captain to the bridge. Astrogation reports the ship is running into spacetime turbulence ahead of expected time—repeat, ahead of expected time." The ship gave a premonitory shudder. "All hands to stations. Captain Tielman to the bridge. Secure all loose—"

Tielman shouted above the commotion, "We'll have to postpone this circus."

Burleigh yelled back, "Captain, there is no later. If we don't get the drive fired up now, we're finished."

The deck beneath their feet convulsed.

Breen shouted, "Captain, we're wasting time. We need the drive. Have I authority to put in the faulty fuse?"

"It's only a two percent chance!" Stolz yelled. "It's suicide!"

"Better two percent than no chance at all with you and your gadgetry!"

Tielman hesitated. Suddenly the decision was on him. "Are you *sure*, Stolz?"

"Captain, I am."

The ship shuddered again. Still the intercom called Tielman's name.

"All right, Stolz. Breen, hand over the fuse." Breen opened his mouth to protest. "Save it. We'll hold an inquest later—if there is a later. Just do it, and give Stolz all the help he needs. Move! Burleigh, you're with me."

The atmosphere on the bridge was taut with energy as Tielman and Burleigh took their posts. The *Pig* shuddered again. Tielman called, "Report!"

Burleigh consulted his readouts. A large tridee screen over the main display tank filled up with an image of a rough sphere of some crawling gray substance. It reminded Tielman of a nest of maggots.

Burleigh said, "This is a visual representation of the quasi-radiation the star's tachy-matter is emitting. It turns spacetime lumpy and turbulent, as you can see."

"And this is what we'll be flying through."

The image abruptly magnified, revealing in detail a small blank gray area. "Astrogation say this is the area we'll hit in three minutes. Astrophysics reports it's a dense knot at the center of the storm of turbulence through which we're flying."

"The eye of the hurricane," Tielman said darkly.

"Yes, sir."

A crewman called out, "Two minutes thirty seconds to that epicenter."

Tielman slammed a button. "Breen! What's going on down there?"

The chief engineer's voice replied, "Stolz's device has produced another copy of the fuse. It looks all right. We're just starting tests before—"

"Two minutes."

"To no-space with tests! Shove that fuse in and get the drive ready to fire. The ship's two minutes—"

"One minute thirty."

"—away from disaster—"

Burleigh caught Tielman's eye. "Captain, the helmsmen are asking if you want to take the wheel yourself."

Tielman looked at the rushing gray clouds on the tridee screen. Even if the drive worked, it would be a rough flight. "Yes. Patch the controls through to this chair."

"One minute."

"Captain! This is Breen. We've got the fuse ready. We can fire the drive on your order."

Tielman hesitated for one precious second. Cursing the chief executive officer, the shareholders of Galactic Technologies, the Coal Sack pirates, cauchium, Prandtl, Stolz, and all the malevolent gods of space, he ordered, *"Fire."*

He waited through a second that seemed as long as an eternity. Then he felt a heavy surge that pushed him into his seat.

The intercom relayed exultant shouts from drive control. "She's holding, Captain!"

Burleigh said, "The wheel's yours, sir."

"Thirty seconds."

Tielman's hands hovered over the joystick and panels set into the arms of his chair. The ship had come alive, but she quivered, as if in fright.

"Twenty seconds. Nineteen—"

"Cut that babble." The bridge fell silent.

Tielman studied the tridee screen. Which way? The "hurricane eye" was a featureless, bland wall, stretching out of sight in all directions—featureless save for a hairline crack in the upper center. How deep was the crack? Was it wide enough? No time, no time! Tielman made his choice and wrenched at the joystick.

An invisible hand forced him deeper into his seat as the ship's nose lifted in a tight, cruel arc.

The *Pig* shot through the crack in the wall of turbulence. Now Tielman flew in a sky through which huge gray masses tumbled, like a fly surrounded by falling elephants. Two immense clouds rushed together from above and below, threatening to crush the ship. Tielman's breath was forced out of his lungs as he dragged the ship through another tight arc. The *Pig* raced out from between the two masses, leaving them to splash together harmlessly. Tielman maintained the curve of the ship's path and piled on still more speed. He was aware of frightened squawks from Engineering but disregarded them. He had to get the ship out of this gray chaos. His eyes probed the tridee display, searching for breaks through which he might reach free space—

A circular breach, fast closing.

Tielman hauled the ship around and called for still more speed, and still more, as he gambled everything in a final race to beat the closure of the gap. The air of the bridge was rent by the thin screams of tortured machinery and tearing metal.

The *Flying Pig* squirted through the gap.

The "progress meeting" in the captain's cabin was going with more of a swing than most parties he remembered. And the guest of honor was, of course, Jordan Stolz.

Tielman said, "All right, Stolz, confession time. Let us in on the secret."

Breen said, "Yes, how did you produce that faultless fuse? If your repair kit swaps damaged objects for earlier editions of themselves—and if every earlier edition of that fuse was imperfect . . ."

Stolz smiled, delighted to be the center of attention. "It's very simple. All the kit needed was a little tinkering. Those old Sirians hadn't built as well as they thought they had, but with the assistance of Jordan Stolz—"

Gregg of Astrogation said, "Yes, yes, but what did you do?"

"I detected a time-symmetry in the governing tau-equations. With a blackboard, I could show you the terms that—" He was shouted down, and continued, "Very well, let's skip the math. After a little thought and a lot of experimentation, I found I could reverse a polarity in the repair kit. This I did, so that now the Kit reaches into the *future* of the damaged artifact, not its past!"

That was greeted by stunned silence.

Horne of Astrophysics said, "But, granting that that's possible—and reaching into the future seems no more absurd than into the past—I don't see how it helps."

Stolz smiled. "Imagine I have the fuse. In the present I hold a damaged copy. In the future, after I have used the kit, I will have an *un*damaged copy, because that is the purpose of the kit. And so there is a point in the future of the fuse after which it will cease to be in a damaged state. Yes? So that if a three-dimensional cross-section is taken from *after* that point, an undamaged copy of the fuse will be retrieved. Well, then, all the kit has to do is to reach into the future *past the moment of its own use* and retrieve a flawless copy. You see? Simple."

Burleigh said, in a weak voice, "Let me get this straight. The kit replaces the damaged object with a copy of itself which resulted from it being replaced by the kit with a copy of itself—did I get that right?"

"Young man," said Stolz, "I've talked to you about this before. You persist in thinking in terms of simple, old-fashioned causality, which is inapplicable. The problem must be considered in terms of a new atemporal causality—in which the kit's function is a neat causal circle."

"Like a chicken hatching out of its own egg," Tielman said.

"Exactly, Captain!"

Breen said sternly, "Oh, I've had enough of this. It's all ridiculous! Quite impossible."

Stolz raised an eyebrow. "Ridiculous it may be. Impossible it is not. I offer you proof in the fact that we are all alive today."

Breen and the others were only just warming up for the fight, but Tielman interrupted. "Gentlemen," he said, pouring another round, "I suggest we stop looking this gift horse in the mouth. The All-Purpose Repair Kit has saved our lives, and that is all that's important. I offer a toast to the inhabitants of Sirius IV, their personal hygiene challenges, and their glorious ancestors."

"I'll drink to that!" said Jordan Stolz.

The party went on all night. But occasionally Burleigh could be heard to mutter stupidly, "But who repaired the fuse?"

STEPHEN BAXTER lives in Northumberland, in the north of England, and has been a full-time writer since 1995. His first stories appeared in *Interzone* in the late 1980s, and he has subsequently published more than twenty novels (two in collaboration with Sir Arthur C. Clarke and five for younger readers), four collections of short fiction, and three nonfiction books. He has won the Philip K. Dick, John W. Campbell Memorial, British Science Fiction Association, Kurd Lasswitz, Seiun, *Locus*, and Sidewise awards. His most recent novels include the Destiny's Children trilogy; the Time Tapestry Quartet, the Time's Odyssey Trilogy (with Sir Arthur C. Clarke); and *The H-Bomb Girl*, a novel for young adults. His stories have been collected in *The Hunters of Pangaea* and *Resplendent*.

His Web site is www.stephenbaxter.co.uk.

AUTHOR'S NOTE

"Repair Kit" is my homage to the great science fiction short stories of the 1940s and 1950s, especially by Robert Sheckley: a genuine SF idea at the core, jeopardy, a ticking clock, a twist, and, above all, humor.

THE DISMANTLED INVENTION OF FATE

Jeffrey Ford

The ancient astronaut, John Gaghn, lived atop a mountain, Gebila, on the southern shore of the Isle of Bistasi. His home was a sprawling, one-story house with whitewashed walls, long empty corridors, and sudden courtyards open to the sky. The windows held no glass, and late in the afternoon the ocean breezes rushed up the slopes and flowed through the place like water through a mermaid's villa. Around the island, the sea was the color of grape jam due to a tiny red organism that, in summer, swarmed across its surface. Exotic birds stopped there on migration, and their high trilled calls mixed with the eternal pounding of the surf were a persistent music heard even in sleep.

Few ever visited the old man, for the mountain trails were, in certain spots, treacherously steep and haunted by predators. Through the years, more than one reporter or historian of space travel had attempted to scale the heights, grown dizzy in the hot island sun, and turned back. Others simply disappeared along the route, never to be heard from again. He'd seen them coming through his antique telescope, laboring in the ascent, appearing no bigger than ants, and smiled ruefully, knowing just by viewing them at a distance which ones would fail and which determined few would make the cool shade and sweet aroma of the lemon groves of the upper slopes. There the white blossoms would surround them like clouds and they might briefly believe that they were climbing into the sky.

On this day, though, Gaghn peered through his telescope and knew the dark figure he saw climbing Gebila would most definitely make the peak by twilight and the rising of the ringed planet in the east. He wanted no visitors, but he didn't care if they came. He had little to say to anyone, for he knew that Time, which he'd spent a life abusing on deep-space voyages sunk in cryogenic sleep and hurtling across galaxies at near the speed of light, would very soon catch up and deliver him to oblivion. If this visitor wanted to know the history of his voyages, he felt he could sum it all up in one sentence and then send the stranger packing. "I've traveled so far and yet never arrived," he would say.

After his usual breakfast of a cup of hot water with a whole lemon squeezed into it, a bowl of tendrils from the telmis bush, and the still-warm heart of a prowling valru, he tottered off, with the help of a cane, into the lemon grove to sit on his observation deck. He settled his frail body gently into a Bentwood rocker and placed upon the table in front of him a little blue box, perfectly square on all sides, with one red dot in the center of the side faceup. His left hand, holding in two fingers a crystal the shape of a large diamond, shook slightly as he reached forward and positioned the point of the clear stone directly above that red dot.

When he drew back his hand, the crystal remained, hovering a hairsbreadth above the box. He cleared his throat and spoke the word—*Zadiiz*—and the many-faceted stone began to spin like a top. He leaned back in the rocker, turning his face, a web of wrinkles, bearing a grin, a wide nose, and a pair of small round spectacles of pink glass, to the sun. As the chair began to move, a peaceful music of flutes and strings seeped out of the blue box and spiraled around him.

He dozed off and dreamed of the planets he'd visited, their landscapes so impossibly varied; the long cold centuries of frozen slumber on deep-space journeys filled with entire dream lives burdened by the unquenchable longing to awake; the wonderful rocket ships he'd piloted; the strange and beautiful aliens he'd befriended, bartered with, eluded, and killed; the suit that preserved his life in hostile atmospheres with its bubble helmet and jet pack for leaping craters. Then he woke for a moment, only to doze again and this time dream of Zadiiz.

He'd come upon her in his youth, on one of the plateaus amidst the sea of three-hundred-foot-high red grass covering the southern continent on the planet Yarmit-Sobit. He'd often wondered if it was random chance or something predestined that he'd have chosen that place at that time of all the places in the universe to set down his shuttle and explore. The village he came upon, comprised of huts woven from the red grass, lying next to a green lake, was idyllic in its serenity.

The people of the village, sleek and supple, the color of an Earth sky, were near-human in form, save for a ridged fin the length of the spine, ending in a short tail, orange eyes without irises, and sharp-sided fingers perfect for cutting grass. In their sensibility, they were more than human, for they were supremely empathetic, even with other species, like his; valued friendships; and had no word for *cruelty.* He stayed among them, fished with them off the platforms that jutted out over the deep sea of grass for the wide winged leviathans they called hurrurati, and joined in their ceremonies of smoke and calculation. Zadiiz was one of them.

From the instant he first saw her, flying one of the orange kites crafted from the inflated bladder of the hurrurati on the open plateau, he had a desire to know her better. He challenged her to a foot race, and she beat him. He challenged her to a wrestling match, and she beat him. He challenged her to a game of tic-tac-toe he taught her using a stick and drawing in the dirt. This he finally won, and it drew a laugh from her—the sound of her joy, the most vibrant thing he'd encountered in all his travels. As the days went on, she taught him her language, showed him how to find roots in the rich loam of the plateau and how to wrangle and ride the giant, single-horned porcine creatures called sheefen, and explained how the universe was made by the melting of an ice giant. In return, he told her about the millions of worlds beyond the red star that was her sun.

Eventually the mother of the village came to him and asked if he would take the challenge of commitment in order to be bonded to Zadiiz for life. He agreed and was lowered by a long rope off the side of the plateau into the depths of the sea of red grass. In among the enormous blades, he discovered schools of birds that swam like fish through the hidden world, and froglike creatures that braved the heights, leaping from one thick strand of red to stick to another. Even deeper down, as he finally touched the ground, where very little sunlight fell, he encountered large white insects that went about on two legs, with antennae and six arms each. He'd hidden his ray gun in his boot and thus had the means to survive for the duration of his stay below the surface.

Upon witnessing the power of his weapon against a carnivorous leething, the white insects befriended him, communicating through unspoken thoughts they fired into his head from their antennae. They showed him the sights of their secret world, cautioned him to always be wary of snakes (which they called weeha), and took him to stay overnight in the skeletal remains of a giant hurrurati, where they fed him a meal of red-grass sugar and revealed their incomprehensible philosophy of the sufficient. When he left, they gave him an object they'd found in the belly of the dead hurrurati, which they had no name for, although he knew it to be some kind of metal gear. Two days later, the rope was again lowered, and he was retrieved back to the plateau. Zadiiz could hardly believe how well he'd survived and was proud of him. During their bonding ceremony, Gaghn placed the curio of the gear, strung on a lanyard, around her neck.

It wasn't long before the astronaut's restlessness, which had flogged him on across the universe, finally returned to displace the tranquility of life on the plateau. He needed to leave, and he asked Zadiiz to go with him. She courageously agreed, even though it was the belief of her people that the dark sea beyond the sky was a sea of death. The entire village gathered around and watched as the shuttle carried them up and away. Legends would be told of the departure for centuries to come.

Gaghn docked the shuttle in the hold of his space vessel, the *Empress*, and when Zadiiz stepped into the metal, enclosed world of the ship, she trembled. They spent some time merely orbiting her planet, so that she might grow accustomed to the conditions and layout of her new home. Then, one day, when he could withstand the impulse to travel no longer, he led her to the cryo-cradle and helped her to lie down inside. He tried to explain that there would be long, intricate dreams that would seem to her she was awake and living her life, and that some could be quite horrendous, but to remember they were only dreams. She nodded. They kissed by fluttering eyelashes together (as was the custom of her people), and he pushed the button that made the top of her berth slide down over her. In the seconds before the gas did its work, he heard her scream and pound upon the lid. Then silence, and with a troubled conscience, he set the coordinates for a distant constellation and went, himself, to sleep.

Upon waking, light years away from Yarmit-Sobit, he opened her cradle and discovered her lifeless. He surmised that a nightmare that attended the frozen sleep had frightened the life out of her. Her eyes were wide, her mouth agape, her fists clenched against some dreamed terror that had stalked her imagination. He took her body down to Eljesh, the planet the *Empress* now orbited, to the lace forest at the bottom of an ancient crater where giant pure white trees, their branches like the entwining arms of so many cosmic snowflakes, reached up into an ashen sky. He'd intended the beauty of this place to be a surprise for her. Unable to contemplate burying her beneath the soil, he laid her next to a milk-white pool on a flat rock, closed her eyes, brushed the hair away from her face, and took with him, as a keepsake, the gear he'd given her.

When he fled Eljesh, it wasn't simply the wanderlust drawing him onward now; he was also pursued with equal ferocity by her memory. He always wondered why he couldn't have simply stayed on the plateau, and that question became his new traveling companion through intergalactic wars, on explorations to the fiery hearts of planets, pirate operations, missions of goodwill, and all the way to the invisible wall at the end of the universe, after which there was no more, and back again.

He knew many, and many millions more knew of him, but he'd never told a soul of any species what he'd done, until one night, high in the frozen mountains, near the pole of the Idiot planet (so named for its harsh conditions and a judgment upon any who would dare to travel there). Somehow he'd wound up in a cave, weathering a blizzard, with a wise old Ketuban, universally considered to be the holiest and most mystical cosmic citizen in existence. This fat old fellow, eyeless, but powerfully psychic, looking like a pile of mud with a gaping mouth, four tentacles, and eight tiny legs, spoke in whispered bursts of air, but spoke the truth.

"Gaghn," said the Ketuban, "you have sorrow."

John understood the language, and moved in close to the lumpish fellow to hear over the howling of the wind. Once he understood the statement, the sheer simplicity of it, the heartfelt tone of it, despite the rude sound that delivered it, he told the story of Zadiiz.

When he was finished, the Ketuban said, "You believe you killed her?"

Gaghn said nothing but nodded.

"Some would call it a sin."

"I call it a sin," said the astronaut.

The storm grew more fierce outside, and the roar of the gale hypnotized Gaghn, making him drowsy. He drifted toward sleep, his memory alive with images of Zadiiz teaching him to fish with spear and rope and tackle, sitting beside him on the plateau beneath the stars, moving around the dwelling they'd shared on a bright warm morning in spring, singing the high-pitched birdsongs of her people. Just before he fell into sleep, he heard his cave-mate's voice mix with the constant rush of the wind. "Rest easy. I will arrange things."

When Gaghn awoke, the storm had abated and the Ketuban had vanished, leaving behind, on the floor of the cave, a crude winged figurine formed from its own mud. He also realized the Ketuban had taken the gear he'd worn around his neck since leaving Zadiiz on Eljesh. As the astronaut made his way cautiously over ice fields fissured with yawning crevices back to his shuttle, he remembered the mystic alien's promise. In the years that followed, though, he found no rest from his need to journey farther or from the memories that tormented him, and he realized that this must be the fate that was arranged—no peace for him, as punishment in payment for his sin.

More memories of his travels ensued as the ancient astronaut woke and slept, the music from the blue box washing over him, the scent of the lemon blossoms, the heat of the sun, his weak heart and failing will to live mixing together into their own narcotic that kept him drowsy. One last image came—his visit to the laboratory of the great inventor Onsing, inside the hollow planet, Simmesia. The aged scientist, whose mind was once ablaze with what many considered the galaxy's greatest imagination, was laid low by the infirmity of age, on the verge of death. The sight of this had frightened John, and he'd thought if he went far enough, fast enough, he'd escape the fate Onsing assured him in labored whispers came to all, and would be protected for all by a great machine of Onsing's invention.

Then Gaghn woke to the late-afternoon wind of the island, saw the ringed planet had risen in the east, and in the failing light, noticed a tall dark figure standing before him.

"I've traveled far and yet never arrived," he said.

The visitor, nearly eight foot, broad as three men, and covered in a long black cloak, the hem of which brushed against the stone of the deck, stepped forward, and the old man saw its face. Not human, but some kind of vague imitation of a human face, like a mask of varnished shell with two dark holes for eyes, a subtle ridge for a nose, and another smaller hole that was the mouth. Atop the smooth head was a pair of horns whose sharp points curved toward each other.

"You may leave now," said the old man.

The tall fellow, his complexion indigo, took two graceful steps forward, stopping next to Gaghn's rocker. The astronaut focused on the empty holes that served as eyes and tried to see if some sign of a personality lurked anywhere inside them. The stranger leaned over, and quicker than a heartbeat, a long tapered nozzle, sharp as the tips of the horns, sprang out of the mouth hole, passed through Gaghn's forehead with the sound of an egg cracking, and stabbed deep into the center of his brain. The astronaut gave a sudden sigh. Then the nozzle retracted as quickly as it had sprung forth. The old man fell forward, dead, across the table, his right arm hitting the blue box sideways, sending the crystal plinking onto the stone floor of the deck.

The indigo figure stepped away from the body and sloughed its long cloak. Once free of the garment, the two wings that had been folded against its back lifted and opened wide. They were sleek, half the creature's height, pointed at the lower tips and ribbed with delicate bone work beneath the slick flesh. Its entire manlike form suggested equal parts reptile and mineral. From down the mountain came the death cry of some creature, from off in the grove came the sorrowful call of the pale night bird, and beneath them both could be heard, in the distance, the persistent pounding of the sea. The visitor crouched, and with great power, leaped into the air. The wings spread out, caught the island wind, and carried it, with powerful thrusts, into the night sky. He flew, silhouetted before the bright presence of the ringed planet from pole to pole, higher and higher, as the figure of John Gaghn receded to a pinpoint, became part of the island, then the ocean, then the night. Hours later, the winged visitor pierced the outer membrane of the planet's atmosphere and was borne into space.

The Aieu, people of the jump bone animal, blended flawlessly with the white trees in the lace forest. A dozen of them—hairless, perfectly pale, crouching still as stone gargoyles among the branches, silently watched the movements of the dark giant. Its wings, its horns, told them it would be a formidable opponent, and they wondered how their enemies had created it. After it had passed beneath them, the elder of their party motioned for the swiftest of them to go quickly and warn the queen of an assassin's approach. The small fellow nodded that he understood the message, and then, on clawed feet, took off, running through the branches, leaping without a sound from tree to tree, in the direction of the hive. The ones that remained behind spread out and followed the intruder, their leader all the while plotting a strategy of offense for when his force would be at full strength.

Zadiiz, the powder-blue queen, sat in her throne at the center of the hive, the children of the Aieu gathered around her feet. Nearly too feeble with age to walk, let alone run and climb, she could no longer lead the war parties or the hunt as she once had. She was not required to do anything at all, as her subjects owed her their very existence, but she wanted to remain useful for as long as she could, both to pass the time and to set an example. She instructed the young ones on everything from the proper way to employ the deadly jump bone against a foe to the nature of existence itself, as she saw it. On this day, it was the latter. In her weak voice, quivering with age, she explained:

"Look around you, my dears. All of you, everything you see, the white forest, the gray sky, your distant past, and whatever future we have left, everything is a dream I am dreaming. As I speak to you, I am really asleep in a great vessel, in the clutch of a cradle that freezes the body but not the dream, flying through the darkness above, amidst the stars, to a far place where I will eventually awake to be with my life companion, John Gaghn."

The children looked into her orange eyes and nodded, although they could hardly understand. One of the brighter ones spoke up. "And what will become of us when you awaken?"

Zadiiz could only speak the truth. "I'm not sure," she said, "but I'll do everything I can to keep you safe inside my memory. You'll know if I've done this when, if I appear to die, you are still alive." Upon her mentioning her own death, the children gasped, but she went on to allay their fears. "I won't have really died, I'll merely have emerged into another dream, or I'll truly have awakened, the vessel having reached its destination." She could see she had confused them and frightened them a little. "Go and think on this for now, and we'll discuss it more tomorrow." The small, dazed faces, which, at one time, back on the plateau of the red grasslands of her own planet, she might have considered ugly, now were precious to her. The children came forward and lightly touched her arms, her legs, her face, before leaving the hive. She watched them scamper out and take to the branches that surrounded her palace in the treetops, and then sat back and tried to understand, for herself, what she had spoken of.

John had warned her that the dreams would come and they would be deep and sometimes terrible, and there were parts of this one she believed herself presently imprisoned in that were, but there was also beauty and the reciprocal love between the Aieu and herself. How many more dream lives would she need to experience, she wondered, before waking. This one began with her opening her eyes, staring up into the pale faces of a hunting party of the people of the jump bone animal. Later, when she'd come to learn their language, they told her that even though many of them thought her dead when they'd found her lying on the flat stone next to the pool, their herb witch listened closely, placing her ear to the blue queen's ear and could hear, though very weak, the faint murmur of thoughts still alive in her head. Then, slowly, employing a treatment of their most powerful natural drugs and constantly moving her limbs, they'd brought her around to consciousness.

Zadiiz was roused from her reverie by the approach of one of her subjects. He was agitated and began spouting in the Aieu gibberish before he'd even reached her side. "An intruder, an assassin," he was shouting, waving his needle-sharp jump bone in the air. She shook her head and put both hands up, palms facing outward to indicate he should slow down. He took a deep breath and bowed, placing his weapon on the floor at her feet. "What is this intruder?" she asked, feeling so weary she could hardly concentrate on his description.

He put the two longest fingers of each of his three-fingered hands, pointing up, atop his wrinkled forehead. She understood and nodded. He then made as blank an expression as he could with his face, closing his eyes, turning his mouth into a perfect O. She nodded. When he saw she was following him, he held his right hand up as high as he could and then leaped up to show the stranger's height. Last he said, "Thula," which meant "deadly." In response, she made a fist, and he responded by lifting his weapon and exiting out upon the treetops to summon the forces of the Aieu.

As old and tired as she was, there still burned within her a spark of envy for those who now swarmed away from the hive to meet the threat of this new enemy. She lit her pipe, ran her hand across the old crone stubble on her chin, and, with a vague smile, found in her memory an image of herself when she could still run and climb and fight. It hadn't taken her long, once the Aieu had brought her around, before she was back on her feet and practicing competing with the best hunters and wrestlers her rescuers had among them. She took to the treetops as though she'd been born in the lace forest, and a few days after they'd demonstrated for her the throwing technique for the jump bone, she was more accurate and deadly with it than those who were still young when the jump bone animal had been hunted to extinction.

But it was in the war against the Fire Hand that she'd proven herself a general of keen strategic insight and unfailing courage. Utilizing the advantage of the treetops, and employing stealth and speed to defeat an enemy of greater number, she'd helped the Aieu turn back the bloodthirsty hordes that had spilled down over the high lip of the crater and flooded the forest. It was this victory that had elevated her to the status of royalty among them. She drew on her pipe, savoring the rush of imagery out of the past. As the smoke twined up toward the center of the hive, a distant battle cry sounded from the forest, and in the confusion of her advanced age, she believed it to be her own.

The victory shouts of the Aieu warriors woke her as they led their prisoner into the hive. The giant indigo creature, wings bound with woven white vine around its chest, hands tied together at the wrists in front, a choker around its muscular neck, strode compliantly forward, surrounded by its captors brandishing jump bones above their heads.

"Bring him into the light," commanded Zadiiz, and they prodded the thing forward to stand in the glow of the two torches that flanked her throne. When she beheld the huge indigo form, she marveled at the effectiveness of her battle training on the Aieu, for it didn't seem possible that all who lived in the treetop complex surrounding the hive could together subdue such a monster. "Good work," she said to her people. Then her gaze came to rest on the emotionless, shell mask of a face with its simple holes for eyes and mouth, and the sight of it startled her. It shared, in its blank expression, the look of another face she could not help but remember.

It was in the dream that preceded her waking into the lace forest and the people of the jump bone animal, the first of her sleeping lives that John Gaghn had promised after he'd closed her in the cradle. In this one, she'd lived alone in a cave on a barren piece of rock, floating through deep space. She spent her time watching the stars, noting, here and there, at great distances, the slow explosions of galaxies, like the blossoming of flowers, and listening to endlessly varied music made by light piercing the darkness. A very long time had passed, and she remembered the weight of her loneliness. Then one day, a figure appeared in the distance, heading for her, and slowly it revealed itself to be a large silver globe. Smoke issued from the back of it and it buzzed horribly, interfering with the natural song of the universe.

The vessel rolled down onto the deep sand beside the entrance to her cave. Moments later, a door opened in the side of it and out stepped a man made of metal. The starlight reflected on his shiny surface, and he gave off a faint glow. At first she was frightened to behold something so peculiar, but the metal man, whose immobile face was cast in an expression of infinite patience, spoke to her in a friendly voice. He told her his name was 49 and asked if he could stay with her until he managed to fix his craft. Zadiiz was delighted to have the company and assured him he could.

She offered him some of the spotted mushrooms that grew on the inner walls of the cave, her only sustenance. They tasted to her like the flesh of the hurrurati. 49 refused, explaining that he was a machine and did not eat. Zadiiz didn't understand the idea of a robot, and so he explained that he was made by a great scientist named Onsing, and that all of his parts were metal. He told her, "I have intelligence, I even have emotion, but I was made to fulfill the need of my inventor, whereas beings like you were made to fulfill your own desires."

"What is your master's need?" asked Zadiiz.

"Onsing has passed on into death," said 49, "but some time ago, while alive, he discovered through intensive calculation—using a mathematical system of his own devising and entering those results into a computer that not only rendered answers as to what was possible but also what could, given an infinite amount of time, be probable—that his sworn enemies, the Ketubans, would someday create a mischievous creature that could very likely manipulate the fate of the universe."

Zadiiz simply stared at 49 for a very long time. "Explain 'infinite' and 'probable,'" she finally said.

The robot explained.

"Explain 'fate,'" she said.

"Fate," said 49, and a whirring sound could be heard issuing from his head as he stared at the ground. Sparks shot from his ears. "Well, it is the series of events beginning at the beginning of everything that will eventually dictate what must be. And all you would need to do to change the universe would be to undo one thing that must be and everything would change."

"Why must it be?" she asked.

"Because it must," said the robot. "So, to prevent this, Onsing created a machine of one thousand parts that could, once its start button was pressed, send out, in all directions, a wave across the universe that would eventually find this creature and melt it. When he had finished the machine, he hoped to always keep it running so that it could forever prevent the Ketubans from undermining fate."

"And did he?" asked Zadiiz.

"Poor Onsing never had a chance to start his machine, because it was destroyed by the evil Ketubans, loathsome creatures, like steaming piles of organic waste with tentacles and too many legs. They used their psychic power to automatically disassemble the machine, and all of its individual parts flew away in as many different directions as there were pieces. Onsing, too determined to give up, but knowing he would not live long enough to rebuild the machine or find all of the parts scattered across the universe, created one thousand robots like me to go out into space and fetch them back. Nine hundred ninety-nine of the robots have found their parts, and they have assembled all of the machine but for one tiny gear that is still missing. That is my part to find, and they wait for my success. Once I find it, I will return with it. It will be fitted into the machine. The robot that has been designed to press the start button on the machine will fulfill his task and the fate of the universe will be protected."

"How long have you searched?" asked Zadiiz.

"Too long," said 49.

Eventually, Zadiiz grew weary, as she always did when eating the mushrooms, and fell asleep. When she awoke, she found that 49 was gone from the cave. She ran outside only to discover that his sphere of a vessel was also gone. Sometime later, she realized that the metal gear that had hung around her neck was missing, and the thought of having to live the rest of that lonely dream life without even the amulet's small connection to John Gaghn sent her into shock. Her mind closed in on itself, shut down, went blank. When she awoke, she was surrounded by the pale faces of the people of the jump bone animal.

She surfaced from her memory again surrounded by the Aieus' pale faces, this time in the hot and crowded hive. They'd been waiting in expectant silence for her to pronounce the fate of the assassin they'd brought before her. Zadiiz realized she'd had a lapse of awareness, and now tried to focus on the situation before her. She looked the horned figure up and down, avoiding another glimpse at the face. She wondered who could have sent this thing. Because of its unknown nature, its obvious power and size, she could not allow it to live. She was about to order that the creature be drowned in the white pool, when she noticed the fingers on its left hand open slightly. Something fell from between them but did not continue on to the floor. It was caught and suspended by a lanyard looped through one of its small openings.

Upon seeing the gear, she gasped and struggled to her feet. The fact that she'd just been thinking of it made her dizzy with its implications. "Where did you get that?" she asked. The implacable face remained silent, but her obvious reaction to the sight of the curio sent a murmur through those assembled. "Who sent you?" she asked. Its eye holes seemed to be staring directly at her. She started down the two steps from her throne, and her people came up on either side to help her approach the creature. As she drew near, she felt a flutter of nervousness in her chest. "Did John send you from his own dream?" she said.

When she was less than a step away from the prisoner, she reached out for the amulet, and that is when the indigo creature inhaled so mightily the ropes binding its wings snapped. In one fluid motion, it ripped its wrists free of their bonds, the vines snapping away as if they were strands of hair, and took Zadiiz by the shoulders. She was too slow to scream, for the prisoner had already leaned forward, and the pointed nozzle had shot forth from its mouth. There was the sound of an egg cracking. The Aieu did not recover from their shock until the nozzle had retracted, and by then the creature had torn the lead from its neck and leaped into the air. At the same moment, Zadiiz fell backward into their waiting arms. Jump bones were thrown, but the assassin flew swiftly up and out of the opening at the top of the hive.

The indigo creature flew on and on for light years through space, past planets and suns, quasars and nebulae, black holes and wormholes, resting momentarily now and then upon an asteroid or swimming down through the atmosphere of a planet to live upon its surface for a year or two, and no matter the incredible sights it witnessed in the centuries it traveled, its expression never once changed. Finally, in a cave whose walls were covered with spotted mushrooms, on an asteroid orbiting a blue-white star, it found what it had been searching for—a large metallic globe and, sitting next to it upon a rock, a robot, long seized with inaction due to the frustration of its inability to accomplish the task its master had set for it.

Dangling the gear upon its lanyard in front of the eye sensors of the robot, the indigo creature brought the man of metal to awareness. Robot 49 reached up for the gear, and the creature placed it easily into his ball-jointed fingers. The two expressionless faces stared at each other for a moment and then each turned away, knowing what needed to be done. The robot moved to his globe of a space vessel, and the indigo creature sprinted from the cave and spread its wings. Even before the sputtering metal ball had exited the cave and set a course for the hollow world, the indigo creature had disappeared into the darkness of space.

On an undiscovered world where a vast ocean of three-hundred-foot-tall red grass lapped the base of a small mountain, the creature landed and set to work. Time, which had passed in long lazy skeins to this point, now was of the essence, and there could be no rest. At the peak of the mountain, the winged being cleared away a tangled forest of vines, telmis, and wild lemon trees, uprooting trunks with its bare hands and knocking down larger ones with its horns. Once the land was cleared, it set about mining blocks of white marble from a site lower down the slope, precisely cutting the hard stone with the nail of its left index finger. These blocks were flown to the peak and arranged so as to build a sprawling, one-story dwelling, with long empty corridors and sudden courtyards open to the sky.

When all was completed upon the mountain peak, the creature entered the white dwelling, passed down the long empty corridors to the bedroom, and sat down upon the edge of a soft mattress of prowling valru hide stuffed with lemon blossoms. It could see through the window opening the ringed planet begin its ascent as the day waned. Twilight breezes from off the sea of red grass rushed up the slopes and swamped the house. The indigo creature folded its wings back and stretched its arms once before lying back upon the wide, comfortable bed it had made.

As the horned head rested upon a pillow, so many light years away, at the center of the hollow planet, Robot 49 fitted the small gear into place within Onsing's remarkable machine. Nine hundred and ninety-nine cheers went up from his metallic brethren gathered behind him. And the 1001st robot, designed only to press the start button on the machine, finally fulfilled its task. A lurching, creaking clang of parts moving emanated from the strange device. Then invisible waves that gave off the sound of a bird's call issued forth, instantly disabling all of the robots, traveling right through the mass of the hollow planet and onward, in all directions across the universe.

The indigo creature heard what it at first believed to be the call of the pale night bird, but soon realized it was mistaken. It then made the only sound it would ever make in its long life, a brief sigh in recognition that it had finally arrived, before it began to melt. Thick droplets of indigo ran from its face and arms and chest, evaporating into night before staining the mattress. Its horns dripped away like lit candles, and its wings became increasingly smaller versions of themselves until they had both run off into puddles of nothing. As the huge dark figure disintegrated, from within its bulk emerged a pair of forms, arms clasped around each other. With the evaporation of the last drop of indigo, John and Zadiiz, again young as the moment they first met, rolled away from each other, dreaming.

In the morning they were awakened by the light of the sun streaming in the window without glass and the sounds of the migrating birds. They discovered each other and themselves but had no memory, save their own names, as to their pasts or how they came to be on the mountain peak. All they remembered was their bond, and although this was an invisible thing, they both felt it strongly.

They lived together for many years in tranquility on the undiscovered planet, and in their fifth year had a child. The little girl had her mother's orange eyes and her father's desire to know what lay out beyond the sky. She was a swift runner and climbed about in the lemon trees like a monkey. The child had a powerful imagination and concocted stories for her parents about men made of metal, and dark winged creatures, about incredible machines and vessels that flew to the stars. At her birth, not knowing exactly why, John Gaghn and Zadiiz settled upon the name of Onsing for her and wondered how that name might direct her fate.

JEFFREY FORD is the author of six novels: *Vanitas*, World Fantasy Award–winner *The Physiognomy*, *Memoranda*, *The Beyond*, *The Portrait of Mrs. Charbuque*, and *The Girl in the Glass*. His short fiction, which has appeared in *Fantasy & Science Fiction*, SCI FICTION, *Black Gate*, *The Green Man*, *Leviathan 3*, *The Dark*, and many year's best anthologies and has won the World Fantasy and Nebula awards, has been collected in World Fantasy Award–winner *The Fantasy Writer's Assistant and Other Stories* and *The Empire of Ice Cream*. Upcoming is a new novel, *The Shadow Year,* and a new collection, *The Night Whiskey*.

He lives in South Jersey with his wife and two sons and teaches writing and literature at Brookdale Community College in Monmouth County, New Jersey.

AUTHOR'S NOTE

My story, "The Dismantled Invention of Fate," was inspired by the fictional work of the writer Michael Moorcock. For readers of the literature of the fantastic who may not have had the opportunity yet to discover this writer, you have literally universes of adventure, imagination, and challenging thought waiting to unfold before you. I could throw out a few titles here, but it's best you find your own portal into Moorcock's cosmos—there must be over a hundred books to choose from. In the field of science fiction, Moorcock is a true visionary. His innovation was to transcend the nuts-and-bolts science of a clockwork, Newtonian conception of the universe, which had long reigned as the accepted approach in the genre, and instead to honor the discovery of quantum physics. His fiction is much less about what is "actual" and far more about what is "probable." There is no telling where his stories are going to take you. Time is a mutable phenomenon, chaos is given its due regard, human imagination is the stuff from which the stars are made, and every outbound adventure is an inward journey. So, I dedicate this story to Moorcock for the generosity of his fiction, and more so for his personal generosity in encouraging and aiding newer writers, groping through the dark in search of their own universes.

ANDA'S GAME

Cory Doctorow

Anda didn't really start to play the game until she got herself a girl-shaped avatar. When Anda was twelve, she met Liza the Organiza, whose avatar was female but had sensible tits and sensible armor and a bloody great sword that she was clearly very good with. Liza came to school after PE, when Anda was massaging her abused podge and hating her entire life. Her PE kit was at the bottom of her school bag and her face was that stupid red color that she *hated*, and now it was stinking math, which was hardly better than PE but at least she didn't have to sweat.

But instead of math, all the girls were called to assembly, and Liza the Organiza stood on the stage in front of Miss Cruickshanks, the principal, and Mrs. Danzig, the useless counselor.

"Hullo, chickens," Liza said. She had an Australian accent. "Well, aren't you lot just precious and bright and expectant with your pink upturned faces like a load of flowers staring up at the sky? Warms me fecking heart it does."

That made Anda laugh, and she wasn't the only one. Miss

Cruickshanks and Mrs. Danzig didn't look amused, but they tried to hide it.

"I am Liza the Organiza, and I kick arse. Seriously." She tapped a key on her laptop and the screen behind her lit up. It was a game—not the one that Anda played, but a space station with a rocket ship in the background. "This is my avatar." Sensible boobs, sensible armor, and a sword the size of the world. "In-game, they call me the Lizanator, Queen of the Spacelanes, El Presidente of the Clan Fahrenheit." The Fahrenheits had chapters in every game. They were amazing and deadly and cool, and to her knowledge, Anda had never met one in the flesh. They had their own *island* in her game. Crikey.

On-screen, the Lizanator was fighting an army of wookie-men, sword in one hand, laser-blaster in the other, rocket-jumping, spinning, strafing, making impossible kills and long shots, diving for power-ups and ruthlessly running her enemies to ground.

"The *whole* Clan Fahrenheit. They voted me in 'cause of my prowess in *combat*. I'm a world champion in six different games. I've commanded armies and I've sent armies to their respawn gates by the thousands. Thousands, chickens: my battle record is 3,522 kills in a single battle. I game for four to six hours nearly every day, and the rest of the time, I do what I like.

"One of the things I like to do is come to girls' schools like yours and let you in on a secret: girls kick arse. We're faster, smarter, and better than boys. We play harder. We spend too much time thinking that we're freaks for gaming, and when we do game, we never play as girls because we catch so much shite for it. Time to turn that around. I am the best gamer in the world and I'm a girl. I started playing at ten, and there were no women in games—you couldn't even buy a game in any of the shops I went to. It's different now, but it's still not perfect. We're going to change that, chickens, you lot and me.

"How many of you game?"

Anda put her hand up. So did about half the girls in the room.

"And how many of you play girls?"

All the hands went down.

"See, that's a tragedy. Practically makes me weep. Gamespace smells like a boy's *armpit.* It's time we girled it up a little. So here's my offer to you: if you will play as a girl, you will be given probationary memberships in the Clan Fahrenheit, and if you measure up, in six months, you'll be full-fledged members."

In real life, Liza the Organiza was a little podgy, like Anda herself, but she wore it with confidence. She was solid, like a brick wall, her hair bobbed bluntly at her shoulders. She dressed in a black jumper over loose dungarees with giant goth boots with steel toes.

She stomped her boots, one-two, *thump-thump*, like thunder on the stage. "Who's in, chickens? Who wants to be a girl out-game and in?"

Anda jumped to her feet. A Fahrenheit, with her own island! Her head was so full of it that she didn't notice that she was the only one standing. The other girls stared at her, a few giggling and whispering.

"That's all right, love," Liza called, "I like enthusiasm. Don't let those staring faces rattle yer: they're just flowers turning to look at the sky. Pink, scrubbed, shining, expectant faces. They're looking at you because *you* had the sense to get to your feet when opportunity came—and that means that someday, girl, you are going to be a leader of women, and men, and you will kick arse. Welcome to the Clan Fahrenheit."

She began to clap, and the other girls clapped too, and even though Anda's face was the color of a lollipop-lady's sign, she felt like she might burst with pride and good feeling and she smiled until her face hurt.

> Anda,

her sergeant said to her,

> how would you like to make some money?

> Money, Sarge?

Ever since she'd risen to platoon leader, she'd been getting more missions, but they paid *gold*—money wasn't really something you talked about in-game.

The Sarge—sensible boobs, gigantic sword, longbow, gloriously orcish ugly phiz—moved her avatar impatiently.

> Something wrong with my typing, Anda?

> No, Sarge.

she typed.

> You mean gold?

> If I meant gold, I would have said gold. Can you go voice?

Anda looked around. Her door was shut and she could hear her parents in the sitting-room watching telly. She turned up her music just to be safe and then slipped on her headset. They said it could noise-cancel a Blackhawk helicopter—it had better be able to overcome the little inductive speakers suction-cupped to the underside of her desk. She switched to voice.

"Hey, Lucy," she said.

"Call me Sarge!" Lucy's accent was American, like an old TV show, and she lived somewhere in the middle of the country where it was all vowels, Iowa or Ohio. She was Anda's best friend in-game, but she was so hardcore it was boring sometimes.

"Hi, Sarge," she said, trying to keep the irritation out of her voice. She'd never smart off to a superior in-game, but v2v it was harder to remember to keep to the game norms.

"I have a mission that pays real cash. Whichever paypal you're using, they'll deposit money into it. Looks fun, too."

"That's a bit weird, Sarge. Is that against Clan rules?" There were a lot of Clan rules about what kind of mission you could accept, and they were always changing. There were curb-crawlers in gamespace and the way that the Clan leadership kept all the mummies, and daddies from going ape-poo about it was by enforcing a boring code of conduct that was meant to ensure that none of the Fahrenheit girlies ended up being virtual prozzies.

"What?" Anda loved how Lucy quacked *What?* It sounded especially American. "No, geez. All the executives in the Clan pay the rent doing missions for money. Some of them are even rich from it, I hear! You can make a lot of money gaming, you know."

"Is it really true?" She'd heard about this, but she'd assumed it was just stories, like the kids who gamed so much that they couldn't tell reality from fantasy. Or the ones who gamed so much that they stopped eating and got all anorexic. She wouldn't mind getting a little anorexic, to be honest. Bloody podge.

"Yup! And this is our chance to get in on the ground floor. Are you in?"

"It's not—you know, *pervy*, is it?"

"Gag me. No. Jeez, Anda! Are you nuts? No—they want us to go kill some guys."

"Oh, we're good at that!"

◉ ◉ ◉

The mission took them far from Fahrenheit Island, to a cottage on the far side of the gameworld. They were spotted by sentries long before they got within sight of the cottage, and they saw the warning spell travel up from the hilltop like a puff of smoke, speeding away toward the cottage. Anda raced up the hill while Lucy covered her with her bow, but that didn't stop the sentries from subjecting Anda to a hail of flaming spears from their fortified position. Anda set up her standard dodge-and-weave pattern, assuming that the sentries were nonplayer characters—who wanted to *pay* to sit around in gamespace watching a boring road all day?—and to her surprise, the spears followed her. She took one in the chest and only some fast work with her shield and all her healing scrolls saved her. As it was, her constitution was knocked down by half, and she had to retreat back down the hillside.

"Get down," Lucy said in her headset. "I'm gonna use the BFG."

Every game had one—the Big Friendly Gun, the generic term for the baddest-arse weapon in the world. Lucy had rented this one from the Clan armory for a small fortune in gold, and Anda had laughed and called her paranoid. It was a huge, demented flaming crossbow that fired five-meter bolts that exploded on impact.

"Fire!" Lucy called, and the game did this amazing and cool animation that it rewarded you with whenever you loosed a bolt from the BFG, making the gamelight dim toward the sizzling bolt as though it were sucking the illumination out of the world as it arced up the hillside, trailing a comet-tail of sparks. The game played them a groan of dismay from their enemies, and then the bolt hit home with a crash that made her point of view vibrate like an earthquake. The roar in her headphones was deafening, and behind it she could hear Lucy on the voice-chat, cheering it on.

"Nuke 'em till they glow and shoot 'em in the dark! Yee-haw!" Lucy called, and Anda laughed and pounded her fist on the desk. Gobbets of former enemy sailed over the treeline dramatically.

Now they had to move fast, for their enemies at the cottage would be alerted to their presence and waiting for them. They spread out into a wide flanking maneuver around the cottage's sides, staying just outside of bow range, using scrying scrolls to magnify the cottage and make the foliage around them fade to translucency.

There were four guards around the cottage, two with nocked arrows and two with whirling slings. One had a scroll out and was surrounded by the concentration marks that indicated spellcasting.

"GO GO GO!" Lucy called.

Anda went! She cast a shield spell. They cost a fortune and burned out fast, but whatever that guard was cooking up, it had to be bad news. She cast the spell as she charged for the cottage, and lucky thing, because there was a fifth guard up a tree who dumped a pot of boiling oil on her that would have cooked her down to her bones in ten seconds if not for the spell.

She reached the fifth man as he was trying to draw his dirk and dagger and lopped his bloody head off in one motion, then back-flipped off the high branch, trusting to her shield to stay intact for her impact on the cottage roof.

The strategy worked—now she had the drop (literally!) on the remaining guards, having successfully taken the high ground. In her headphones, she could hear the sound of Lucy making mayhem, the grunts as she pounded her keyboard mingling with the in-game shrieks as her arrows found homes in the chests of two more of the guards.

Shrieking a berzerker wail, Anda jumped down off of the roof and landed on one of the two remaining guards, plunging her sword into his chest and pinning him in the dirt. Her sword stuck in the ground, and she hammered on her keys, trying to free it, while the remaining guard ran for her on-screen. Anda pounded her keyboard, but it was useless: the sword was good and stuck. Poo. She'd blown a small fortune on spells and rations for this project, with the expectation of getting some real cash out of it, and now it was all lost.

She moved her hands to the part of the keypad that controlled motion and began to run, waiting for the guard's sword to find her avatar's back and knock her into the dirt.

"Got 'im!" It was Lucy, in her headphones. She wheeled her avatar about so quickly it was nauseating and saw that Lucy was on her erstwhile attacker, grunting as she engaged him close-in. Something was wrong, though: despite Lucy's avatar's awesome stats and despite Lucy's own skill at the keyboard, she was being taken to the cleaners. The guard was kicking her ass. Anda went back to her stuck sword and recommenced whanging on it, watching helplessly as Lucy lost her left arm, then took a cut on her belly, then another to her knee.

"Shit!" Lucy said in her headphones as her avatar began to keel over. Anda yanked her sword free—finally—and charged at the guard, ululating her war cry. He managed to get his sword up before she reached him, but she got in a lucky swing and danced back before he could counterstrike. Now she closed carefully, moving in for a fast kill.

"Lucy?"

"Call me Sarge!"

"Sorry, Sarge. Where'd you respawn?"

"I'm all the way over at Body Electric—it'll take me hours to get there. Do you think you can complete the mission on your own?"

"Uh, sure." Thinking, *Crikey, if that's what the guards* outside *were like, how'm I gonna get past the* inside *guards?*

"You're the best, girl. Okay, enter the cottage and kill everyone there."

"Uh, sure."

She wished she had another scrying scroll in inventory so she could get a look inside the cottage before she beat its door in, but she was fresh out of scrolls and just about everything else.

She kicked the door in and her fingers danced. She'd killed four of her adversaries before she even noticed that they weren't fighting back.

In fact, they were generic avatars, maybe even nonplayer characters. They moved like total noobs, milling around in the little cottage. Around them were thousands and thousands of shirts. Incredibly, some noobs were still sitting, crafting more shirts, ignoring the swordswoman who'd just butchered their companions.

She took a careful look at all the avatars in the room. None of them were armed. Tentatively, she walked up to one of the players and cut his head off. The player next to him moved clumsily to one side, and she followed him.

"Are you a player or a bot?" she typed.

The avatar did nothing. She killed it.

"Lucy, they're not fighting back."

"Good, kill them all."

"Really?"

"Yeah—that's the orders. Kill them all and then I'll make a

phone call and some guys will come by and verify it and then you haul ass back to the island. I'm coming out there to meet you, but it's a long haul from the respawn gate. Keep an eye on my stuff, okay?"

"Sure," Anda said, and killed two more. That left ten. *One two one two and through and through,* she thought, lopping their heads off. One left. He stood off in the back.

> no porfa necesito mi plata

Spanish. She could always paste the text into a translation bot on one of the chat channels, but who cared? She cut his head off.

"They're all dead," she said into her headset.

"Good job!" Lucy said. "Okay, I'm gonna make a call. Sit tight."

Bo-ring. The cottage was filled with corpses and shirts. The kind of shirts you crafted when you were down at Level 0 and trying to get basic skillz. Add it all together and you barely had two thousand gold.

Just to pass the time, she pasted the Spanish into the chatbot.

> no [colloquial] please, I need my [colloquial] [money/silver]

Pathetic. A few thousand golds—he could make that much by playing a couple of the beginner missions. Crafting shirts!

She left the cottage and patrolled around it. Twenty minutes later, two more avatars showed up. More generics.

> are you players or bots?

she typed, though she had an idea they were players. Bots moved better.

> any trouble?

Well, all right then.

> no trouble

> good

One player entered the cottage and came back out again. The other player spoke.

> you can go now

"Lucy?"

"What's up?"

"Two blokes just showed up and told me to piss off. They're noobs, though. Should I kill them?"

"No! Jeez, Anda, those are the contacts. They're just making sure the job was done. Get my stuff and meet me at Marionettes Tavern, okay?"

As she made her way home, she snuck a peek back at the cottage. It was in flames, the two noobs standing amid them, burning slowly along with the cottage and a few thousand golds' worth of badly crafted shirts.

That month, she fought her way through six more missions, and the paypal she used filled with real, honest-to-goodness cash, pounds sterling that she could withdraw from the cashpoint situated exactly 501 meters away from the school gate, next to the candy shop that was likewise 501 meters away.

"Anda, I don't think it's healthy for you to spend so much time with your game," her da said, prodding her bulging podge with a finger. "It's not healthy."

"Daaaa!" she said, pushing his finger aside. "I go to PE every stinking day. It's good enough for the Ministry of Education."

"I don't like it," he said. He was no movie star himself, with a little potbelly that he wore his belted trousers high upon, a wobbly extra chin. She pinched his chin and wiggled it.

"I get loads more exercise than you, Mr. Pot."

"But I pay the bills around here, little Miss Kettle."

"You're not seriously complaining about the cost of the game?" she said, infusing her voice with incredulity. "Ten quid a week, and I get unlimited calls, texts, and messages! Plus play, of course, and the in-game encyclopedia and spellchecker and translator bots!" (Every member of the Fahrenheits memorized this for dealing with recalcitrant parental units.) "Fine then. If the game is too dear for you, Da, let's set it aside and I'll just start using a normal phone; is that what you want?"

Her da held up his hands. "I surrender, Miss Kettle. But *do* try to get a little more exercise, please? Fresh air? Sport? Games?"

"Getting my head trodden on in the hockey pitch, more like," she said darkly.

"Zackly!" he said, prodding her podge anew. "That's the stuff! Getting my head trodden on was what made me the man I are today!"

Her da could bluster all he liked about paying the bills, but she had pocket money for the first time in her life: not book-tokens and fruit-tokens and milk-tokens that could be exchanged for "healthy" snacks and literature. She had real money, cash money that she could spend outside of the five-hundred-meter sugar-free zone around her school.

"Go get a BFG," Lucy said. "We're going on a mission."

Lucy's voice in her ear was a constant companion in her life now. When she wasn't on Fahrenheit Island, she and Lucy were running missions into the wee hours of the morning. The Fahrenheit armorers, nonplayer characters, had learned to recognize her, and they had the Clan's BFGs oiled and ready for her when she showed up.

"Sarge?"

"Yes, Anda?"

"I just can't understand why anyone would pay us cash for these missions."

"You complaining?"

"No, but—"

"Anyone asking you to cyber some old pervert?"

"No!"

"Okay then. I don't know either. But the money's good. I don't care. Hell, probably it's two rich gamers who pay their butlers to craft for them all day. One's fucking with the other one and paying us."

"You really think that?"

Lucy sighed a put-upon, sophisticated, American sigh. "Look at it this way. Most of the world is living on, like, a dollar a day. I spend five dollars every day on a Frappuccino. Some days, I get two! Dad sends mom three thousand a month in child support—that's a hundred bucks a day. So, if a day's money here is a hundred dollars, then to an African or whatever, my Frappuccino is worth, like, *five hundred dollars.* And I buy two or three every day.

"And we're not rich! There's craploads of rich people who wouldn't think twice about spending five hundred bucks on a coffee—how much do you think a hot dog and a Coke go for on the space station? A thousand bucks!

"So that's what I think is going on. There's someone out there, some Saudi or Japanese guy or Russian mafia kid who's so rich that this is just chump change for him, and he's paying us to mess around with some other rich person. To them, we're like the Africans making a dollar a day to craft—I mean, sew—T-shirts. What's a couple hundred bucks to them? A cup of coffee."

"Three o'clock," Anda said, and aimed the BFG again. More snipers *pat-patt*ed in bits around the forest floor.

"Nice one, Anda."

"Thanks, Sarge."

They smashed half a dozen more sniper outposts before coming upon the cottage.

"Bloody hell," Anda breathed. The cottage was ringed with guards, forty or fifty of them, with bows and spells and spears, in entrenched positions.

"This is nuts," Lucy agreed. "I'm calling them. This is nuts."

There was a muting click as Lucy rang off, and Anda used up a scrying scroll on the guards. They were loaded down with spells, a couple of them were guarding BFGs and the fabled BFG10K, something that was removed not long after gameday one, as too disruptive to the balance of power. Supposedly, one or two existed, but that was just a rumor. Wasn't it?

"Okay," Lucy said. "Okay, this is how this goes. We've got to do this. I just called in three squads of Fahrenheit veterans and their noob prentices for backup." Anda summed that up in her head to a hundred player characters and maybe three hundred nonplayer characters: familiars, servants, demons . . .

"That's a lot of shares to split the pay into," Anda said.

"Oh ye of little tits," Lucy said. "I've negotiated a bonus for us if we make it—a million gold and three missions' worth of cash. The Fahrenheits are taking payment in gold—they'll be here in an hour."

This wasn't a mission anymore, Anda realized. It was war. Gamewar. Hundreds of players converging on this shard, squaring off against the ranked mercenaries guarding the huge cottage over the hill.

"On my signal," Lucy said. The voice chat was like a wind tunnel from all the unmuted breathing voices, hundreds of girls in hundreds of bedrooms like Anda's all over the world, some sitting down before breakfast, some just coming home from school, some roused from sleep by their ringing game-sponsored mobiles. "GO GO GO!"

They went, roaring, and Anda roared too, heedless of her parents downstairs in front of the blaring telly, a Fahrenheit in berzerker rage, sword swinging. She made straight for the BFG10K. She spelled the merc who was cranking it, rolled, and rolled again to dodge arrows and spells, healed herself when an arrow found her leg and sent her tumbling, springing to her feet before another arrow could strike home, watching her hit points and experience points move in opposite directions.

HERS! She vaulted the BFG10K and snicker-snacked her sword through two mercs' heads. Two more appeared—they had the thing primed and aimed at the main body of Fahrenheit fighters, and they could turn the battle's tide just by firing it—and she killed them, slamming her keypad, howling, barely conscious of the answering howls in her headset.

Now *she* had the BFG10K, though more mercs were closing on her. She disarmed it quickly and spelled at the nearest bunch of mercs, then had to take evasive action against the hail of incoming arrows and spells. It was all she could do to cast healing spells fast enough to avoid losing consciousness.

"LUCY!" she called into her headset. "LUCY, OVER BY THE BFG10K!"

Lucy snapped out orders, and the opposition before Anda thinned as Fahrenheits fell on them from behind. In short order, every merc was butchered or run off.

Anda waited by the BFG10K while Lucy paid off the Fahrenheits and saw them on their way. "Now we take the cottage," Lucy said.

"Right," Anda said. She set her character off for the doorway. Lucy brushed past her.

"I'll be glad when we're done with this—that was nutso." She opened the door and her character disappeared in a fireball that erupted from directly overhead. A door-curse.

"SHIT!" Lucy said in her headset.

Anda giggled. "Teach *you* to go rushing into things," she said. She used a scrying scroll, making sure that there was nothing else in the cottage save for millions of shirts and thousands of unarmed noob avatars that she'd have to mow down like grass to finish out the mission.

She descended upon them like a reaper, swinging her sword heedlessly, taking five or six out with each swing. When she'd been a noob in the game, she'd had to endure endless "grappling" with piles of leaves, just to get enough experience points to have a chance of hitting anything. This was every bit as dull.

Her wrists were getting tired and her chest heaved and her hated podge wobbled as she worked the keypad.

> Wait, please, don't—I'd like to speak with you

It was a noob avatar, just like the others, but not just like them after all, for it moved with purpose, backing away from her sword. And it spoke English.

> nothing personal

she typed.

> just a job

> There are many here to kill—take me last at least. I need to talk to you.

> talk, then

she typed. Meeting players who moved well and spoke English was hardly unusual in gamespace, but here in the cleanup phase, it felt out of place. It felt *wrong*.

> My name is Raymond, and I live in Tijuana. I am a labor organizer in the factories here. What is your name?

> i don't give out my name in-game

> What can I call you?

> kali

It was a name she liked to use in-game: Kali, Destroyer of Worlds, like the Hindu goddess.

> Are you in India?

> london

> You are Indian?

> naw im a whitey

She was halfway through the room, mowing down the noobs in twos and threes. She was hungry and bored and this Raymond was weirding her out.

> Do you know who these people are that you're killing?

She didn't answer, but she had an idea. She killed four more and shook out her wrists.

> They're working for less than a dollar a day. The shirts they make are traded for gold and the gold is sold on eBay. Once their avatars have leveled up, they too are sold off on eBay. They're mostly young girls supporting their families. They're the

lucky ones: the unlucky ones work as prostitutes.

Her wrists *really* ached. She slaughtered half a dozen more.

> The bosses used to use bots, but the game has countermeasures against them. Hiring children to click the mouse is cheaper than hiring programmers to circumvent the rules. I've been trying to unionize them because they've got a very high rate of injury. They have to play for 18-hour shifts with only one short toilet break. Some of them can't hold it in and they soil themselves where they sit.

> look

she typed, exasperated.

> it's none of my lookout, is it. the world's like that. lots of people with no money. im just a kid, theres nothing i can do about it.

> When you kill them, they don't get paid.

no porfa necesito mi plata

> When you kill them, they lose their day's wages. Do you know who is paying you to do these killings?

She thought of Saudis, rich Japanese, Russian mobsters.

> not a clue

> I've been trying to find that out myself, Kali.

They were all dead now. Raymond stood alone amongst the piled corpses.

> Go ahead

he typed,

> I will see you again, I'm sure.

She cut his head off. Her wrists hurt. She was hungry. She was alone there in the enormous woodland cottage, and she still had to haul the BFG10K back to Fahrenheit Island.

"Lucy?"

"Yeah, yeah, I'm almost back there, hang on. I respawned in the ass end of nowhere."

"Lucy, do you know who's in the cottage? Those noobs that we kill?"

"What? Hell, no. Noobs. Someone's butler. I dunno. Jesus, that spawn gate—"

"Girls. Little girls in Mexico. Getting paid a dollar a day to craft shirts. Except they don't get their dollar when we kill them. They don't get anything."

"Oh, for chrissakes, is that what one of them told you? Do you believe everything someone tells you in-game? Christ. English girls are so naïve."

"You don't think it's true?"

"Naw, I don't."

"Why not?"

"I just don't, okay? I'm almost there, keep your panties on."

"I've got to go, Lucy," she said. Her wrists hurt, and her podge overlapped the waistband of her trousers, making her feel a bit like she was drowning.

"What, now? Shit, just hang on."

"My mum's calling me to supper. You're almost here, right?"

"Yeah, but—"

She reached down and shut off her PC.

Anda's da and mum were watching the telly again, with a bowl of crisps between them. She walked past them like she was dreaming and stepped out the door onto the terrace. It was nighttime, eleven o'clock, and the chavs in front of the council flats across the square were kicking a football around and swilling lager and making rude noises. They were skinny, wearing shorts and string vests, with strong, muscular limbs flashing in the streetlights.

"Anda?"

"Yes, Mum?"

"Are you all right?" Her mum's fat fingers caressed the back of her neck.

"Yes, Mum. Just needed some air is all."

Anda's mum licked a finger and scrubbed it across Anda's neck. "Gosh, you're dirty—how did you get to be such a mucky puppy?"

"Owww!" she said. Her mum was scrubbing so hard it felt like she'd take her skin off.

"No whingeing," her mum said sternly. "Behind your ears too! You are *filthy*."

"Mum, *owwww*!"

Her mum dragged her up to the bathroom and went at her with a flannel and a bar of soap and hot water until she felt boiled and raw.

"What *is* this mess?" her mum said.

"Lilian, leave off," her dad said, quietly. "Come out into the hall for a moment, please."

The conversation was too quiet to hear, and Anda didn't want to, anyway: she was concentrating too hard on not crying—her ears *hurt*.

Her mum enfolded her shoulders in her soft hands again. "Oh, darling, I'm sorry. It's a skin condition, your father tells me, acanthosis nigricans—he saw it in a TV special. We'll see the doctor about it tomorrow after school. Are you all right?"

"I'm fine," she said, twisting to see if she could see the "dirt" on the back of her neck in the mirror. It was hard because it was an awkward placement—but also because she didn't like to look at her face and her soft extra chin, and she kept catching sight of it.

She went back to her room to Google *acanthosis nigricans*.

A condition involving darkened, thickened skin. Found in the folds of skin at the base of the back of the neck, under the arms, inside the elbow and at the waistline. Often precedes a diagnosis of type-2 diabetes, especially in children.

Obesity-related diabetes. They had lectures on this every term in health class—the fastest-growing ailment among British teens—accompanied by photos of orca-fat sacks of lard sitting up in bed surrounded by an ocean of rubbery, flowing podge. Anda prodded her belly and watched it jiggle.

It jiggled. Her thighs jiggled. Her chins wobbled. Her arms sagged.

She grabbed a handful of her belly and *squeezed it* as hard as she could, until she had to cry out. She'd left livid red fingerprints in the rolls of fat and she was crying now, from the pain and the shame and oh, God, she was a fat girl with diabetes—

"Jesus, Anda, where the hell have you been?"

"Sorry, Sarge," she said. "My PC's been broken. . . ." Well, out of service, anyway. Under lock and key in her dad's study. Almost a month now of medications and no telly and no gaming and double PE periods at school with the other whales.

"Well, you should have found a way to let me know. I was getting worried about you, girl."

"Sorry, Sarge," she said again. The PC baang was filled with stinky, spotty boys—literally stinky, it smelled like a train-station toilet—being obnoxious. The headphones provided were as greasy as a slice of pizza, and the mouthpiece was sticky with excited boy-saliva from past games.

"Well, I've got four missions we can do today if you're game."

"Four missions! How on earth will we do four missions? That'll take days!"

"We'll take the BFG10K." Anda could hear the savage grin in her voice.

The BFG10K simplified things quite a lot. Find the cottage, aim the BFG10K, fire it, whim-wham, no more cottage.

"I met a guy after the last campaign," Anda said. "One of the noobs in the cottage. He said he was a union organizer."

"Oh, you met Raymond, huh?"

"You knew about him?"

"I met him too. He's been turning up everywhere. What a creep."

"So you knew about the noobs in the cottages?"

"Um. Well, yeah, I figured it out mostly on my own, and then Raymond told me a little more."

"And you're fine with depriving little kids of their wages?"

"Anda," Lucy said, her voice brittle. "You like gaming, right, it's important to you?"

"Yeah, 'course it is."

"How important? Is it something you do for fun, just a hobby you waste a little time on? Are you just into it casually, or are you *committed* to it?"

"I'm committed to it, Lucy, you know that." God, without the game, what was there? PE class? Stupid acanthosis nigricans and, someday, insulin jabs every morning? "I love the game, Lucy. It's where my friends are."

"I know that. That's why you're my right-hand woman, why I want you at my side when I go on a mission. We're badass, you and me, as badass as they come, and we got that way through discipline and hard work and really *caring* about the game, right?"

"Yes, right, but—"

"You've met Liza the Organiza, right?"

"Yes, she came by my school."

"Mine too. She asked me to look out for you because of what she saw in you that day."

"Liza the Organiza goes to Ohio?"

"Idaho. Yeah. She's amazing, and she cares about the game too—that's what makes us all Fahrenheits: we're committed to each other, to teamwork, and to fair play."

Anda had heard these words—lifted from the Fahrenheit mission statement—many times, but now they made her swell a little with pride.

"So, these people in Mexico or wherever, what are they doing? They're earning their living by exploiting the game. *We* would never trade cash for gold or *buy* a weapon—it's cheating. You get gold and weapons through hard work and hard play. But those Mexicans spend all day, every day, crafting stuff to turn into gold to sell off on the exchange. That's how rich noobs can buy their way into the game that we had to play hard to get into.

"If we keep burning the factories down, they'll shut them down and those kids'll find something else to do for a living, and the game will be better. If no one does that, the game will get less and less fun.

"These people *don't* care about the game. To them, it's just a place to suck a buck out of. They're not players, they're leeches, here to suck all the fun out."

They had come upon the cottage now, the fourth one, having exterminated four different sniper nests on the way.

"Are you in, Anda? Or are you so worried about these leeches on the other side of the world?"

"I'm in, Sarge," Anda said. She armed the BFGs and pointed them at the cottage.

"Boo-yah!" Lucy said. Her character nocked an arrow.

> Hello, Kali

"Oh, Christ, he's back," Lucy said. Raymond's avatar had snuck up behind them.

> Look at these

he said, and his character set something down on the ground and backed away. Anda edged up on them.

"Come on, it's probably a booby trap. We've got work to do," Lucy said.

They were photos. She examined them. The first showed ranked little girls in clean and simple T-shirts, skinny as anything, sitting at generic white-box PCs, hands on the keyboards. They were hollow-eyed and grim, and none of them older than she.

The next showed a shantytown, tin shacks made of corrugated aluminum and trash, muddy trails between them, spray-painted graffiti, rude boys loitering, rubbish and carrier bags blowing.

The next showed the inside, three little girls and a little boy sitting together on a battered sofa, their mother serving them something on plastic plates. Their brave smiles were heartbreaking.

> That's who you're about to deprive of a day's wages

"Oh, hell, *no*," Lucy said. "Not again. I killed him last time and I said I'd do it again. That's it, he's dead." Her character turned toward him, putting away her bow and drawing a short sword. Raymond's character backed away quickly.

"Lucy, don't," Anda said. She interposed her avatar between Lucy's and Raymond. "Don't do it. He deserves to have a say."

"God *damn* it, Anda, what is *wrong* with you? Did you come here to play the game, or to screw around with this pervert dork?"

> what do you want from me raymond?

> Don't kill them—let them have their wages. Go play somewhere else.

> They're leeches

Lucy typed,

> they're wrecking the game economy and they're providing a gold-for-cash supply that lets rich assholes buy their way in. They don't care about the game and neither do you

> If they don't play the game, they don't eat. They care about the game as much as you do. You're being paid cash to kill them, yes? So you need to play for your money too. I think that makes you and them a little the same.

> go screw yourself

Raymond's character was so far away now that his texting came out in tiny type, almost too small to read. Lucy drew her bow again and nocked an arrow.

"Lucy, *don't*!" Anda cried. Her hands moved of their own volition and her character followed, clobbering Lucy barehanded so that her avatar reeled and dropped its bow.

"You *bitch*!" Lucy said. She drew her sword.

"I'm sorry, Lucy," Anda said, stepping back out of range. "But I don't want you to hurt him. I want to hear him out."

Lucy's avatar came on fast, and there was a click as the voicelink dropped. Anda typed one-handed while she drew her own sword.

> dont lucy come on talk2me

Lucy slashed at her twice and she needed both hands to defend herself. Anda blew out through her nose and counterattacked, fingers pounding the keyboard. Lucy had more experience points than she did, but she was a better player, and she knew it. She hacked away at Lucy, driving her back and back, back down the road they'd marched together.

Abruptly, Lucy broke and ran, and Anda thought she was going away and decided to let her go, no harm no foul, but then she saw that Lucy wasn't running away, she was running *toward* the BFGs, armed and primed.

"Bloody hell," she breathed, as a BFG swung around to point at her. Her fingers flew. She cast the fireball at Lucy in the same instant that she cast her shield spell. Lucy loosed the bolt at her a moment before the fireball engulfed her, cooking her down to ash, and the bolt collided with the shield and drove Anda high into the air, and the shield spell wore off before she hit ground, scattering her inventory.

"Lucy?"

There was no reply.

> I'm very sorry you and your friend quarreled.

She felt numb and unreal. There were rules for Fahrenheits, lots of rules, and the penalties for breaking them varied, but the penalty for attacking a fellow Fahrenheit was—she couldn't think the word, she closed her eyes, but there it was in big glowing letters: EXPULSION.

But Lucy had started it, right? It wasn't her fault.

But who would believe her?

She opened her eyes. Her vision swam through incipient tears. Her heart was thudding in her ears.

> The enemy isn't your fellow player. It's not the players guarding the fabrica, it's not the girls working there. The people who are working to destroy the game are the people who pay you and the people who pay the girls in the fabrica, who are the same people. You're being paid by rival factory owners, you know that? THEY are the ones who care nothing for the game. My girls care about the game. You care about the game. Your common enemy is the people who want to destroy the game and who destroy the lives of these girls.

"Anda, dear, there's a phone call for you."

Her eyes stung. She'd been lying in her darkened bedroom for hours now, snuffling and trying not to cry, trying not to look at the empty desk where her PC used to live.

Her da's voice was soft and caring, but after the silence of her room, it sounded like a rusting hinge.

"Anda?"

She opened her eyes. He was holding a cordless phone, silhouetted against the open doorway.

"Who is it?"

"Someone from your game, I think," he said. He handed her the phone.

"Hullo?"

"Hullo, chicken." It had been a year since she'd heard that voice, but she recognized it instantly.

"Liza?"

"Yes."

Anda's skin seemed to shrink over her bones. This was it: expelled. Her heart felt like it was beating once per second; time slowed to a crawl.

"Hullo, Liza."

"Can you tell me what happened today?"

She did, stumbling over the details, backtracking and stuttering. She couldn't remember, exactly—did Lucy move on Raymond and Anda asked her to stop and then Lucy attacked her? Had Anda attacked Lucy first? It was all a jumble. She should have saved a screenmovie and taken it with her, but she couldn't have taken anything with her, she'd run out—

"I see. Well, it sounds like you've gotten yourself into quite a pile of poo, haven't you, my girl?"

"I guess so," Anda said. Then, because she knew that she was as good as expelled, she said, "I don't think it's right to kill them, those girls. All right?"

"Ah," Liza said. "Well, funny you should mention that. I happen to agree. Those girls need our help more than any of the girls anywhere else in the game. The Fahrenheits' strength is that we are cooperative—it's another way that we're better than the boys. We care. I'm proud that you took a stand when you did—glad I found out about this business."

"You're not going to expel me?"

"No, chicken, I'm not going to expel you. I think you did the right thing—"

That meant that Lucy would be expelled. Fahrenheit had

killed Fahrenheit—something had to be done. The rules had to be enforced. Anda swallowed hard.

"If you expel Lucy, I'll quit," she said, quickly, before she lost her nerve.

Liza laughed. "Oh, chicken, you're a brave thing, aren't you? No one's being expelled, fear not. But I want to talk to this Raymond of yours."

Anda came home from remedial hockey sweaty and exhausted, but not as exhausted as the last time, nor the time before that. She could run the whole length of the pitch twice now without collapsing—when she'd started out, she could barely make it halfway without having to stop and hold her side, kneading her loathsome podge to make it stop aching. Now there was noticeably less podge, and she found that with the ability to run the pitch came the freedom to actually pay attention to the game, to aim her shots, to build up a degree of accuracy that was nearly as satisfying as being really good in-game.

Her dad knocked at the door of her bedroom after she'd showered and changed. "How's my girl?"

"Revising," she said, and hefted her math book at him.

"Did you have a fun afternoon on the pitch?"

"You mean 'did my head get trod on?'"

"Did it?"

"Yes," she said. "But I did more treading than getting trodden on." The other girls were *really* fat, and they didn't have a lot of team skills. Anda had been to war: she knew how to depend on someone and how to be depended upon.

"That's my girl." He pretended to inspect the paint-work around the light switch. "Been on the scales this week?"

She had, of course: the school nutritionist saw to that, a morning humiliation undertaken in full sight of all the other fatties.

"Yes, Dad."

"And . . . ?"

"I've lost a stone," she said. A little more than a stone, actually. She had been able to fit into last year's jeans the other day.

She hadn't been to the sweets shop in a month. When she thought about sweets, it made her think of the little girls in the sweatshop. Sweatshop, sweetshop. The sweets shop man sold his wares close to the school because little girls who didn't know better would be tempted by them. No one forced them, but they were *kids*, and grown-ups were supposed to look out for kids.

Her da beamed at her. "I've lost three pounds myself," he said, holding his tum. "I've been trying to follow your diet, you know."

"I know, Da," she said. It embarrassed her to discuss it with him.

The kids in the sweatshops were being exploited by grown-ups too. It was why their situation was so impossible: the adults who were supposed to be taking care of them were exploiting them.

"Well, I just wanted to say that I'm proud of you. We both are, your mum and me. And I wanted to let you know that I'll be moving your PC back into your room tomorrow. You've earned it."

Anda blushed pink. She hadn't really expected this. Her fingers twitched over a phantom game controller.

"Oh, Da," she said. He held up his hand.

"It's all right, girl. We're just proud of you."

She didn't touch the PC the first day, or the second. The kids in the game—she didn't know what to do about them. On the third day, after hockey, she showered and changed and sat down and slipped the headset on.

"Hello, Anda."

"Hi, Sarge."

Lucy had known the minute she entered the game, which meant that she was still on Lucy's buddy list. Well, that was a hopeful sign.

"You don't have to call me that. We're the same rank now, after all."

Anda pulled down a menu and confirmed it: she'd been promoted to sergeant during her absence. She smiled.

"Gosh," she said.

"Yes, well, you earned it," Lucy said. "I've been talking to Raymond a lot about the working conditions in the factory, and, well—" She broke off. "I'm sorry, Anda."

"Me too, Lucy."

"You don't have anything to be sorry about," she said.

They went adventuring, running some of the game's standard missions together. It was fun, but after the kind of campaigning they'd done before, it was also kind of pale and flat.

"It's horrible, I know," Anda said. "But I miss it."

"Oh, thank God," Lucy said. "I thought I was the only one. It was fun, wasn't it? Big fights, big stakes."

"Well, poo," Anda said. "I don't wanna be bored for the rest of my life. What're we gonna do?"

"I was hoping you knew."

She thought about it. The part she'd loved had been going up against grown-ups who were not playing the game, but *gaming* it, breaking it for money. They'd been worthy adversaries, and there was no guilt in beating them, either.

"We'll ask Raymond how we can help," she said.

"I want them to walk out—to go on strike," he said. "It's the only way to get results: band together and withdraw your labor." Raymond's voice had a thick Mexican accent that took some getting used to, but his English was very good—better, in fact, than Lucy's.

"Walk out in-game?" Lucy said.

"No," Raymond said. "That wouldn't be very effective. I want them to walk out in Ciudad Juarez and Tijuana. I'll call the press in; we'll make a big deal out of it. We can win—I know we can."

"So what's the problem?" Anda said.

"The same problem as always. Getting them organized. I thought that the game would make it easier: we've been trying to get these girls organized for years: in the sewing shops, and the toy factories, but they lock the doors and keep us out and the girls go home and their parents won't let us talk to them. But in the game, I thought I'd be able to reach them. . . ."

"But the bosses keep you away?"

"I keep getting killed. I've been practicing my swordfighting, but it's so hard. . . ."

"This will be fun," Anda said. "Let's go."

"Where?" Lucy said.

"To an in-game factory. We're your new bodyguards." The bosses hired some pretty mean mercs, Anda knew. She'd been one. They'd be *fun* to wipe out.

Raymond's character spun around on the screen, then planted a kiss on Anda's cheek. Anda made her character give him a playful shove that sent him sprawling.

"Hey, Lucy, go get us a couple BFGs, okay?"

CORY DOCTOROW, self-described "renaissance geek," is probably best known for his Web site boingboing.net and for his work with the Electronic Frontier Foundation. Raised by Trotskyist schoolteachers in the wilds of Canada, Doctorow began selling fiction when he was seventeen, and published a small handful of stories through the early and mid-1990s. His best-known story, "Craphound," appeared in 1998, and he won the John W. Campbell Award for Best New Writer in 2000. Doctorow's first novel, *Down and Out in the Magic Kingdom*, was published to good reviews in early 2003 and was followed by collections *A Place So Foreign and Eight More* and *Overclocked*, and novels *Eastern Standard Tribe* and *Someone Comes to Town, Someone Leaves Town*. Doctorow is currently working on three novels: *usr/bin/god*, *Themepunks*, and *Little Brother.* He is also the coauthor of *The Complete Idiot's Guide to Writing Science Fiction* with Karl Schroeder.

"Anda's Game" is the first in a series of stories that play off the titles of famous SF short stories. Doctorow began this series after Ray Bradbury voiced his disapproval of filmmaker Michael Moore appropriating the title of Bradbury's novel *Fahrenheit 451*. The ongoing series includes Hugo Award nominee "I, Robot" and "I, Rowboat," both of which play off the name and concepts in Isaac Asimov's famous short story, "I, Robot."

AUTHOR'S NOTE

"Anda's Game" is meant to tackle some of the themes in Orson Scott Card's *Ender's Game*, a wildly popular novel that talks a lot about how gaming can numb kids to violence so that they end up committing unspeakable acts of violence. I wanted to talk a little about how games can arouse compassion, community, and fellow-feeling:

I was practically raised online and made some of my most important friendships that way. I think that networked communications can be magnificent for bringing people together.

Another important theme in this story is obesity. The World Health Organization predicts that by the year 2015, 1.5 billion people will be obese, many of them in the developing world. There are a lot of reasons for this, but laziness and lack of virtue aren't among them. Obesity is an epidemic and needs to be studied like one, with an eye to the social/medical causes of its spread. In particular, I believe that industrial food products like high-fructose corn syrup and palm oil are basically toxic waste that unscrupulous food manufacturers add to their products, guaranteeing that their customers will become unhealthily fat.

SUNDIVER DAY

Kathleen Ann Goonan

Most of our brain is dedicated to vision. Did you know that?

My big brother Sam told me that. Before he died. He was a secret kite scout somewhere in the Middle East.

Right now, my name is Sundiver Day. I live in Key West. I just turned sixteen. Ever since Sam died—or disappeared—last March, I have to get out on the water a lot.

My father died when I was ten. We still have his parrots, the brilliant Esmeralda and the shy Evylyn and the really cranky Ed. They live practically forever. I used to go around Key West with one or the other on my shoulder, usually Esmeralda. So my other name, the name my friends call me, is Parrot Girl. And I have cloned a parrot, little Alouicious, who also lives in the backyard with the others. Alouicious is what made me famous. Wow, they all said. All the adults, anyway. I was in the *Key West Citizen* and *Science News* and won a science prize.

But I'm tired of being Parrot Girl. I have a new name now, although I haven't told anyone. It's nobody's business. They used to make fun of me and call me "Miss Smarty," but I beat up the ringleader of that crowd, Marcy Phipps, when I was fourteen, and after that nobody bothered me. Sam taught me how to fight. It seems childish now, but it was worth it at the time. And Parrot Girl is better than Eelie.

People say my mother is eccentric, but she's not. She studies orchids and has to go all over the world and leaves me with my aunt Cicily, who has a Café Cubano shop, even though she's not Cuban but originally from Iowa. She's my mother's twin. She was a biologist and did cloning things. Famous cloning things. Things people got mad at her for doing. Even her husband, who divorced her. So now she has Café Cubano. Her work is on the Internet. I've been reading it a lot lately. She would be surprised at what I know.

We live in an old house. The wide front porch is decorated with wiggly white gingerbread. They call old houses "Conch houses" here, and they call the people who have lived in the Keys a long time Conchs. I guess we're Conchs, although my dad was a hippie, too, and got thrown in jail a lot when he was young, in places like Chicago and Washington, D.C. My mother said they came down here because it was cheap and because she grew up here, in this house, and because people wouldn't talk about them taking experimental life-extension drugs. Everybody takes them now; they've been FDA approved, and Key West isn't cheap anymore. Our neighbor Millie, who is a real estate agent, keeps wanting to list our house. "It's worth well over a million now, Hannah," I heard her telling my mom one night in the living room. "Eelie needs a better place to grow up. A place where she can use her intellectual talents. She's turning into a wild girl."

I kind of liked hearing that. Wild girl, that's me. My mother says, of course, that I need as normal a life as possible and it's pretty normal here, and Millie laughs.

But Eelie? That's what they call me. The adults. Short for Elendilia. They said that I called myself Eelie when I was a baby. It's not quite fair. I had no idea what I was doing. It's no wonder I haven't really settled on a suitable name just yet.

After Sam disappeared I started using his Zodiac boat and found my own secret creek hidden in the mangroves, where gray snappers flock beneath the sea roots, silent-colored like wolves, brushing over and around one another in slow light.

They say he's missing in action, but Mom says that we have to accept that he's dead. It's been eight months now. She only said that once, and really quietly at night when she came into my room and tucked me in, like she hadn't done since I was little, and then kissed me, and then went away fast because she was crying.

Sometimes I think I see my brother up in the sky, drifting past, red hair streaming out, his eyes two blue stars and one of them *winks* at me.

Sometimes I hope, sometimes I think, that the whole world is his wink to me, his way of saying, "I'm still here, sis." And that's when I'm glad that most of my brain is for vision, because then it's full of Sam.

If I didn't think that, I couldn't get out of bed in the morning. I can barely move a finger. I've tried thinking that the world isn't Sam's wink, his way of staying with me always. I am much too heavy to move then, even though my mother worries and calls me her Thin Stick, and Louisa the Cuban therapist says that I have to find new ways of thinking.

They say his wings failed. That's how they described it. But it wasn't "they." It was just one tall black woman wearing a uniform.

Most people when they walk up to our house from the street hesitate because the front yard is a private jungle and it's hard to see the house, and it looks kind of haunted to my friends. A ghost lived here one time, a German ghost, my friend Janet, who is a true Conch, says, but I don't believe it. This is a friendly house with big square rooms, tall wavy windows, and tilted wood floors.

And there are no ghosts.

Lobster claw helliconias drop down their yellow-orange flowers, hard and triangular like the claws they're named for. White birds-of-paradise thrust their beaks between elephant ears as big as the front window. That morning our jungle was cool and dripping from the shower that usually passes over the island just before dawn, when the sky is the color between night and day; the color of no. Nautical twilight is that color, when you can't tell a white thread from a black thread, when you have to start worrying about whether or not you will be able to see, and turn on your mast light if you are in a sailboat at anchor.

So I am sitting on a rocker on the front porch reading my messages and I glimpse her at the gate, looking worried. I think she is lost and yell, "Can I help you?"

"Is this the Wheeler residence?"

My father never liked to tell anybody anything; he said that if they didn't know they shouldn't be there, and maybe they were trying to serve a warrant or something. But I just say, "Yes, it is."

"Is your mother home?" She unhooks the crooked wire gate, and Alpha, who is a very old dog, wakes up from under the cool plants and whoofs her way to the woman's knees.

"She won't hurt you."

"Hello?" Mom comes out the door carrying her big straw bag stuffed with papers and her computer and who knows what, ready for class. She's teaching this semester; then she's going to Bali.

Mom is pretty, but she needs help. She has long flyaway reddish hair and blue eyes and laughed and laughed when I gave her some expensive wrinkle pills with hormones in them one Christmas. Go figure. And I went all the way to Miami on the bus to get them so that she wouldn't see them come in the mail, like she would have if I had ordered them online. She could use them. She needs a good haircut, too, and she needs to dress up more. Right now she's wearing thrift-store jeans, a tie-dye T-shirt, and zoris. Sometimes I'm embarrassed to be around her. All the mothers of my friends dress like they're on a permanent cruise. Their hair is perfect and their high heels are tall even when they're grocery shopping; their clothes are never wrinkled, and little diamonds wink at their neck.

The woman looks at me as she says to Mom, "I have something to tell you. In private."

Mom looks like she is going to melt. She blinks, puts her bag down on the dark green porch floor, and says, "Come in." The screen door shuts, and I go over and listen while the woman tells Mom that Sam is missing in action.

He is some kind of scout. The Third Middle East War has lasted for five years now, and he was—he *is*—a kitesurfer, a champion kite-surfer, and that's why he was picked for the special flying division. They wear nanotech camouflage and fly through the mountains silent as the air on solar wings that change with the terrain and sky. The scouts record everything with cameras in their eyes. He enlisted, and Mom was very, very angry and said that his father would be very disappointed in him, and he said that he wanted to get the implants and the training and be able to earn a living now, not after years and years of college. It sounded very sensible to me. Our mother is not that sensible, I must say. I am trying to think of something sensible to do myself, but the only thing that comes to mind is cloning Sam like Aunt Cicily cloned the famous Mitisent Baby.

It's not really sensible. And it's against the law. Plus, he would be a baby and not Sam at all. He'd just look like Sam. It wouldn't be fair to expect him to be anything like Sam. That's what Aunt Cicily told me when I suggested it. I think I started to scream at one point and that's when she hugged me so tight that I couldn't breathe. I'm sorry I mentioned it to her in the first place. She said, with tears in her eyes and so fiercely that I thought she was mad at me at first, "Do you think I haven't thought of that myself?"

I'm over that now. I would love him like himself. I wouldn't even call him Sam. I could just look at him, though, and see Sam, a little Sam I never knew. I would take care of him. I would never, never let him go to war.

Later I asked Mom why they couldn't find him, if where he went that night wasn't on the GPS or transmitted by his eye-camera, and she said she wondered that too and was trying to find out, but that it was all a big f-word secret. She says the f-word when she gets very angry, which is about once a year.

"Oh God, honey," she said. "I didn't mean to say that." She shook her head and wandered into the kitchen to eat ice cream. That's all she eats anymore. Mint chocolate chip. Breakfast, lunch, and dinner. And talk about thin. If I'm a thin stick then she's a fragile baby twig about to break. I heard her start to play the grand piano that sits in the living room. A Bach two-piece invention, one that I used to love to play too. Now it sounds like dust. It sounds like no.

I do want to get better. I think that little Sam—little not-Sam, will help. He will help us all.

Today I wake from the dream of Sam smashing into sharp dry mountain peaks and there is nobody in the kitchen; Mom has left for work, and Aunt Cicily is getting dressed. I eat half an oatmeal muffin and some almonds.

I am supposed to be in school today, but instead I grab some Cokes from the refrigerator and climb into Sam's Zodiac boat, a big puffy inflatable that's good for getting into small, shallow spaces, and untie it from the dock cleats. It has a tiny two-stroke solar Honda; the whole boat is a solar collector, and I move quietly down the green canal while Aunt Cicily runs out into the backyard and yells at me until her voice gets little. They will give me a hard time, but I will tell them that I was working on my science project. I am cloning fish now. There's a big market for perfect cloned fish. I am looking for something rare—at least, that's what I tell them. Doctor Harris is helping me with the project. Her son would like me to come over to their house, but I can't stand him. I used to think I loved Jim Johnson, who is also a Conch and a great sailor and has gorgeous green eyes, but he doesn't have a clue. I used to walk past his house and stare at his window, but I don't have time for that kind of stuff anymore.

Now I just meet Doctor Harris at the lab. She's a fertility doctor and does research. I'm getting college credits for my work. The adults like it. They say it's "keeping me busy."

I am very busy. Cloning Sam is a big project.

There are a lot of famous clones. The Tred-Bleck quintet. A

Britney Spears, a Marilyn Monroe, many Elvises, and other more mundane clones, all cloned before it was illegal in the U.S. The Britney Spears was cloned by the original Britney, and she's kind of a Britney slave, bringing in money for the first one. She's trademarked, and they have some kind of contract. Mom says there are probably lots of clones that nobody even knows about, and that all the things that Aunt Cicily went through aren't fair, and that if she wanted to move to Sweden she'd be able to work again.

I'm not sure how I'll get him into my uterus, the clone of Sam. It's actually pretty weird when I think about it. I guess I'd have to steal the fertility drugs from Dr. Harris's lab, which bothers me. But I'll figure something out. Maybe some woman who can't have a baby would want him. Maybe I can pay someone to do it. A surrogate mother. That might be the best idea. I'm not allowed to make money from fish cloning, because it's research through the college, but I've got a lot of babysitting money saved up. I've been babysitting forever. I could run an ad in the *Key West Citizen*. It would be better, I think, if Mom would consent to carrying him, but I'm pretty sure she wouldn't. She would raise holy hell if she knew. Besides, even though she takes the longevity drug, she's old. She's probably too tired to have a baby.

I don't care what they say. I don't care if they arrest me. In fact, I'd like to see the trial. "Gifted Girl Clones Brother; Government Confesses That He Is Still Alive." The article would talk about how I could have been a prize-winning piano player but was driven to give it up by the biological research I had to do. That's what Mom and Aunt Cicily and Luisa the Cuban therapist, who I've had since I was ten and Dad died, complain about—I don't play the piano anymore because I'm obsessed with science. Then the government would tell us the truth, wouldn't they? I know Sam is still alive. My friends think I'm crazy, so I just don't talk to them anymore. They don't know anything. They're all dating and talking about their boyfriends and getting nanotech communication implants put in without their parents' permission, which is easy if you just go to Cuba on the hydro ferry for a day. I'd rather be alone.

Babies are a lot of work. I know this. Sometimes when I think about this plan, I see little Melanie Eddleson, four months old and screaming with something that turned out to be an earache, when I finally got hold of her mother and she rushed home and took her to the doctor. I felt completely helpless as she lay there kicking and punching, her little face bright red, and even scared that she might die suddenly and it would all be my fault. I know about morning sickness. I know about changing diapers. But would it be the same if I couldn't leave? I would be the one crazy with worry, calling the doctor. And I might have to put off college, for a little while, anyway.

It doesn't really matter. I have to do it.

I can't go very fast on the canal because you're not supposed to cause a wake—plus, there might be manatees. I slowly pass *Double Ace*, *Toad Hall*, *Windly*. You could cruise all the way to Africa in any one of them. White monsters. They each hold a thousand gallons of gas. After I leave Aunt Cicily behind, I pass *Pieces of Eight* and John Kred's little sailboat *Sly Skimmer* and all the regular-sized weekender fishing boats with puns in their names like *Reel Incredible*. I pass Jane Alberson's house and whistle to her potbellied Vietnamese pig snuffling around in the yard, and he raises his head and looks at me with his smart little eyes. Mr. Albert waves to me from his backyard where he's watering his bromeliads and then I'm out into the bay. I put on my CoolBrite sunglasses and polarize the world into brilliant greens and blues.

The bay is flat as a single diamond facet because there is no wind today. And enormous, like the sky, and filled with mangrove islands. It never gets deep. In most places it is about a foot, and it's easy to run aground, unless you're in a little boat like mine. It is also very easy to get lost. All the islands look the same, low and gray and floating today on a lime green band that divides the bay from the sky.

I speed up, fast as flying, and the wind pushes back my hair. I go through Toilet Seat Cut, where people have decorated toilet seats by painting and writing on them and stuck them on posts. Sam has one here. I cross the Intracoastal Waterway where the big boats roar from marker to marker, on their way to somewhere as fast as they can go.

Five minutes later I pass the boundary sign that says EVERGLADES NATIONAL PARK, mounted on a metal post sticking up out of the water. I turn northwest, sixty degrees, and head for a white stick I pounded into the mud a while back. I can't see it yet but I know where it is. When I get an implant, when I'm eighteen (my mom won't give permission for *anything*, even if, as I tell her, it might save my life), it's not going to be for cosmetic purposes. It will be a global positioning system. I don't want to put this spot into a handheld GPS right now. If they got their hands on the GPS they could find me. And I don't want to be found.

I skim over the shallow water, blue and green like a liquid quilt, so clear I can see the seagrass below, pulled like long hair across the bottom by the outgoing tide rushing through narrow channels to the Atlantic. There are low gray islands everywhere, and they all look alike, kind of fluffy and very small. You can't land on them because they are park. A fishhawk flies overhead, and a pair of white egrets, and doves making their weird, low dinosaur cry. Gulls chase me for a moment, hoping for food, then drop back.

I'm surrounded by islands now, and sandbars, and I can't see Key West anymore. If a boat with a bigger draft wandered into this mile-wide basin, they'd have a hard time finding their way back out. They'd run aground and have to call Sea Tow. Golden brown sandbars glimmer in strips around me. Out on the water it's hard to tell how far away anything is. When I reach my white stick, I turn the boat at a precise angle, and suddenly a channel, two feet deep and brilliant green, appears before me. If you aren't headed right into it, you can't see it at all. That's the thing about the bay. You really have to know what you're doing, and I do. This is where Sam and I grew up, on the water, with Dad teaching us where to go and how to survive, and then just us two after he died.

The mouth of my little creek is hidden by mangroves. I look around before I go in, but I see no one except a flats fisherman way, way off. I duck beneath the branches and the leaves scratch my face. Then I'm in the creek.

It's only about ten feet wide, with a sandy bottom over which snapper and bonefish phantoms glide. A few yellow mangrove leaves drift past on the surface. I can see every pebble, every branch that has fallen into the water. It's a crystal place, and utterly quiet except for birds. Sometimes porpoises come into the canal, hunting. They make a snorting sound with their airholes, like hogs, and come up to the boat and look at me.

Mangroves are peculiar plants. Their roots drop down into the water, looking like gray scribbles, but when you look at a single tree carefully, you can see that the roots arch out, dive straight down, then split at a precise angle. My mother could tell you the angle. The water flows through their roots. There are three kinds of mangroves—red, white, and black. They mostly look the same, though, except for subtle differences. This is a black mangrove hammock.

I turn off the engine and float but don't throw in the anchor. It is hot and damp and still.

There's a lot to think about out here. You can think about waves that pass through a medium. Like light through the air, like motion through the water. Ripples draw reflections into bands of straight colored lines—green, silver, blue, like their edges were drawn with a ruler. A pelican dives straight down into the water with a big loud smash and surfaces, swimming. He didn't catch anything. Light wavers and twists on the creek bottom in a diamond pattern.

You can think about cells, and zygotes, but I don't feel like it right now. I think about circles. Have you ever noticed how people are always telling you about how things like light and sound are organized in circles? If you paint, there is the color wheel. If you play the piano, you have to learn the circle of fifths so you can transpose like mad, change anything into any other key right away.

I do like to transpose. I want to transpose the whole world. I want to transpose it to the world where Sam is, to take all the light and dive into it and see him there, where he always calls me Sundiver. It's his name for me. But it's only his. The Day part, the last name, is mine. Making Sam again would be like a circle, wouldn't it? A new Sam, in a new time.

I take off all my clothes and sit naked in the hot sun because, as I now realize, I didn't have time to grab my bathing suit. I pull my snorkel on over my head and get my neon green flippers out from under the seat.

I look up and the sky is no longer blue. It is the color of no. A cloud covers the sun.

Sometimes when I am very sad, a face cries inside me. Tears flow there. But they do not flow outside, anymore.

Then sunlight shoots out and the world winks back at me. I fall into the other world below me, a sundiver. Sam is the triangles of light. He is the color wheel. He is the universe of transposed notes, winking at me.

He is colors I don't yet know. I am inventing them. I am giving him a new self.

If anybody found out, they'd kill me.

Millicent Swartz, our neighbor, is a real estate agent, as I mentioned before. She sits in the living room now, wearing a red, vaguely Western hat from which shimmering things dangle, shaking whenever she moves her head, which is often because that's how she talks. Her hands dance around; she just can't sit still, and she's tiny, like a human flea with wild, frizzy black hair. She gives belly-dancing lessons on the side, and I took some last year. It was fun. She has a big mirror in her living room, and you have to do a lot of exercises. She's drinking a cold Cuban beer. My mother, wearing shorts and a halter top, sits in a leather club chair with her long brown legs stretched out on an ottoman. She is drinking red wine from a glass etched with palm trees.

I'm in the dining room, working on my computer at the table of my grandparents. It is mahogany, heavy and showy and brilliantly shining where it is not scratched. I think it got here on a Spanish galleon or something. Key West was once the largest city in Florida, back in the 1860s. I'm not kidding. The whole rest of Florida was impenetrable jungle (excpet for a few places) full of gators and wild pigs and mosquitoes. The land turned the people back big-time. But Key West has a great harbor.

Actually, I'm not working at all. I'm just listening to them talk. There's a heavy wind out of the southwest today, so their words are interlaced with the thrashing of the palm trees right outside the window and cranky Ed croaking, "Up against the wall! Up against the wall!" He used to say, "Up against the wall, mother f-word," but Mom made Dad train it out of him.

"I had them this close!" says Millicent, hat jewels shimmering. She holds up a finger and a thumb to indicate a quarter inch. "This close! But that asshole just didn't want to close the deal. Two weeks wasted."

Mom nods and sips her wine. She looks tired, as usual. I'm afraid that she's sick or something. Alpha snoozes on the tattered Tibetan rug next to her chair. Her muzzle is gray. Mom and I have had arguments about giving her the longevity drug. I don't see why anyone has to die, even dogs.

"I think I'm going to get out of this business." She says this once a week. Then she makes a big haul, closes a huge deal. It's like fishing. You never know what you're going to catch. "One of those Argentineans at the closing last week pulled a gun on us."

"Really."

"Of course, Bob took his own out of his desk drawer, and it was a draw." Millecent laughs. "It's hard to outgun Southernmost Realty. We should put that in our ad!" She intones, "It's Hard to Outgun Southernmost Realty. We've Got Your Deal in Our Sights."

She hoots. Sometimes Millicent snorts, sometimes she hoots, sometimes she guffaws. One thing about Millicent, she is always really, really amused by just about everything.

Mom says that Alfred, her broker, made all his money by smuggling drugs back in the teens. Endorphins, I think. "Oh, it's probably better to ambush everyone, wouldn't you say?"

I roll up my tiny computer, which is just a piece of nanocrystal as thin as paper. Rolling it up turns it off. I tuck it under my arm. It's time to go to the lab.

As I pass through the living room, I say, "Hi."

"Hi, honey," says Millicent. "Why don't you play something for us?"

For a moment I am struck by how strange the idea seems to me. There is no music in me. Doesn't anyone understand?

My computer slips lightly to the floor as I slide onto the piano bench, wrench open the top, and smash my fingers onto the keys, fierce and hard. *Dunn dun da dun/Dun ta dun ta dun ta dun*, the big minor chords and slow cadence of the death march.

Mom is out of her seat in a flash, her wine aslosh and her eyes very, very angry, like scary angry. "You apologize to Millie immediately, young lady! Do you understand?"

I turn to Millie. She looks like I punched her in the stomach. I know she was just trying to make me feel better. "I'm sorry." And I am. I have to stop saying and doing what I think. I lean down and give her a tight hug around her neck.

"It's okay," she says, and pats my back. "It's okay."

A powerful gray-black cloud is being pushed across the sky by the wind, a dark ribbon winding across the blue sky behind. A cold front is coming and evidently is almost here. Each gust of wind has some cold air in it, like an ice cube in a drink. I wish I was wearing jeans instead of shorts.

Mike Sledge is coming up Caroline Street now. The sidewalks are tilty, no good for skating, crazed with cracks and heaved slabs. He's wearing the usual: a muscle shirt with something about fish on it; teeny shorts. He has a scruffy gray beard, kind of long, and somehow he finds the energy to shave his head, which is as darkly tanned as the rest of his skinny self. He wears no shoes. Raises his hand in greeting. "Hey, little girl. Howzit going?"

I stop for a moment to talk. "Not bad, Mike."

"Hear about Sam?"

"Nothing new. Still missing." No matter what Mom says, I will never say he's dead until they show me a body. And that might be never.

"Ah. He's a good kid. Smart. He'll turn up. Don't you worry now, missy."

Mike does two things: drinks, and fixes houses. He is very much in demand—not because he's dependable, which he isn't, but because he does such an incredible job when he's there. I've decided that he's an obsessive, which is what drove him to drink and fine carpentry. I'm an obsessive myself. I'm so obsessive that sometimes I'm afraid to start something because it will have to be absolutely perfect and will take forever and everybody will get mad at me for falling into some detail that gets bigger and bigger until it's all I can see.

Biology is perfect, though. It's already here. We just have to tweak it, which is easy, because it's always changing anyway. It's called evolution.

"Your mom ready for that new kitchen yet?" His seamed, dried-up face, half-hidden with beard, is the face of a lot of people in Key West. Except for the mothers of my former friends. Unlike Mike, who wouldn't do it anyway, they can afford all kinds of treatments to deal with the results of their perpetual tans. I think the latest is just growing a new face at a spa in Cuba.

"I don't know. She's going to Bali next month."

"Oh, perfect time, perfect time. It'd drive her nuts to have the work done while she's living there."

"I'll be living there. Aunt Cicily will be living there."

"Oh my God, not *you* two!" He rolls his eyes. "It'll never happen." He ambles off down the tilted sidewalk, on his way to the infinite happy hour on Duval Street.

Mike used to be a commercial fisherman, until the IRS took his boat. He used to take Sam and me out, showed us the secret places and the ways to catch certain fish. He might drink a lot, but funny thing, he's always there when you need him, just knows and shows up somehow, and never gets mean like some people do. I mean, I've never seen him staggering across the street at three in the afternoon, and he's always sweet.

Mike's all right.

Cold raindrops flick over me, and I run the last two blocks to the lab.

Mothertime Clinic is in a big old mansion. I like going up the walk to the broad steps. Cushioned garden chairs and chaises sit on brick pads here and there in the garden. I wave to a clearly pregnant man lying on one, covered with a blanket and reading. He's been in the *Key West Citizen*. Famous, like me, ha ha.

Up the big steps, through the glass doors, past the plush waiting rooms where some decorator managed to cover everything from the sofas to the lampshades with images of palm trees. This was the Kingsley Mansion; they made their fortune in the eighteen hundreds by salvaging from wrecked ships.

I climb the wide mahogany staircase and look at a spot next to the door frame. The retina scan opens the door to the smooth, shiny lab.

It's not hard. Cloning. You just take an egg and suck out the nucleus with a pipette, which is a little glass straw, and put in the DNA of choice. In this case, it is DNA from Sam's hair.

When I'm ready, I'll have to get an ovum from somewhere. Of course, the lab is full of them; in fact, Dr. Harris subscribes to a bank and orders them whenever she needs them. I could probably find out all the codes and go online and order some myself. Although that doesn't really seem right. I mean, Dr. Harris trusts me, and she would get in a lot of trouble if anyone found out about that, or if anyone found out about Sam. Which they would. It's hard to hide a baby.

That's one of the problems I have. It's not that it can't be done. It's that everything has to be a secret. I'm not sure if that's a good idea, or even possible. Sometimes it scares me.

But then I think of Sam. The world winks, like it does now. It winks from the cold machines and from the lab glass and from the tall locked cabinets, and Sam is there saying, *It's the right thing, sis*, through all of the colors and the shapes around me.

And so, I have to.

Dr. Harris comes in. "Hi, Eelie. I didn't know if I'd see you today."

"Hi, Dr. Harris."

She has a little frown on her freckled face. Her frizzy blonde hair is not very long, but long enough to pull back in a bun. She is tall and reminds me of a sailboat mast. It holds the sail and has a light at the top. It's the most important part of a sailboat.

"I heard you missed school the other day."

"I was looking for wrasses."

"Look for them on Saturday." She opens a refrigerator door—there are lots of refrigerators in the lab—and pulls out a bottle of spring water, and the lid makes a slight snapping sound as she twists it off. She leans back against the counter and takes a swig. "Look, Eelie, I do have some responsibilities here. I'm supervising you." She looks at me with serious blue eyes between white eyelashes and pale blonde eyebrows and somehow I think that maybe she knows what I'm up to, which is impossible. I haven't told a soul.

I am running through the rain. Running, running, running, down Duval Street, dodging slow, oblivious, probably drunk tourists. I hear my feet pound; they glance at me from beneath parrot-colored umbrellas because my long hair and all of me is soaked and because I must look so glad and they are all pissed because it's a cold front and they've spent big bucks to come down here in winter and bask in hot subtropical sunlight. I feel water stream from my face because my very speed, my ecstatic celebratory speed, pushes it backward almost as if I were taking flight myself, Flying Girl, Sundiver Day, my arms pushed against my side as I leave the ground and fly out over the Everglades. But my feet still touch the sidewalk. Breathless, I round a corner and the center of my chest is a bright, glowing sun, and I run past the World-Famous Oyster Bar and the absurdly expensive Frank's and onto the concrete dock past millionaires' yachts and then pound onto the narrow wooden extension where Sam and I used to meet, him in the Zodiac and me just out of school, and thread through the harbor full of anchored sailboats, pass the Glittering Isle of Incredible Wealth, and speed out into the Everlasting Everglades.

"I did it!" I stop (if I had wheels they would screech) at the end of the dock, wavering, almost pitching forward into the cold water. Again, I shout, "I did it I did it I did it I *did* it!" My breath comes from way down deep, from running. A gust of cold wind sprays wavelet salt over me. "You did it, Sam." I am whispering now, and shivering, and my tears surprise me. "It's *you*. You're going to be born again. In eight months."

And then I really do fly off the end of the dock, up into the drizzle, and circle over the yachts and the Magic Penny Water Taxi making its way across the harbor, and then it takes off too and I know I'm dreaming and wake up.

Moonlight filters through the Bahama shutters on my windows, and a breeze flits through the room. Palm fronds move languidly outside, and their shadows modulate shadow and light into even thinner slivers. The sweet smell of night-blooming jasmine is heavy in the air. Esmeralda moves back and forth on her perch, squawks, ruffles her feathers, dozes off again.

I get up and open the top drawer of my dresser, paw away the underwear, get out the kit.

Now that I have it, I am afraid.

I got it from a sales rep. Phizer-Wellbourne-Merce, whose sample fertility kits the rep carried with her in a large leather case, had probably paid to have her face regrown, and her right eyebrow was a tiny bit lower than her left. She looked very striking, though, with her hard blue eyes, black eyebrows (one crooked), and smooth, smooth, smooth blonde hair. She wore a green tropical suit and lots of gold and the highest heels I'd ever seen. Dr. Harris had gone to a meeting for a week and so the rep pitched to me.

"Just for practice," she said, grinning.

"I'm Dr. Harris's research assistant." In case she thought I was a kid doing cleaning work, despite the crisp lab coat I wore with my name sewn in blue above the pocket.

She looked skeptical. I slouched back against a soapstone lab table and crossed my arms. "We use the Bathfeldt Xygote Kit. It is extremely dependable and our birth rate is the highest in the world, for what we do."

"Oh. Really." She arched her highest eyebrow at me. "Well, this kit is a breakthrough."

"In what way?"

"I'm not sure you'd understand, but these hormones help the zygote implant in the womb at a much higher rate."

By the time she was gone, I had convinced her to leave four sample kits. They were off the record, unlike everything else in the lab, which was all meticulously accounted for down to the last Chinese nano-suture kit, which knits incisions seamlessly, and, probably, the last lowly, old-fashioned aspirin.

I felt a little bit sick, then, alone in the shining lab with my wrasses languidly swimming in their aquarium and Sam-in-the-Hair-Shaft, whom I had the power to make into two cells, then four, then eight. . . .

I stuffed one of the kits into my pack and ran home. Without changing, I jumped into my Zodiac and sped through the canal, ignoring Mr. Albert in bathing suit and fish tank top, brandishing a beer can and yelling, "For God's sake, Eelie! Slow down!" as my wake smacked into neighbors' docks, making their boats buck and test their lines like wild ponies bent on escape. The day seemed way too sunny and bright, the bay too stunningly blue and green, the mangrove islands too filled with white herons.

When I got to my creek, I was soaked from spray. I threw my lab coat into a corner, crumpled up and getting engine grease on it, and wondered why I wanted to stomp on it.

I sat there in the stillness, waiting for the world to wink.

It didn't.

I saw the same mangroves and snappers and the same brilliant sky with clouds teetering on the edge of green-hued crystal that he had seen. But it did not move. It might have been painted there. I sat within a postcard of our past.

Then a pelican plummeted, far off, and the world resumed.

I have to do this, I told myself, I have to.

If I don't do it, I am killing Sam. He'll die.

Completely and for always.

They wouldn't put me in jail—after all, I was way too young to know what I was doing. Wasn't I? Of course, they might put my mother in jail. Or Dr. Harris.

And who was Sam, anyway?

My big brother. Sitting across from me in the bow on this day's twin sister, taking pictures with his eyes that he would later download by pressing his index finger onto his photo touchpad. He could zoom, adjust the f-stop, perform any function of the fanciest digital camera by touching one or another of his fingers to his thumb in a particular cadence. Staring and staring. I hadn't known that he was playing with war toys. I hadn't known that he had already been recruited. Neither had Mom.

But oh, he wanted to go. He wanted the fanciest and most powerful enhancements available. Binocular eyes, night-vision eyes, nanotech cells with memory, everlasting life. "Look, sis!" Pulling his screen from his shirt pocket and snapping it open as we sat on shaded benches in the park. "Look at what humans can be now!"

I peered at the tiny images. "That's in the future, Sam."

He looked at me with serious eyes. "No, Sundiver. This is the present. But the only people who can use them are the people who go to war. It's military stuff. That's the way this happens. It's who pays for this stuff, how it is developed."

I bent over the screen, watching a tiny figure metamorph from human to man-bird, from man-bird to man-fish.

"Where are the girls?" Woman into fishhawk, woman into dolphin and back again to woman, that's what I longed to see. My grown-up self diving into sky and diving into sea and diving back into air. Swimming in all mediums. Collecting information with my new eyes, clacking my beak in cadence, squeaking commands to my onboard organic computers.

He ran through the options. "Good point. They aren't here, are they? Girls can do all this, though. Maybe they give a different one to female recruits."

"I'm going to do it too."

His tight hug squeezed me sideways for an instant, then he let go. "You'll do it for science, Sunny. For fun. Not for war."

"But you're—"

He furled his screen and stuck it in his shirt pocket. "This is from the army. I shouldn't be showing it to you. Right now this is all experimental. It could be dangerous. No one really knows what will happen to people yet. It's like genetic engineering, this bio-nanotech stuff. You know something about that, eh? How will the smallest, most beneficial-seeming change affect us down the line?"

"Machines 'R' us."

"R you R." He poked me with his elbow.

"R we ever what we seem?" I was thinking of all those unexpressed genes, everywhere, waiting.

We had this conversation for two months, and finally he told Mom what he'd done. She just said sadly, "Oh, Sam." She bowed her head. Tears flowed down her face, but it was the oddest kind of crying, because her face didn't move, she was so stunned. My chest squeezed in pain. I had to go out on the porch, with my parrots.

Ed greeted me. "Up against the wall. Up against the wall."

"I think so," I told Ed. "I guess you're right after all."

We were at the harbor. "Once I get back, Sundiver, I'll be able to fly. You'll be underwater with gills, and I'll be in the air, your mirror. We'll *speed*." He told me this on the dock before his transport ship pulled out and got tiny on the horizon and then vanished. He hugged me tight. He was eighteen, old and wise and stupid and young. "Bye, Sundiver."

Bye.

"Mom, have you ever thought of having another baby?"

She whirls in the kitchen in the morning sunlight, which dapples the old, tall glass-door cupboards, the twentieth-century porcelain sink, the Art Deco light fixture that always reminds me of speed, velocity. Coffee sloshes over the edge of her cup, and she makes an odd sound, kind of like laughing but kind of like choking. Then she gets serious.

"Honey, I'm pretty old."

"Not really. I mean, you could have one if you wanted, couldn't you?"

"I guess. Let's sit down for a while."

The kitchen table is an old wooden one, painted white, covered with a vintage tablecloth. Gigantic pink hibiscus wave outside the screen door, their huge faces impassive. I take a slice of coffee cake from the platter and slather it with butter. Mom rests her arms on the table, leaning forward, holding her coffee cup in both hands. Earnest. She bows her head, thinking, then looks at me levelly. "I'm a little worried about you, Eelie."

"I'm okay." I take a bite of coffee cake and drop crumbs everywhere.

"Dr. Harris says that—"

I leap out of my chair like a spring toy, dropping the coffee cake on the floor, shouting, "What is she doing? Spying on me for you?"

"Sit down, sit down. Of course not."

I don't sit down. "It looks like it to me."

"We can't bring Sam back."

"Yes we *can*!" Suddenly I am, like, five years old. I want to fling myself on the floor and scream. "We can!"

"Technically, yes. Of course we can. We can clone him." Her tone of voice is so reasonable. "It's a possibility."

I stare at her.

"I clone orchids all the time. It's easy. But they aren't as complicated as humans. They have no emotions. They have no brain. Not only do we have a brain, we have frontal lobes. We think. We grieve. We feel joy. We have memory."

"*Find* Sam then! Take his memory back! The one the army gave him!" I am screaming, furious, and suddenly my tears are on the outside, hot on my face. "Put it in the new Sam!"

She looks amused, which makes me even angrier. "Does that seem quite fair to you?" She quirks her head sideways. "How about we find it and put it in you?"

"No! I'm not Sam! I'm *Sundiver Day*!"

"You're my fierce Eelie." She gets up and hugs me, tight. "My wonderful, beautiful, brilliant girl. Think about what you just said." She takes her cup of coffee and steps out the back door into the garden, shutting the screen door behind her so gently it only makes a slight *clunk*.

I get out the hormone kit and leave it on my nightstand.

Mom seems to take a few days to notice it, but I'm sure she noticed it the first morning. She picks it up, turns it over, and reads the back of the package. "I hear these are really good." Then she sets it back down and kisses my forehead. "It's your choice, honey. I'll support you whatever you do."

When she leaves, it is as if the sun is huge and golden, infusing the entire room. Alouicious and Esmeralda lock beaks as they perch on the back of a chair, making funny little squawks, and the red and blue and green and yellow of them are astonishingly bright, so bright that it hurts my eyes and the rainbow vision swims in tears. A warm gust of wind blows through the room, and outside my little balcony the tops of palm trees dance their clicking tango, fronds flung this way and that like the long hair of little girls. The plumeria tree is in bloom, and rich perfume flows inside for just a second before it is borne away by the antic bright wind, the loud, tropical jubilation of the day.

The possibility of Sam sits there, and I can use it whenever I want.

It's funny. Just knowing that seems to be the most important thing.

They do find him, a few months later, and his memory. They give us back the unclassified pictures and movies. There are lots and lots of me.

I'm a stranger to myself, seeing me through his eyes. In one movie we're out on the reef, snorkeling. I laugh and argue about something, I can't quite hear my words because it's so loud out there, with the wind and the waves. I look very, very young. I fling back my head and dive sideways into the sun's reflection on the water.

"I love you, Sundiver!" he shouts when I surface out at the reef after swirling to look at a vast ray, its wingspan at least twenty feet long, and flip to swim with it for a few feet. I remember how fast it was, and how I managed to touch its speckled wingtip, unafraid of its legendary stinging tail. "Don't be mad!"

I see myself, and it's odd, my face still covered with the mask, treading water. I spit out my snorkel mouthpiece. "It's so beautiful," I shout back, my voice small in the roar of the wind and the sound of waves slapping the boat.

As I watch these pictures, sometimes in the garden, sometimes at night when I wake up at three, and the only thing I see is the glowing screen in my hands, the world does slowly wink again, and deepens somehow, and Ed stirs on his perch and sometimes flies to my shoulder to watch with me. "Sammy," he croaks. "Sammy."

The world brims with tears, and I feel them all. It's a miracle. I don't know how it happened.

KATHLEEN ANN GOONAN has been a packer for a moving company, a vagabond, a madrigal singer, a painter of watercolors, and is a fiercely omnivorous reader. She has a degree in English and Association Montessori Internationale certification. After teaching for thirteen years, ten of them in her own one-hundred-student school, she began writing. She has published over twenty short stories in venues such as *Omni*, *Asimov's*, *F&SF*, *Interzone*, scifi.com, and a host of others. Her Nanotech Quartet includes *Queen City Jazz*, *Mississippi Blues*, *Crescent City Rhapsody*, and *Light Music*; the latter two were both shortlisted for the Nebula Award. *The Bones of Time*, shortlisted for the Arthur C. Clarke Award, is set in Hawaii. Her most recent novel is *In War Times*. Her novels and short stories have been published in France, Poland, Russia, Great Britain, the Czech Republic, Spain, Italy, and Japan. "Literature, Consciousness, and Science Fiction" recently appeared in the *Iowa Review* online journal. She speaks frequently at various universities about nanotechnology and literature.

Her Web site is www.goonan.com.

AUTHOR'S NOTE

I have lived in the Florida Keys for the past fifteen years. "Sundiver Day" is an outgrowth of a YA novel I have been working on, *The Water Rats*, in which four teenaged girls of various backgrounds, living in the Florida Keys, have access to stunningly beautiful, sometimes treacherous Florida Bay, which they explore at every opportunity in their own small boat. This life on the water exposes them to danger and mysteries and magnifies their own ever-changing relationship to each other, to the world around them, and to the adult world, which they soon must enter. At sixteen, Eelie is utterly devastated by her brother's death; "Sundiver Day" is essentially a story about dealing with the fact of death and newly available choices in a world that is becoming increasingly science fictional.

THE DUST ASSASSIN

Ian McDonald

When I was a small, a steel monkey would come into my room. My *ayah* put me to bed early, because a growing girl needed sleep, big sleep. I hated sleep. The world I heard beyond the carved stone *jali* screens of my verandah was too full of things for sleep. My *ayah* would set the wards, but the steel monkey was one of my own security robots and invisible to them. As I lay on my side in the warmth and perfume of dusk, I would see first its little head, then one hand, then two appear over the lip of my balcony, then all of it. It would crouch there for a whole minute, then slip down into the night shadows filling up my room. As my eyes grew accustomed to the dark, I would see it watching me, turning its head from one side to the other. It was a handsome thing, metal shell burnished as soft as skin (for in time it came close enough for me to slip a hand through my mosquito nets to stroke it) and adorned with the symbol of my family and its make and serial number. It was not very intelligent, less smart than the real monkeys that squabbled and fought on the rooftops, but clever enough to climb and hunt the assassin robots of the Azads along the ledges and turrets and carvings of the Jodhra Palace. And in the morning I would see the steel monkeys lining the ledges and rooftops with their solar cowls raised, and then they did not seem to me like monkeys at all, but cousins of the sculpted gods and demons among which they sheltered, giving salutation to the sun.

You never think your life is special. Your life is just your life, your world is just your world, even lived in a Rajput Palace defended by machine monkeys against an implacable rival family. Even when you are a weapon.

Those four words are my memory of my father: his face filling my sight like the Marwar moon, his lips, full as pomegranates, saying down to me, *You are a weapon, Padmini, our revenge against the Azads.* I never see my mother's face there: I never knew her. She lived in seclusion in the *zenana*, the women's quarters. The only woman I ever saw was my *ayah*, mad Harpal, who every morning drank a steaming glass of her own piss. Otherwise, only men. And Heer, the *khidmutgar*, our steward. Not man, not woman: other. A *nute*. As I said, you always think your life is normal.

Every night, the monkey-robot watched me, turning its head this way, that way. Then one night it slipped away on its little plastic paws and I slid out of my nets in my silk pajamas after it. It jumped up on the balcony, then in two leaps it was up the vine that climbed around my window. Its eyes glittered in the full moon. I seized two handfuls of tough, twisted vine, thick as my thigh, and was up after it. Why did I follow the steel monkey? Maybe because of that moon on its titanium shell. Maybe because that was the moon of the great kite festival, which we always observed by flying a huge kite in the shape of a man with a bird's tail and outstretched wings for arms.

My father kept all the festivals and rituals, the feasts of the gods. It was what made us different from, better than, the Azads. That man with wings for arms, flying up out of the courtyard in front of my apartment with the sun in his face, could see higher and farther than I, the only daughter of the Jodhras, ever could.

By the moonlight in the palace courtyard I climbed the vine, like something from one of *ayah*'s fairy tales of gods and demons. The steel monkey led on, over balconies, along ledges, over carvings of heroes from legends and full-breasted *apsara* women. I never thought how high I was: I was as light and luminous as the man-bird. Now the steel monkey beckoned me, squatting on the parapet with only the stars above it. I dragged myself up onto the roof. Instantly an army of machine monkeys reared up before me like Hanuman's host. Metal gleamed; they bared their antipersonnel weapons—needle throwers tipped with lethal neurotoxins. My family has always favored poison. I raised my hand and they melted away at the taste of my body chemistry, all but my guide. It skipped and bounded before me. I walked barefoot through a moonlit world of domes and turrets, with every step drawn closer to the amber skyglow of the city outside.

Our palace presented a false front of bays and windows and *jharokas* to the rude people in the street: I climbed the steps behind the façade until I stood on the very top, the highest balcony. A gasp went out of me. Great Jaipur lay before me, a hive of streetlights and pulsing neons, the reds and white and blinking yellows of vehicles swarming along the Johan Bazaar, the trees hung with thousands of fairy lights, like stars fallen from the night, the hard fluorescent shine of the open shop fronts, the glowing waver of the *tivi* screens, the floodlight pools all along the walls of the old city: all, all reflected in the black water of the moat my father had built around his palace. A moat, in the middle of a drought.

The noise swirled up from the street: traffic, a hundred musics, a thousand voices. I swayed on my high perch but I was not afraid. Softness brushed against my leg, my steel monkey pressed close, clinging to the warm pink stone with plastic fingers. I searched the web of light for the sharp edges of the Jantar Mantar, the observatory my ancestors had built three hundred years before. I made out the great wedge of the Samrat Yantra, seven stories tall, the sundial accurate to two seconds; the floodlit bowls of the Jai Prakash Yantra, mapping out the heavens on strips of white marble. The hot night wind tugged at my pajamas; I smelled biodiesel, dust, hot fat, spices carried up from the thronged bazaar. The steel monkey fretted against my leg, making a strange keening sound, and I saw out on the edge of the city, a slash of light down the night, curved like a sail filled with darkness. A tower, higher than any of the others of the new industrial city on the western edges of Jaipur. The glass tower of the Azads, our enemies, as different as could be from our old-fashioned, Rajput-style palace—glowing from within with blue light. And I thought, *I am to bring that tower to the ground.*

Then, voices. Shouts. *Hey, you. Up there. Where? There. See that? What is it? Is it a man? I don't know. Hey, you, show yourself.* I leaned forward, peered carefully down. Light blinded me. At the end of the flashlight beams were two palace guards in combat armor, weapons trained on me. *It's all right, it's all right, don't shoot, for god's sake, it's the girl.*

"Memsahib," a soldier called up. "*Memsahib*, stay exactly where you are, don't move a muscle, we're coming to get you."

I was still staring at the glowing scimitar of the Azad tower when the roof door opened and the squad of guards came to bring me down.

Next morning I was taken to my father in his audience *Diwan*. Climate-mod fields held back the heat and the pollution; the open, stone-pillared hall was cool and still. My father sat on his throne of cushions between the two huge silver jars, taller than two of me, that were always filled with water from the holy river Ganga. My father drank a glass at every dawn every morning. He was a very traditional Rajput. I saw the plastic coil of his lighthoek behind his ear. To him his *Diwan* was full of attendants; his virtual aeai staff, beamed through his skull into his visual centers, busy busy busy on the affairs of Jodhra Water.

My brothers had been summoned and sat uncomfortably on the floor, pulling at their unfamiliar, chafing, old-fashioned costumes. This was to be a formal occasion. Heer knelt behind him, hands folded in yts sleeves. I could not read yts eyes behind yts polarized black lenses. I could never read anything about Heer. Not man, not woman—*yt*—yts muscles lay in unfamiliar patterns under yts peach-smooth skin. I always felt that yt did not like me.

The robot lay on its back, deactivated, limbs curled like the dry dead spiders I found in the corners of my room where *ayah* Harpal was too lazy to dust.

"That was a stupid, dangerous thing to do," my father said. "What would have happened if our *jawans* had not found you?"

I set my jaw and flared my nostrils and rocked on my cushions.

"I just wanted to see. That's my right, isn't it? It's what you're educating me for, that world out there, so it's my right to see it."

"When you are older. When you are a . . . woman. The world is not safe, for you, for any of us."

"I saw no danger."

"You don't need to. All danger has to do is see you. The Azad assassins . . ."

"But I'm a weapon. That's what you always tell me, I'm a weapon, so how can thc Azads harm me? How can I be a weapon if I'm not allowed to see what I'm to be used against?"

But the truth was I didn't know what that meant, what I was meant to do to bring that tower of blue glass collapsing down into the pink streets of Jaipur.

"Enough. This unit is defective."

My father made a gesture with his fingers and the steel monkey sprang up, released. It turned its head in its this-way, that-way gesture I knew so well, confused. In the same instant, the walls glittered with light reflecting from moving metal as the machines streamed down the carved stonework and across the pink marble courtyard. The steel monkey gave a strange, robot cry and made to flee, but the reaching plastic paws seized it and pulled it down and turned it on its back and circuit by circuit, chip by chip, wire by wire, took it to pieces. When they had finished, there was no part of my steel monkey left big enough to see. I felt the tightness in my chest, my throat, my head of about-to-cry, but I would not, I would never, not in front of these men. I glanced again at Heer. Yts black lenses gave nothing, as ever. But the way the sun glinted from those insect eyes told me yt was looking at me.

My life changed that day. My father knew that something between us had been taken apart like the artificial life of the steel monkey. But I had seen beyond the walls of my life, so I was allowed out from the palace a little way into the world: with Heer, and guards, in armored German cars to bazaars and malls; by tilt-jet to family relatives in Jaisalmer and Delhi; to festivals and *mela*s and *puja*s in the Govind temple. I was still schooled in the palace by tutors and aeai artificial intelligences, but I was presented with my new friends, all the daughters of high-ranking, high-caste company executives, carefully vetted and groomed. They wore all the latest fashions and makeup and jewelry and shoes and tech. They dressed me and styled me and wove brass and amber beads into my hair; they took me to shops and pool parties—in the heart of a drought—and cool summer houses up in the mountains, but they were never comfortable like friends, never free, never friends at all. They were afraid of me. But there were clothes and trips and Star Asia tunes and celebrity *gupshup*, and so I forgot about the steel monkey that I once pretended was my friend and that was taken to pieces by its brothers.

Others had not forgotten.

They remembered the night after my fourteenth birthday. There had been a *puja* by the Govind priest in the *Diwan*. It was a special age, fourteen, the age I became a woman. I was blessed with fire and ash and light and water and given a *sari*, the dress of a woman. My friends wound it around me and decorated my hands with *mehndi*, intricate patterns in dark henna. They set the red *bindi* of the *kshatriya* caste over my third eye and led me out through the rows of applauding company executives and then to a great party. There were gifts and kisses, the food was laid out the length of the courtyard, and there were press reporters and proper French champagne, which I was allowed to drink because I was now a woman. My father had arranged a music set by MTV star Anila—real, not artificial intelligence—and in my new woman's finery, I jumped up and down and screamed like any of my teenage girlfriends. At the very end of the night, when the staff took the empty silver plates away and Anila's roadies folded up the sound system, my father's *jawans* brought out the great kite of the Jodhras, the winged man-bird the color of fire, and sent him up, shining, into the night above Jaipur, up toward the hazy stars. Then I went to my new room, in the *zenana*, the women's quarter, and old disgusting *ayah* Harpal locked the carved wooden door to my nursery.

It was that that saved me, when the Azads struck.

I woke an instant before Heer burst through the door, but in that split-second was all the confusion of waking in an unfamiliar bed, in a strange room, in an alien house, in a body you do not fully know as your own.

Heer. Here. Not Heer. Dressed in street clothes. Men's clothes. Heer, with a gun in yts hand. The big gun with the two barrels, the one that killed people and the one that killed machines.

"*Memsahib*, get up and come with me. You must come with me."

"Heer . . ."

"Now, *memsahib.*"

Mouth working for words, I reached for clothes, bag, shoes, things. Heer threw me across the room to crash painfully against the Rajput chest.

"How dare—" I started, and as if in slow motion, I saw the gun fly up. A flash like lightning in the room. A metallic squeal, a stench of burning, and the smoking steel shell of a defense robot went spinning across the marble floor like a burning spider. Its tail was raised, its stinger erect. Not knowing if this was some mad reality or if I was still in a dream, I reached my hand toward the dead machine. Heer snatched me away.

"Do you want to die? It may still be operational."

Yt pushed me roughly into the corridor, then turned to fire a final e-m charge into the room. I heard a long, keening wail like a cork being turned in a bottle, which faded into silence. In that silence I heard for the first time the sounds. Gunfire, men shouting, men roaring, engines revving, aircraft overhead, women crying. Women wailing. And everywhere, above and below, the clicking scamper of small plastic feet.

"What's going on?" Suddenly I was chilled and trembling with dread. "What's happened?"

"The House of Jodhra is under attack," Heer said.

I pulled away from yts soft grip.

"Then I have to go, I have to fight, I have to defend us. I am a weapon."

Heer shook yts head in exasperation and with yts gun hand struck me a ringing blow on the side of my side.

"Stupid, stupid! Understand! The Azads, they are killing everything! Your father, your brothers! The Azads are killing everyone. They would have killed you, but they forgot you moved to a new room."

"Dada*ji*? Arvind, Kiran?"

Heer tugged me along, still reeling, still dizzy from the blow but more dazed, more stunned by what the *nute* had told me. My father, my brothers . . .

"Mama*ji*?" My voice was three years old.

"Only the gene-line."

We rounded a corner. Two things happened at the same time. Heer shouted "Down!" and as I dived for the smooth marble, I glimpsed a swarm of monkey-machines bounding toward me, clinging to walls and ceiling. I covered my head and cried out with every shot as Heer fired and fired and fired until the gas-cell canister clanged to the floor.

"They hacked into them and reprogrammed them. Faithless, betraying things. Come *on*." The smooth, manicured hand reached for me, and I remember only shards of noise and light and dark and bodies until I found myself in the backseat of a fast German car, Heer beside me, gun cradled like a baby. I could smell hot electricity from the warm weapon. Doors slammed. Locks sealed. Engine roared.

"Where to?"

"The Hijra Mahal."

As we accelerated through the gate, more monkey-robots dropped from the *naqqar ḳhana*. I heard their steel lives crack and burst beneath our wheels. One clung to the door, clawing at the window frame until the driver veered and scraped it off on a streetlight.

"Heer . . ."

Inside, it was all starting to burst, to disintegrate into the colors and visions and sounds and glances of the night. *My father my head my brothers my head my mother my family my head my head my head.*

"It's all right," the *nute* said, taking my hand in yts. "You're safe. You're with us now."

The house of Jodhra, which had endured for a thousand years, fell, and I came to the house of the *nute*s. It was pink, as all the great buildings of Jaipur were pink, and very discreet. In my life *before*, as I now thought of it, I must have driven past its alleyway a hundred times without ever knowing the secret it concealed: cool marble rooms and corridors behind a façade of orioles and turrets and intricately carved windows, courts and tanks and water gardens open only to the sky and the birds. But then the Hijra Mahal had always been a building apart. In another age it had been the palace of the *hijra*s, the eunuchs. The un-men, shunned yet essential to the ritual life of Rajput Jaipur, living in the very heart of the old city, yet apart.

There were six of them: Sul the *janampatri* seer, astrologer to celebs as far away as the movie boulevards of Mumbai; Dahin the plastic surgeon, who worked on faces on the far side of the planet through remote machines accurate to the width of an atom; Leel the ritual dancer, who performed the ancient *Nautch* traditions and festival dances; Janda the writer, whom half of India knew as Queen Bitch of *gupshup* columnists; Suleyra, whose parties and events were the talk of society from Srinagar to Madurai; and Heer, once *khidmutgar* to the House of Jodhra. My six guardians bundled me from the car wrapped in a heavy *chador* like a Muslim woman and took me to a domed room of a hundred thousand mirror fragments. Their warm, dry hands gently held me on the divan—I was thrashing, raving as the shock hit me—and Dahin the face surgeon deftly pressed an efuser to my arm.

"Hush. Sleep now."

I woke among the stars. For an instant I wondered if I was dead, stabbed in my sleep by the poison needle of an Azad assassin robot that had scaled the hundred windows of the Jodhra Mahal. Then I saw that they were the mirror shards of the roof, shattering the light of a single candle into a hundred thousand pieces. Heer sat cross-legged on a *dhuri* by my low bedside.

"How long . . . ?"

"Two days, child."

"Are they . . . ?"

"Dead. Yes. I cannot lie. Every one."

But even as the House of Jodhra fell, it struck back like a cobra, its back broken by a stick. Homing missiles, concealed for years, clinging like bats under shop eaves and bus shelters, unfolded their wings and lit their engines and sought out the pheromone profiles of Azad vehicles. Armored Lexuses went up in fireballs in the middle of Jaipur's insane traffic as they hooted their ways toward the safety of the airport. No safety even there, a Jodhra missile locked on to the company tilt-jet as it lifted off, hooked into the engine intake with its titanium claws until the aircraft reached an altitude at which no one could survive. The blast cast momentary shadows across the sun-dials of the Jantar Mantar, marking the moment of Jodhra revenge. Burning debris set fires all across the *basti* slums.

"Are they . . . ?"

"Jahangir and the Begum Azad died in the tilt-jet attack, and our missiles took out much of their board, but their countermeasures held off our attack on their headquarters."

"Who survived?"

"Their youngest son, Salim. The line is intact."

I sat up in my low bed, which smelled of sandalwood. The stars were jewels around my head.

"It's up to me then."

"Memsahib . . ."

"Don't you remember what he said, Heer? My father? *You are a weapon; never forget that*. Now I know what I am a weapon for."

"*Memsahib* . . . Padmini." The first time yt had ever spoken my name. "You are still in shock, you don't know what you're saying. Rest. You need rest. We'll talk in the morning." Yt touched yts forefinger to yts full lips, then left. When I could no longer hear soft footfalls on cool marble, I went to the door. Righteousness, rage, and revenge were one song inside me. Locked. I heaved, I beat, I screamed. The Hijra Mahal did not listen. I went to the balcony that hung over the alley. Even if I could have shattered the intricate stone *jali*, it was a ten-meter drop to street level, where the late-night hum of *phatphat* autorickshaws and taxis was giving way to the delivery drays and cycle-vans of the spice merchants. Light slowly filled up the alley and crept across the floor of my bedroom: by its gathering strength I could read the headlines of the morning editions. WATER WARS: DOZENS DEAD IN CLASH OF THE RAJAS. JAIPUR REELS AS JODHRAS ANNIHILATED. POLICE POWERLESS AGAINST BLOODY VENDETTA.

In Rajputana, now as always, water is life, water is power. The police, the judges, the courts: we owned them. Us, and the Azads. In that we were alike. When gods fight, what mortal would presume to judge?

"A ride in triumph, a fall through a window into love, a marriage, and a mourning?" I asked. "That's it?"

Sul the astrologer nodded slowly. I sat on the floor of yts observatory. Incense rose on all sides of me from perforated brass censors. At first glance the room was so simple and bare that even a *sadhu* would have been uncomfortable, but as my eyes grew accustomed to the shadow in which it must be kept to work as a prediction machine, I saw that every centimeter of the bare pink marble was covered in curving lines and Hindi inscriptions, so small and precise they might be the work of tiny gods. The only light came from a star-shaped hole in the domed ceiling: Sul's star chamber was in the topmost turret of the Hijra Mahal, closest to heaven. As yt worked with yts palmer and made the gestures in the air of the *janampatri* calculations, I watched a star of dazzling sunlight crawl along an arc etched in the floor, measuring out the phases of the House of Meena. Sul caught me staring at yt, but I had only been curious to see what another *nute* looked like, close up. I had only ever known Heer. I had not known there could be as many as six nutes in the whole of India, let alone Jaipur. Sul was fat and had unhealthy yellow skin and eyes and shivered a lot as yt pulled yts shawl around yt, though the turret room directly under the sun was stifling hot. I looked for clues to what yt had been before: woman, man. *Woman,* I thought. I had always thought of Heer as a man—an ex-man, though yt never mentioned the subject. I had always known it was taboo. When you Stepped Away, you never looked back.

"No revenge, no justice?"

"If you don't believe me, see for yourself."

Fingers slipped the lighthoek behind my ear and the curving lines on the floor leaped up into mythical creatures studded with stars. Makara the crocodile, Vrishaba the Bull, the twin fishes of Meena: the twelve *rashi*. Kanya the dutiful daughter. Between them the twenty-seven *nakshatars* looped and arced, each of them subdivided into four *padas*; wheels within wheels within wheels, spinning around my head like blades as I sat on Sul's marble floor.

"You know I can't make any sense out of this," I said, defeated by the whirling numbers. Sul leaned forward and gently touched my hand.

"A ride in triumph, a fall through a window into love, a marriage, and a mourning. Window to widow. Trust me."

"Young girls are truly beautiful on the inside." Dahin the dream doctor's voice came from beyond the bank of glaring surgical lights as the bed on which I lay tilted back. "No pollution, no nasty, dirty hormones. Everything clean and fresh and lovely. Most of the women who come here, I never see any deeper than their skin. It is a rare privilege to be allowed to look inside someone."

It was midnight in the chrome and plastic surgery in the basement of the Hijra Mahal, a snatched half hour between the last of the consultations (society ladies swathed in veils and *chador*s to hide their identities) and Dahin hooking into the global web, settling the lighthoek over the visual center in yts brain and pulling on the manipulator gloves connected to surgical robots in theaters half a world away. So gentle, so deft; too agile for any man's hands. Dahin of the dancing hands.

"Have you found it yet?" I asked. My eyes were watering from the lights. Something in them, something beyond them, was looking into my body and displaying it section by section, organ by organ, on Dahin's inner vision. Traditionally, the *hijra*s were the only ones allowed to examine the bodies of the *zenana* women and reported their findings to the doctors outside.

"Found what? Finger lasers? Retractable steel claws? A tabletop nuke wired into your tummy?"

"My father said over and over, I'm a weapon, I'm special . . . I will destroy the house of Azad."

"*Cho chweet*, if there's anything there, this would have shown it to me."

My eyes were watering. I pretended it was the brightness of the light.

"Maybe there's something . . . smaller, something you can't see, like . . . bugs. Like a disease."

I heard Dahin sigh and imagined the waggle of yts head.

"It'll take a day or two but I can run a diagnostic." Tippy-tapping by the side of my head. I turned my head and froze as I saw a spider robot no bigger than my thumb move toward my throat. It was a month since *the night*, but still I was distrustful of robots. I imagined I always would be. I felt a little flicking needle pain in the side of my neck, then the robot moved over my belly. I cringed at the soft spiking of its sharp, precise feet. I said, "Dahin, do you mind me asking, did you do this?"

A short jab of pain in my belly.

"Oh yes, *baba*. All this, and more. Much, much more. I only work on the outside, the externals. To be like me—to become one of us—you have to go deep, right down into the cells."

Now the robot was creeping over my face. I battled the urge to sweep it away and crush it on the floor. I was a weapon, I was special. This machine would show me how.

"Woman, man, that's not a thing easily undone. They take you apart, *baba*. Everything, hanging there in a tank of fluid. Then they put you back together again. Different. Neither. Better."

Why, I wanted to ask, *why do this thing to yourself?* But then I felt a tiny scratch in the corner of my eye as the robot took a scrape from my optic nerve.

"Three days for the test results, *baba*."

Three days, and Dahin brought the results to me as I sat in the Peacock Pavilion overlooking the bazaar. The wind was warm and smelled of ashes of roses as it blew through the *jali* and turned the delicately handwritten sheets. No implants. No special powers or abilities. No abnormal neural structures, no tailored combat viruses. I was a completely normal fourteen-year-old Kshatriya girl.

• • •

I leaped over the swinging stick. While still in the air, I brought my own staff up low, catching the Azad's weapon between his hands. It flew from his grasp, clattered across the wooden floor of the hall. He threw a kick at me, rolled to pick up his pole, but my swinging tip caught him hard against the temple, send him down to the floor like dropped laundry. I vaulted over him, swung my staff high to punch its brass-shod tip into the nerve cluster under the ear. Instant death.

"And finish."

I held the staff millimeters away from my enemy's brain. Then I slipped the lighthoek from behind my ear and the Azad vanished like a *djinn*. Across the practice floor, Leel set down yts staff and unhooked yts hoek. In yts inner vision yts representation of me—enemy, sparring partner pupil—likewise vanished. As ever at these practice sessions, I wondered what shape Leel's avatar took. Yt never said. Perhaps yt saw me.

"All fighting is dance, all dance is fighting." That was Leel's first lesson to me on the day yt agreed to train me in Silambam. For weeks I had watched yt from a high balcony practice the stampings and head movements and delicate hand gestures of the ritual dances. Then one night after yt had dismissed yts last class, something told me, *stay on*, and I saw yt strip down to a simple *dhoti* and take out the bamboo staff from the cupboard and leap and whirl and stamp across the floor in the attacks and defenses of the ancient Keralan martial art.

"Since it seems I was not born a weapon, then I must become a weapon."

Leel had the dark skin of a southerner, and I always felt that yt was very much older than yt appeared. I also felt—again with no evidence—that yt was the oldest inhabitant of the Hijra Mahal, that yt had been there long before any of the others came. I felt that yt might once have been a *hijra* and that the dance moves yt practiced and taught were from the days when no festival or wedding was complete without the outrageous, outcast eunuchs.

"Weapon, so? Cut anyone tries to get close you, then when you've cut everyone, you cut yourself. Better things for you to be than a weapon."

I asked Leel that same question every day until one evening thick with smog and incense from the great Govind festival, yt came to me as I sat in my window reading the *chati* channels on my lighthoek.

"So. The stick fighting."

That first day, as I stood barefoot on the practice floor in my Adidas baggies and stretchy sports top trying to feel the weight and heft of the fighting staff in my hands, I had been surprised when Leel fitted the lighthoek behind my ear. I had assumed I would spar against the guru ytself.

"Vain child. With what I teach you, you can kill. With one blow. Much safer to fight your image, in here." Yt tapped yts forehead. "As you fight mine. Or whatever you make me."

All that season I learned the dance and ritual of Silambam, the leaps and the timings and the sweeps and the stabs. The sharp blows and the cries. I blazed across the practice floor, yelling Kerala battle hymns, my staff a blur of thrusts and parries and killing strokes.

"Heavy child, heavy. Gravity has no hold on you—you must fly. Beauty is everything. See?" And Leel would vault on yts staff and time seemed to freeze around yt, leaving yt suspended there, like breath, in midair. And I began to understand about Leel, about all the *nute*s in this house of *hijra*s. Beauty was everything, a beauty not male, not female; something else. A third beauty.

The hard, dry winter ended and so did my training. I went down in my Adidas gear and Leel was in yts dance costume, bells ringing at yts ankles. The staffs were locked away.

"This is so unfair."

"You can fight with the stick, you can kill with a single blow; how much more do you need to become this weapon you so want to be?"

"But it takes years to become a master."

"You don't need to become a master. And that is why I have finished your training today, because you should have learned enough to understand the perfect uselessness of what you want to do. If you can get close, if you ever learn to fly, perhaps you might kill Salim Azad, but his soldiers will cut you apart. Realize this, Padmini Jodhra. It's over. They've won."

In the morning when the sun cast pools of light in the shapes of birds onto the floor of the little balcony, Janda would drink coffee laced with *paan* and, lazily lifting a finger to twirl away another page in yts inner vision, survey the papers the length and breadth of India, from the Rann of Kutch to the Sundarbans of Bengal.

"Darling, how can you be a bitch if you don't *read*?"

In the afternoon over *tiffin*, Janda would compose yts scandalous gossip columns: who was doing what with whom where and why, how often and how much, and what all good people should think. Yt never did interviews. Reality got in the way of creativity.

"They love it, sweetie. Gives them an excuse to get excited and run to their lawyers. First real emotion some of them have felt in years."

At first I had been scared of tiny, monkeylike Janda, always looking, checking, analyzing from yts heavily kohled eyes, seeking weaknesses for yts acid tongue. Then I saw the power that lay in yts cuttings and clippings and entries, taking a rumor here, a whisper there, a suspicion yonder and putting them together into a picture of the world. I began to see how I could use it as a weapon. Knowledge was power. So, as dry winter gave way to thirsty spring and the headlines in the streets clamored MONSOON SOON? and RAJPUTANA DEHYDRATES, Janda helped me build a picture of Salim Azad and his company. Looking beyond those sensationalist headlines to the business sections, I grew to recognize his face beneath the headlines: AZAD PLUNDERS CORPSE OF RIVALS. SALIM AZAD: REBUILDER OF A DYNASTY. AZAD WATER IN FIVE RIVERS PROJECT. In the society section, I saw him at weddings and parties and premiers. I saw him skiing in Nepal and shopping in New York and at the races in Paris. In the stock market feeds, I watched the value of Azad Water climb as deals were struck, new investments announced, takeovers and buyouts made public. I learned Salim Azad's taste in pop music, restaurants, tailors, designers, *filmi* stars, fast fast cars. I could tell you the names of the people who hand-sewed his shoes, who wrote the novel on his bedside table, who massaged his head and lit cones of incense along his spine, who flew his private tilt-jets and programmed his bodyguard robots.

One smoggy, stifling evening as Janda cleared away the *thalis* of sweetmeats yt gave me while I worked ("Eat, darling, eat and act"), I noticed the lowlight illuminate two ridges of shallow bumps along the inside of yts forearm. I remembered them on Heer all my life and had always known they were as much a part of a *nute* as the absence of any sexual organs, as the delicate bones and the long hands and the bare skull. In the low, late light they startled me because I had never asked, *What are they for?*

"For? Dear girl." Janda clapped yts soft hands together. "For love. For making love. Why else would we bear these nasty, ugly little goose bumps? Each one generates a different chemical response in our brains. We touch, darling. We play each other like instruments. We feel . . . things you cannot. Emotions for which you have no name, for which the only name is to experience them. We step away to somewhere not woman, not man, to the *nute* place."

Yt turned yts arm wrist upward to me so that yts wide sleeve fell away. The two rows of mosquito-bite mounds were clear and sharp in the yellow light. I thought of the harmonium the musicians would play in the old Jodhra Palace, fingers running up and down the buttons, the other hand squeezing the bellows. Play any tune on it. I shuddered. Janda saw the look on my face and snatched yts arm back into yts sleeve. And then, laid out in the newspaper in front of me was an emotion for which I had no name, which I could only know by experiencing it. I thought no one knew more than I about Salim Azad, but here was a double spread of him pushing open the brass-studded gates of the Jodhra Mahal, my old home, where his family annihilated mine, under the screaming headline: AZAD BURIES PAST, BUYS PALACE OF RIVALS. Below that, Salim Azad standing by the pillars of the *Diwan*, shading his eyes against the sun, as his staff ran our burning sun-man-bird kite up above the turrets and battlements into the hot yellow sky.

In the costume and makeup of Radha, divine wife of Krishna, I rode the painted elephant through the pink streets of Jaipur. Before me the band swung and swayed, its clarinets and horns rebounding from the buildings. Around and through the players danced Leel and the male dancer in red, swords flashing and clashing, skirts whirling, bells ringing. Behind me came another twenty elephants, foreheads patterned with the colors of Holi, howdahs streaming pennons and gold umbrellas. Above me robot aircraft trailed vast, gossamer-light banners bearing portraits of the Holy Pair and divine blessings. Youths and children in red wove crimson patterns with smoke-sticks and threw handfuls of colored powder into the crowd. *Holi Hai! Holi Hai!* Reclining beside me on the golden howdah, Suleyra waved yts flute to the crowd. Jaipur was an endless tunnel of sound: people cheering, holiday shouts, the hooting of *phatphat* horns.

"Didn't I tell you you needed to get out of that place, *cho chweet*?"

In the blur of days inside the Hijra Mahal, I had not known that a year had passed without me setting foot outside its walls. Then Suleyra, the fixer, the jester, the party maker, had come skipping into my room, pointed yts flute at me, and said, "Darling, you simply must be my wife," and I had realized that it was Holi, the Elephant Festival. I had always loved Holi, the brightest, maddest of festivals.

"But someone might see me. . . ."

"*Baba*, you'll be blue all over. And anyway, no one can touch the bride of a god on her wedding day."

And so, blue from head to toe, I reclined on gilded cushions beside Suleyra, who had been planning this public festival for six months, equally blue and not remotely recognizable as anything human—man, woman, or *nute*. The city was clogged with people, the streets were stifling hot, the air was so thick with hydrocarbon fumes that the elephants wore smog goggles, and I loved every bit of it. I was set free from the Hijra Mahal.

A wave of Suleyra/Krishna's blue hand activated the chips in the elephant's skull and turned it left through the arched gateway to the Old City, behind the boogieing band and the leaping, sword-wielding dancers. The crowds spilled off the arcades, onto the street, ten, twenty deep. Every balcony was lined; women and children threw handfuls of color down on us. Ahead I could see a platform and a canopy. The band was already marching in place while Leel and yts partner traded mock blows.

"Who is up there?" I asked, suddenly apprehensive.

"A most important dignitary," said Suleyra, taking the praise of the spectators. "A very rich and powerful man."

"Who is he, Suleyra?" I asked. Suddenly, I was cold in the stinking heat of Jaipur. *"Who is he?"*

But the dancers and the band had moved on, and now our elephant took their place in front of the podium. A tap from Suleyra's Krishna-flute: the elephant wheeled to face the dais and bent its front knees in a curtsey. A tall young man in a Rajput costume with a flame-red turban stood up to applaud, face bright with delight.

I knew that man's shoe size and star sign. I knew the tailor who had cut his suit and the servant who wound his turban. I knew everything about him, except that he would be here, reviewing the Holi parade. I tensed myself to leap. One blow; Suleyra's Krishna-flute would suffice as a weapon. But I did nothing, for I saw a thing more incredible. Behind Salim Azad, bending forward, whispering in his ear, eyes black as obsidian behind polarizing lenses, was Heer.

Salim Azad clapped his hands in delight.

"Yes, yes, this is the one! Bring her to me. Bring her to my palace."

So I returned from the Palace of the Hijras to the Palace of the Jodhras, which was now the Palace of the Azads. I came through the brass gates under the high tower from which I had first looked out across Jaipur on the night of the steel monkey, across the great courtyard. The silver jars of holy Ganga water still stood on either side of the *Diwan* where my father had managed his water empire. Beneath the gaze of the gods and the monkeys on the walls, I was dragged out of the car by Azad *jawan*s and carried, screaming and kicking, up the stairs to the *zenana*. "My brother lay there, so-and-so died there, my father died there," I shouted at them as they dragged me along the same corridor down which I had fled a year before. The marble floors were pristine, polished. I could not remember where the blood had been. Women retainers waited for me at the entrance to the *zenana*, for men could not enter the women's palace, but I flew and kicked and punched at them with all the skills Leel had taught me. They fled shrieking, but all that happened was the soldiers held me at gunpoint until house robots arrived. I could kick and punch all I liked and never lay a scratch on their spun-diamond carapaces.

In the evening I was brought to the Hall of Conversations, an old and lovely room where women could talk and gossip with men across the delicate stone *jali* that ran the length of the hall. Salim Azad walked the foot-polished marble. He was dressed as a Rajput, in the traditional costume. I thought he looked like a joke. Behind him was Heer. Salim Azad paced up and down for five minutes, studying me. I pressed myself to the *jali* and tried to stare him down.

Finally he said, "Do you have everything you want? Is there anything you need?"

"Your heart on a *thali*," I shouted. Salim Azad took a step back.

"I'm sorry about the necessity of this. . . . But please understand, you're not my prisoner. Both of us are the last. There has been enough death. The only way I can see to finish this feud is to unite our two houses. But I won't force you—that would be . . . impolite. Meaningless. I have to ask and you have to answer me." He came as close to the stonework as was safe to avoid my Silambam punch. "Padmini Jodhra, will you marry me?"

It was so ridiculous, so stupid and vain and so impossible, that in my shock, I felt the word *yes* in the back of my throat. I swallowed it down, drew back my head, and spat long and full at him. The spit struck a molding and ran down the carved sandstone.

"Understand I have nothing but death for you, murderer."

"Even so, I shall ask every day, until you say yes," Salim Azad said. With a whisk of robes, he turned and walked away. Heer, hands folded in yts sleeves, eyes pebbles of black, followed.

"And you, *hijra*," I yelled, reaching a clawing hand through the stone *jali* to seize, to rip. "You're next, traitor."

That night, I thought about starving myself to death, like the great Gandhi*ji* when he battled the British to make India free, and their Empire had stepped aside for one old, frail, thin, starving man. I forced my fingers down my throat and puked up the small amount of food I had forced myself to eat that evening. Then I realized that starved and dead I was no weapon. The House of Azad would sail undisturbed into the future. It was the one thing that kept me alive, kept me sane in those first days in the *zenana*—my father's words: *You are a weapon*. All I had to discover was what kind.

In the night a small sweeper came and cleaned away my puke.

It was as he said. Every evening as the sun touched the battlements of the Nahargarh Fort on the hill above Jaipur, Salim Azad came to the Hall of the Conversations. He would talk to me about the history of his family, back twenty generations to central Asia, from where they had swept down into the great river plains of Hindustan to build an empire of unparalleled wealth and elegance and beauty. They had not been warriors or rulers. They had been craftsmen and poets, makers of exquisite fine miniatures and jewel-like verses in Urdu, the language of poets. As the great Mughals erected their forts and palaces and fought their bloody civil wars, they had advanced from court painters and poets to court advisors, then to viziers and *khidmutgar*s, not just to the Mughals, but to the Rajputs, the Marathas, and later to the East India Company and the British Raj. He told me tales of illustrious ancestors and stirring deeds; of Aslam, who rode out between the armies of rival father and son emperors and saved the Panjab; of Farhan, who carried love notes between the English resident of Hyderabad and the daughter of the Nizam and almost destroyed three kingdoms; of Shah Hussain, who had struggled with Gandhi against the British for India, who had been approached by Jinnah to support partition and the creation of Pakistan but who had refused, though his family had all but been annihilated in the ethnic holocaust following independence. He told me of Elder Salim, his grandfather, founder of the dynasty, who had come to Jaipur when the monsoon failed the first terrible time in 2008 and set up village water reclamation schemes that over the decades became the great water empire of the Azads. Strong men, testing times, thrilling stories. And every night he said as the sun dipped behind Nahargarh Fort, "Will you marry me?" Every night I turned away from him without a word. But night by night, story by story, ancestor by ancestor, he chipped away at my silence. These were people as real, as vital as my own family. Now their stories had all ended. We were both the last.

I tried to call Janda at the Hijra Mahal, to seek wisdom and comfort from my sister/brothers, to find out if they knew why Heer had turned and betrayed me, but mostly to hear another voice than the sat channels or Salim Azad. My calls bounced. White noise: Salim had my apartments shielded with a jamming field. I flung the useless palmer against the painted wall and ground it under the heel of my jeweled slipper. I saw endless evenings reaching out before me. Salim would keep coming, night after night, until he had his answer. He had all the time in the world. Did he mean to drive me mad to marry him?

Marry him. This time I did not push the thought away. I turned it this way, that, studied it, felt out its implications. Marry him. It was the way out of this marble cage.

In the heat of the midday, a figure in voluminous robes came hurrying down the cool corridor to the *zenana*. Heer. I had summoned yt. Because yt was not a man yt could enter the *zenana*, like the eunuchs of the Rajput days. Yt did not fear the skills Leel had taught me. Yt knew. Yt *namasted*.

"Why have you done this to me?"

"*Memsahib*, I have always been, and remain, a loyal servant of the House of Jodhra."

"You've given me into the hands of my enemies."

"I have saved you from the hands of your enemies, Padmini. It would not just be the end of this stupid, pointless bloody vendetta.

He would make you a partner. Padmini, listen to what I am saying; you would be more than just a wife. Azad Jodhra. A name all India would learn."

"Jodhra Azad."

Heer pursed yts rosebud lips.

"Padmini, Padmini, always, this pride."

And yt left without my dismissal.

That night in the blue of the magic hour Salim Azad came again to the *zenana*, a pattern of shadows beyond the *jali*. I saw him open his lips. I put a finger up to mine.

"Ssh. Don't speak. Now it's time for me to tell you a story, my story, the story of the House of Jodhra."

So I did, for one hundred and one nights, like an old Muslim fairy tale, seated on cushions leaning up against the *jali*, whispering to Salim Azad in his Rajput finery wonderful tales of dashing Kshatriya cavalry charges and thousand-cannon sieges of great fortresses, of handsome princes with bold mustaches and daring escapes with princesses in disguise in baskets over battlements, of princedoms lost over the fall of a chessman and Sandhurst-trained *sowar* officers more British than the British themselves and air-cav raids against Kashmiri insurgents and bold antiterrorist strikes, of great polo matches and spectacular *durbar*s with a hundred elephants and the man-bird-sun kite of the Jodhras sailing up into the sky over Jaipur, for a thousand years our city. For one hundred nights I bound him with spells taught to me by the *nute*s of the Hijras Mahal; then on the one hundred and first night, I said, "One thing you've forgotten."

"What?"

"To ask me to marry you."

He gave a little start, then waggled his head in disbelief and smiled. He had very good teeth.

"So, will you marry me?"

"Yes," I said. "Yes."

The day was set three weeks hence. Sul had judged it the most propitious for a wedding of dynasties. Suleyra had been commissioned to stage the ceremony: Muslim first, then Hindu. Janda had been asked to draw on yts celebrity inside knowledge to invite all India to the union of the houses of Azad and Jodhra. *This is the wedding of the decade,* yt cried in yts *gupshup* columns. *Come or I will bad-mouth you*. Schedules of the great and glorious were rearranged, aeai *soapi* stars prepared avatars to attend, as did those human celebs who were unavoidably out of the subcontinent. From the shuttered *jharoka*s of the *zenana* I watched Salim order his staff and machines around the great court, sending architects here, fabric designers there, pyrotechnicians yonder. Marquees and pavilions went up; seating was laid out, row upon row, carpet laid, patterns drawn in sand to be obliterated by the feet of the processional elephants. Security robots circled among the carrion-eating black kites over the palace; camera drones flitted like bats around the great court, seeking angles. Feeling my eyes on him, Salim would glance up at me, smile, lift his hand in the smallest greeting. I glanced away, suddenly shy, a girl-bride. This was to be a traditional Rajputana wedding. I would emerge from *purdah* only to meet my husband. For those three weeks, the *zenana* was not a marble cage but an egg from which I would hatch. Into what? Power, unimaginable wealth, marriage to a man who had been my enemy. I still did not know if I loved him or not. I still saw the ghost shadows on the marble where his family had destroyed mine. He still came every night to read me Urdu poetry I could not understand. I smiled and laughed, but I still did not know if what I felt was love or just my desperation to be free. I still doubted it on the morning of my wedding.

Women came at dawn to bathe and dress me in wedding yellow and make up my hair and face and anoint me with turmeric paste. They decked me with jewels and necklaces, rings and bangles. They dabbed me with expensive perfume from France and gave me good-luck charms and advice. Then they threw open the brass-studded doors of the *zenana* and, with the palace guard of robots, escorted me along the corridors and down the stairs to the great court. Leel danced and somersaulted before me; no wedding could be lucky without a *hijra*, a *nute*.

All of India had been invited, and all of India had come, in flesh or in avatar. People rose, applauding. Cameras swooped on ducted fans. My *nute*s, my family from the Hijra Mahal, had been given seats at row ends.

"How could I improve on perfection?" said Dahin the face doctor as my bare feet trod rose petals toward the dais.

"The window, the wedding!" said Sul. "And, pray the gods, many, many decades from now, a very old and wise widow."

"The setting is nothing without the jewel," exclaimed Suleyra Party Arranger, throwing pink petals into the air.

I waited with my attendants under the awning as Salim's retainers crossed the courtyard from the men's quarters. Behind them came the groom on his pure white horse, kicking up the rose petals from its hooves. A low, broad *ooh* went up from the guests, then more applause. The *maulvi* welcomed Salim onto the platform. Cameras flocked for angles. I noticed that every parapet and carving was crowded with monkeys—flesh and machine—watching. The *maulvi* asked me most solemnly if I wished to be Salim Azad's bride.

"Yes," I said, as I had said the night when I first accepted his offer. "I do, yes."

He asked Salim the same question, then read from the holy Quran. We exchanged contracts; our assistants witnessed. The *maulvi* brought the silver plate of sweetmeats. Salim took one, lifted my gauze veil, and placed it on my tongue. Then the *maulvi* placed the rings upon our fingers and proclaimed us husband and wife. And so were our two warring houses united, as the guests rose from their seats cheering and festival crackers and fireworks burst over Jaipur and the city returned a roaring wall of vehicle horns. Peace in the streets at last. As we moved toward the long, cool pavilions for the wedding feast, I tried to catch Heer's eye as yt paced behind Salim. Yts hands were folded in the sleeves of yts robes, yts head thrust forward, lips pursed. I thought of a perching vulture.

We sat side by side on golden cushions at the head of the long, low table. Guests great and good took their places, slipping off their Italian shoes, folding their legs, and tucking up their expensive Delhi frocks as waiters brought vast *thali*s of festival food. In their balcony overlooking the *Diwan*, musicians struck up, a Rajput piece older than Jaipur itself. I clapped my hands. I had grown up with this tune. Salim leaned back on his bolster.

"And look."

Where he pointed, men were running up the great sun-bird-man kite of the Jodhras. As I watched, it skipped and dipped on the erratic winds in the court; then a stronger draught took it soaring up into the blue sky. The guests went *oooh* again.

"You have made me the happiest man in the world," Salim said.

I lifted my veil, bent to him, and kissed his lips. Every eye down the long table turned to me. Everyone smiled. Some clapped.

Salim's eyes went wide. Tears suddenly streamed from them. He rubbed them away, and when he put his hands down, his eyelids were two puffy, blistered boils of flesh, swollen shut. He tried to speak but his lips were bloated, cracked, seeping blood and pus. Salim tried to stand, push himself away from me. He could not see, could not speak, could not breathe. His hands fluttered at the collar of his gold-embroidered *sherwani.*

"Salim!" I cried. Leel was already on yts feet, ahead of all the guest doctors and surgeons as they rose around the table. Salim let out a thin, high-pitched wail, the only scream that would form in his swollen throat. Then he went down onto the feast table.

The pavilion was full of screaming guests and doctors shouting into palmers and security staff locking the area down. I stood useless as a butterfly in my makeup and wedding jewels and finery as doctors crowded around Salim. His face was like a cracked melon, a tight bulb of red flesh. I swatted away an intrusive hovercam. It was the best I could do. Then I remember Leel and the other *nute*s taking me out into the courtyard, where a tilt-jet was settling, engines sending the rose petals up in a perfumed blizzard. Paramedics carried Salim out from the pavilion on a gurney. He wore an oxygen rebreather. There were tubes in his arms. Security guards in light-scatter armor pushed the great and the celebrated aside. I struggled with Leel as the medics slid Salim into the tilt-jet, but yt held me with strange, withered strength.

"Let me go, let me go, that's my husband. . . ."

"Padmini, Padmini, there is nothing you can do."

"What do you mean?"

"Padmini, he is dead. Salim, your husband, is dead."

Yt might have said that the moon was a great mouse in the sky.

"Anaphylactic shock. Do you know what that is?"

"Dead?" I said simply, quietly. Then I was flying across the court toward the tilt-jet as it powered up. I wanted to dive under its engines. I wanted to be scattered like the rose petals. Security guards ran to cut me off, but Leel caught me first and brought me down. I felt the nip of an efuser on my arm, and everything went soft as the tranquilizer took me.

After three weeks I called Heer to me. For the first week the security robots had kept me locked back in the *zenana* while the lawyers argued. I spent much of that time out of my head, part grief-stricken, part insane at what had happened. Just one kiss. A widow no sooner than I was wed. Leel tended to me; the lawyers and judges reached their legal conclusions. I was the sole and lawful heir of Azad-Jodhra Water. The second week I came to terms with my inheritance: the biggest water company in Rajputana, the third largest in the whole of India. There were contracts to be signed, managers and executives to meet, deals to be set up. I waved them away, for the third week was my week, the week in which I understood what I had lost. And I understood what I had done, and how, and what I was. Then I was ready to talk to Heer.

We met in the *Diwan*, between the great silver jars that Salim, dedicated to his new tradition, had kept topped up with holy Ganga water. Guard-monkeys kept watch from the rooftops. My monkeys. My *Diwan*. My palace. My company, now. Heer's hands were folded in yts sleeves. Yts eyes were black marble. I wore widow's white—a widow, at age fifteen.

"How long had you planned it?"

"From before you born. From before you were even conceived."

"I was always to marry Salim Azad."

"Yes."

"And kill him."

"You could not do anything but. You were designed that way."

Always remember, my father had said, here among these cool, shady pillars, *you are a weapon*. A weapon deeper, subtler than I had ever imagined, deeper even than Dahin's medical machines could look. A weapon down in the DNA: designed from conception to cause a fatal allergic reaction in any member of the Azad family. An assassin in my every cell, in every pore and hair, in every fleck of dust shed from my deadly skin.

I killed my beloved with a kiss.

I felt a huge, shuddering sigh inside me, a sigh I could never, must never utter.

"I called you a traitor when you said you had always been a loyal servant of the House of Jodhra."

"I was, am, and will remain so, please God." Heer dipped yts hairless head in a shallow bow. Then yt said, "When you become one of us, when you Step Away, you Step Away from so much, from your own family, from the hope of ever having children . . . You are my family, my children. All of you, but most of all you, Padmini. I did what I had to for my family, and now you survive, now you have all that is yours by right. We don't live long, Padmini. Ours lives are too intense, too bright, too brilliant. There's been too much done to us. We burn out early. I had to see my family safe, my daughter triumph."

"Heer . . ."

Yt held up a hand, glanced away; I thought I saw silver in the corners of those black eyes.

"Take your palace, your company; it is all yours."

That evening I slipped away from my staff and guards. I went up the marble stairs to the long corridor where my room had been before I became a woman, and a wife, and a widow, and the owner of a great company. The door opened to my thumbprint; I swung it open into dust-hazy golden sunlight. The bed was still made, mosquito nets neatly knotted up. I crossed to the balcony. I expected the vines and creepers to have grown to a jungle; with a start I realized it was just over a year since I had slept here. I could still pick out the handholds and footholds where I had followed the steel monkey up onto the roof. I had an easier way to that now. A door at the end of the corridor, previously locked to me, now opened onto a staircase. Sentry robots immediately bounced up as I stepped out onto the roof, crests raised, dart-throwers armed. A *mudra* from my hand sent them back into watching mode.

Once again I walked between the domes and turrets to the balcony at the very top of the palace façade. Again, Great Jaipur at my bare feet took my breath away. The pink city kindled and burned in the low evening light. The streets still roared with traffic. I could smell the hot oil and spices of the bazaar. I now knew how to find the domes of the Hijra Mahal among the confusion of streets and apartment buildings. The dials and half domes and buttresses of the Jantar Mantar threw huge shadows over each other, a confusion of clocks. Then I turned toward the glass scimitar of the Azad

Headquarters—my headquarters now, my palace as much as this dead old Rajput pile. I had brought that house crashing down, but not in any way I had imagined. I wanted to apologize to Salim as he had apologized to me, every night when he came to me in the *zenana*, for what his family had done. *They made me into a weapon and I did not even know.*

How easy to step out over the traffic, step away from it all. Let it all end, Azad and Jodhra. Cheat Heer of yts victory. Then I saw my toes with their rings curl over the edge and I knew I could not, must not. I looked up and there, at the edge of vision, along the bottom of the red horizon, was a line of dark. The monsoon, coming at last. My family had made me one kind of weapon, but my other family, the kind, mad, sad, talented family of the *nute*s, had taught me, in their various ways, to be another weapon. The streets were dry, but the rains were coming. I had reservoirs and canals and pumps and pipes in my power. I was Maharani of the Monsoon. Soon the people would need me. I took a deep breath and imagined I could smell the rain. Then I turned and walked back through the waiting robots to my kingdom.

IAN McDONALD was born in 1960 in Manchester and moved to Northern Ireland in 1965. He is the author of ten novels, most notably *Desolation Road*, *Out on Blue Six*, Philip K. Dick Award winner *King of Morning*, *Queen of Day*, *Chaga*, and *Ares Express*. His most acclaimed, novel is British SF Award winner and Hugo and Arthur C. Clarke award nominee *River of Gods*. His short fiction has won the Sturgeon and British Science Fiction awards and been nominated for the Nebula, World Fantasy, and Tiptree awards, and is collected in *Empire Dreams* and *Speaking in Tongues*. His most recent book is the novel *Brasyl*.

His Web journal is at ianmcdonald.livejournal.com.

AUTHOR'S NOTE

The future hits all of us. In the West we're used to feeling we're the cutting edge and the future is going to be just like us. But this is a wired, small planet, and the new technology that catches on in Boston or Birmingham appears simultaneously on the streets of Bangalore and Beijing.

The future is not necessarily American or European. The future may be shaped as much by the CRIB group: China, Russia, India, Brazil—huge countries with huge populations developing at an incredible rate. It's a big, thrilling planet out there, full of life, movement, passion, color. We've taught ourselves over the past few years to be afraid of it. The way to beat fear is understanding, and to understand we need to look outside ourselves.

I've been writing about a big, powerful, future hi-tech India in my book *River of Gods* and the Cyberabad sequence of stories, of which this is one. It's a vast, endlessly fascinating country. But in the end, despite all the seeming strangenesses of Padmini and her world in "The Dust Assassin," we are all people with the same needs and desires. There is no Third World: there is just One World.

THE STAR SURGEON'S APPRENTICE

Alastair Reynolds

Through the bar's windows, Juntura Spaceport was an endless grid of holding berths, launch gantries, and radiator fins, coiling in its own pollution under a smeared pink sky. The air crackled with radiation from unshielded drives. It was no place to visit, let alone stay.

"I need to get out of here," I said.

The shipmaster sneered at my remaining credit. "That won't get you to the Napier Belt, kid, let alone Frolovo."

"It's all I've got."

"Then maybe you should spend a few months working in the port, until you can pay for a ride."

The shipmaster—he was a cyborg, like most of them—turned away with a whine of his servo-driven exoskeleton.

"Wait," I said. "Please . . . just a moment. Maybe this makes a difference."

I pulled a black bundle from inside my jacket, peeling back enough of the cloth to let him see the weapon. The shipmaster—

his name was Master Khorog—reached out one iron gauntlet and hefted the prize. His eye-goggle clicked and whirred into focus.

"Very nasty," he said appreciatively. "I heard someone used one of these against Happy Jack." The eye swiveled sharply onto me. "Maybe you know something about that?"

"Nothing," I said easily. "It's just an heirloom."

The heirloom was a bone gun. Kalarash Empire tech: very old, very difficult to pick up in security scans. Not much of it around anymore, which is why the gun cost me so much. It employed a sonic effect to shatter human bone, turning it into something resembling sugar. Three seconds was all it needed to do its work. By then the victim no longer had anything much resembling a skeletal structure.

You couldn't live long like that, of course. But you didn't die instantly either.

"The trick—so they say—is not to dwell on the skull," Khorog mused. "Leave enough cranial structure for the victim to retain consciousness. And the ability to hear, if you want to taunt them. There are three small bones in the ear. People usually forget those."

"Will you take the gun or not?"

"I could get into trouble just looking at it." He put the gun back onto the cloth. "But it's a nice piece. Warm, too. It might make a difference. There used to be a good market for antique weapons on Jelgava. Maybe there still is."

I brightened. "Then you can give me a berth?"

"I only said it makes a difference, kid. Enough that you can pay off the rest aboard the *Iron Lady*."

I could already feel Happy Jack's button men pushing their way through the port, asking urgent questions. Only a matter of time before they hit this bar and found me.

"If you can get me to the Frolovo Hub, I'll take it."

"Maybe we're not going to Frolovo. Maybe we're going to the Bafq Gap, or the Belterra Sphere."

"Somewhere nearby, then. Another hub. It doesn't matter. I just have to get off Mokmer."

"Show us your mitts." Before I could say yes, Khorog's metal hands were examining my skin-and-bone ones, splaying the fingers with surprising gentleness. "Never done a hard day's work in your life, have you? But you have good fingers. Hand-to-eye coordination okay? No neuromotor complications? Palsy?"

"I'm fine," I said. "And whatever it is you want me to do, I can learn."

"Mister Zeal—our surgeon—needs an assistant. It's manual labor, mostly. Think you can handle it?"

Jack's men, closer now. "Yes," I said. By then I'd have said anything to get off Mokmer.

"There'll be no freezer berth: the *Iron Lady* doesn't run to them. You'll be warm the whole trip. Two and a half years subjective, maybe three, till we make the next orbitfall. And once Zeal's trained you up, he won't want you leaving his service at the first port of call. You'll be looking at four or five years aboard the *Lady*; maybe longer if he can't find another pair of hands. Doesn't sound so sweet now, does it?"

No, I thought, but then neither did the alternative.

"I'm still willing."

"Then be at shuttle dock nine in twenty minutes. That's when we lift for orbit."

We lifted on time.

I didn't see much of the ship from the shuttle: just enough to tell that the *Iron Lady* looked much the same as all the other ramscoops parked in orbit around Mokmer: a brutalist gray cylinder, swelling to the armored mouth of the magnetic field intake at the front, tapering to the drive assembly at the back. Comms gear, radiators, docking mechanisms, and modular cargo containers ringed the ship around its gently in-curving waist. It was bruised and battered from endless near-light transits, with great scorch marks and impact craters marring much of the hull.

The shuttle docked with just Khorog and me aboard. Even before I had been introduced to the rest of the crew—or even the surgeon—the *Iron Lady* was moving.

"Sooner than I expected," I said.

"Complaining?" Khorog asked. "I thought you wanted to get away from Mokmer as soon as possible."

"No," I said. "I'm glad we're under way." I brushed a wall panel as we walked. "It's very smooth. I expected it to feel different."

"That's because we're only on in-system motors at the moment."

"There's a problem with the ramscoop?"

"We don't switch on the scoop until we're well beyond Mokmer—or any planet, for that matter. We're safe in the ship—life quarters are well shielded—but outside, you're looking at the strongest magnetic field this side of the Crab pulsar. Doesn't hurt *wetheads* like you all that much . . . but us, that's different." He knuckled his fist against his plated cranium. "Cyborgs like me . . . cyborgs like everyone else you'll meet aboard this ship, or in any kind of space environment—we feel it. Get within a thousand kilometers of a ship like this . . . it warms up the metal in our bodies. Inductive heating: we fry from the inside. That's why we don't light the scoop: it ain't *neighborly*."

"I'm sorry," I said, realizing that I'd touched the cyborg equivalent of a nerve.

"We'll light in good time." Khorog hammered one of the wall plates. "Then you'll feel the old girl shiver her timbers."

On the way to the surgeon, we passed other members of the *Iron Lady*'s redoubtable crew, none of whom Khorog saw fit to introduce. They were a carnival of grotesques, even by the standards of the cyborgs I'd seen around the spaceport. One man consisted of a grinning, cackling, gap-toothed head plugged into a trundling life-support mechanism that had apparently originated as a cleaning robot: in place of wheels, or legs, he moved on multiple spinning brushes, polishing the deck plates behind him. A woman glanced haughtily at me as she passed: normal enough except that the upper hemisphere of her skull was a glass dome, in which resided a kind of ticking orrery: luminous planetary beads orbiting the bright lamp of a star. As she walked she rubbed a hand over the swell of her belly and I understood—as I was surely *meant* to—that her brain had been relocated there for safekeeping. Another man moved in an exoskeleton similar to the one Khorog wore, but in this case there was very little man left inside the powered frame: just a desiccated wisp, like something that had dried out in the sun. His limbs were like strands of rope, his head a piece of shriveled, stepped-on fruit. "You'll be the new mate, then," he said in a voice that sounded as if he was trying to speak while being strangled.

"If Zeal agrees to it," Khorog said back. "Only then."

"What if Mister Zeal doesn't agree to it?" I asked, when we were safely out of earshot.

"Then we'll find you something else to do," Khorog replied. "Always plenty of jobs on the . . ." And then he halted, as if he'd been meaning to say something else but had caught himself in time.

By then we'd reached the surgeon.

Mister Zeal occupied a windowless chamber near the middle of the ship. He was working on one of his patients when Khorog showed me in. Hulking surgical machines loomed over the operating table, carrying lights, manipulators, and barbed, savage-looking cutting tools.

"This is the new assistant," Khorog said. "Has a good pair of hands on him, so try and make this one last."

Zeal looked up from his work. He was a huge, bald, thick-necked man with a powerful jaw. There was nothing obviously mechanical about him: even the close-up goggle he wore over his left eye was strapped into place, rather than implanted. He wore a stiff leather apron over his bare, muscular chest, and he glistened with sweat and oil.

His voice was a low rumble. "Just a pup, Master Khorog. I asked for a man."

"Beggars can't be choosers, Mister Zeal. This is what was on offer."

Zeal stood up from the table and studied me with a curl on his lips, wiping his right hand against his apron. He pushed his left hand against the rust-dappled side of one of the surgical machines, causing it to move back on a set of caterpillar tracks. He stepped over a body that happened to be lying on the floor, scuffing his boot heel against the chest.

The voice rumbled again. "What's your name, lad?"

"Peter," I said, fighting to keep my nervousness in check. "Peter Vandry."

He pushed the goggle off his eye, up onto his forehead.

"Your hands."

"I'm sorry?"

He roared, "Show me your damned hands, boy!"

I stepped closer to the surgeon and offered him my hands. Zeal examined them with a particular attentiveness, his scrutiny more thorough, more methodical, than Khorog's had been. He looked at my tongue. He peeled back my eyelids and looked deep into my eyes. He sniffed as he worked, the curl never leaving his lips. All the while I tried to ignore the semihuman thing laid out on the operating table, horrified that it was still breathing, still obviously alive. The crewman's torso was completely detached from his hips and legs.

"I need a new mate," Zeal told me. He kicked the body on the floor. "I've been trying to manage ever since with this *lobot*, but today . . ."

"Temper got the better of you, did it?" Khorog asked.

"Never mind my temper," Zeal said warningly.

"Lobots don't grow on trees, Mister Zeal. There isn't an inexhaustible supply."

The surgeon snapped his gaze back onto me. "I'm a pair of hands down. Do you think you can do better?"

My throat was dry, my hands shaking. "Master Khorog seemed to think I could do it." I held out my hand, hoping he didn't notice the tremble. "I'm steady."

"Steadiness is a given. But do you have the stomach for the rest?"

"I've seen worse than that," I said, glancing at the patient. But only today, I thought, only since I left Happy Jack flopping and oozing on the carpet.

Zeal nodded at the other man. "You may leave us now, Master Khorog. Please ask the captain to delay drive start-up until I'm finished with this one, if that isn't too much trouble?"

"I'll do what I can," Khorog said.

Zeal turned smartly back to me. "I'm in the middle of a procedure. As you can tell from the lobot, things took a turn for the worse. You'll assist in the completion of the operation. If things conclude satisfactorily . . . well, we'll see." The curl became a thin, uncharitable smile.

I stepped over the dead lobot. It was common knowledge that space crews made extensive use of lobots for menial labor, but quite another to see the evidence. Many worlds saw nothing wrong in turning criminals into lobotomized slave labor. Instead of the death sentence, they got neurosurgery and a set of implants so that they could be puppeted and given simple tasks.

"What do you want me to do?" I asked.

Zeal lowered his goggle back into place, settling it over his left eye.

"Looking in the rough direction of the patient would be a start, lad."

I forced myself to take in the bloody mess on the table: the two detached body halves, the details of meat and bone and nervous system almost lost amid the eruptive tangle of plastic and metal lines spraying from either half, carrying pink-red arterial blood, chemical green pneumatic fluid. The tracked machines attending to the operation were of ancient, squalid provenance. Nothing in Zeal's operating room looked newer than a thousand years old.

Zeal picked up the end of one segmented chrome tube. "I'm trying to get this thoracic line in. There was a lot of resistance . . . the lobot kept fumbling the job. I'm assuming you can do better."

I took the end of the line. It was slippery between my fingers. "Shouldn't I . . . wash, or something?"

"Just hold the line. Infection's the least of his worries."

"I was thinking of me."

Zeal made a small guttural sound, like someone trying to cough up an obstruction. "The least of yours as well."

I worked as best I could. We got the line in, then moved on to other areas. I just did what Zeal told me, while he watched me with his one human eye, taking in every slip and tremor of my hand. Once in a while he'd dig into the wide leather pocket sewn across the front of his apron and come out with some new blade or tool. Occasionally a lobot would arrive to take away some piece of equipment or dead flesh, or arrive with something new and gleaming on a plate. Now and then the tracked robot would creep forward to assist in a procedure. I noticed, with skin-crawling horror, that its dual manipulator arms ended in a pair of perfect female human hands, long fingered and elegant and white as snow.

"Forceps," he'd say. "Laser scalpel." Or, sometimes, "Soldering iron."

"What happened to this man?" I asked, feeling I ought to be showing interest in more than just the mechanics of the operation.

"Hold that down," Zeal said, ignoring my question completely. "Cut there. Now make a knot and tie off. God's teeth, *careful*."

A little while later, the engine lit up. The transition to thrust weight was sudden and unannounced. The floor shook violently. Equipment clattered off trays. Zeal slipped with a knife, ruining half an hour's work, and swore in one of the ancient trade languages.

"They've lit the drive," he said.

"I thought you asked . . ."

"I did. Now apply pressure *here*."

We kept on working, even as the ship threatened to shake itself to bits. Scoop instability, Zeal said: it was always rough at first, before the fields settled down. My back began to ache from all the leaning over the table. Yet after what felt like many hours, we were done: the two halves reunited, the interconnects joined, the bone and flesh encouraged to fuse across the divide.

The patient was sewn up, rebooted, and restored to consciousness. I rubbed my back as Zeal spoke softly to the man, answering his questions and nodding now and then.

"You'll be all right," I heard him say. "Just keep away from any cargo lifts for a while."

"Thanks," the cyborg said.

The crewman got up off the table, whole again—or as whole as he would ever be. He walked stiffly to the door, pawing at his healed injuries in a kind of stunned wonderment, as if he had never expected to leave the operating table.

"It wasn't as bad as it looked," Zeal told me, when the patient had gone. "Stick with me, and you'll see a lot worse."

"Does that mean you'll let me stay?"

Zeal picked up an oily rag and threw it my way. "What else would it mean? Clean yourself up and I'll show you to your quarters."

It was a job, and it had got me off Mokmer. As gruesome as working for Zeal might have been, I kept reminding myself that it was a lot better than dealing with Happy Jack's button men. And in truth, it could have been a lot worse. Gruff as he had been to start with,

Zeal gradually opened up and started treating me . . . not exactly as an equal, but at least as a promising apprentice. He chided me when I made mistakes but was also careful to let me know when I had done something well—when I'd sewn up a wound nicely or when I'd wired in a neuromotor implant without causing too much surrounding brain damage. He wouldn't say anything, but the curl of his lip would soften and he'd favor my efforts with a microscopic nod of approval.

Zeal, I came to learn, enjoyed an uneasy relationship with the rest of the *Iron Lady*'s crew. It must have always been that way for ship's surgeons. They were there to keep the crew healthy, and much of their work was essentially benign: the treating of minor ailments, the prescribing of restorative drugs and diets. But occasionally they had to do unspeakable things, things that inspired dread and horror. And no one was beyond the surgeon's reach, not even the captain. If a crewman needed treatment, he was going to get it—even if Zeal and his lobots had to drag the man screaming and kicking to the table.

Most of the accidents, though, tended to happen during port time. Now that we were under flight, sucking interstellar gases into the ramscoop field, climbing inexorably closer to the speed of light, Zeal's work tended to minor operations and adjustments. Days went by with nobody to treat at all. During these intervals, Zeal would have me practicing on the lobots, refining my techniques.

Three or four years, Khorog had said. Longer, if Zeal couldn't find a replacement. With only a week under my belt, it seemed like a life sentence aboard the *Iron Lady*. But I would get through it, I promised myself. If conditions became intolerable, I would just jump ship in the next port of call.

In the meantime I got to know as much of my new home as I was allowed. Large areas of the *Iron Lady* were out-of-bounds: the rear section was deemed too radioactive, while the front was closed to low-ranking crew members like myself. I never saw the captain, never learned his name. But that still left a labyrinth of rooms, corridors, and storage bays in which I was allowed to roam during my off-duty hours. Now and then I would pass other crew members, but apart from Khorog, none of them ever gave me the time of day. Zeal told me not to take it to heart: it was just that I was working for *him* and would always be seen as the butcher's boy.

After that, I began to take a quiet pride in the fear and respect Zeal and I enjoyed. The other crew might loathe us, but they needed us as well. Our knives gave us power.

The lobots were different: they neither feared nor admired us but simply did what we wanted with the instant obedience of machines. They didn't have enough residual personality to feel emotions. That was what I'd been told, anyway, but I still found myself wondering. There were nine of them on the *Iron Lady*: five men and four women. Looking into their slack, sleepwalker faces, I couldn't help wondering what kind of people they had been before, what kinds of lives they had led. It was true that they must have all committed capital crimes to have become lobots in the first place. But not every planet defined capital crimes in exactly the same way.

I knew there were nine, and only nine, because they came through Zeal's room on a regular basis, for minor tweaks to their control circuitry. I got to know their faces, got to recognize their slumping, shuffling gait as they walked into a room.

One day, however, I saw a tenth.

Zeal had sent me off on an errand to collect replacement parts for one of his machines. I'd taken a wrong turn, then another one, and before I realized quite how lost I was, I had ended up in an unfamiliar part of the *Iron Lady*. I stayed calm at first, expecting that after ten or twenty minutes of random wandering, I'd find a corridor I recognized.

I didn't.

After thirty minutes became an hour, and every new corridor looked less familiar than the last, I began to panic. There were no markings on the walls, no navigation consoles or color-coordinated arrows. The ship's dark architecture seemed to be rearranging itself as I passed, confounding my attempts at orientation. My panic changed to dread as I considered my plight. I might starve before I found my way back to the part of the ship I knew. The *Iron Lady* was huge, and its living crew tiny. If they had little cause to visit these corridors, it might be years before they found my dead body.

I turned another corner, more in desperation than hope, and faced yet another unrecognized corridor. But there was someone standing at the end of it. The harsh overhead light picked out only her face and shoulders, with the rest of her lost in shadow. I could see from her collar that she wore the same kind of overall as the other lobots. I could also see that she was quite pretty. The lobots were usually shaved to the scalp, to make life easier when their heads had to be opened. This one had a head of hair. It grew out ragged and greasy, tangled like the branches of an old tree, but it was still hair. Beneath it was a pale, almond-shaped face half lost in shadow.

She started back from me, vanishing into deeper shadow and then around a bend at her end of the corridor.

"Wait!" I called. "I'm lost! I need someone to show me the way out of here!"

Lobots never spoke, but they understood spoken instructions. The girl should have obeyed me instantly. Instead she broke into a running shuffle. I heard her shoes scuffing on the deck plating.

I chased after her, catching up with her easily before she reached the end of the next corridor. I seized her by the left arm and forced her to look at me.

"You shouldn't have run. I just need to know how to get out of here. I'm *lost.*"

She looked at me from under the stiff, knotted overhang of her hair. "Who you?" she asked.

"Peter Vandry, surgeon's mate," I said automatically, before frowning. "You talk. You're not *meant* to talk."

She lifted up her right arm, the sleeve of her overall slipping down to reveal a crude mechanical substitute for a hand. This claw-like appendage was grafted onto her forearm, held in place by a tight black collar. I thought for a moment that she meant to shock me, but then I realized that she was only making a human gesture, touching the tip of her mechanical hand against the side of her head.

"I . . . talk. Still . . . something left."

I nodded, understanding belatedly. Some of the lobots were clearly allowed to retain more mental faculties than others. Presumably these were the lobots that needed to engage in more complex tasks, requiring a degree of reciprocal communication.

But why had I never seen this one before?

"What are you doing here?" I asked.

"I . . . tend." She screwed up her face. Even this stripped-down approximation of normal speech was costing her great effort. "*Them*. Keep *them* . . . working."

"What do you mean, them?"

She cocked her head behind us, in the direction of wall plating. "Them."

"The engine systems?" I asked.

"You . . . go now." She nodded back the way I had chased her. "Second . . . left. Third right. Then you . . . know."

I let go of her, conscious that I had been holding her arm too tightly. I saw then that both her hands had been replaced by mechanical substitutes. With a shudder my thoughts raced back to the surgical machine in Zeal's operating room, the one with the feminine hands.

"Thank you," I said softly.

But before I could leave her, she suddenly reached out her left hand and touched the metal to the side of my head, running her fingers against the skin. "Wethead," she said, with something like fascination. "Still."

"Yes," I said, trying not to flinch against the cold touch. "Zeal's talked about putting some implants into me soon, to help with the surgery . . . nothing irreversible, he says . . . but he hasn't done it yet."

Why was I talking to her so openly? Because she was a girl. Because it had been a long time since I'd seen someone who looked even remotely human, let alone someone pretty.

"Don't let," she said urgently. "Don't let. *Bad thing* happen soon. You okay now. You *stay* okay."

"I don't understand."

"You stay wethead. Stay wethead and get off ship. Soon as can. Before *bad thing*."

"How am I supposed to get off the ship? We're in interstellar space!"

"Your problem," she said. "Not mine."

Then she turned away, the sleeves of her overalls falling down to hide her hands.

"Wait," I called after her. "Who are you? What is . . . what *was* your name?"

She paused in her stiff shuffle and looked back at me. "My name . . . gone." Then her eyes flashed wild in the shadows. "Second left. Third right. Go now, Peter Vandry. Go now then *get off ship*."

Zeal and I were midway through another minor procedure when the engagement began. The *Iron Lady* shook like a struck bell. "God's teeth!" Zeal said, flinging aside his soldering iron. "What now?"

I picked up the iron and wiped sandpaper across its tip until it was bright again. "I thought the scoop fields were supposed to have settled down by now."

"That didn't feel like a field tremor to me. Felt more like an attack. Pass me the iron: we'll sew this one up before things get worse."

"An attack?" I asked.

Zeal nodded grimly. "Another ship, probably. They'll be after our cargo."

"Pirates, you mean?"

"Aye, son. Pirates. If that's what they are."

We tidied up the patient as best we could, while the ship continued to shudder. Zeal went to an intercom, bent a stalk to his lips, and spoke to the rest of the crew before returning to me. "It's an attack," he said. "Just as I reckoned. Apparently we've been trying to outrun the other ship for weeks. Quite why no one thought to *tell* me this . . ." He shook his head ruefully, as if he expected no better.

We were a long way in from the hull, but the impacts still sounded like they were happening next door. I shuddered to think of the energies being flung against the *Iron Lady*'s already bruised armor. "How long can we hold?" I asked.

"Come with me," Zeal said, pushing the goggle up onto his forehead. "There's a reinforced observation bubble not far from here. It's not often you'll get to see close action, so you might as well make the most of it."

Something in Zeal's tone surprised me. He'd been annoyed at the interruption to his surgical work, but he still did not sound particularly alarmed at the fact that we were being shot at by another ship.

What did Zeal know that I didn't?

As he led me to the observation bubble, I finally found the nerve to ask the question I had been meaning to put to him ever since I met the girl in the corridor, several weeks ago. Now that he was distracted with the battle, I assumed he wouldn't dwell overlong on my questions.

"Mister Zeal . . . that lobot we were just working on . . ."

He looked back at me. "What about it?"

"It seems funny that we can do so much to their brains . . . put stuff in, take stuff out . . ."

"Go on."

"It seems funny that we never give them *language*. I mean, they can understand us . . . but wouldn't it be easier if they could talk to us as well? At least that way we'd know that they'd understood our instructions."

"Language modules are too expensive. The captain has one, but that's only because a hull spar took out his speech center."

"I'm not talking about cyber modules."

Zeal halted and looked back at me again. Around us, the ship rocked and roared. Emergency alarms sounded from the distance. A mechanical voice intoned warning messages. I heard the shriek of a severed air line.

"What, then?"

"Why do we take out the language center in the first place? I mean, why not just leave it intact?"

"We take the lobots as we get 'em, son. If the speech center's been scooped out . . . it isn't in our power to put it back again."

I steadied myself against a bulkhead, as the floor bucked under us. "Then they're all like that?"

"Unless you know otherwise." Zeal studied me with chilling suspicion. "Wait," he said slowly. "This line of questioning . . . it wouldn't be because you've seen *her*, would it?"

"'Her,' Mister Zeal?"

"You know who I mean. The other lobot. The tenth one. You've met her, haven't you?"

"I . . ." Zeal had the better of me. "I got lost. I bumped into her somewhere near the back of the ship."

The curl of his lip intensified. "And what did she say?"

"Nothing," I said hurriedly. "Nothing. Just . . . how to find my way back. That's all I asked her. That's all she said."

"She's out of control," he said, more to himself than me. "Becoming trouble. Needs something done to her."

I sensed further questions would be unwise, bitterly regretting that I had raised the subject in the first place. At least the battle was still ongoing, with no sign of any lessening in its intensity. Difficult as it was to look on that as any kind of positive development, it might force Zeal's mind onto other matters. If we had a rush of casualties, he might forget that I'd mentioned the girl at all.

Some chance, I thought.

We reached the observation bubble, Zeal silent and brooding at first. He pulled back a lever, opening an iron shutter. Beyond the glass, closer than I'd expected, was the other ship. It couldn't have been more than twenty or thirty kilometers from us.

It was another ramscoop, shaped more or less like the *Iron Lady*. We were so close that the magnetic fields of our scoops must have been meshed together, entangled like the rigging of two sailing ships exchanging cannon fire. Near the front of the other ship, where the scoop pinched to a narrow mouth, I could actually *see* the field picked out in faint purple flickers of excited, inrushing gas. Behind the other ship was the hot spike of its drive flame: the end result of all that interstellar material being sucked up in the first place, compacted and compressed to stellar core pressures in her drive chamber. A similar flame would have been burning from the *Iron Lady*'s stern, keeping us locked alongside.

The other ship was firing on us, discharging massive energy and projectile weapons from hull emplacements.

"They must be pirates," I said, bracing myself as the ship took another hit. "I'd heard they existed but never really believed it until now."

"Start believing it," Zeal grunted.

"Could that ship be the *Devilfish*?"

"And what have you heard about the *Devilfish*?"

"If you take the stories seriously, that's the ship they say does most of the pirating between here and the Frolovo Hub. I suppose if pirates exist, then there's a good chance the *Devilfish* does as well."

The hull shook again, but it was a different kind of vibration than before: more regular, like the steady chiming of a great clock.

"That's us firing back," Zeal said. "About bloody time."

I watched our weapons impact across the hull of the other ship, flowering in a chain. Huge blasts . . . but not enough to stop a wave of retaliatory fire.

"She's switched to heavy slugs," Zeal said. "We'll feel this."

We did. It was worse than anything we had experienced before, as if the entire ship were being shaken violently in a dog's jaw. By now the noise from the klaxons and warning voices had become deafening. Through the window I saw huge scabs of metal slam past.

"Hull plating," Zeal said. "Ours. That'll take some fixing."

"You don't seem all that worried."

"I'm not."

"But we're being shot to pieces here."

"We'll hold," he said. "Long enough."

"Long enough for what?"

I felt a falling sensation in my gut. "That's our drive flame stuttering," Zeal reported, with no sense of alarm. "Captain's turned off our scoop. We'll be on reserve fuel in a moment."

Sure enough, normal weight returned. The two ships were still locked alongside each other.

"Why's he done that?" I asked, fighting to keep the terror from my voice, not wanting to show myself up before Zeal. "We won't be able to burn reserve fuel for very long without the scoop to replenish . . ."

"Scoop's down for a reason, son."

I followed Zeal's gaze back to the other ship. Once again, I saw the hot gases ramming into the engine mouth, flickering purple. But now there was something skewed about the geometry of the field, like a candle flame bending in a draught. The distortion to the field intensified, and then snapped back in the other direction.

"What's happening?"

"Her fieldmaster's trying to compensate," Zeal said. "He's pretty good, give him that."

Now the ramscoop field was oscillating wildly, caught between two distorted extremes. The pinched gas flared hotter—blue white, shifting into the violet.

"What's happening to them? Why doesn't the fieldmaster shut down the field, if he's losing control of it?"

"Too scared to. Most ships can't switch to reserve fuel as smoothly as we can."

"I still don't see . . ."

That was when the field instabilites exceeded some critical limit. Gobbets of hot gas slammed into the swallowing mouth. An eyeblink later, an explosion ripped from the belly of the other ship. Instantly her drive flame and scoop field winked out.

She began to fall behind us.

We cut our engines and matched her velocity. The other ship was a wreck: a huge hole punched amidships, through which I saw glowing innards and pieces of tumbling debris, some of which looked horribly like people.

"She's dead now," I said. "We should leave, get out of here as quickly as we can. What if they repair her?"

Zeal looked at me and shook his head slowly. "You don't get it, do you? They weren't the pirates. They were just trying to get away from us."

"But I thought you said . . ."

"I was having some fun. This was a scheduled interception—always was. It just happened a bit sooner than the captain told me."

"But then if they're not the pirates . . ."

"Correct, lad. We are. And this isn't really the *Iron Lady*. That's only a name she wears in port." He tapped a hand against the metal framing of the bubble. "You're on the *Devilfish*, and that makes you one of us."

A week passed, then another. I learned to stop asking questions, afraid of where my tongue might take me. I kept thinking back to the girl in the corridor and the cryptic warning she had given me. About how I should get off the ship as soon as possible, before Mister Zeal put machines in my head or the *bad thing* happened. Well, a bad thing had certainly happened. The *Iron Lady*, or the *Devilfish* as I now had to think of her, had attacked and crippled another ship. Her holds had been looted for cargo. A handful of her crew had managed to escape in cryopods, but most had died in the explosion when her drive core went critical. I did not know what had happened to the few survivors, but it could not have been coincidence that I suddenly noticed we were carrying three new lobots. I had played no part in converting them, but it would not have taxed Zeal to do the surgery on his own. I knew my way around his operating room by now, knew what was difficult and what was easy.

So we had murdered another ship and taken some of her crew as prize. Every hour that I stayed aboard the *Devilfish* made me complicit in that crime and any other attacks that were yet to take place. But where could I run to?

We were between systems, in deep interstellar space.

Get off ship. Before bad thing happens.

Had she meant the attack, or was she talking about something else, something yet to happen?

I had to find her again. I wanted to ask her more questions, but that wasn't the only reason. I kept seeing her face, frozen in the corridor lights. I knew nothing about her except that I wanted to know more. I wanted to touch that face, to pull back that messy curtain of hair and look into her eyes.

I fantasized about saving her: how I'd do the bare minimum in Zeal's service, just enough to keep him happy, and then jump ship at the first opportunity. Jump and run, and take the lobot girl with me. I'd outrun Happy Jack's button men; I could outrun the crew of the *Devilfish*.

But it wasn't going to be that easy.

"I've got a job for you," Zeal said. "Nice and easy. Then you can have the rest of the day off."

"A job?" I ventured timidly.

"Take this." He delved into his apron pocket and passed something to me: a gripped thing shaped a little like the soldering iron. "It's a tranquilizer gun," he said.

"What do you want me to do?"

"I want you to bring the girl back in."

"The girl?"

"Don't try my patience, Peter." He closed my hand around the grip. "You know where she haunts. Find her, or let her find you. Shouldn't be too hard."

"And when I've found her?"

"Then you shoot her." He raised a warning finger. "Not to kill, just to incapacitate. Aim for a leg. She'll drop, after a minute or so. Then you bring her back to me."

He'd cleared the operating table. I knew from our work schedule that we were not expecting any more patients today.

"What do you want her for?" I asked.

"Always been a bit too chirpy, that one. She has a job to do . . . a certain job that means she has to be brighter than the other lobots. But not *that* much brighter. I don't like it when they answer back, and I definitely don't like it when they start showing notions of free will." He smiled. "But it's all right. Nothing we can't fix, you and I."

"Fix?"

"A few minutes under the knife, is all."

My hand trembled on the gun. "But then she won't be able to talk."

"That's the idea."

"I can't shoot her," I said. "She's still a person. There's still something left of who she was."

"How would you know? All she told you was how to get back home. Or did you talk more than you said?"

"No," I said, cowed. "Only what I told you."

"Good. Then you won't lose any sleep over it, will you?"

With gun in my hand I considered turning it on Mister Zeal and putting him under and then killing him. With the rest of the crew still alive, my chances of stopping the *Devilfish* (let alone making it off the ship in one piece) were practically zero. It would be a futile gesture, nothing more. Without Zeal the crew would be inconvenienced, but most of them would still survive.

I still wanted to stop them, but the gun wasn't the answer. And she *was* just a lobot, after all. She hadn't even remembered her name. What kind of person did that make her?

I slipped the gun into my belt.

"Good lad," Zeal said.

I found her again. It didn't take all that long, considering. I kept a careful note on the twists and turns I took, doubling back every now and then to make sure the ship really wasn't shifting itself around me. That much had always been my imagination, and now that I was revisiting the zone where I had been lost before, it all looked a degree more familiar. Now that I had been given license to enter this part of the ship, I felt more confident. I still wasn't happy about shooting the girl . . . but then it wasn't as if Zeal was going to *kill* her. When so much had already been taken from her, what difference did a little bit more make?

I turned a corner and there she was. She wolfed vile-looking paste into her mouth from some kind of spigot in the wall, the stuff lathering her metal hands.

My hand tightened on the gun, still tucked into my belt. I took a pace closer, hoping she would stay engrossed in her meal.

She stopped eating and looked at me. Through the tangled fringe of her hair, eyes shone feral and bright.

"Peter Vandry," she said, and then did something horrible and unexpected, something no lobot should ever do.

She smiled.

It was only a flicker of a smile, quickly aborted, but I had still seen it. My hand trembled as I withdrew the gun and slipped off the safety catch.

"No," she said, backing away from the spigot.

"I'm sorry," I said, aiming the gun. "It isn't personal. If I don't do it, Zeal'll kill me."

"Don't," she said, raising her hands. "Not shoot. Not shoot me. Not *now. Not now.*"

"I'm sorry," I said again.

My finger tightened on the trigger. Two things made me hesitate, though. The first was: what did she mean: *not now*? What did it matter to her if I shot her now, rather than later? The second thing was those fierce, beautiful eyes.

My hesitation lasted an instant too long.

"Baby," she said.

The gun quivered in my hand, and then leapt free with painful force, nearly snapping my fingers as it escaped my grip. It slammed into the wall, the impact smashing it apart. The metal remains hovered there for an agonizing instant, before dropping—one by one—to the floor.

I looked on, stunned at what had just happened.

"Warn . . . you," she said. "Warn you good, Peter Vandry. Warn you . . . get off ship. Stay wethead. Soon *bad thing* happen and you still here."

I pushed my hand against my chest, trying to numb the pain in my forefinger, where it had been twisted out of the trigger grip.

"The bad thing already happened," I said, angry and confused at the same time. "We took out a ship . . . killed its crew."

"No," she said, shaking her head gravely. "That not what I mean. I mean *real bad thing. Real bad thing* happen *here*. Here and soon. *This ship*."

I looked at the remains of the gun. "What just happened?"

"She save me."

I frowned. "She?"

For a moment the girl seemed torn between infinite opposed possibilities.

"You try shoot me, Peter Vandry. I trust you and you try *shoot* me."

"I'm sorry. I didn't want to . . . it's just that I need to keep on Mister Zeal's good side."

"Zeal bad man. Why you work for Zeal?"

"I didn't have a choice. They tricked me aboard. I didn't know this was a pirate ship. I just needed a ticket off Mokmer."

"What happen on Mokmer?"

"Bad thing," I said, with half a smile.

"Tell."

"A man called Happy Jack did something to my sister. I got even with Happy Jack. Unfortunately, that meant I couldn't stick around."

"Happy Jack bad man?"

"As bad as Zeal."

She looked at me, hard and deep and inquiring, and then said, "I hope you not lie, Peter Vandry."

"I'm not lying."

She showed me her hands, giving me time to admire the crudity of their function, the brutal way they'd been grafted to her arms. "Zeal did this."

"I figured."

"Once I work for Zeal. All go well . . . until one day. Then I make mistake. Zeal get angry. Zeal take hands. Zeal say 'more use on end of machine.'"

"I'm sorry."

"Zeal got temper. One day Zeal get angry with *you*."

"I'll be off the ship before then."

"You hope."

Now it was my turn to sound angry. "What does it matter? There's nowhere for me to go. I have no choice but to work with Zeal."

"No," she said. "You have choice."

"I don't see that I do."

"I show. Then you understand. Then you help."

I looked at her. "I just tried to shoot you. Why would you still trust me?"

She cocked her head, as if my question made only the barest sense to her. "You ask me . . . what my name *is*." She blinked, screwing up her face with the effort of language. "What my name *was*."

"But you didn't know."

"Doesn't matter. No one else . . . ever ask. Except you, Peter Vandry."

She took me deeper into the ship, into the part I had always been told was off-limits because of its intense radiation. Dimly, it began to dawn on me that this was just a lie to dissuade the curious.

"Zeal not happy, you not bring me in," she said.

"I'll make something up. Tell him I couldn't find you, or that you tricked me and destroyed the gun."

"Not work on Zeal."

"I'll think of something," I said glibly. "In the meantime . . . you can just hide out here. When we dock, we can both make a run for it."

She laughed. "I not get off *Devilfish*, Peter Vandry. I die here."

"No," I said. "It doesn't have to happen like that."

"Yes, it does. Nearly time now."

"Back there," I said. "When you did that thing with the gun . . . what did you mean when you said 'baby'?"

"I mean this," she said, and opened a door.

It led into a huge and bright room: part of the engine system. Since my time on the ship, I had learned enough of the ramscoop design to understand that the interstellar gases collected by the magnetic scoop had to pass through the middle of the ship to reach the combustion chamber at the rear . . . which was somewhere near where we were standing.

Overhead was a thick, glowing tube, running the length of the room. That was the fuel conduit. With the drive off, the glass lining the tube would have been midnight black. Only a fraction of the glow from the heated gases shone through . . . but it was still enough to bathe the room in something like daylight.

But that wasn't the only bright thing in the room.

We walked along a railinged catwalk, high above the floor. Below, but slightly off to one side, was a thick metal cage in the form of a horizontal cylinder. The cage flickered with containment fields.

Something huge floated in the cage. It was a creature: sleek and elongated, aglow with its own fierce, brassy light. Something like a whale but carved from molten lava. Quilted in fiery platelets that flexed and undulated as the creature writhed in the field's embrace. Flickering with arcs and filaments of lightning, like a perpetual dance of St. Elmo's fire.

I squinted against the glare from the alien thing.

"What . . . ?" I asked, not needing to say any more.

"Flux Swimmer," she said. "*Devilfish* found her . . . living in outflow jet from star. Didn't evolve there. Migrated. Star to star, billions of years. Older than Galaxy."

I stared, humbled, at the astonishing thing. "I've heard of such things. In the texts of the Kalarash . . . but everyone always assumed they were legendary animals, like unicorns, or dragons, or tigers."

"Real," she said. "Just . . . rare."

The creature writhed again, flexing the long, flattened whip of its body. "But why? Why keep it here?"

"*Devilfish* needs Flux Swimmer," she said. "Flux Swimmer . . . has power. Magnetic fields. Reaches out . . . shapes. *Changes*."

I nodded slowly, beginning to understand. I thought back to the engagement with the other ramscoop; the way its intake field had become fatally distorted.

"The Flux Swimmer is the *Devilfish*'s weapon against other ships," I said, speaking for the girl. "She reaches out and twists their magnetic fields. Zeal always knew we were going to win." I looked down at the creature again, looking so pitiful in its metal cage. I did not have to read the animal's mind to know that it did not want to be held here, locked away in the heart of the *Devilfish*.

"They . . . make her do this," the girl said.

"Torture?"

"No. She could always . . . choose to die. Easier for her."

"How, then?"

She led me along an extension to the catwalk, so that we walked directly over the trapped animal. It was then that I understood how the crew exerted their control on the alien.

Hidden from view before, but visible now, was a smaller version of the same cage. It sat next to the Flux Swimmer. It held another version of the alien animal, but one that was much tinier than the first. Probes reached through the field, contacting the fiery hide of the little animal.

"Baby," the girl said. "Hurt baby. Make mother shape field, or hurt baby even more. *That* how it works."

It was all too much. I closed my eyes, numbed at the implicit horror I had just been shown. The baby was not being hurt now, but that was only because the *Devilfish* did not need the mother's services. But when another ship needed to be destroyed and looted . . . then the pain would begin again, until the mother extended her alien influence beyond the hull and twisted the other ship's magnetic field.

"I see why the captain cut our field now," I said. "It was so she could reach through it."

"Yes. Captain clever."

"Where do you come into it?" I asked.

"I look after them. Tend them. Keep them alive." She nodded upward, to where smaller conduits branched off the main fuel line. "Swimmers drink plasma. Captain lets them have fuel. Just enough . . . keep alive. No more."

"We've got to stop this ever happening again," I said, reopening my eyes. Then a thought occurred to me. "But she *can* stop it, can't she? If the mother has enough influence over magnetic fields to twist the ramscoop of a ship thirty kilometers away . . . surely she can stop the captain and his crew? They're cyborgs, after all. They're practically made of metal."

"No," she said, shaking her head in exasperation—either with the situation, or her own limitations. "Mother . . . too strong. Long range . . . good control. Smash other ship, easy. Short range . . . bad. Too near."

"So what you're saying is . . . she can't exercise enough local control, because she's too strong?"

"Yes," she said, nodding emphatically. "Too strong. Too much danger . . . kill baby."

So the mother was powerless, I thought: she had the ability to destroy another ramscoop, but not to unshackle herself from her own chains without harming her child.

"Wait, though. The thing with the gun . . . *that* took some precision, didn't it?"

"Yes," she said. "But not mother. Baby."

She had said it with something like pride. "The baby can do the same trick?"

"Baby weak . . . for now. But I make baby stronger. Give baby more fuel. They say starve baby . . . keep baby alive, but *just*." She clenched her fist and snarled. "I disobey. Give baby more food. Let baby get stronger. Then one day . . ."

"The baby will be able to do what the mother can't," I said. "Kill them all. That's the bad thing, isn't it? That's what you were warning me about. Telling me to get off the ship before it happened. And to make sure Zeal didn't put implants in my head. So I'd have a chance."

"Someone . . . live," she said. "Someone . . . come back. Find *Devilfish*. Let mother and baby go. Take them home."

"Why not you?"

She touched the side of her head. "I, lobot."

"Oh, no."

"When bad thing happen, I go too. But you live, Peter Vandry. You *wethead*. You come back."

"How soon?" I breathed, not wanting to think about what she had just said.

"Soon. Baby stronger . . . hour by hour. Control . . . improving. See, feel, all around it. *Empathic*. Know what to do. Understand good." Again that flicker of pride. "Baby *clever*."

"Zeal's on to you. That's why he sent me here."

"That why . . . has to happen soon. Before Zeal take away . . . *me*. What left behind after . . . not care about baby."

"And now?"

"I care. I *love*."

"Well, isn't that heartwarming," said a voice behind us.

I turned around, confronted by the sight of Mister Zeal blocking the main catwalk, advancing toward us with a heavy gun in his human hand: not a tranquilizer this time. He shook his head disappointedly. "Here was I, thinking maybe you needed some help . . . and when I arrive I find you having a good old chinwag with the lobot!"

"Zeal make you lobot too," she said. "He train you now . . . just to build up neuromotor patterns."

"Listen to her," Zeal said mockingly. "Step aside now, Peter. Let me finish the job you were so tragically incapable of completing."

I stood my ground. "Is that right, Zeal? Were you going to make me into one of them as well, or were you just planning on taking my hands?"

"Stand aside, lad. And it's *Mister* Zeal to you, by the way."

"No," I said. "I'm not letting you touch her."

"Fine, then."

Zeal aimed the gun and shot me. The round tore through my leg, just below the knee. I yelped and started to fold as my leg buckled under me. By tightening my grip on the railings I managed not to slip off the catwalk.

Zeal advanced toward me, boots clanging on the catwalk. I could barely hold myself up now. Blood was drooling down my leg from the wound. My hands were slippery on the railing, losing their grip.

"I'm trying not to do too much damage," Zeal said, before leveling the gun at me again. "I'd still like to be able to salvage something."

I steeled myself against the shot.

"Baby," the girl called.

Zeal's arm swung violently aside, mashing against the railing. His hand spasmed open to drop the gun. It clattered to the deck of the catwalk, then dropped all the way to the floor of the chamber, where it smashed apart.

Zeal grunted in anguish, using his good hand to massage the fingers of the other.

"Nice trick," he said. "But it'll only make it slower and messier for both of you."

With both hands—he couldn't have been hurt that badly—he delved into the pocket on the front of his apron. He came out with a pair of long, vicious-looking knives, turning them edge-on so that we'd see how sharp they were.

"Baby . . ." I called.

But Zeal kept advancing, sharpening the knives on each other, showing no indication that the baby was having any effect on his weapons. It was only then that I realized that the knives were not necessarily made of metal.

Baby wasn't going to be able to do anything about them.

Zeal's huge boots clanged ponderously closer. The pain in my leg was now excruciating, beginning to dull my alertness. Slumped down on the deck, I could barely reach his waist, let alone the knives.

"Easy now, lad," he said as I tried to block him. "Easy now, and we'll make it nice and quick when it's your turn. How does that sound?"

"It sounds . . ."

I pawed ineffectually at the leather of his apron, slick with blood and oil. I couldn't begin to get a grip on it, even if I'd had the strength to stop him.

"Now lad," he said, sounding more disappointed than angry. "Don't make me slash at your hands. They're too good to waste like that."

"You're not getting any part of me."

He clucked in amusement and knelt down just far enough to stab the tip of one of the knives—the one he held in his right hand—against my chest. "Seriously, now."

The pressure of the knife made me fall back, so that my back was on the deck. That was when I touched the deck with my bare hand and felt how warm it was.

Warm and getting hotter.

Inductive heating, I thought: Baby's magnetic field washing back and forth over the metal, cooking it.

I twisted my neck to glance back at the girl and saw her pain. She held her hands in front of her, like someone expecting a gift. Baby must have been warming her hands as well as the deck.

Baby couldn't help it.

Flat on the deck now, Zeal lowered his heel onto my chest. "Yes, the deck's getting hotter. I can just feel it through the sole of my shoe."

"Don't you touch her."

He increased the pressure on my chest, crushing the wind from my lungs. "Or what, exactly?"

I didn't have the strength to answer. All I could do was push ineffectually against his boot, in the hope of snatching a breath of air.

"I'll deal with you in a moment," Zeal said, preparing to move on.

But then he stopped.

Even from where I was lying, I saw something change on his face. The cocky set of his jaw slipped a notch. His eyes looked up, as if he'd seen something on the ceiling.

He hadn't. He was looking at his goggle, pushed high onto his forehead.

Nothing about the goggle had changed, except for the thin wisp of smoke curling away from it where it contacted his skin.

It was beginning to burn its way into his forehead, pulled tight by the strap.

Zeal let out an almighty bellow of pain and fury: real this time. His hands jerked up reflexively, as if he meant to snatch the goggle away. But both hands were holding knives.

He screamed, as the hot thing seared into his forehead like a brand.

He lowered his hands, and tried to fumble one of the knives into his apron pocket. His movements were desperate, uncoordinated. The knife tore at the leather but couldn't find its way home. Finally, shrieking, he simply dropped the weapon.

It fell to the decking. I reached out and took it.

Zeal reached up with his bare hand and closed his fingers around the goggle. Instantly I heard the sizzle of burning skin. He tried to pull his hand away, but his fingers appeared to have stuck to the goggle. Thrashing now, he reached up with the other knife—still unwilling to relinquish it—and tried to use its edge to lever the offending mass of fused metal and skin from his forehead.

That was when I plunged the other knife into his shin, and twisted. Zeal teetered, fighting for balance. But with one hand stuck to his forehead and the other holding the knife, he had no means to secure himself.

I assisted him over the edge. Zeal screamed as he fell. Then there was a clatter and a sudden, savage stillness.

For what seemed like an age I lay on the catwalk, panting until the pain lost its focus.

"It won't be long before the rest of the crew comes after us," I told the girl.

She was still holding her metal hands before her: I could only imagine her pain.

"Need to make baby strong now," she said. "Feed it more." She moved to a console set into a recess in the railing itself. She touched her claws against the controls, and then gasped, unable to complete whatever action she'd had in mind.

I forced myself to stand, putting most of my weight on my good leg. My arm was in a bad way, but the fingers still worked. If I splinted it, I ought to be able to grip something.

I lurched and hobbled until I was next to her.

"Show me what to do."

"Give Baby more fuel," she said, indicating a set of controls. "Turn that. All the way."

I did what she said. The decking rumbled, as if the ship itself had shuddered. Overhead, I noticed a dimming in the glow of the pipe after the point where the smaller lines branched out of it.

"How long?" I said, pushing my good hand against the slug wound to keep the blood at bay.

"Not long. Ship get slower . . . but not enough for captain to notice. Baby drink. Then . . . *bad thing*."

"Everyone aboard will die?"

"Baby kill them. Fry them alive, same way as Zeal. Except you."

I thought of all that the *Devilfish* had done. If only half of those stories were true, it was still more than enough to justify what was about to happen.

"How long?" I repeated.

"Thirty . . . forty minutes."

"Then it's time enough," I said.

She looked at me wonderingly. "Time enough . . . for what?"

"To get you to the surgeon's room. To get you on the table and get those implants out of your head."

Something like hope crossed her face. It was there, fleetingly. Then it was gone, wiped away. How often had she dared to hope, before learning to crush the emotion before it caused any more pain? I didn't want to know . . . not yet.

"No," she said. "Not time."

"There is time," I said. If I could extract those implants in time, and remove those metal hands, she would weather Baby's magnetic storm when it ripped through the rest of the crew. There was nothing I could do for the other lobots, not in the time that was left. And maybe there was nothing anyone could do for them now.

But the girl was different. I knew there was something more in there . . . something that hadn't been completely erased. Maybe she didn't remember her name now, but with time . . . with patience . . . who knew what was possible?

But first we had to save the aliens. And we would, too. We'd have the *Devilfish* to ourselves. If we couldn't work out how to fly the aliens home, we could at least let them go. They were creatures of space: all that they really craved was release.

Then . . . once the Flux Swimmers were taken care of . . . we'd find a cryopod and save ourselves. So what if it took a while before anyone found us?

"No time," she said again.

"There is," I said. "And we're doing this. You're my patient, and I'm not giving up on you. I'm Peter Vandry, surgeon."

"Surgeon's mate," she corrected.

I looked down at Zeal's spread-eagled, motionless form and shook my head. "Surgeon, actually. Someone just got a promotion."

ALASTAIR REYNOLDS was born in Barry, South Wales, in 1966. He has lived in Cornwall, Scotland, and—since 1991—the Netherlands, where he spent twelve years working as a scientist for the European Space Agency. He became a full-time writer in 2004, and recently married his longtime partner, Josette. Reynolds has been publishing short fiction since his first sale to *Interzone* in 1990. Since 2000 he has published seven novels: the Inhibitor trilogy (*Revelation Space*, *Redemption Space*, and *Absolution Gap*), British Science Fiction Association Award winner *Chasm City*, *Century Rain*, *Pushing Ice*, and *The Prefect*. His short fiction has been collected in *Zima Blue and Other Stories* and *Galactic North*. In his spare time he rides horses.

His Web site is members.tripod.com/~voxish/

AUTHOR'S NOTE

I had the title for "The Star Surgeon's Apprentice" a long time before I had the story itself, but that's often the way it goes. My hard drive is full of empty Word files with titles that I hope will—one day, somewhere down the line—become finished stories. It doesn't matter to me if it takes a year or ten years—just as long as someone else doesn't get there first! But "Star Surgeon" goes back even further than that, at least insofar as I've made several abortive stabs at a story concerning a young man who finds himself aboard a ship crewed by an assortment of less-than-pleasant cyborg grotesques. I think my first stab at it was about twenty years ago, before I'd sold a word. Now I've finished it, though, and I can move on to another of those empty Word files. So keep an eye out for "Monsters of Rock" somewhere around 2016. . . .

AN HONEST DAY'S WORK

Margo Lanagan

Jupi's talkie-walkie crackled beside his plate. Someone jabbered out of it, "You about, chief?"

All four of us stopped chewing. We'd been eating slowly, silently. We all knew that this was nearly the last of our peasepaste and drumbread.

Jupi raised his eyebrows and finished his mouthful. "Harrump." He brushed the flour from the drumbread off his fingers. He picked up the talkie and took it out into the courtyard. Jumi watched him go, eyes glittering, hands joined and pointing to her chin.

"Couldn't have come at a better time," said Dochi. "Eat something other than pease for a change." He rolled his eyes at me.

"Eh. Pease is better than nothing, like some people have," I said, but mildly. You don't pick a fight with the prince of the household.

"Sh!" said Jumi, leaning toward the courtyard door.

"Why don't you go out?" Dochi pushed his face at her. "Listen right up close?" Dochi was sound in body, so could get away with rudeness. With my withered leg I had to be more careful.

"Sh!" she said again, and we listened.

From the squeal of the voice and the way it worried on and on, it was Mavourn on the other end—and from Jupi's barking answers—"Yup . . . I'll be there . . . I'll fetch him on the way . . . Yup." Behind his voice, blue-daubs buzzed in the neighbor's bananas, tearing strings off the leaves for nesting. Farther away were the cries of sea-birds, and of that family down the lane that always fought, that no one spoke the names of.

Then Jupi was in the doorway, the talkie clapped closed in his hand, his arms spread as if to receive, as only his due, this gift from heaven.

Jumi smiled frightenedly. "Incoming?" she said.

Jupi tipped his head.

"A big one?"

"Mavourn says one leg and one arm, but sizable. Good big head, good sex. Not junk, he says."

Jumi clapped her hands, sparkling. Then she went modest, pulled the cloth farther forward around her face, and ushered our emptied plates toward herself. The anxiety that had been tightening her like slow-wrung laundry these past weeks was gone.

And for us, too, all of a sudden the evening's heat and approaching darkness weren't oppressive anymore. We didn't need to flee from worried thoughts into sleep.

"So I can be useful too?" I said. "If it's sizable?"

Dochi snorted, but Jupi blessed me with a nod. "Amarlis can have work too, as I arranged with A. M. Agency Limited. Just as I arranged it, it comes to be, does it not?"

Jumi pushed the pease bowl and the bread platter toward him. "Eat," she said. "You will need your strength for working."

• • •

So we went to the office of A. M. Agency Limited and saw their hiring officer, and I was taken on as a team-onlooker, and put my mark on the dotted line.

"Well, there is no problem with the boy's hand, at least," said the hirer's assistant. He thought it was a kind of joke.

Jupi could have said, "Oh no, he makes a good mark." Or, "That's right, every other part of him is fine and sound." Or, "There are many activities for which two good legs are not needed." Instead he went icy quiet beside me.

I didn't mind what the man said. I was too happy to mind. I had a contract and I was going to do a useful job like any man—why would I care what anyone said? It was a nuisance, only, because Jupi minded so much that I had to mind on *his* behalf, and because, when we had finished our business, I had to swing along so fast and chatter so hard to make Jupi give up his minding with a laugh and hurry after me, and answer my questions.

Next morning before dawn, we took my job-ticket to the Comm-store, and in the middle of the wonderful bustle there I was issued my onlooker's whistle and megaphone. Jumi had plaited me a neck-cord for the megaphone, which would hold it close on my back while I walked so I could manage the crutches, and loose at my hip when I stood at my work and might need to reach for it fast.

Then we went down to number 17 plan to await the incoming.

The boss-men and the gangers grouped themselves, tense and sober, around my Jupi and his crackling talkie. My brother, Dochi, and his friends formed another group, as they did outside the Lips Club most nights, only without the showy bursts of laughter. They were tired; they were missing their sleep-in.

I was in the main crowd of workers. As soon as the general shape and proportions of the incoming were clear, we'd be teamed up. There was not much talk, just watching the bay and shivering in the breeze. Many of us wore the new Commstore shirts, bought on credit when the news came yesterday. The dull pink and mauve stripes were invisible in the dusky light, but the hot green-blue stripes glowed, slashing down a man's left chest, maybe, with another spot on his right collar. To my eyes, as I read the plan over and over, trying to make it real, trying to believe my luck, the crowd was sticks and spots floating in darkness, with a movement to it like long grass in a slow wind.

Every now and then another team-onlooker would come clearer against the others, his whistle a gleam, his megaphone swinging in his hand. These men I examined keenly; I was one of them now. I thought they all looked very professional. Their heads must be full of all manner of lore and experience, I was sure, and my own memory seemed very empty by comparison. Home life at my Jumi's side was all I knew; I felt as if I ought to be ashamed of it, even as a pang of missing-Jumi made me move uncomfortably on the plan's damp concrete.

Won't this house be quiet without my little monkey! she had said this morning.

Which had made me feel peculiar—guilty because I'd not even thought about how Jumi might feel, that I was going to work; flustered and a little angry, it must be confessed, because it seemed that I could do no right. I could be a sort of stay-at-home, embarrassing half-person by her side, or I could be a cruel son leaving her lonely.

While I was feeling all this, Dochi gave one of his awful laughs. *Yes, he's such a screecher of a monkey,* he said. *So loud as he swings from tree to tree!*

Jumi gave him her mildest reproving look. She broke the soft-boiled egg and laid it on top of my soup in the bowl and pushed it toward me, under Dochi's laughing at his own joke, which she was not stopping.

Thank you, Jumi, I said.

The joke was that I was so quiet and so little trouble, anyone could ignore me if they chose. The joke was that, after some years of trying, of lashing out at Dochi with my crutches and being beaten for it, I would rather sit as I did now at my food, wearing a blank look, and let the laughter pass by.

The incoming appeared on the horizon like a small, weak sunrise. The workers stirred and gestured, and another layer bobbed above the shirt-stripes, of smiling teeth, of wide, bright eyes. My Jupi barked into the talkie, and the two tugboats crawled out from the headland's shadow. They sent back on the breeze a whiff of diesel, and many noses drew it in with delight—a breakyard is *supposed* to be all smells and activity. How long had it been since Portellian smelled right and busy? Long enough for all our savings to be spent. Long enough for us to be half a sack of pease, a quarter of a sack of drumflour away from starting starving.

At first, all we could see was the backlit bulk of the thing, with a few bright rags of aura streaming in the wind, thinning as it came closer. The light from the sun, which as yet was below the horizon, made the thick shroud glow, and the body shape was a dark blur within it. I thought I could see a head against a bigger torso. But you can't be sure with these things; they're never the same twice in their build and features, in their arrangement of limbs.

What kind of people could afford to send craft up into the ether to find and kill such beasts? They must be so rich! A boy born bung-legged to those people would be no shame or disadvantage, I was sure—they would get him a new leg and sew that on. Or they would get him a little car to drive himself around on their smooth roads. There would be so many jobs for him, his leg wouldn't matter; he might do finecrafts with his hands or grow a famous brain or work with computers. Nobody would be anxious for him or disappointed; he wouldn't have to forever apologize for himself and make up to his family for having come out wrong.

"It's a long-hair, I think," said someone near me. "I think I can see hair around that head—if it *is* the head."

"Hair? That's good."

"Oh, every part of it is good."

"It's low in the water," said another. "Good and fresh. Quality cuttings. Everything cheaper to process. Bosses will be happy."

"Everyone will be happy!"

People laughed. Now we could see that the thing was more than rumor and hope.

"I will be happy when I hold that new reel of net-yarn in my hands."

"I will be happy when I'm seated in the club with the biggest plate of charfish and onion in front of me—"

"And Cacohao, he'll be happy when he's lying in the dirt *behind* the club—won't you, Caco?—singing love songs to a bottle of best throb-head."

"Oh. I can see her beautiful face now!"

People were spending their day-wage all around me. But when the incoming reached the tugs and they attached their ropes and lined it up for the tide to bring it onto number 17, all fell quiet. The beast's head loomed, a soft dark shape inside the radiant shroud, which had protected the skin from damage during the burning of the aura. The shape beyond the head was long, narrow, uneven, with a lump at the foot. Jupi jabbered nervously on the talkie to the tugs, checked the time on the clock tower, and his gang around him grew now murmurous with advice, now silent with attention. Things could go wrong at this point; the moment must be judged exactly.

A breeze came ahead of the beast. Our shirts rattled on us; the hems of pants and loongies stung our calves. The air stank of the burnt plastics of the aura, a terrible smell that all the children of Portellian learned early to love, because it meant full bellies, smiling jupis and jumis. Coming in from the ether burnt the aura to almost nothing, to the pale dust we'd seen on the wind—all gone now—to this nasty smell. The sun crept up and took a chink out of the horizon. A lot of the men had gone forward into the mauve and silver wavelets that crawled up the plan.

The tugs, now unhooked from the beast, rode beside it, their engines laboring against the tide. Jupi stood with his arms folded, chewing his lip with the responsibility. The tugs retreated to the beast's far end, and with Jupi warning and checking them through the talkie, helped the tide move the great shape the last little way to the plan. The head began to rise independently of the body, nudged upward by the plan's slope. A cheer went up; the beast had arrived.

Teams were forming. Horse-piecers gathered with their spades at the head of the plan near the winches. Mincers, some with their own knives, drifted toward the try-house where the copper pots and boilers glowed in the shadows. Gangers came through the crowd shouting, claiming the workers they knew were good. As a team-onlooker, I didn't have to jump and wave my arms and call out gangers' names. I was a contractor, not a loose day-job man dependent on luck and favor. I could stand calm in the middle of the scramble.

As the incoming edged up the plan, the cutting-teams threw grapplers and swung themselves up the cloudy gel. Though they mustn't drop any gel while the beast was moving, they could make all their preparatory slits. This they did with ropes and weights, pulling the ropes through the gel just the way a merchant cuts wax-cheese with a wire. The shroud began to look fringed about the head and shoulders. The nimble rope-clippers darted in and out; chanters' voices rang on the stinking air from high on the beast's torso.

The message came through on the talkie: the tugs were done. The beast was beached, all head to foot of it. Jupi walked up the plan and signaled the bell-man. The bell clanged, the teams cheered, the ground teams scuttled away from the body. Great strips of the gel began tumbling from above. They splashed in the shallows and bounced and jounced and sometimes leaped into curls across the other strips. Hookmen straightened them flat on the ground, making a wide platform on which the beast's parts could be deposited.

Another smell took over from the burnt-shroud odor. I had smelt it before as I helped Jumi, as I cleaned and cooked and span. She would lift her head, happy because the work—Jupi's and Dochi's work—was going on, and if one of the other mothers was there, she would say, *Smell that? It always reminds me of the smell of Dochi when he was born. Like inside-of-body, but clean, clean. New.*

Smell of clean, warm womb, the other might say.

Yes, and hot, too! Hot from me and hot from him.

When I was born to her, I must have smelled not so good, not so enchanting, for it was always Dochi she mentioned. Maybe it was only the firstborn who brought out the clean smell with him. I did not want the details of in what way I had smelt bad—or perhaps, how she had not noticed my smell from being in such horror at my leg. So I never asked.

Anyway, there would be other smells soon against this one: oil and fuel, sweat and scorched rope, hot metal, sawn bone, sea and mud and stirred-up putrefaction.

"Amarlis?"

The way I sprang to face Mavourn showed that I'd been waiting not moments but *years* to hear my name, to be called to usefulness.

"I'm putting you on a thigh-team," he said. "It's got a good man, Mister Chopes, heading it. Are you happy with that?"

"Very happy, sir!"

"There is Mister Chopes with the kerchief on his head. I've told him you're on your way."

"And I am!"

I swung myself across the watery plan, watching Mister Chopes count heads, scan the hopping hopefuls, pick out a good clean man and give him a job-ticket, shoo away a sneaky-looking boy. The team's chanter stood with his drum and beaters, wrapped in his white cloth and his dignity. He too was a contractor; he had no need to fuss.

Mister Chopes counted again, then sent them off for their hooks and spades, and turned and saw me. "You Amarlis?"

"I am, sir, Mister Chopes!"

"You ready to look sharp?"

"Sharp as a shark-tooth, sir!"

"Mavourn says you'll be good, but you're new, right?"

"That's right, sir. This is my first day ever."

"I'll give you plenty of advice, then. You won't sulk at that, boy? You'll take that in good spirit?"

"I'll be grateful for all you can give me."

"Then we'll do fine. Main thing, no one gets hurt. All those boys have mothers. All those men have wives and children waiting on them, right? Your job's to make sure they come home on their own legs, right? Not flat and busted by beast-bits. This here is Trawbrij; he's our chanter."

"How do you do, Trawbrij?" I shook hands with him.

"Twenty years on the plans," said Mister Chopes. "He'll tell you anything more you need to know. Now, let's get down the thigh." Because all the team was tooled-up and running back to us.

Some of the hopefuls, lingering nearby in case Mister Chopes changed his mind, cast jealous looks at me. They were angry, no doubt, that someone so clearly handicapped could gain a job when they, able-bodied, could not. I swung away from them.

Trawbrij the chanter gave us a beat; I walked with him, behind the twenty-five chosen workers, while Mister Chopes went ahead. The knee-team preceded us, with their chanter and their onlooker; I tried to hold my head as high and my back as straight as their onlooker's, to look as casual and unself-conscious as he.

We took a safe path wide of the torso, well behind the row of waiting hookmen. Slabs of shroud slapped down and jiggled on the plan, sending wavelets over the hookmen's feet.

I had watched other incomings, up with the women and children on the hill behind town. What you don't see from there are the surfaces of things: the coarse head-hair, which is like a great tangle of endless curving double-edged combs—with fish in there, too, and seaweed; the damp, waxy skin, pale as the moon, hazed with its own form of hair, dewy with packaging fluid; the eye, the ear-hole, and the mouth-slit, all sealed with gray gum by the hunters. What you don't see from the hills is the *size*, is the *wall* of the cheek going up, behind the heaps of the hair, which themselves tower three houses high above the running workers. My eyes couldn't believe what was in front of them.

"He's enormous, isn't he?" said Trawbrij beside me.

"He makes us look like ants," I said. "Smaller than ants, even. Just look how much of the sky he takes up!"

"And yet we smaller-than-ants, we little crawling germs, we're going to set upon him, and pull him apart and bring him down and saw him into plates, and melt him into pots and pints, and there'll be nothing left of him in three weeks' time."

"Is there any part of him that's not useful to someone?" I turned to look properly at the chanter. He was slender and white haired and wise looking.

"I have only ever seen tumor rocks left lying on the plan, though even these reduce in time, and become parts of people's walls and houses, though they do not export. And sometimes if an organ bursts, or if the tides delay the incoming and the beast is putrefying on arrival, there may be lumps of dirty gel that won't melt, that sit about for a while."

As we came level with the thigh, the first of our team threw up his grappler and shinnied up the rope, chopping footholds as he went. Others followed, each just far enough behind the previous man not to be kicked in the head. In this way we quickly had half a team at the top.

Mister Chopes turned with his foot in the first slot. "Where's my looker? Amarlis."

"Here," I said.

"What do you reckon your job is?"

"Keep an eye out down here."

"'S right. Main thing is, teams getting in each other's ways. So, stand well back, watch how stuff falls, and give a hoy before someone gets hurt."

"I'm on it."

I swung around, passed Trawbrij tucking up his robes for the climb, and went back as far as the other onlookers. There I could see right to the edges of my team's activities, and keep track of Mister Chopes and the team up on top. I blew my whistle straightaway, and the whole ground-team turned as if I had them on strings.

I cleared my throat. "Back up," I said clearly through the megaphone, and waved them toward me. "Back to where these other teams are standing." And up they came to safety, which seemed a wonder to me, a great respectful gesture. I tried not to smile, not to look surprised.

The shroud on the side of the thigh, because it was so flat, could be cut away in a single piece. When it came down—with a smack and two bounces that I felt up my spine and in my armpits through the crutches—there above it was the white-clay wall of the thigh, height of a tanker ship, running with pack-fluid. That clean, warm, newborn-Dochi smell was all there was to breathe now. The fluid ran off, and the skin-hairs lifted from the skin, then separated from each other, gleaming in the early sun. And as I watched, the side-lit skin covered itself with little bluish triangles, bluish scallops of shadow, as if the hairs were not just drying and springing free but pulling bumps up on the skin, in the sudden chill of the sea-breeze.

But then, without warning, the whole leg sprang free of the plan. Daylight shone underneath it, and water-splash, and I saw the tiny black feet of the far thigh-team fleeing—and in my fright I forgot about the gooseflesh on the thigh.

The limb smacked back down and did not move again.

One man on my team had been shaken loose. He hung swinging and screaming from the cutting-rope. Several farther down the limb had fallen right off the top. Some had hit the gel; two had bounced from it onto the plan. Out of all the sounds that happened in those few moments, I managed to hear the ones their heads made breaking on the ground two teams away. It sounded unremarkable, like wooden mallets striking the concrete, but of course they were not tools but people who struck, not wood but brother or father or son, as Mister Chopes had said. My heart rushed out—but less to the fallen ones than to their onlooker. He could have done nothing, poor man, it had happened so quickly. How anguished he must be! What a failure I would feel, if that were me! And then relief swept through me, a professional relief, that it had *not* been me, here on my first day.

All our team, except for those helping the hanging worker, were clawing gel, or each other, or watery ground, trying to hold the world steady. "How can such a thing happen?" I said to the man nearest me.

"It's a nerve thing," he said. "I've heard of it. It's electricity. It's metal on a nerve. It'll be that team on the knee. See how they've just shot their cap-lever in there? You can do the same thing to a dead frog. Poke it in the nerve and the leg jumps, though the heart is still and the head is cut right off."

"Don't the bosses know about that nerve?" I said. "Shouldn't they have the knee team do their work first, rather than endanger so many workers?"

The man shrugged. "When no two beasts are quite the same, how is anyone to learn all the nerves?"

A boss and some stretcher-men had run past us toward the

shin, followed by day-jobbers eager to offer themselves as replacements for the dead and the injured. Mister Chopes got his top-team up and moving again. The hip-men were back at work; the knee-people cleavered open flesh so that the knee-cap could be brought free; the wall of the thigh was smooth, sunlit. The hairs had a slight red-gold tint; perhaps that was why the flesh looked so rosy in the strengthening sun.

Once all the shroud was off the thigh, our job was a plain job, a meat job. The top-team cut blanket pieces of thigh flesh and lowered them to the ground-team. Hooked ropes were brought along from the winches at the top of the plan, and the ground-team hooked the flesh on, then jumped aside as it slid away, followed by the flesh from the calf-cutters, smaller and more shaped pieces than ours.

The hip-team to our left didn't send anything up on the first load rope, or the second. Theirs was more technical work, cutting away the bags and scrags that were the beast's sex, sewing and sealing up the bags and passing them down in tarpaulin sheathing so that not a drop of the profitable aphrodisiacs could seep out and be wasted on the plan, on our splashing feet, on the sea. Then they must excavate the pelvis, which was complicated—valuable organs lay there and must not be punctured in the processing.

"That's a lot of muck, on the shroud," someone said as the smallest of the three toes, on the last few rope hooks, slid up past us.

"'Cause it's so fresh," came the satisfied answer. "Them star-men done a good job this time. They're getting more efficienter with every beast, I say."

"Do we *want* it this fresh?" said the first. "Seems like a lot of the good oils coming dribbling and drabbling out of the thing, that could be bottled and used and profited from."

"Ah, but what's left must be such quality!" The man kissed his fingers. "Unearthly good. Purest essence of money, trickling into the bosses' pockets—"

And then the bell rang, from the top of the plan, mad and loud and on and on.

The whole crowd of workers swayed shoreward as if a gust of wind had bent them. Many day-jobbers broke and ran for shore, shouting.

A slow shiver went through the whole length of the beast. At its foot, water splashed up from the drumming of its heel on the plan.

The knee-team's onlooker, whom I had thought so professional looking this morning, flashed by, alone.

"Down the ropes!" Mister Chopes shouted.

My men, their knees bent to spring into a run, looked to me for the word.

"Back up here!" I megaphoned through the noise. A man fleeing past me clapped his hand to his ear and scowled as he ran on. "We'll wait for the boss!"

But Mister Chopes, tiny on top of the quaking beast, was swinging his arms as if he would scoop us all up and *throw* us toward the head. "We'll go," I said. "On boss's orders. Form up and I'll be the chanter."

And so my men—all of them older than me, because it's the younger and limberer workers who go up top—made two lines in front of me. I used my whistle like a chanter's drum and held them to a rhythm. It was a fast one, but still I kept swinging nearly into the rearmost men—a crutch-pace is longer than a normal stride. We passed a man in the water, neither standing nor crouching, excrement running down his legs and dripping from the hem of his loongy. His wide eyes were fixed on the vast shuddering shadow looming over us all, and his lips had drawn right back from his big, sticking-out teeth. Beyond him some stretcher-men were busy lifting a misshapen, screaming thing with red spikes coming out of it. I tried to watch only the water shooting out flat to the sides when my men's feet hit it.

"Is it electricity?" one of my men asked the knowledgeable one, as we ran.

"Is *what* electricity?"

"With the dead frog. Has somebody hit a nerve?"

"A nerve? There's no nerve in a body can make the whole thing shake like that."

When we got to the head end, people in the beast's shadow were calling for help, but no stretcher-men ran to them. The harvested hair made a mountain on the plan, winched halfway to the hair-shed, strands trailing behind like giant millipedes. The shorn scalp had been taken off, and the sawyers had cut the full oval in the braincase. As we hurried past—we were not close; it only *felt* close because the head was so big—the beast's convulsions made this dish of bone tip slowly outward.

My rhythm went ragged, but my men kept it anyway, bringing *me* back into rhythm though it should have been me bringing *them*.

At the top of the plan near the steamer-sheds was a thick, panicky crowd, all trying not to be the outermost layer. I drew my team up on number 18 plan. Our formation was all gone to beggary, but we were together, tight together; none of us was missing, don't worry. From number 17 we must have looked like a row of heads upon a single candy-striped body.

"Is that Mister Chopes?" I looked back down the plan. I wanted a boss. I wanted to be in charge of nothing, no one.

"Look at them! And look at those raggedy foot-people coming after! Chopes will get commended for this, being so neat and ordered."

"If he doesn't die."

"If we don't all die."

"Look! Look at the stuff inside!"

The bone lid had tipped right out from the beast's head. The head-contents sat packed in their cavity. They were supposed to be gray, a purplish gray. Once, I had seen some damaged ones go past, on a lorry; the good ones were shipped across to the Island for sterile processing.

Frog eggs, I thought. Sheep eyes. A lightning storm.

Inside each giant cell floated two masses of blackness, joined by a black bar. Through each cell, and among them, pulsed, flashed, webs, veins, sheets, streaks, and sparks of light. Each flicker and pass began yellow, flashed up to white, faded away through yellow again—and so quickly that it took me many flickers to see this, to separate single flashes from the patterns, from the maps the light fast drew, then fast redrew.

"That's the brain," said Trawbrij the chanter. "Those lights must be its thinking. It's alive. They've not killed it properly."

"They've taken their economizing too far," said Mister Chopes. "They've skimped on the drug."

All workers were clear of the beast now, except for the dead, the injured, and two laden stretcher-teams splashing up the plan through the shallows. The lightning storm flickered and played in the head, now in fine, clear webs at the surface, now deeper and vaguer.

The beast lifted its upper limb, a giant unsteady thing with three clasping digits at the end, from its far side to its head. It felt, with delicate clumsiness, the bald skin above the ear, the angled dish of the skull top.

One of the digits slipped into the cavity, dislodging a single globe there, and whatever tension had held the cells in position was broken. The head-contents collapsed like a fruit stack from a market stall. Many rolled right out of the skull, onto the plan.

The beast tried to paw the spilt cells back into its skull. Some it retrieved; others it knocked farther away, and they sat gray and lightless on the plan. Like a flirty old drunk man fumbling for his fancy Western hat, it groped for its skull-dish. It clamped it back onto its head—but crookedly. Several cells were crushed. Their contents burst out; the black barbells cringed and withered, the oils spread upon the seawater; the rest of the filling lay jellied against the casing.

Holding its head together, the beast used a great contraction of its as-yet-uncut abdomen to curve itself up, to roll itself onto its single foot.

Oh my, I thought. It could be mistaken for a person, this one. Like what you see of a person sidling in through a nearly closed door.

"It can crush the whole town," said Trawbrij. "If it falls that way."

The thing turned from the sun to the land. There it stood, on its crooked hind limb, loose pieces of gel sliding off it. How many houses high was it, how many hills? Its chest and limbs were patterned with rectangular excavations like a rock quarry; our last unfinished blanket of thigh flesh drooped, dripping. There was a neatly cut cavity where the sex had been, full of drips and runnels like a grotto in the hill caves. Its eye was still sealed, its mouth torn partly open. Brain-fluid and matter ran down either side of the gray-stopped nose, in the high sun.

My own head felt light and hollow. Good, was the only thought in it. My heart thumped hard and burned red. Crush the whole town. And the plan, too, and everyone on it. Do that.

Three small, ornamental picture frames appeared in my mind, around three faces—Jumi's, Dochi's, Jupi's—all looking downward, or to the side. Far overhead, guilt whipped at me as always, but it barely stung. I was deep in my insides; against my cheek and ear, some black inner organ, quite separate from my body's functioning, turned and gleamed.

It's only fair.

The beast managed, though one-legged, to take a kind of step. But it sagged toward the missing toe; it gripped and tried to hold itself upright with a toe that wasn't there. Then the weakened knee gave, and the creature jerked and wobbled tremendously above us. And fell—of course it fell. But it fell away from us, stretching itself out across the farther plans.

And it lay still.

There were several moments of silence. Nothing moved but eyes.

Then there was an explosion around me, a fountain of striped shirts and shouting mouths, a surge forward.

I knew what they meant; I myself was hot bowelled and shaking with relief. But I didn't surge or shout or leap; I couldn't quite believe. So vast a creature and so strange, and yet the life in it was one-moment-there, next-moment-gone, just as for a dog under a bus wheel, or a chicken that a jumi pulls the neck of. And the world adjusts around it like water; as soon as the fear is gone, as soon as the danger is passed, normalness slips in on all sides, to cover up that any life was ever there.

The plan-workers rushed in. People came exclaiming into the yards from the town—those who had not seen had certainly heard, had felt the ground jump as the beast collapsed. Women and children crowded at the plan gates, and some of the little boys were allowed to run in because they were not bad luck like the girls and women.

Lots of people—and I was one of these—felt we had to approach the beast and touch it. Lots of us felt compelled to walk its length and see its motionlessness end to end for ourselves, see its dead face.

"Oh, oh," I said, to no one, as I walked, as I stroked the skin. "All my Jupi's careful work."

All the plans from 16 to 13 were cracked clean through. The beast had crushed plan 13's steamer-shed to splinters, its try-pots to copper pancakes; it had filled plan 12's hair-shed to the rafters with brain-spheres—dead spheres, gray-purplish spheres, spheres that held nothing unexpected.

The stretcher-men went to and fro with their serious faces, bearing their serious loads. The bosses withdrew; theirs was the most urgent work. The rest of us could do nothing until they had bargained our jobs back into being, weighed up the damage and set it against the value of the beast and parceled everything out appropriately. Yet we couldn't leave, could only wander dazed, and examine, and exclaim.

Finally they made us go, because some of the day-jobbers were found snipping pieces of hair, or taking chunks of eyeball or some such, and they put ribbons and guards all around the beast and brought the soldiers in to clear the plans and keep them clear.

So Jupi and Dochi and I, we walked, still all wobbly, back to our uncrushed home. There was Jumi, waiting to be told, and Jupi described how he had seen it, and Dochi how it had looked from his position up on the forelimb, and I told her yes, between them that was pretty much how it had seemed to me. There was too much to say, and yet none of it would tell properly what had happened, even to people who'd been there too.

Still people tried and tried. They came and went—we came and went ourselves—and everyone kept trying.

"How would it be!" said Mavourn.

We were all in the beer-shanty by then. I looked down at the thin foam on the beer he had bought me, and smelled the smell, and thought how I didn't want *ever* to like drinking beer.

"How would it be," he said, "to be a beast, to wake up and find yourself chopped half to pieces, and not in the ether anymore, and with no fellow beast to hear your cry?"

"No one can know that, Mavourn," said Jupi. "No one can know how a beast thinks, what a beast feels."

I looked around the table. My colleagues shook their heads, some of them muzzy with the beer. Some were my family—there was Jupi here, and two distant cousins across from me. I had wanted them all crushed, a few hours ago; what on earth made me want that, in the moment when the beast wavered, and the future was not set?

I could not say. That moment had gone, and the heat in my heart had gone with it. I picked up the beer. I closed my nose to the smell; I looked beyond the far rim so as not to see the slick on the surface from the unclean cup. And I sipped and swallowed, and I put the cup down, and I shook my head along with the other men.

MARGO LANAGAN was born in 1960 and grew up in the Hunter Valley (New South Wales) and Melbourne, Australia. She traveled a bit, studied history at university in Perth and Sydney, and has worked as a kitchen hand and encyclopedia seller, as well as spending ten years as a freelance book editor. She is now a technical writer as well as a creative one. She has written three books of junior fiction—*Wild Game*, *The Tankermen*, and *Walking Through Albert*—and two books of YA realistic fiction—*The Best Thing* and *Touching Earth Lightly*. Her short fiction has been collected in *White Time* and World Fantasy Award winner *Black Juice*. Her most recent book is the collection *Red Spikes*.

She lives in Sydney with her partner and their two sons. Her Web site is www.amongamidwhile.blogspot.com.

AUTHOR'S NOTE

"An Honest Day's Work" is directly inspired by photographs (particularly Edward Burtynsky's photographs) and a documentary I saw on TV about shipbreaking yards in India and Bangladesh, where retired ships are taken apart by workers using only the most basic equipment—such as their own bare hands. The workplaces are highly dangerous and thoroughly contaminated with asbestos, heavy metals, and poisons. The main causes of death and injury are explosions or fires, falls, being hit by falling steel plates and the like, suffocation, and the inhalation of carbon dioxide.

This is also a whaling-station story—I have stolen some of the tools and jargon from whalers—only the "whales" are larger than oil tankers and similar in nature to humans.

It's also about communities that operate on the fringes (and largely out of sight and out of mind) of more prosperous, more technologically advanced nations than themselves—how they manage to survive and how they regard themselves and their invisible, distant bosses.

But mainly it's about sense of scale, about tiny humans working on vast objects that they only partly understand.

LOST CONTINENT

Greg Egan

1

Ali's uncle took hold of his right arm and offered it to the stranger, who gripped it firmly by the wrist.

"From this moment on, you must obey this man," his uncle instructed him. "Obey him as you would obey your father. Your life depends on it."

"Yes, Uncle." Ali kept his eyes respectfully lowered.

"Come with me, boy," said the stranger, heading for the door.

"Yes, haji," Ali mumbled, following meekly. He could hear his mother still sobbing quietly in the next room, and he had to fight to hold back his own tears. He had said good-bye to his mother and his uncle, but he'd had no chance for any parting words with his cousins. It was halfway between midnight and dawn, and if anyone else in the household was awake, they were huddled beneath their blankets, straining to hear what was going on but not daring to show their faces.

The stranger strode out into the cold night, hand still around Ali's wrist like an iron shackle. He led Ali to the Land Cruiser that sat in the icy mud outside his uncle's house, its frosted surfaces glinting in the starlight, an apparition from a nightmare. Just the smell of it made Ali rigid with fear; it was the smell that had presaged his father's death, his brother's disappearance. Experience had taught him that such a machine could only bring tragedy, but his uncle had entrusted him to its driver. He forced himself to approach without resisting.

The stranger finally released his grip on Ali and opened a door at the rear of the vehicle. "Get in and cover yourself with the blanket. Don't move, and don't make a sound, whatever happens. Don't ask me any questions, and don't ask me to stop. Do you need to take a piss?"

"No, haji," Ali replied, his face burning with shame. Did the man think he was a child?

"All right, get in there."

As Ali complied, the man spoke in a grimly humorous tone. "You think you show me respect by calling me 'haji'? Every old man in your village is 'haji'! I haven't just been to Mecca. I've been there in the time of the Prophet, peace be upon him." Ali covered his face with the ragged blanket, which was imbued with the concentrated stench of the machine. He pictured the stranger standing in the darkness for a moment, musing arrogantly about his unnatural pilgrimage. The man wore enough gold to buy Ali's father's farm ten times over. Now his uncle had sold that farm, and his mother's jewelry—the hard-won wealth of generations—and handed all the money to this boastful man, who claimed he could spirit Ali away to a place and a time where he'd be safe.

The Land Cruiser's engine shuddered to life. Ali felt the vehicle moving backward at high speed, an alarming sensation. Then it stopped and moved forward, squealing as it changed direction; he could picture the tracks in the mud.

It was his first time ever in one of these machines. A few of his friends had taken rides with the Scholars, sitting in the back in the kind with the uncovered tray. They'd fired rifles into the air and shouted wildly before tumbling out, covered with dust, alive with excitement for the next ten days. Those friends had all been Sunni, of course. For Shi'a, rides with the Scholars had a different kind of ending.

Khurosan had been ravaged by war for as long as Ali could remember. For decades, tyrants of unimaginable cruelty from far in the future had given their weapons to factions throughout the country, who'd used them in their squabbles over land and power. Sometimes the warlords had sent recruiting parties into the valley to take young men to use as soldiers, but in the early days the villagers had banded together to hide their sons, or to bribe the recruiters to move on. Sunni or Shi'a, it made no difference; neighbor had worked with neighbor to outsmart the bandits who called themselves soldiers and keep the village intact.

Then four years ago, the Scholars had come, and everything had changed.

Whether the Scholars were from the past or the future was unclear, but they certainly had weapons and vehicles from the future. They had ridden triumphantly across Khurosan in their Land Cruisers, killing some warlords, bribing others, conquering the bloody patchwork of squalid fiefdoms one by one. Many people had cheered them on, because they had promised to bring unity and piety to the land. The warlords and their rabble armies had kidnapped and raped women and boys at will; the Scholars had hung the rapists from the gates of the cities. The warlords had set up checkpoints on every road, to extort money from travelers; the Scholars had opened the roads again for trade and pilgrimage in safety.

The Scholars' conquest of the land remained incomplete, though, and a savage battle was still being waged in the north. When the Scholars had come to Ali's village looking for soldiers themselves, they'd brought a new strategy to the recruitment drive: they would take only Shi'a for the front line, to face the bullets of the unsubdued warlords. Shi'a, the Scholars declared, were not true Muslims, and this was the only way they could redeem themselves: laying down their lives for their more pious and deserving Sunni countrymen.

This deceit, this flattery and cruelty, had cleaved the village in two. Many friends remained loyal across the divide, but the old trust, the old unity was gone.

Two months before, one of Ali's neighbors had betrayed his older brother's hiding place to the Scholars. They had come to the farm in the early hours of the morning, a dozen of them in two Land Cruisers, and dragged Hassan away. Ali had watched helplessly from his own hiding place, forbidden by his father to try to intervene. And what could their rifles have done against the Scholars' weapons, which sprayed bullets too fast and numerous to count?

The next morning, Ali's father had gone to the Scholars' post in the village to try to pay a bribe to get Hassan back. Ali had waited, watching the farm from the hillside above. When a single Land Cruiser had returned, his heart had swelled with hope. Even when the Scholars had thrown a limp figure from the vehicle, he'd thought it might be Hassan, unconscious from a beating but still alive, ready to be nursed back to health.

It was not Hassan. It was his father. They had slit his throat and left a coin in his mouth.

Ali had buried his father and walked half a day to the next village, where his mother had been staying with his uncle. His uncle had arranged the sale of the farm to a wealthy neighbor, then sought out a *mosarfar-e-waqt* to take Ali to safety.

Ali had protested, but it had all been decided, and his wishes had counted for nothing. His mother would live under the protection of her brother, while Ali built a life for himself in the future. Perhaps Hassan would escape from the Scholars, God willing, but that was out of their hands. What mattered, his mother insisted, was getting her youngest son out of the Scholars' reach.

In the back of the Land Cruiser, Ali's mind was in turmoil. He didn't want to flee this way, but he had no doubt that his life would be in danger if he remained. He wanted his brother back and his father avenged, he wanted to see the Scholars destroyed, but their only remaining enemies with any real power were murderous criminals who hated his own people as much as the Scholars themselves did. There was no righteous army to join, with clean hands and pure hearts.

The Land Cruiser slowed, then came to a halt, the engine still idling. The *mosarfar-e-waqt* called out a greeting, then began exchanging friendly words with someone, presumably a Scholar guarding the road.

Ali's blood turned to ice; what if this stranger simply handed him over? How much loyalty could mere money buy? His uncle had made inquiries of people with connections up and down the valley and had satisfied himself about the man's reputation, but however much the *mosarfar-e-waqt* valued his good name and the profits it brought him, there'd always be some other kind of deal to be made, some profit to be found in betrayal.

Both men laughed, then bid each other farewell. The Land Cruiser accelerated.

For what seemed like hours, Ali lay still and listened to the purring of the engine, trying to judge how far they'd come. He had never been out of the valley in his life, and he had only the sketchiest notion of what lay beyond. As dawn approached, his curiosity overwhelmed him, and he moved quietly to shift the blanket just enough to let him catch a glimpse through the rear window. There was a mountain peak visible to the left, topped with snow, crisp in the predawn light. He wasn't sure if this was a mountain he knew, viewed from an unfamiliar angle, or one he'd never seen before.

Not long afterward they stopped to pray. They made their ablutions in a small, icy stream. They prayed side by side, Sunni and Shi'a, and Ali's fear and suspicion retreated a little. However arrogant this man was, at least he didn't share the Scholars' contempt for Ali's people.

After praying, they ate in silence. The *mosarfar-e-waqt* had brought bread, dried fruit, and salted meat. As Ali looked around, it was clear that they'd long ago left any kind of man-made track behind. They were following a mountain pass, on higher ground than the valley but still far below the snow line.

They traveled through the mountains for three days, finally emerging onto a wind-blasted, dusty plain. Ali had grown stiff from lying curled up for hours, and the second time they stopped on the plain, he made the most of the chance to stretch his legs and wandered away from the Land Cruiser for a minute or two.

When he returned, the *mosarfar-e-waqt* said, "What are you looking for?"

"Nothing, haji."

"Are you looking for a landmark, so you can find this place again?"

Ali was baffled. "No, haji."

The man stepped closer, then struck him across the face, hard enough to make him stagger. "If you tell anyone about the way you came, you'll hear some more bad news about your family. Do you understand me?"

"Yes, haji."

The man strode back to the Land Cruiser. Ali followed him, shaking. He'd had no intention of betraying any detail of their route, any secret of the trade, to anyone, but now his uncle had been named as hostage against any indiscretion, real or imagined.

Late in the afternoon, Ali heard a sudden change in the sound of the wind, a high-pitched keening that made his teeth ache. Unable to stop himself, he lifted his head from beneath the blanket.

Ahead of them was a small dust storm, dancing across the ground. It was moving away from them, weaving back and forth as it retreated, like a living thing trying to escape them. The Land Cruiser was gaining on it. The heart of the storm was dark, thick with sand, knotted with wind. Ali's chest tightened. This was it: the *pol-e-waqt*, the bridge between times. Everyone in his village had heard of such things, but nobody could agree what they were: the work of men, the work of djinn, the work of God. Whatever their origin, some men had learned their secrets. No *mosarfar-e-waqt* had ever truly tamed them, but nobody else could find these bridges or navigate their strange depths.

They drew closer. The dust rained onto the windows of the Land Cruiser, as fine as any sand Ali had seen, yet as loud as the hailstones that fell sometimes on the roof of his house. Ali forgot all about his instructions; as they vanished into the darkness, he threw off the blanket and started praying aloud.

The *mosarfar-e-waqt* ignored him, muttering to himself and consulting the strange, luminous maps and writing that changed and flowed in front of him through some magic of machinery. The Land Cruiser ploughed ahead, buffeted by dust and wind but palpably advancing. Within a few minutes, it was clear to Ali that they'd traveled much farther than the storm's full width as revealed from the outside. They had left his time and his country behind, and were deep inside the bridge.

The lights of the Land Cruiser revealed nothing but a handsbreadth of flying dust ahead of them. Ali peered surreptitiously at the glowing map in the front, but it was a maze of branching and reconnecting paths that made no sense to him. The *mosarfar-e-waqt* kept running a fingertip over one path, then cursing and shifting to another, as if he'd discovered some obstacle or danger ahead. Ali's uncle had reassured him that at least they wouldn't run into the Scholars in this place, as they had come to Khurosan through another, more distant bridge. The entrance to that one was watched over night and day by a convoy of vehicles that chased it endlessly across the desert, like the bodyguards of some staggering, drunken king.

A hint of sunlight appeared in the distance, then grew slowly brighter. After a few minutes, though, the *mosarfar-e-waqt* cursed and steered away from it. Ali was dismayed. This man had been unable to tell his uncle where or when Ali would end up, merely promising him safety from the Scholars. Some people in the village—the kind with a friend of a friend who'd fled into the future—spoke of a whole vast continent where peace and prosperity reigned from shore to shore. The rulers had no weapons or armies of their own but were chosen by the people for the wisdom, justice, and mercy they displayed. It sounded like paradise on Earth, but Ali would believe in such a place when he saw it with his own eyes.

Another false dawn, then another. The body of the Land Cruiser began to moan and shudder. The *mosarfar-e-waqt* cut the engine, but the vehicle kept moving, driven by the wind or the ground itself. Or maybe both, but not in the same direction: Ali felt the wheels slipping over the treacherous river of sand. Suddenly there was a sharp pain deep inside his ears, then a sound like the scream of a giant bird, and the door beside him was gone. He snatched at the back of the seat in front of him, but his hands closed over nothing but the flimsy blanket as the wind dragged him out into the darkness.

Ali bellowed until his lungs were empty. But the painful landing he was braced for never came: the blanket had snagged on something in the vehicle, and the force of the wind was holding him above the sand. He tried to pull himself back toward the Land Cruiser, hand over hand, but then he felt a tear run through the blanket. Once more he steeled himself for a fall, but then the tearing stopped with a narrow ribbon of cloth still holding him.

Ali prayed. "Merciful God, if you take me now, please bring Hassan back safely to his home." For a year or two his uncle could care for his mother, but he was old, and he had too many mouths to feed. With no children of her own, her life would be unbearable.

A hand stretched out to him through the blinding dust. Ali reached out and took it, grateful now for the man's iron grip. When the *mosarfar-e-waqt* had dragged him back into the Land Cruiser, Ali crouched at the stranger's feet, his teeth chattering. "Thank you, haji. I am your servant, haji." The *mosarfar-e-waqt* climbed back into the front without a word.

Time passed, but Ali's thoughts were frozen. Some part of him had been prepared to die, but the rest of him was still catching up.

Sunlight appeared from nowhere: the full blaze of noon, not some distant promise. "This will suffice," the *mosarfar-e-waqt* announced wearily.

Ali shielded his eyes from the glare, then when he uncovered them the world was spinning. Blue sky and sand, changing places.

The bruising thud he'd been expecting long before finally came, the ground slapping him hard from cheek to ankle. He lay still, trying to judge how badly he was hurt. The patch of sand in front of his face was red. Not from blood: the sand itself was red as ocher.

There was a sound like a rapid exhalation, then he felt heat on his skin. He raised himself up on his elbows. The Land Cruiser was ten paces away, upside down, and on fire. Ali staggered to his feet and approached it, searching for the man who'd saved his life. Behind the wrecked vehicle, a storm like the one that the mouth of the bridge had made in his own land was weaving drunkenly back and forth, dancing like some demented hooligan pleased with the havoc it had wreaked.

He caught a glimpse of an arm behind the flames. He rushed toward the man, but the heat drove him back.

"Please, God," he moaned, "give me courage."

As he tried again to breach the flames, the storm lurched forward to greet him. Ali stood his ground, but the Land Cruiser spun around on its roof, swiping his shoulder and knocking him down. He climbed to his feet and tried to circle around to the missing door, but as he did the wind rose up, fanning the flames.

The wall of heat was impenetrable now, and the storm was playing with the Land Cruiser like a child with a broken top. Ali backed away, glancing around at the impossible red landscape, wondering if there might be anyone in earshot with the power to undo this calamity. He shouted for help, his eyes still glued to the burning wreck in the hope that a miracle might yet deliver the unconscious driver from the flames.

The storm moved forward again, coming straight for the Land Cruiser. Ali turned and retreated; when he looked over his shoulder, the vehicle was gone and the darkness was still advancing.

He ran, stumbling on the uneven ground. When his legs finally failed him and he collapsed onto the sand, the bridge was nowhere in sight. He was alone in a red desert. The air was still, now, and very hot.

After a while he rose to his feet, searching for a patch of shade where he could rest and wait for the cool of the evening. Apart from the red sand there were pebbles and some larger, cracked rocks, but there was no relief from the flatness: not so much as a boulder he could take shelter beside. In one direction there were some low, parched bushes, their trunks no thicker than his fingers, their branches no higher than his knees. He might as well have tried to hide from the sun beneath his own thin beard. He scanned the horizon, but it offered no welcoming destination.

There was no water for washing, but Ali cleaned himself as best he could and prayed. Then he sat cross-legged on the ground, covered his face with his shawl, and lapsed into a sickly sleep.

He woke in the evening and started to walk. Some of the constellations were familiar, but they crossed the sky far closer to the horizon than they should have. Others were completely new to him.

There was no moon, and though the terrain was flat he soon found that he lost his footing if he tried to move too quickly in the dark.

When morning came, it brought no perceptible change in his surroundings. Red sand and a few skeletal plants were all that this land seemed to hold.

He slept through most of the day again, stirring only to pray. Increasingly, his sleep was broken by a throbbing pain behind his eyes. The night had been chilly, but he'd never experienced such heat before. He was unsure how much longer he could survive without water. He began to wonder if it would have been better if he'd been taken by the wind inside the bridge or perished in the burning Land Cruiser.

After sunset, he staggered to his feet and continued his hopeful but unguided trek. He had a fever now, and his aching joints begged him for more rest, but he doubted if he'd wake again if he resigned himself to sleep.

When his feet touched the road, he thought he'd lost his mind. Who would take the trouble to build such a path through a desolate place like this? He stopped and crouched down to examine it. It was gritty with a sparse layer of windblown sand; beneath that was a black substance that felt less hard than stone, but resilient, almost springy.

A road like this must lead to a great city. He followed it.

An hour or two before dawn, bright headlights appeared in the distance. Ali fought down his instinctive fear; in the future such vehicles should be commonplace, not the preserve of bandits and murderers. He stood by the roadside awaiting its arrival.

The Land Cruiser was like none he'd seen before, white with blue markings. There was writing on it, in the same European script as he'd seen on many machine parts and weapons that had made their way into the bazaars, but no words he recognized, let alone understood. One passenger was riding beside the driver; he climbed out, approached Ali, and greeted him in an incomprehensible tongue.

Ali shrugged apologetically. *"Salaam aleikom,"* he ventured. *"Bebakhshid agha, mosarfar hastam. Ba tawarz' az shoma moharfazat khahesh mikonam."*

The man addressed Ali briefly in his own tongue again, though it was clear now that he did not expect to be understood any more than Ali did. He called out to his companion, gestured to Ali to stay put, then went back to the Land Cruiser. His companion handed him two small machines; Ali tensed, but they didn't look like any weapons he'd seen.

The man approached Ali again. He held one machine up to the side of his face, then lowered it again and offered it to Ali. Ali took it, and repeated the mimed action.

A woman's voice spoke in his ear. Ali understood what was happening; he'd seen the Scholars use similar machines to talk with each other over great distances. Unfortunately, the language was still incomprehensible. He was about to reply, when the woman spoke again in what sounded like a third language. Then a fourth, then a fifth. Ali waited patiently, until finally the woman greeted him in stilted Persian.

When Ali replied, she said, "Please wait." After a few minutes, a new voice spoke. "Peace be upon you."

"And upon you."

"Where are you from?" To Ali, this man's accent sounded exotic, but he spoke Persian with confidence.

"Khurosan."

"At what time?"

"Four years after the coming of the Scholars."

"I see." The Persian speaker switched briefly to a different language; the man on the road, who'd wandered halfway back to his vehicle and was still listening via the second machine, gave a curt reply. Ali was amazed at these people's hospitality: in the middle of the night, in a matter of minutes, they had found someone who could speak his language.

"How did you come to be on this road?"

"I walked across the desert."

"Which way? From where? How far did you come?"

"I'm sorry, I don't remember."

The translator replied bluntly, "Please try."

Ali was confused. What did it matter? One man, at least, could see how weary he was. Why were they asking him these questions before he'd had a chance to rest?

"Forgive me, sir. I can't tell you anything; I'm sick from my journey."

There was an exchange in the native language, followed by an awkward silence. Finally the translator said, "This man will take you to a place where you can stay for a while. Tomorrow we'll hear your whole story."

"Thank you, sir. You have done a great thing for me. God will reward you."

The man on the road walked up to Ali. Ali held out his arms to embrace him in gratitude. The man produced a metal shackle and snapped it around Ali's wrists.

2

The camp was enclosed by two high fences topped with glistening ribbons of razor-sharp metal. The space between them was filled with coils of the same material. Outside the fences there was nothing but desert as far as the eye could see. Inside, there were guards, and at night everything was bathed in a constant harsh light. Ali had no doubt that he'd come to a prison, though his hosts kept insisting that this was not the case.

His first night had passed in a daze. He'd been given food and water, examined by a doctor, then shown to a small metal hut that he was to share with three other men. Two of the men, Alex and Tran, knew just enough Persian to greet Ali briefly, but the third, Shahin, was an Iranian, and they could understand each other well enough. The hut's four beds were arranged in pairs, one above the other; Ali's habit was to sleep on a mat on the floor, but he didn't want to offend anyone by declining to follow the local customs. The guards had removed his shackles, then put a bracelet on his left wrist—made from something like paper, but extraordinarily strong—bearing the number 3739. The last numeral was more or less the same shape as a Persian nine; he recognized the others from machine parts, but he didn't know their values.

Every two hours, throughout the night, a guard opened the door of the hut and shone a light on each of their faces in turn. The first time it happened, Ali thought the guard had come to rouse them from their sleep and take them somewhere, but Shahin explained that these "head counts" happened all night, every night.

The next morning, officials from the camp had taken Ali out

in a vehicle and asked him to show them the exact place where he'd arrived through the bridge. He'd done his best, but all of the desert looked the same to him. By midday, he was tempted to designate a spot at random just to satisfy his hosts, but he didn't want to lie to them. They'd returned to the camp in a sullen mood. Ali couldn't understand why it was so important to them.

Reza, the Persian translator who'd first spoken with Ali through the machine, explained that he was to remain in the camp until government officials had satisfied themselves that he really was fleeing danger and hadn't merely come to the future seeking an easy life for himself. Ali understood that his hosts didn't want to be cheated, but it dismayed him that they felt the need to imprison him while they made up their minds. Surely there was a family in a nearby town who would have let him stay with them for a day or two, just as his father would have welcomed any travelers passing through their village.

The section of the camp where he'd been placed was fenced off from the rest and contained about a hundred people. They were all travelers like himself, and they came from every nation Ali had heard of, and more. Most were young men, but there were also women, children, entire families. In his village, Ali would have run to greet the children, lifted them up and kissed them to make them smile, but here they looked so sad and dispirited that he was afraid the approach of even the friendliest stranger might frighten them.

Shahin was a few years older than Ali, but he had spent his whole life as a student. He had traveled just two decades through time, escaping a revolution in his country. He explained that the part of the camp they were in was called "Stage One"; they were being kept apart from the others so they wouldn't learn too much about the way their cases would be judged. "They're afraid we'll embellish the details if we discover what kind of questions they ask, or what kind of story succeeds."

"How long have you been here?" Ali asked.

"Nine months. I'm still waiting for my interview."

"Nine months!"

Shahin smiled wearily. "Some people have been in Stage One for a year. But don't worry, you won't have to wait that long. When I arrived here, the Center Manager had an interesting policy: nobody would have their cases examined until they asked him for the correct application form. Of course, nobody knew that they were required to do that, and he had no intention of telling them. Three months ago, he was transferred to another camp. When I asked the woman who replaced him what I needed to do to have my claims heard, she told me straightaway: ask for Form 866."

Ali couldn't quite follow all this. Shahin explained further.

Ali said, "What good will it do me to get this piece of paper? I can't read their language, and I can barely write my own."

"That's no problem. They'll let you talk to an educated man or woman, an expert in these matters. That person will fill out the form for you, in English. You only need to explain your problem, and sign your name at the bottom of the paper."

"English?" Ali had heard about the English; before he was born they'd tried to invade both Hindustan and Khurosan, without success. "How did that language come here?" He was sure that he was not in England.

"They conquered this country two centuries ago. They crossed the world in wooden ships to take it for their king."

"Oh." Ali felt dizzy; his mind still hadn't fully accepted the journey he'd made. "What about Khurosan?" he joked. "Have they conquered that as well?"

Shahin shook his head. "No."

"What is it like now? Is there peace there?" Once this strange business with the English was done, perhaps he could travel to his homeland. However much it had changed with time, he was sure he could make a good life there.

Shahin said, "There is no nation called Khurosan in this world. Part of that area belongs to Hindustan, part to Iran, part to Russia."

Ali stared at him, uncomprehending. "How can that be?" However much his people fought among themselves, they would never have let invaders take their land.

"I don't know the full history," Shahin said, "but you need to understand something. This is not your future. The things that happened in the places you know are not a part of the history of this world. There is no *pol-e-waqt* that connects past and future in the same world. Once you cross the bridge, everything changes, including the past."

With Shahin beside him, Ali approached one of the government officials, a man named James, and addressed him in the English he'd learned by heart. "Please, Mr. James, can I have Form 866?"

James rolled his eyes and said, "Okay, okay! We were going to get around to you sooner or later." He turned to Shahin and said, "I wish you'd stop scaring the new guys with stories about being stuck in Stage One forever. You know things have changed since Colonel Kurtz went north."

Shahin translated all of this for Ali. "Colonel Kurtz" was Shahin's nickname for the previous Center Manager, but everyone, even the guards, had adopted it. Shahin called Tran "The Rake," and Alex was "Denisovich of the Desert."

Three weeks later, Ali was called to a special room, where he sat with Reza. A lawyer in a distant city, a woman called Ms. Evans, spoke with them in English through a machine that Reza called a "speakerphone." With Reza translating, she asked Ali about everything: his village, his family, his problems with the Scholars. He'd been asked about some of this the night he'd arrived, but he'd been very tired then and hadn't had a chance to put things clearly.

Three days after the meeting, he was called to see James. Ms. Evans had written everything in English on the special form and sent it to them. Reza read through the form, translating everything for Ali to be sure that it was correct. Then Ali wrote his name on the bottom of the form. James told him, "Before we make a decision, someone will come from the city to interview you. That might take a while, so you'll have to be patient."

Ali said, in English, "No problem."

He felt he could wait for a year, if he had to. The first four weeks had gone quickly, with so much that was new to take in. He had barely had space left in his crowded mind to be homesick, and he tried not to worry about Hassan and his mother. Many things about the camp disturbed him, but his luck had been good: the infamous "Colonel Kurtz" had left, so he'd probably be out in three or four months. The cities of this nation, Shahin assured him, were mostly on the distant coast, an infinitely milder place than the desert around the camp. Ali might be able to get a laboring job while studying English at night, or he might find work on a farm. He hadn't quite started his new life yet, but he was safe, and everything looked hopeful.

◉ ◉ ◉

By the end of his third month Ali was growing restless. Most days he played cards with Shahin, Tran, and a Hindustani man named Rakesh, while Alex lay on his bunk reading books in Russian. Rakesh had a cassette player and a vast collection of tapes. The songs were mostly in Hindi, a language that contained just enough Persian words to give Ali some sense of what the lyrics were about: usually love, or sorrow, or both.

The metal huts were kept tolerably cool by machines, but there was no shade outside. At night the men played soccer, and Ali sometimes joined in, but after falling badly on the concrete, twice, he decided it wasn't the game for him. Shahin told him that it was a game for grass; from his home in Tehran, he'd watched dozens of nations compete at it. Ali felt a surge of excitement at the thought of all the wonders of this world, still tantalizingly out of reach: in Stage One, TV, radio, newspapers, and telephones were all forbidden. Even Rakesh's tapes had been checked by the guards, played from start to finish to be sure that they didn't contain secret lessons in passing the interview. Ali couldn't wait to reach Stage Two, to catch his first glimpse of what life might be like in a world where anyone could watch history unfolding and speak at their leisure with anyone else.

English was the closest thing to a common language for all the people in the camp. Shahin did his best to get Ali started, and once he could converse in broken English, some of the friendlier guards let him practice with them, often to their great amusement. "Not every car is called a Land Cruiser," Gary explained. "I think you must come from Toyota-stan."

Shahin was called to his interview. Ali prayed for him, then sat on the floor of the hut with Tran and tried to lose himself in the mercurial world of the cards. What he liked most about these friendly games was that good and bad luck rarely lasted long, and even when they did it barely mattered. Every curse and every blessing was light as a feather.

Shahin returned four hours later, looking exhausted but satisfied. "I've told them my whole story," he said. "It's in their hands now." The official who'd interviewed him had given him no hint as to what the decision would be, but Shahin seemed relieved just to have had a chance to tell someone who mattered everything he'd suffered, everything that had forced him from his home.

That night Shahin was told that he was moving to Stage Two in half an hour. He embraced Ali. "See you in freedom, brother."

"God willing."

After Shahin was gone, Ali lay on his bunk for four days, refusing to eat, getting up only to wash and pray. His friend's departure was just the trigger; the raw grief of his last days in the valley came flooding back, deepened by the unimaginable gulf that now separated him from his family. Had Hassan escaped from the Scholars? Or was he fighting on the front line of their endless war, risking death every hour of every day? With the only *mosarfar-e-waqt* Ali knew now dead, how would he ever get news from his family or send them his assistance?

Tran whispered gruff consolations in his melodic English. "Don't worry, kid. Everything okay. Wait and see."

Worse than the waiting was the sense of waste: all the hours trickling away, with no way to harness them for anything useful. Ali tried to improve his English, but there were some concepts he could get no purchase on without someone who understood his own language to help him. Reza rarely left the government offices for the compound, and when he did he was too busy for Ali's questions.

Ali tried to make a garden, planting an assortment of seeds that he'd saved from the fruit that came with some of the meals. Most of Stage One was covered in concrete, but he found a small patch of bare ground behind his hut that was sheltered from the fiercest sunlight. He carried water from the drinking tap on the other side of the soccer ground and sprinkled it over the soil four times a day. Nothing happened, though. The seeds lay dormant; the land would not accept them.

Three weeks after Shahin's departure, Alex had his interview, and left. A week later, Tran followed. Ali started sleeping through the heat of the day, waking just in time to join the queue for the evening meal, then playing cards with Rakesh and his friends until dawn.

By the end of his sixth month, Ali felt a taint of bitterness creeping in beneath the numbness and boredom. He wasn't a thief or a murderer, he'd committed no crime. Why couldn't these people set him free to work, to fend for himself instead of taking their charity, to prepare himself for his new life?

One night, tired of the endless card game, Ali wandered out from Rakesh's hut earlier than usual. One of the guards, a woman named Cheryl, was standing outside her office, smoking. Ali murmured a greeting to her as he passed; she was not one of the friendly ones, but he tried to be polite to everyone.

"Why don't you just go home?" she said.

Ali paused, unsure whether to dignify this with a response. He'd long ago learned that most of the guards' faces became stony if he tried to explain why he'd left his village; somewhere, somehow it had been drummed into them that nothing their prisoners said could be believed.

"Nobody invited you here," she said bluntly. "We take twelve thousand people from the UN camps every year. But you still think you're entitled to march right in as if you owned the place."

Ali had only heard mention of these "UN camps" since his arrival here. Shahin had explained that there'd probably been a dusty tent-city somewhere on the border of his country, where—if he'd survived the journey across the Scholars' heartland—he could have waited five, or ten, or fifty years for the slim chance that some beneficent future government might pluck him from the crowd and grant him a new life.

Ali shrugged. "I'm here. From me, big tragedy for your nation? I'm honest man and hard worker. I'm not betray your hospitality."

Cheryl snickered. Ali wasn't sure if she was sneering at his English or his sentiments, but he persisted. "Your leaders did agreement with other nations. Anyone asking protection gets fair hearing." Shahin had impressed that point on Ali. It was the law, and in this society the law was everything. "That is my right."

Cheryl coughed on her cigarette. "Dream on, Ahmad."

"My name is Ali."

"Whatever." She reached out and caught him by the wrist, then held up his hand to examine his ID bracelet. "Dream on, 3739."

James called Ali to his office and handed him a letter. Reza translated it for him. After eight months of waiting, in six days' time he would finally have his interview.

Ali waited nervously for Ms. Evans to call him to help him prepare, as she'd promised she would when they'd last spoken, all those months before. On the morning of the appointed day, he was summoned again to James's office, and taken with Reza to the room with the speakerphone, the "interview room." A different lawyer, a man called Mr. Cole, explained to Ali that Ms. Evans had left her job and he had taken over Ali's case. He told Ali that everything would be fine, and he'd be listening carefully to Ali's interview and making sure that everything went well.

When Cole had hung up, Reza snorted derisively. "You know how these clowns are chosen? They put in tenders, and it goes to the lowest bidder." Ali didn't entirely understand, but this didn't sound encouraging. Reza caught the expression on Ali's face, and added, "Don't worry, you'll be fine. Fleeing from the Scholars is flavor of the month."

Three hours later, Ali was back in the interview room.

The official who'd come from the city introduced himself as John Fernandez. Reza wasn't with them; Fernandez had brought a different interpreter with him, a man named Parviz. Mr. Cole joined them on the speakerphone. Fernandez switched on a cassette recorder and asked Ali to swear on the Quran to give truthful answers to all his questions.

Fernandez asked him for his name, his date of birth, and the place and time he'd fled. Ali didn't know his birthday or his exact age; he thought he was about eighteen years old, but it was not the custom in his village to record such things. He did know that at the time he'd left his uncle's house, twelve hundred and sixty-five years had passed since the Prophet's flight to Medina.

"Tell me about your problem," Fernandez said. "Tell me why you've come here."

Shahin had told Ali that the history of this world was different from his own, so Ali explained carefully about Khurosan's long war, about the meddlers and the warlords they'd created, about the coming of the Scholars. How the Shi'a were taken by force to fight in the most dangerous positions. How Hassan was taken. How his father had been killed. Fernandez listened patiently, sometimes writing on the sheets of paper in front of him as Ali spoke, interrupting him only to encourage him to fill in the gaps in the story, to make everything clear.

When he had finally recounted everything, Ali felt an overwhelming sense of relief. This man had not poured scorn on his words the way the guards had; instead, he had allowed Ali to speak openly about all the injustice his family and his people had suffered.

Fernandez had some more questions.

"Tell me about your village, and your uncle's village. How long would it take to travel between them on foot?"

"Half a day, sir."

"Half a day. That's what you said in your statement. But in your entry interview, you said a day." Ali was confused. Parviz explained that his "statement" was the written record of his conversation with Ms. Evans, which she had sent to the government; his "entry interview" was when he'd first arrived in the camp and been questioned for ten or fifteen minutes.

"I only meant it was a short trip, sir, you didn't have to stay somewhere halfway overnight. You could complete it in one day."

"Hmm. Okay. Now, when the smuggler took you from your uncle's village, which direction was he driving?"

"Along the valley, sir."

"North, south, east, west?"

"I'm not sure." Ali knew these words, but they were not part of the language of everyday life. He knew the direction for prayer, and he knew the direction to follow to each neighboring village.

"You know that the sun rises in the east, don't you?"

"Yes."

"So if you faced in the direction in which you were being driven, would the sun have risen on your left, on your right, behind you, where?"

"It was nighttime."

"Yes, but you must have faced the same direction in the valley in the morning, a thousand times. So where would the sun have risen?"

Ali closed his eyes and pictured it. "On my right."

Fernandez sighed. "Okay. Finally. So you were driving north. Now tell me about the land. The smuggler drove you along the valley. And then what? What kind of landscape did you see, between your valley and the bridge?"

Ali froze. What would the government do with this information? Send someone back through their own bridge, to find and destroy the one he'd used? The *mosarfar-e-waqt* had warned him not to tell anyone the way to the bridge. That man was dead, but it was unlikely that he'd worked alone; everyone had a brother, a son, a cousin to help them. If the family of the *mosarfar-e-waqt* could trace such a misfortune to Ali, the dead man's threat against his uncle would be carried through.

Ali said, "I was under a blanket, I didn't see anything."

"You were under a blanket? For how many days?"

"Three."

"Three days. What about eating, drinking, going to the toilet?"

"He blindfolded me," Ali lied.

"Really? You never mentioned that before." Fernandez shuffled through his papers. "It's not in your statement."

"I didn't think it was important, sir." Ali's stomach tightened. What was happening? He was sure he'd won this man's trust. And he'd earned it: he'd told him the truth about everything, until now. What difference did it make to his problem with the Scholars, which mountains and streams he'd glimpsed on the way to the bridge? He had sworn to tell the truth, but he knew it would be a far greater sin to risk his uncle's life.

Fernandez had still more questions, about life in the village. Some were easy, but some were strange, and he kept asking for numbers, numbers, numbers: how much did it weigh, how much did it cost, how long did it take? What time did the bazaar open? Ali had no idea, he'd been busy with farmwork in the mornings, he'd never gone there so early that it might have been closed. How many people came to Friday prayers in the Shi'a mosque? None, since the Scholars had arrived. Before that? Ali couldn't remember. More than a hundred? Ali hesitated. "I think so." He'd never counted them, why would he have?

When the interview finished, Ali's mind was still three questions behind, worrying that his answers might not have been clear enough. Fernandez was rewinding the tapes, shaking his hand formally, leaving the room.

Mr. Cole said, "I think that went well. Do you have any questions you want to ask me?"

Ali said, "No, sir." Parviz had already departed.

"All right. Good luck." The speaker phone clicked off. Ali sat at the table, waiting for the guard to come and take him back to the compound.

3

Entering Stage Two, Ali felt as if he had walked into the heart of a bustling town. Everything was noise, shouting, music. He'd sometimes heard snatches of this cacophony wafting across the fenced-off "sterile area" that separated the parts of the camp, but now he was in the thick of it. The rows of huts, and the crowds moving between them, seemed to stretch on forever. There must have been a thousand people here, all of them unwilling travelers fleeing the cruelties of their own histories.

He'd moved his small bag of belongings into the hut allocated to him, but none of his new roommates were there to greet him. He wandered through the compound, dizzy from the onslaught of new sights and sounds. He felt as if he'd just had a heavy cloth unwound from around his head, and his unveiled senses were still struggling to adjust. If he was reeling from this, how would he feel when he stepped onto the streets of a real city, in freedom?

The evening meal was over, the sun had set, and the heat outside had become tolerable. Almost everyone seemed to be out walking, or congregating around the entrances of their friends' huts, taped music blaring through the open doorways. At the end of one row of huts, Ali came to a larger building, where thirty or forty people were seated. He entered the room and saw a small box with a window on it, through which he could see an oddly-colored, distorted, constantly changing view. A woman was dancing and singing in Hindi.

"TV," Ali marveled. This was what Shahin had spoken about; now the whole world was open to his gaze.

An African man beside him shook his head. "It's a video. The TV's on in the other common room."

Ali lingered, watching the mesmerizing images. The woman was very beautiful, and though she was immodestly dressed by the standards of his village, she seemed dignified and entirely at ease. The Scholars would probably have stoned her to death, but Ali would have been happy to be a beggar in Mumbai if the streets there were filled with sights like this.

As he left the room, the sky was already darkening. The camp's floodlights had come on, destroying any hope of a glimpse of the stars. He asked someone, "Where is the TV, please?" and followed their directions.

As he walked into the second room, he noticed something different in the mood at once; the people here were tense, straining with attention. When Ali turned to the TV, it showed an eerily familiar sight: an expanse of desert, not unlike that outside the camp. Helicopters, four or five, flew over the landscape. In the distance, a tight funnel of swirling dust, dancing across the ground.

Ali stood riveted. The landscape on the screen was brightly lit, which meant that what he was watching had already happened: earlier in the day, someone had located the mouth of the bridge. He peered at the small images of the helicopters. He'd only ever seen a broken one on the ground, the toy of one warlord brought down by a rival, but he recognized the guns protruding from the sides. Whoever had found the bridge, it was now in the hands of soldiers.

As he watched, a Land Cruiser came charging out of the storm. Then another, and another. This was not like his own arrival; the convoy was caked with dust, but more or less intact. Then the helicopters descended, guns chattering. For a few long seconds Ali thought he was about to witness a slaughter, but the soldiers were firing consistently a meter or so ahead of the Land Cruisers. They were trying to corral the vehicles back into the bridge.

The convoy broke up, the individual drivers trying to steer their way past the blockade. Curtains of bullets descended around them, driving them back toward the meandering storm. Ali couldn't see the people inside, but he could imagine their terror and confusion. This was the future? This was their sanctuary? Whatever tyranny they were fleeing, to have braved the labyrinth of the *pol-e-waqt* only to be greeted with a barrage of gunfire was a fate so cruel that they must have doubted their senses, their sanity, their God.

The helicopters wheeled around the mouth of the bridge like hunting dogs, indefatigable, relentless in their purpose. Ali found the grim dance unbearable, but he couldn't turn away. One of the Land Cruisers came to a halt; it wasn't safely clear of the storm, but this must have seemed wiser than dodging bullets. Doors opened and people tumbled out. Weirdly, the picture went awry at exactly that moment, clumps of flickering color replacing the travelers' faces.

Soldiers approached, guns at the ready, gesturing and threatening, forcing the people back into the car. A truck appeared, painted in dappled green and brown. A chain was tied between the vehicles. Someone emerged from the Land Cruiser; the face was obscured again, but Ali could see it was a woman. Her words could not be heard, but Ali could see her speaking with her hands, begging, chastising, pleading for mercy. The soldiers forced her back inside.

The truck started its engines. Sand sprayed from its wheels. Two soldiers climbed into the back, their weapons trained on the Land Cruiser. Then they towed their cargo back into the storm.

Ali watched numbly as the other two Land Cruisers were rounded up. The second stalled, and the soldiers descended on it. The driver of the third gave up and steered his own course into the mouth of the bridge.

The soldiers' truck emerged from the storm, alone. The helicopters spiraled away, circling the funnel at a more prudent distance. Ali looked at the faces of the other people in the room; everyone was pale, some were weeping.

The picture changed. Two men were standing, indoors somewhere. One was old, white haired, wizened. In front of him a younger man was talking, replying to unseen questioners. Both were smiling proudly.

Ali could only make sense of a few of the words, but gradually he pieced some things together. These men were from the government, and they were explaining the events of the day. They had sent the soldiers to "protect" the bridge, to ensure that no more criminals and barbarians from the past emerged to threaten the peaceful life of the nation. They had been patient with these intruders for far too long. From this day on, nobody would pass.

"What about the law?" someone was asking. An agreement had been signed: any traveler who reached this country and asked for protection had a right to a fair hearing.

"A bill has been drafted, and will be introduced in the House tomorrow. Once passed, it will take force from nine o'clock this morning. The land within twenty kilometers of the bridge will, for the purposes of the Act, no longer be part of this nation. People entering the exclusion zone will have no basis in law to claim our protection."

Confused, Ali muttered, *"Chi goft?"* A young man sitting nearby turned to face him. *"Salaam, chetori? Fahim hastam."*

Fahim's accent was unmistakably Khurosani. Ali smiled. *"Ali hastam. Shoma chetori?"*

Fahim explained what the man on the TV had said. Anyone emerging from the mouth of the bridge, now, might as well be on the other side of the world. The government here would accept no obligation to assist them. "If it's not their land anymore," he mused, "maybe they'll give it to us. We can found a country of our own, a tribe of nomads in a caravan following the bridge across the desert."

Ali said nervously, "My interview was today. They said something about nine o'clock—"

Fahim shook his head dismissively. "You made your claim months ago, right? So you're still covered by the old law."

Ali tried to believe him. "You're still waiting for your decision?"

"Hardly. I got refused three years ago."

"Three years? They didn't send you back?"

"I'm fighting it in the courts. I can't go back; I'd be dead in a week." There were dark circles under Fahim's eyes. If he'd been refused three years before, he'd probably spent close to four years in this prison.

Fahim, it turned out, was one of Ali's roommates. He took him to meet the other twelve Khurosanis in Stage Two, and the whole group sat together in one of the huts, talking until dawn. Ali was overjoyed to be among people who knew his language, his time, his customs. It didn't matter that most were from provinces far from his own, that a year ago he would have thought of them as exotic strangers.

When he examined their faces too closely, though, it was hard to remain joyful. They had all fled the Scholars, like him. They were all in fear for their lives. And they had all been locked up for a very long time: two years, three years, four years, five.

In the weeks that followed, Ali gave himself no time to brood on his fate. Stage Two had English classes, and though Fahim and the others had long outgrown them, Ali joined in. He finally learned the names for the European numbers and letters that he'd seen on weapons and machinery all his life, and the teacher encouraged him to give up translating individual words from Persian, and reshape whole sentences, whole thoughts, into the alien tongue.

Every evening, Ali joined Fahim in the common room to watch the news on TV. There was no doubt that the place they had come to was peaceful and prosperous; when war was mentioned, it was always in some distant land. The rulers here did not govern by force; they were chosen by the people, and even now this competition was in progress. The men who had sent the soldiers to block the bridge were asking the people to choose them again.

When the guard woke Ali at eight in the morning, he didn't complain, though he'd had only three hours' sleep. He showered quickly, then went to the compound's south gate. It no longer seemed strange to him to move from place to place this way: to wait for guards to come and unlock a succession of doors and escort him through the fenced-off maze that separated the compound from the government offices.

James and Reza were waiting in the office. Ali greeted them, his mouth dry. James said, "Reza will read the decision for you. It's about ten pages, so be patient. Then if you have any questions, let me know."

Reza read from the papers without meeting Ali's eyes. Fernandez, the man who'd interviewed Ali, had written that there were discrepancies between things Ali had said at different times, and gaps in his knowledge of the place and time he claimed to come from. What's more, an expert in the era of the Scholars had listened to the tape of Ali talking, and declared that his speech was not of that time. "Perhaps this man's great-grandfather fled Khurosan in the time of the Scholars, and some sketchy information has been passed down the generations. The applicant himself, however, employs a number of words that were not in use until decades later."

Ali waited for the litany of condemnation to come to an end, but it seemed to go on forever. "I have tried to give the applicant the benefit of the doubt," Fernandez had written, "but the overwhelming weight of evidence supports the conclusion that he has lied about his origins, his background, and all of his claims."

Ali sat with his head in his hands.

James said, "Do you understand what this means? You have seven days to lodge an appeal. If you don't lodge an appeal, you will have to return to your country."

Reza added, "You should call your lawyer. Have you got money for a phone card?"

Ali nodded. He'd taken a job cleaning the mess; he had thirty points in his account already.

Every time Ali called, his lawyer was busy. Fahim helped Ali fill out the appeal form, and they handed it to James two hours before the deadline. "Lucky Colonel Kurtz is gone," Fahim told Ali. "Or that form would have sat in the fax tray for at least a week."

Wild rumors swept the camp: the government was about to change, and everyone would be set free. Ali had seen the government's rivals giving their blessing to the use of soldiers to block the bridge; he doubted that they'd show the prisoners in the desert much mercy if they won.

When the day of the election came, the government was returned, more powerful than ever.

That night, as they were preparing to sleep, Fahim saw Ali

staring at the row of white scars that criss-crossed his chest. "I use a razor blade," Fahim admitted. "It makes me feel better. The one power I've got left: to choose my own pain."

"I'll never do that," Ali swore.

Fahim gave a hollow laugh. "It's cheaper than cigarettes."

Ali closed his eyes and tried to picture freedom, but all he saw was blackness. The past was gone, the future was gone, and the world had shrunk to this prison.

4

"Ali, wake up, come see!"

Daniel was shaking him. Ali swatted his hands away angrily. The African was one of his closest friends, and there'd been a time when he could still drag Ali along to English classes or the gym, but since the appeal tribunal had rejected him, Ali had no taste for anything. "Let me sleep."

"There are people. Outside the fence."

"Escaped?"

"No, no. From the city!"

Ali clambered off the bunk. He splashed water on his face, then followed his friend.

A crowd of prisoners had gathered at the southwest corner of the fence, blocking the view, but Ali could hear people on the outside, shouting and banging drums. Daniel tried to clear a path, but it was impossible. "Get on my shoulders." He ducked down and motioned to Ali.

Ali laughed. "It's not that important."

Daniel raised a hand angrily, as if to slap him. "Get up, you have to see." He was serious. Ali obeyed.

From his vantage, he could see that the crowd of prisoners pressed against the inner fence was mirrored by another crowd struggling to reach the outer one. Police, some on horses, were trying to stop them. Ali peered into the scrum, amazed. Dozens of young people, men and women, were slithering out of the grip of the policemen and running forward. Some distance away across the desert stood a brightly colored bus. The word *freedom* was painted across it, in English, Persian, Arabic, and probably ten or twelve languages that Ali couldn't read. The people were chanting, "Set them free! Set them free!" One young woman reached the fence and clung to it, shouting defiantly. Four policemen descended on her and tore her away.

A cloud of dust was moving along the desert road. More police cars were coming, reinforcements. A knife twisted in Ali's heart. This gesture of friendship astonished him, but it would lead nowhere. In five or ten minutes, the protesters would all be rounded up and carried away.

A young man outside the fence met Ali's gaze. "Hey! My name's Ben."

"I'm Ali."

Ben looked around frantically. "What's your number?"

"What?"

"We'll write to you. Give us your number. They have to deliver the letters if we include the ID number."

"Behind you!" Ali shouted, but the warning was too late. One policeman had him in a headlock, and another was helping wrestle him to the ground.

Ali felt Daniel stagger. The crowd on his own side was trying to fend off a wave of guards with batons and shields.

Ali dropped to his feet. "They want our ID numbers," he told Daniel. Daniel looked around at the melee. "Got anything to write on?"

Ali checked his back pocket. The small notebook and pen it was his habit to carry were still there. He rested the notebook on Daniel's back, and wrote, "Ali 3739 Daniel 5420." Who else? He quickly added Fahim and a few others.

He scrabbled on the ground for a stone, then wrapped the paper around it. Daniel lofted him up again.

The police were battling with the protesters, grabbing them by the hair, dragging them across the dirt. Ali couldn't see anyone who didn't have more pressing things to worry about than receiving his message. He lowered his arm, despondent.

Then he spotted someone standing by the bus. He couldn't tell if it was a man or a woman. He, or she, raised a hand in greeting. Ali waved back, then let the stone fly. It fell short, but the distant figure ran forward and retrieved it from the sand.

Daniel collapsed beneath him, and the guards moved in with batons and tear gas. Ali covered his eyes with his forearm, weeping, alive again with hope.

GREG EGAN was born in Perth, Western Australia, in 1961 and earned a bachelor of science in mathematics from the University of Western Australia before attending the National Film and Television School. He gave up a career in filmmaking, which inspired his surreal early novel *An Unusual Angle*, for science fiction, and has supported himself as a computer programmer when not writing full-time.

While Egan began publishing short fiction in the pages of *Interzone* and *Asimov's Science Fiction Magazine* in the 1980s, his most impressive work is the extensive body of short fiction published during the 1990s, which includes "Reasons To Be Cheerful," "Learning To Be Me," "Cocoon," "Luminous," and Hugo Award–winning story "Oceanic"—and has established him as one of the world's most important writers of science fiction. He is a frequent contributor to *Interzone* and *Asimov's*; has made sales to *Pulphouse*, *Analog*, *Aurealis*, *Eidolon*, and *New Legends*; and has been represented in every volume of the U.S.-based *Year's Best Science Fiction* since 1991. Egan's short fiction has been collected in *Axiomatic* and *Luminous*.

Egan's first major novel—the first of his "Nature of Consciousness" novels—was *Quarantine*, and it was followed by John W. Campbell Memorial Award winner *Permutation City*, *Distress*, *Diaspora*, *Teranesia*, and the radical space opera *Schild's Ladder*. After a lengthy break from writing, when he focused on political issues related to refugees in Australia, he has recently published a new novel, *Incandescence*.

His Web site is www.gregegan.net.

INCOMERS

Paul McAuley

If the three friends had seen the man in one of the malls or plazas of the new city, they wouldn't have spared him a second glance, but in the old part of Xamba, the largest city on Saturn's second-largest moon, where the weird was commonplace and the commonplace weird, he was as exotic as a tiger strolling down Broadway in old New York. People born and raised in the weak or nonexistent gravity of the various moons, orbital habitats, and ships of the outer reaches of the solar system—Outers—were generally taller than basketball stars and skinny as rails, and most citizens of old Xamba were of pale-skinned, blond, blue-eyed Nordic stock. This man, with a compact build, a shaven head, a neatly pointed black beard, and skin the color of old teak, was definitely no Outer. So why was he sitting at a tiny stall near the bottom of the produce market's spiral walkway, a place where most incomers never ventured, selling bundles of fresh herbs and various blends of herb tea?

Jack Miyata said that he was probably a harmless eccentric; Mark Griffin was convinced that he was some kind of exiled pervert or criminal; Sky Bolofo, who had filled the quantum processor of his large, red-framed spex with all kinds of talents and tricks, used a face-recognition program to identify the fellow, then pulled up his public page.

"His name is Algren Rees. He lives right here in the old city. He sells herbs and he also fixes up pets."

Jack said, "Is that it? No links to family or friends or favorites?"

Sky shrugged.

"He has to be hiding something," Mark said. "What about his private files?"

"No problem," Sky said complacently, but ran into heavy security as soon as he tried to hack into Algren Rees's password-protected files, and had to back out in a hurry.

Jack suggested that he could be a retired spy—just before the Quiet War kicked off, all of the Outer Colonies had been lousy with spies masquerading as diplomats and businesspeople—and Mark jumped all over the idea.

"Maybe he's still active," he said. "Selling herbs is his cover. What he's actually doing is gathering information. Keeping watch for terrorists and so-called freedom fighters."

Sky, his fingers pecking at the air in front of his face, using his spex's virtual keyboard to erase his electronic trail in case Algren Rees's security followed it, said that if the fellow wanted real cover, he should have made himself taller and skinnier, which cracked up the other two.

They were all the same age, fourteen, and went to the same school and lived in the same apartment complex in the new part of Xamba. They were also Quiet War buffs who restaged campaigns, sieges, and invasions on a war-gaming network, which was how

Jack had hooked up with the other two. Jack Miyata had moved to Xamba, Rhea, just two months ago. Unlike most city-states in the Saturn system, Xamba had remained neutral during the Quiet War. After the war had ended in defeat for every one of the rebellious Outer Colonies, Earth's Three Powers Alliance had settled the bulk of its administration there, building a new city of towers and domes above Xamba's underground chambers. Seven years later, New Xamba was still growing—Jack's engineer parents were involved in the construction of a thermal-exchange plant that would tap the residual heat of the little moon's rocky core and provide power for a brand-new sector.

Very few incomers from Earth ever ventured beyond their apartment complexes, malls, and leisure parks, but Jack had caught the exploration bug from his parents. He'd roamed through much of the old and new parts of Xamba, and after passing a pressure-suit training course had taken several long hikes through the untouched wilderness in the southern half of the big crater in which the city was located and from which it took its name, had climbed to the observatory at the top of the crater's central peak, and had visited the memorial at the crash site of a spaceship that had attempted to break the blockade during the war. It had been Jack's idea to take his two new friends to his latest discovery, the produce market in the oldest chamber of old Xamba. As far as Jack was concerned, the market was a treasure house of marvels, but as they'd wandered between stalls and displays of strange flowers and fruits and vegetables, streamers of dried waterweed, tanks of fish and shrimp, caged birds and rats, and bottle vivariums in which stag beetles lumbered like miniature rhinoceroses through jungles of moss and fern, Mark and Sky quickly made it clear that they thought it was smelly, horribly crowded with strangely dressed, alarmingly skinny giants, and, quite frankly, revoltingly primitive. When food makers could spin anything from yeast and algae, why would anyone want to eat the meat of real live animals, especially as they would have to kill them first? Kill and gut them and God knew what else. But all three agreed that there was definitely something intriguing about the herb seller, Algren Rees.

"Maybe he's a double agent," Jack said. "He's in the pay of the Three Powers, but he's gone over to the Outers, and they're using him to feed our side false information."

Mark nodded. "There's plenty of people who want to sabotage the reconstruction. Look at that blowout at the spaceport last month."

"The newsfeeds said it was an accident," Sky said. "Someone fitted some kind of widget upside down or the wrong way round."

"Of course they *said* it was an accident," Mark said scornfully. "It's the official line. But it doesn't mean it really *was* an accident."

He was a stocky boy who, with his pale skin, jet-black hair, and perpetual scowl, looked a lot like his policeman father. His mother was in the police too, in charge of security at the spaceport. He had a vivid imagination and an opinion about everything.

Jack wanted to know if Mark had inside information about the accident, and Mark smiled and said that maybe he didn't and maybe he did. "I had a feeling there was something wrong with Mr. Algren Rees as soon as I saw him. All good police have what they call gut instinct, and my gut very definitely told me that this fellow is a wrong one, and Sky's run-in with his over-the-top security confirmed it. It's up to all of us to find out exactly who he is, and why he's living here. It's our *duty*."

Jack and Mark quickly decided that they would follow Algren Rees—or "Algren Rees" as Mark called him, drawing quotation marks in the air with his little finger—and made Sky promise that he would use his data miners to ferret out anything and everything about the man. They were fourteen years old, secret masters of all they surveyed, possessed by restless energies and impulses that war gaming was no longer enough to satisfy, and hungry for adventure, for anything that would fill up the desert of the school holidays. Following Algren Rees and uncovering his secrets was just the beginning.

Algren Rees had no fixed routine. He spent only an hour or so at his stall in the produce market (which explained why Jack hadn't seen him there before); he tended the little garden where he grew his herbs; he sat outside the door of his apartment, a one-room efficiency on a terrace directly above the market, drinking tea or homemade lemonade and watching people go by; he took long, rambling walks through the old city. Jack saw more of the place in the three days he spent following the man, sometimes with Mark, sometimes on his own, than he had in the past two months.

The cylindrical chambers of old Xamba were buried inside the rock-hard water ice of the crater's eastern rimwall like so many bottles in a snowbank, and most had transparent endwalls facing what was generally reckoned to be one of the most classically beautiful views on all of Saturn's family of moons, across slumped terraces and flat, dusty plains toward the crater's central peak, which stood right at the edge of the close, curved horizon. In the little moon's microgravity, just 3 percent of Earth's, there was little difference between horizontal and vertical. Inside the old city's chambers, apartments, shops, cafés, workshops, and gardens were piled on top of each other in steep, terraced cliffs, rising up on either side of skinny, landscaped parks and canals in steep-sided troughs. Apart from the boats in the canals that linked the chambers, traffic was entirely pedestrian. Jack had no problem blending into the crowds as he trailed Algren Rees through markets and malls, parks and plazas, up and down ropeways, chutes, and chairlifts.

Although Mark insisted on teaching him some basic tradecraft (he claimed to have learnt it from his parents, but more likely had gotten it from some text), Jack figured out most of his moves for himself. Staying well behind his quarry and trying to anticipate his every move, walking straight past him or dodging up a ropeway or down a chute if he stopped to talk to someone, lurking inconspicuously when he lingered over a bulb of coffee at a café or a tube of beer at a bar. It was a lot more exciting than any war game, and a lot scarier, too. There was no wizard to ask for a clue or hint about what to do next, every decision was unconditionally permanent, and any mistake would be his last, game over. But Algren Rees seemed quite unaware that he was being followed, and by the third day Jack plucked up the courage to chat with the woman behind the counter of the café where the man ate his lunch and breakfast, learning that he had moved to Rhea two years ago and that he was originally from Greater Brazil, where he'd worked in the emergency relief services as a paramedic and helicopter pilot. He seemed well liked. He always stopped to talk to his neighbors when he met them as he went about his errands, and had long conversations with people who bought herbs or herb tea at his stall. He was a regular at the café and several bars in various parts of the city, trading fresh herbs for food and drink, and apart from eating out, his life seemed as austere as any monk's. Still, Jack didn't see how he could stretch the minuscule income from his market stall and fixing broken pets to cover the rent on his apartment, and his power and water and air taxes.

"I guess he must have some kind of private income," Jack said to Mark.

"He has secrets, is what he has," Mark said. "We don't even know if 'Algren Rees'"—he did the thing with his little fingers—"is his real name, no thanks to Sky for bailing on us. Some hacker he turned out to be, when it came down to it."

"He was majorly spooked when he ran up against our friend's electronic watchdogs," Jack said.

"Which also proves our friend has something to hide, or why else would he be using military-grade security?"

It was late in the evening. The city's sky lighting was beginning to dim. The two boys were sitting in a little park near the top of the east side of the chamber, taking turns with a pair of binoculars to keep watch on Algren Rees's apartment, which was near the top of the west side. Across the wide gulf of air, the man was sitting on the little raised porch outside his front door, wearing shorts and nothing else and reading a book. Books printed on paper were a quirky tradition in old Xamba. Algren Rees read slowly, licking the top of his thumb before turning each page. Yellow light from inside the apartment spilled around him. Pretty soon, judging by the last three days, Algren Rees would turn in. He wasn't a night owl.

"What we need to do," Mark said, "is take this to the next level."

Jack felt a tingling rush of anticipatory excitement. "What do you mean?"

"I mean we have to get into his apartment."

"You're kidding."

Mark had a determined look, a jut of his heavy jaw like a dog gripping a bone it isn't willing to let go of. "It's what real spies would do. I bet he has all kinds of stuff stashed away in there. Stuff that would crack this case wide open."

"He probably has all kinds of security, too," Jack said.

"Oh, I can handle that."

"Right."

"It's simply a matter of police tradecraft," Mark said.

"Right."

"I'd like to tell you more, but if I did, I'd have to kill you afterward," Mark said. Like his father, he never smiled when he made a joke.

They decided to do it the very next day, even though it was a Monday, the one day in the week when the produce market was closed, when Algren Rees wouldn't be safely occupied at his stall for an hour or so. Jack would find some way of keeping the man at the café where he ate breakfast; meanwhile, Mark would break into the apartment, to see what he could see.

It wasn't much of a plan, but Jack couldn't think of anything better. He was pretty sure that Algren Rees wasn't any kind of spy, but he'd developed a curious feeling of kinship with the man during the time he'd spent trailing him around the chambers of old Xamba. Yet although he'd spent a couple dozen hours in his company, he still knew almost nothing about him. It had become a matter of pride to find out who Algren Rees really was, and why he had chosen to come here, and live amongst the Outers.

◆ ◆ ◆

When they met up early the next morning, Mark wanted to know what was in the box Jack was clutching to his chest. Jack told him that it was a foolproof way of keeping the man busy.

"I'll tell you what it is if you'll tell me how you're going to break into his apartment."

"I'm not going to break in," Mark said with a sly smile. "Are you sure you can keep him busy for half an hour?"

"Absolutely," Jack said, tapping the top of the plastic box, feeling what was inside stir, a slow, heavy movement that subsided after a moment.

Actually, he wasn't sure at all. He'd slept badly, his mind spinning, tracing and retracing every part of a plan that seemed increasingly silly and flimsy. Two hours later, when Algren Rees finally left his apartment and he followed him to the café, the muscles of Jack's legs felt watery and his stomach was doing somersaults. But it was too late to back out. As Jack skimmed up a short ropeway to the café, he knew that Mark would be breaking into the apartment.

The café was little more than a bamboo counter in the shade of a huge fig tree, with half a dozen stools, a hot plate, and a hissing coffee machine that the owner, a very tall, incredibly skinny woman with long snow-white hair, had built herself, using a design centuries old. The food was prepared from whatever was in season in the garden spread on either side of the fig tree, and whatever came in trade—the citizens of old Xamba had a complicated economy based on barter of goods and services.

It was the middle of the morning. Algren Rees and Jack were the only customers. Jack set the plastic box on the counter and asked the owner for an orange juice, then turned to the man and said as casually as he could manage that he'd heard that he treated sick pets.

"Who told you that?"

Algren Rees, hunched over a bowl of porridge flecked with nuts and seeds, didn't look up when he spoke. He had a husky voice and a thick accent: the voice of a villain from some cheap virtuality.

"She did," Jack said, nodding to the owner of the café, who was filling a blender with orange segments and a handful of strawberries.

"I guess I did," the woman said with cheerful carelessness, and switched on the blender. She'd braided her hair into a pigtail that twitched down her back as she moved about in the narrow space behind the counter.

"Stop by my apartment when you've had your breakfast," Algren Rees told Jack. "It's just around the corner, down the ropeway, past a clump of black bamboo. The one with the red door."

He was eating his porridge slowly but steadily. In a few minutes he would be finished. He'd walk back to his apartment, find that red door open . . .

Jack pushed the box an inch along the counter and said, "I have it right here."

"So I see," Algren Rees said, although he still hadn't looked up. "And I have my breakfast right here, too."

"It belongs to my little sister," Jack said, the little lie sliding out with surprising ease. He added, "She loves it to bits, but we're scared that it's dying."

"Why don't you take a look, Al," the woman said as she placed the bulb of orange juice in front of Jack. "The worst that can happen is that it'll improve your karma."

"It will need much more than fixing a pet to do that," Algren Rees said, smiling at her.

The woman smiled, too, and Jack was reminded of the way his parents shared a private joke.

"All right, kid," Algren Rees said. "Show me what you got."

It was a mock turtle, a halflife creature that produced no waste or unpleasant odors and needed only a couple of hours of trickle charge and a cupful of water a day. It had large, dark, soulful eyes, a soft yellow beak, a shell covered in pink fur, and a fifty-word vocabulary. Although it didn't belong to Jack's wholly imaginary little sister but to the youngest daughter of Jack's neighbors, it really was sick. It had grown slow and sluggish, its fur was matted and threadbare, its eyes were filmed with white matter, and its breath was foully metallic.

Algren Rees studied it for a moment, then took a diagnostic pen from one of the many pockets of his brocade waistcoat, lifted the mock turtle from the box and turned it upside down, and plugged the instrument into the socket behind its front leg.

"Tickles," the turtle complained, working its stubby legs feebly.

"It's for your own good," Algren Rees told it. "Be still."

He had small, strong hands and neatly trimmed fingernails. There were oval scars on the insides of his wrists; he'd had neural sockets once upon a time, the kind that interface with smart machinery. He squinted at the holographic readout that blossomed above the shaft of the diagnostic pen, then asked Jack, "Do you know what a prion is?"

Jack's mind went horribly blank for a moment; then a fragment of a biology lesson surfaced, and he grabbed at it gratefully. "Proteins have to fold up the right way to work properly. Prions are proteins that fold up wrongly."

Algren Rees nodded. "The gene wizard who designed these

things used a lot of freeware, and one of the myoelectric proteins has a tendency to turn prions. That's what's wrong with your sister's pet. It's a self-catalyzing reaction—do you know what that means?"

"It spreads like a fire. Prions turn ordinary proteins into more prions."

Algren Rees unplugged the diagnostic pen and settled the mock turtle in the box. "The myoelectric proteins are what powers it. When they fold the wrong way they can no longer hold a charge, and when enough have folded wrongly, it will die."

"Can you fix it?"

Algren Rees shook his head. "The best thing would be to put it to sleep."

He looked genuinely sorry, and Jack felt a wave of guilt pass through him. Right now, Mark was breaking into the man's apartment, rifling through his possessions . . .

"If you like, I can do it right now," Algren Rees said.

"I'll have to tell my sister first."

Algren Rees shrugged and started to push away from the counter, saying, "I'm sorry I couldn't help you, kid."

"Wait," Jack said desperately, knowing that Mark must still be in the apartment. Adding, when Algren Rees looked at him, "I mean, I want to ask you, why is someone like you living here?"

"Why does who I am have anything to do with where I live?"

There was a sudden sharpness in the man's voice.

"Well, I mean, you're an incomer. From Earth," Jack said, feeling the heat of a blush rise in his face. "And incomers, they all live in the new city, don't they? But you live here, you sell herbs . . ."

"You seem to know an awful lot about me, kid. Why the interest?"

"I saw you at the produce market," Jack said, blushing harder, certain that he'd been caught out.

Algren Rees studied him for a moment, pinching the point of his neat black beard between finger and thumb. Then he smiled and said, "I had the feeling I'd seen you before. You like the market, huh?"

"It's one of my favorite places in the old city."

"And you like the old city?"

Jack nodded.

"Most incomers don't much care for it."

Jack nodded again.

"So maybe we have something in common, you and I. Think about it, kid," Algren Rees said. "If you can figure it out, stop by my stall sometime. But right now I have an appointment to keep."

The woman behind the counter asked him to have a good thought on her behalf, and then he was skimming away. Not toward his apartment, but in the opposite direction, toward the chute that dropped to the floor of the chamber.

Jack didn't dare ask the woman (who refused his offer to pay for his juice, telling him that he could bring her some sour oranges next time he visited the produce market) where Algren Rees was headed, who he was going to meet. As he set off after the man, he called Mark, told him about the conversation, told him that he believed that Algren Rees was going to meet someone. Mark said that he'd catch up, and ten minutes later arrived breathless and excited at the canalside jetty just as Algren Rees was climbing into one of the dinghies that ferried people around the city's waterways.

"He's a spy, all right," he told Jack.

"You found something. What did you find?"

Mark patted the pouch of his jumper. "I'll show you after we get going."

There were several high-sided dinghies waiting at the jetty. Jack and Mark jumped into one, and Mark stuck something in a slot in the fat sensor rod that stuck up at its prow and ordered it to follow the boat that had just left.

As their dinghy headed toward the tunnel that linked the chamber with its neighbor, rising and falling on the tall, sluggish, low-gravity waves that rolled along the canal, Jack said, "That's how you got into his apartment, isn't it? You used that card on the lock."

He was sitting in the stern, the plastic box with the mock turtle inside it on his knees.

Mark, standing at the prow with one hand on top of the sensor rod, said, "Of course I did."

"I suppose you stole it."

"No one stole anything," Mark said. "I borrowed my mother's card last night, and Sky cloned it."

"If she finds out—"

"As long as I don't get into trouble, my parents don't care what I do. They're too busy with their jobs, too busy *advancing their careers*, too busy *making money*," Mark said. He had his back to Jack, but Jack could hear the bitterness in his voice. "Which is fine with me, because once they make enough, we'll leave this rotten little ball of ice and go back to Earth."

There was a short silence. Jack was embarrassed, feeling that he'd had an unwanted glimpse of his friend's true feelings through a crack in his armor of careless toughness. At last, he said, "If we prove that Algren Rees really is a spy, your parents will be proud of you."

Mark turned around and said carelessly, "Oh, he's a spy, all right. Guess what I found in his apartment?"

It was the kind of question you were bound to fail to answer correctly, so Jack shrugged.

Mark, smiling a devilish smile, reached into the pouch of his jumper and drew out a small silvery gun.

Jack was shocked and excited. "Is it real?"

"Of course it is. And it's charged, too," Mark said, pointing to a tiny green light that twinkled above the crosshatched grip.

He explained that it was a railgun that used a magnetic field to fire metal splinters tipped with explosive or toxin, and showed Jack the Navy sigil stamped on top of its reaction chamber.

"If he's a spy, why does he have a Navy sidearm?" Jack said.

"Maybe he was in the Navy before he became a spy. Or he killed someone in the Navy, and kept this as a souvenir," Mark said.

Discovering the gun had made him bold and reckless. He talked about catching Algren Rees in the middle of some act of sabotage, about arresting him and forcing him to tell everything about the conspiracy in which he was clearly involved.

Although Jack was excited, too, he could see that his friend was getting carried away. "This doesn't change our plan," he said. "We follow the man and see what he gets up to, and then we decide what to do."

Mark shrugged and said blithely, "We'll see what we'll see."

"We shouldn't just charge in," Jack said. "For one thing, if he really is a spy, he's dangerous. Spies were hardwired with all kinds of wild talents."

"If you're scared, you can get off the boat anytime you want."

"Of course I'm not scared," Jack said, even though he was, more than he cared to admit. "All I'm saying is that we have to be careful."

Algren Rees's dinghy stopped three times, dropping people off and picking up others, before it headed down a long transparent tunnel, with Mark and Jack's dinghy following a couple hundred meters behind it. The tunnel was laid along the edge of a steep cliff, with a stunning view of the crater. It was the middle of Rhea's night. Saturn hung full and huge overhead in the black sky like God's own Christmas ornament, the razor-thin line of his rings stretching out on either side of his banded face, his smoggy light laid across terraced icefields. Jack leaned back, and for the ten minutes it took to traverse the tunnel was lost in wonder at the intricate beauty of the gas giant's yellow and dirty-white and salmon-pink bands, their frills and frozen waves, forgetting all about the gun in Mark's pouch, forgetting all about following Algren Rees.

At the end of the tunnel, the canal entered a skinny lake pinched between two steep slopes of flowering meadows and stands of trees and bamboos. It was the city's cemetery, where bodies were buried in soil and trees planted over them, so that their freight of carbon and nitrogen and phosphorous and other useful elements could reenter the loop of the city's ecosystem.

It was a quiet, beautiful place, artificially lit in the even golden tones of a late summer afternoon. On one steep slope was the black pyramid, hewn from crystalline iron mined from the heart of an asteroid, that commemorated those who had died in accidents during the construction of the old city; on the other was a slim white column topped by an eternal blue flame, the monument to the citizens of Xamba who had been killed during the Quiet War. For although the city had remained neutral, more than a thousand of its citizens had died because they'd been trapped in sieges in rebellious cities, or in ships crippled by neutron lasers, microwave bursters, and EMP mines. Apart from these two monuments, and the bone-white paths that wandered here and there, the woods and meadows seemed untouched by human hands, a tame wilderness where birds and cat-sized deer and teddy bear–sized pandas roamed freely.

Algren Rees and two women disembarked at a jetty of black wood with a red-painted Chinese arch at one end. The two women went off along the lakeshore; Algren Rees started up a steep path that bent around a grove of shaggy cypress trees. As soon as their dinghy nudged the jetty, Mark sprang out, bounded through the arch, and set off up the path after Algren Rees. Jack had to hurry to catch up with him. They went around the cypress grove, climbed a ropeway alongside a tiny stream that ran over white rocks speckled with chunky black shards of shock quartz, followed Algren Rees as he cut through a belt of pines.

Beyond the trees, a lumpy heath of coarse tussock grass and purple heather and clumps of flowering gorse rose in steep terraces to meet the edge of the chamber's curved blue roof. The flame-topped white column of the monument to Xamba's war dead stood halfway between the pines and the painted sky. Algren Rees stood in front of it, still as a statue, his bald head bowed.

Crouched behind a pine tree, Jack and Mark discussed what they'd do when Algren Rees's coconspirator appeared, agreeing that they might have to split up, follow the men separately, and meet up again later. But no one came. Big silver and gold butterflies tumbled over each other above a clump of gorse; rabbits emerged from their burrows and began to nibble at the grass. At last, Algren Rees turned from the monument and moved on up the slope, silhouetted against the solid blue sky for a moment when he reached the top, then dropped out of sight.

Rabbits leaped away in huge, graceful arcs as Jack and Mark followed the man. Jack still hadn't quite mastered the art of moving quickly in low gravity, and Mark outpaced him at once, making a bounding run up the rough slope, disappearing between rocks spattered with orange lichens. Jack hauled himself through the rocks, discovered a narrow stairway down to the floor of a narrow gully, and saw Algren Rees and Mark facing each other in front of a steel door set in a wide frame painted with yellow-and-black warning chevrons—the entrance to an airlock. Mark was pointing the pistol at Algren Rees's chest, but the stocky man was ignoring him, looking instead at Jack as he came down the stairs, saying mildly, "Tell your friend he has made a mistake."

"Kneel down," Mark said. He was wavering like a sapling in a high wind, but he held the pistol steady, bracing his right wrist with his left hand. "Kneel down and put your hands on your head."

Algren Rees didn't move, saying, "I believe that is mine. How did you get it?"

"Just kneel down."

"I must suppose that you broke into my apartment while your friend"—he looked at Jack again, a sharp, unfriendly look—"kept me busy. What is this about? What silly game are you playing?"

"It's no game," Mark said. "We know you're a spy."

Algren Rees laughed.

"Shut up!"

Mark screamed it so loudly it echoed off the blue sky curving overhead.

Jack, clutching the plastic box to his chest, frightened that his friend would shoot Algren Rees there and then, said, "You said that you had an appointment with someone. Who is it?"

"Is that what this is about? Yes, I visit someone. I visit her every Monday. Everyone knows that." Algren Rees looked at Mark and said, "Hand over the pistol, kid. Give it to me before you get into trouble."

"You're a spy," Mark said stubbornly. "I'm arresting you. Kneel down—"

There was a blur of movement, a rush of air. Mark was knocked into Jack, they both fell down, and Algren Rees was standing a yard away, the pistol in his hand. He was sweating and trembling lightly all over, like a horse that had just run the hardest race of its life. He stared at the two boys, and Jack felt a spike of fear cleave right through him, thinking that the man was going to shoot them and dump their bodies in some deep crevasse outside. But then the man tucked the pistol in the waistband of his shorts and said, "My nervous system was rewired when I was in the Navy. A long time ago, but it still works. Go home, little boys. Go back to your brave new city. Never let me see you again, and I won't tell anyone about this. But if I find you following me again, I will have a long hard talk with your parents, and with the police, too. Go!"

Jack and Mark picked themselves up, and ran.

On the boat ride back, Mark vented his anger and fear and shame by making all kinds of plans and boastful threats. He promised vengeance. He promised to find out the truth. He promised to bring the man to justice. He told Jack that if he said so much as *one word* about this, he'd get into so much trouble he'd never find his way out again.

Jack, with the cold clarity that fear sometimes brings, told Mark that he was being a fool. Even if Algren Rees was a spy, there was nothing they could do about it because they were outside the law, too. If they went to the police, how were they going to explain that they'd broken into his apartment, stolen his gun, and threatened him with it?

"*If* he's a spy?" Mark said. "The gun *proves* he's a spy!"

"Does it? The gun is a Navy sidearm—you showed me the sigil yourself. And he said that he was in the Navy."

Mark sneered. "I suppose you believe him."

"And if he really was a spy, he would have shot us after he took it back."

"Yes, and he used some kind of wild talent to take it back. He speeded up. Which also proves that he's a spy."

"He took his own gun back, Mark. The gun you stole from his apartment. And we can't do anything about it because he threatened to go to our parents."

"It's an empty threat," Mark said stubbornly. "He can't go to our parents, or to the police, either, because if he did, it would blow his cover. It's a deadlock, don't you see? And we have to figure out how to turn it to our advantage."

Jack couldn't get Mark to promise that this was an end to it, and spent the next few days in a misery of fear and guilty anticipation. He avoided his parents as much as he could, either hiding away in his room, halfheartedly fiddling with his virtual model of the invasion of Paris, Dione (but after his adventure had gone so badly wrong, playing at soldiers no longer had the appeal it once did), or mooching around the apartment complex's mall.

That was where he met Sky Bolofo. Sky wanted to know what had made Mark so terminally pissed off with Algren Rees, and eventually got Jack to confess everything.

"Wow. You're lucky the guy didn't report you," Sky said when Jack was finished.

"I know," Jack said. "The problem is, Mark still thinks he's some kind of spy. I think he's going to do something stupid."

They were sitting in the mall's food court. The chatter of the people around them rose through the fronds of tall palms toward the glass dome. Sky studied Jack through his red-framed spex and said, "I think so, too."

"You do? What's Mark been saying?"

That was when Jack learned that their friend had told Sky that he was going to settle things once and for all, and had asked for Sky's help.

Sky told Jack, "I said good luck, but it was nothing to do with me." And then, "Hey, where are you going?"

"I have to settle something, too," Jack said.

He tried to phone Mark, but Mark was screening his calls and wouldn't answer his door when Jack went to his apartment. But by then Jack had more or less worked out what Mark was planning to do. Each and every Monday, Algren Rees had a mysterious appointment. And Jack and Mark had confronted him at the entrance to an airlock, which meant that it was probably somewhere outside the city, on the surface . . .

Jack knew that he couldn't tell either his parents or Mark's parents about what had happened, and what he believed Mark was planning. He was just as guilty as Mark, and would get into just as much trouble. He'd have to sort it out himself, and because Mark was refusing to talk to him, he'd have to catch him in the act, stop him before he did something really dumb.

When he asked Sky to help him out, Sky naturally refused at

first, just as he'd refused to help Mark, but quickly changed his mind when Jack reminded him that if Mark was caught, *everything* would come out, including the police card that Sky had cloned. After Jack explained what he thought Mark was planning to do, Sky said that in the three years he'd been living in New Xamba, he'd never once stepped outside and didn't intend to break that record now, but he could download a hack into Jack's spex that would give him full access to the city's CCTV system so that Jack could use it to follow Mark wherever he went.

"I'll patch in a demon with a face-recognition program. It'll alert you if Mark gets anywhere near an airlock. And that's *all* I'm doing. And if anyone asks you where you got this stuff, tell them it's freeware."

"Absolutely," Jack said. "I know all of this is my fault. If I hadn't taken him to the market, and agreed that there was something funny about the guy selling herbs—"

"Don't beat yourself up," Sky said. "Mark would have got into trouble all by himself sooner or later. He's bored, he hates living here, and he doesn't exactly get on with his parents. It's quite obvious that this whole thing is some kind of silly rebellion."

"You hate living here, too," Jack said. "But you didn't break into someone's apartment and steal a gun."

"I don't much care for the place," Sky said, "but as long as I'm left alone to get on with my own thing, it doesn't matter where I live. Mark, though, he's like a tiger in a cage. Be careful, Jack. Don't let him get you into any more trouble."

The demon woke Jack in the early hours of Monday morning. He fumbled for his spex, shut off the alarm, stared dazedly at a skewed video picture of Mark sitting in a dressing frame that was assembling a pressure suit around him, then realized with a surge of adrenaline that this was it. That Mark really was going through with it.

The main airlocks of the apartment complex were in an ancillary structure reached by a long, slanting tunnel. Mark was long gone by the time Jack reached it, but despite his bladder-burning need to follow his friend, Jack remembered his training. When you went out onto the airless surface, even the slightest oversight or equipment malfunction could be deadly. Once the dressing frame had fitted him with a pressure suit, he carefully checked the suit's power systems and lifesystem, and because he didn't know how long he was going to be outside, took time to hook up a spare air pack before making his way through the three sets of doors.

The outer door of the airlock opened onto a flat, dusty apron trodden everywhere with cleated bootprints, reminding Jack of the snow around the ski lifts at the mountain resort where he and his parents had several times gone on holiday. Inside the city, which kept Earth time, it was six in the morning; outside, it was the middle of Rhea's 108-hour-long day. Saturn's slender crescent was cocked overhead, lassoed by the slender ellipse of his rings. The sun was a brilliant diamond whose cold light gleamed on the towers and domes of the new city and the great curve of the rimwall behind them. Although the rimwall was more than three miles away, the sculpted folds of its cliffs and its gently undulating crest stood sharp and clear against the black, airless sky.

Jack tried and failed to pick up the radio transponder of Mark's pressure suit—Mark must have switched it off, but that didn't matter, because Jack knew exactly where his friend was going. He walked around the side of the airlock to the racks where the cycles were charging, and found to his surprise that every rack was occupied. Then he realized that Mark, like most incomers, had never taken a pressure-suit training course (he must have used the cloned police card to force the dressing frame to fit him with a suit) and had never before taken a single step outside the city, so there was no reason why he should know about the cycles.

They were three-wheeled, with fat, diamond-mesh tires, a low-slung seat, and a simple control yoke. Jack pulled one from the rack, clambered onto it, and, feeling a blithe optimism, set off toward the cemetery chamber at the eastern end of the old city. He was on a cycle, and Mark was on foot. It was no contest.

He followed a polymer-sealed track that, throwing wide loops around cone-shaped rockfalls, cut through the fields of boulders that stretched out from the base of the rimwall's steep cliffs. He drove slowly, scanning the jumbled wilderness, and after ten minutes spotted a twinkle of movement amongst the tan boulders and ink-black shadows. He stopped the cycle, used the magnification feature of his visor, and saw a figure in a white pressure suit moving in a kind of slow-motion kangaroo hop. Jack plotted a course and drove half a mile along the track before turning toward the cliffs, intending to intercept Mark when he reached the cemetery chamber's airlock.

The going was easy at first, with only a few outlying boulders to steer around, but then the ground began to rise up and down in concentric ridges like frozen waves, and the rubble fallen from the cliffs grew denser, tumbled blocks of dirty ice of every size, some as big as houses, all frozen harder than granite. Jack kept losing sight of Mark, and piled on the speed in the broad dips between the ridges, anxious that he'd lose sight of him completely. To his left, the rumpled plain of the crater floor stretched away toward the central peak; to his right, the lighted circles of the endwalls of the old city's buried chambers glowed with green light in the face of the rimwall cliffs, like the portholes of a huge ocean liner or the windows of a giant's aquarium. He was driving toward the crest of the fifth or sixth ridge when the razor-sharp, jet black shadow between two shattered blocks turned out to be a narrow but deep crevice that neatly trapped the cycle's front wheel. The cycle slewed, Jack hit the brakes, everything tipped sideways with a bone-rattling shock, and then he was hanging by his safety harness, looking up at the black sky and Saturn's ringed crescent. He managed to undo the harness's four-way clasp and scramble free, and checked the integrity of his pressure suit before he heaved the cycle's front tire out of the crevice. Its mesh was badly flattened along one side, and the front fork was crumpled beyond easy repair. There was no way the machine was going to take him any farther.

Well, his suit was fine, he wasn't injured, he had plenty of air and power, and if he got into trouble, he could always phone for help. There was nothing for it. He was going to have to follow Mark on foot.

It took two hours to slog four miles across the rough terrain, skirting around huge chunks and blocks, crabbing down uneven slopes into the dips between ridges and climbing back out again, finding a way around jagged crevices. Sometimes Jack glimpsed Mark's pressure-suited figure plodding no more than four or five hundred yards ahead of him, but for most of the time he had only his suit's navigation system to guide him. He was drenched with sweat, his ankles and knees were aching, and he had just switched to his reserve air pack when at last he reached the track that led to the airlock of the cemetery chamber. Jack went slowly through the rubble at the edge of the track, creeping from shadow to shadow, imagining Mark crouched behind a boulder with a gun he'd stolen from his mother or father, waiting for Algren Rees . . .

But there was no need for caution. Mark's white pressure suit was sprawled on the track just two hundred yards from the airlock, a red light flashing on its backpack. Adrenaline kicked in: Jack reached Mark in three bounds, managed to roll him onto his side. Behind the visor of the suit's helmet, Mark's face was tinged blue, and although his eyes were open, their pupils were fixed and unseeing.

Jack switched on his distress beacon and began to drag Mark's pressure-suited body toward the yellow-painted steel door of the airlock. He was halfway there when the door slid open and a figure in a pressure suit stepped out.

"You kids again," Algren Rees's voice said over the phone link. "I swear you'll be the death of me."

Two days later, after the medivac crew had whisked Mark away to the hospital (when its oxygen supply had run dangerously low, his pressure suit had put him in a coma and cooled him down to keep him alive for as long as possible, but it had been a close thing), after Jack had confessed everything to his parents, Algren Rees took him to see the place he visited each and every week.

There was a kind of ski lift that carried them half a mile up a sheer face of rock-hard black ice to the top of the rimwall, and a diamond-mesh path that climbed a frozen ridge to a viewpoint that looked across slopes of ejecta toward a flat, cratered plain. Jack had been there before. He had seen the yard-high steel pillar before, had read the three simple, moving sentences on the plaque set into its angled top, had listened to the brief story its induction loop had played on his pressure suit's phone, the story of how the freighter pilot Rosa Lux had saved Xamba in the last seconds of her life. But even if he hadn't been there, he wouldn't have needed to read the plaque or listen to the looped message; the story was part of the reason why Algren Rees came here every week.

"She was flying one of those little freelance freighters that are mostly engine, with a tiny internal hold and a cabin not much bigger than a coffin," Algren Rees said. "She was hauling a special cargo—the mayor of the city of Camelot, Mimas. He had been one of the leaders of the rebellion that started the Quiet War. When Camelot fell, he managed to escape, and if he had reached Xamba, he would have been granted political asylum and could have caused all kinds of trouble.

"I was a singleship pilot, part of the picket which orbited Rhea to prevent ships leaving or arriving. When Rosa Lux's freighter was detected, mine was the only ship able to intercept her, and even then I had to burn almost all my fuel to do it. She was a daring pilot and had come in fast and low, skimming the surface of Rhea just a mile up and using its gravity to slow her so that she could enter into a long orbit and come in to land when she made her second pass. That was what she was doing when my orbit intercepted hers. I had only one chance to stop her, and I made a mess of it.

"I fired two missiles, and both were confused by her countermeasures. One hit the surface; the other missed her ship by a few hundred yards but managed to blow itself up as it zoomed past. It damaged her main drive and changed her vector—her course. She was no longer heading for Xamba's spaceport, but for the rimwall, and the city. I saw her fire her maneuvering thrusters. I saw her dump fuel from her main tank. I saw her sacrifice herself so that she would miss the city. Everything happened in less than five seconds, and she barely missed the top of the rimwall, but miss it she did. And crashed here, and died."

It was early in the morning. The brilliant star of the sun was low in the black sky, throwing long, tangled shadows across the moonscape, but the long scar left by Rosa Lux's ship was clearly visible, a gleaming sword aimed at the eastern horizon.

Algren Rees said, "Rosa Lux had only five seconds to live, and she used that little time to save the lives of a hundred thousand people. The funny thing was, the mayor of Camelot survived. He was riding in a coffin filled with impact gel, cooled down much the same way your friend was cooled down. When the ship crashed, his coffin was blasted free and pinwheeled across the landscape, but it survived more or less intact. The mayor was revived and successfully claimed asylum. He still lives in Xamba—he married a local woman, and runs the city's library. The memorial doesn't tell you that, and there's something else it doesn't tell you, either."

There was silence. Jack watched the scar shine in the new sunlight, waited for Algren Rees to finish his story. He was certain that there would be a moral; it was the kind of story that always had a moral. But the silence stretched, and at last Jack asked the man why he'd come to Rhea.

"After the war, I left the Navy and went back to Greater Brazil, trained as a paramedic, and got on with my life. Then my wife was killed in a train crash. It was more life-changing than the war. I decided to make a last visit to the place where the most intense and most important thing in my life had happened. And soon after I arrived, I fell in love with someone. You have met her, actually."

"The woman who owns the café!"

There was another silence. Then Algren Rees said, "You've been here before."

"Sure."

"And I bet it was your idea to visit the produce market."

"I guess," Jack said cautiously, wondering where this was going.

"You're an unusual boy, Jack. Unusual for an incomer, that is. Most of them don't set foot outside the new city. The Three Powers Alliance won the war, but it doesn't know what to do with what it won. That's why it will lose control of it, by and by. And when the Outers realize that, there could be another war. Unless there are more people like you, Jack. Incomers who reach out. Who try to understand the strange moons and habitats of the Outer System. People like you and me. People like Rosa Lux."

"She was an incomer, too?"

"She was born on Earth and moved to Saturn five years before the Quiet War began. The memorial doesn't tell you that because as far as the Outers are concerned, Rosa Lux was one of them. But she was an incomer, just like us.

"I fell in love when I returned to Dione, Jack, and even though it didn't last, I decided to make a home here. But what brought me here to begin with was a chance encounter with another woman—the bravest person I know about. A chance encounter, an instant's decision, can change a single life, or even change history. Perhaps you're too young to know it, but I think something like that has already happened to you."

Jack thought about this, thought about all that had happened in the past week, and realized that his new friend might be right. Time would tell.

PAUL McAULEY was born in England in 1955 and currently lives in London. He worked as a researcher in biology at various universities and then lectured in botany at University of St Andrews for six years, before becoming a full-time writer.

McAuley's first novel, *Four Hundred Billion Stars*, was published in 1988 and was followed by a string of cutting-edge science fiction novels, including *Red Dust*, *Pasquale's Angel*, the Confluence Trilogy, and *Fairyland*. In the past few years he's focused more on sophisticated science thrillers like *The Secret of Life*, *Whole Wide World*, and *Mind's Eye*. He has won the Philip K. Dick Memorial Award, the Arthur C. Clarke Award, and the John W. Campbell Memorial Award. His short fiction has been collected in *The King of the Hill* and *Little Machines*. His most recent novel is *Cowboy Angels*.

His Web site is www.omegacom.demon.co.uk.

AUTHOR'S NOTE

If you've ever had to move to a new town, maybe one just ten miles down the road, maybe one on the other side of the country, you'll know that the basic things in life don't change. Traffic keeps to the same side of the street; the supermarkets and chain stores look more or less the same, and sell the same kinds of things; electrical sockets, national holidays, the alphabet, and the price of stamps . . . all of that kind of stuff is the same. Pretty soon you've worked out where everything is, made some new friends, and learned all the stories that make one place different from the next; pretty soon it seems like you've lived there all your life.

But suppose you move to another country, on the other side of the world. Maybe the language is different; the money definitely is, and cars are driving on the wrong side of the road, and they're smaller, too. It's hotter than you're used to, or colder and wetter. Christmas is in the middle of summer, and people celebrate it at barbecue parties on the beach. Or it's in the middle of winter, and people sit around in overheated houses and eat too much and watch too much TV. Well, people can adapt to all kinds of things, even driving on the left instead of the right. It'll take you a while to settle into your new way of life, but you'll manage it, in the end.

Now, suppose you move to a different world . . .

Science fiction is all about changes as big as moving to a new world—or even bigger. Although it's firmly grounded in what's possible (the impossible, such as dragons or magic, is the realm of fantasy), it deals with new ideas and weird and wonderful things capable of creating new worlds or new ways of living or thinking that don't yet exist. Rhea, the world Jack Miyata has moved to, is real enough. It's the second-biggest moon of Saturn. On a clear night when Saturn is above the horizon, you can catch a glimpse of it with a good but not especially powerful telescope. NASA robots such as Voyager and Cassini have taken photographs of its surface. But in this story, Rhea and the other moons of Saturn (Saturn has more moons than the Sun has planets, and they're all different) have been changed because people are living on them. And the people who live on the moons of Saturn have been changed, too. Not only because they live in a place where the gravity is so much less than the earth's, and anyone who wants to take a stroll in the countryside around the city must remember to take enough air with them, but because their history and their stories are different and new. After all, science fiction isn't only about the future and new worlds; like this story, it's also about the people who have to make their homes there.

POST-IRONIC STRESS SYNDROME

Tricia Sullivan

Diego gave me the M-ask at a window booth in Friendly's. I didn't look at it right away. It sat on the red formica between us, cushioned by a Friendly's napkin. It was matte black and virtually featureless. It looked more like a hockey mask than an actual face.

It was waiting for me to put it on and make it my own.

"Okay," Diego said. "Final version. Let's see how it fits."

I glanced over Diego's shoulder. There was a cute guy with blond dreads two tables away. Maybe a college student, or a senior at Midland Park—they're allowed to go out for lunch. But it was strange that he was alone. He was sketching left-handed in a notebook, using rapid, intense strokes. He had nice legs, and I wondered what sport he played.

Diego poked the whipped cream on his sundae with a long-handled spoon, but he didn't eat. He leaned toward me.

"It's costing us a fortune to secure this timespace," he muttered. "Could you do it, already?"

"I'm not putting it on here," I said.

"It's perfectly safe."

"I'll do it in private," I said.

"I need to see it on you."

I shook my head. "No."

"No? What do you mean, 'no'?"

"No."

"I'm not happy."

"So spank me," I said. "I want to put it on in private."

"There is no such thing as private, under that M-ask," Diego said. "Get used to it."

I glanced at Cute Blond Guy again and caught him looking back at me. He quickly looked away.

"Maja!" Diego nudged my foot under the table.

I took a long breath, like a free diver. I picked up the M-ask. It smelled of apricots and weighed almost nothing. My fingers left greasy sweat marks on it.

Under the M-ask I stretch like Silly Putty. My awareness shoots across space. All I have to do is think of a location, and I'm there.

The sensation of freedom is overwhelming, until I remember my training and set about performing the routine assessments that will test the fit of the M-ask. I go to the most distant point of the Scatter to view our current status.

It could be better. . . . The insurgents have cut a swath across the far side of the Scatter. Long-haul flesh carriers move inward in a steady stream: settlers abandoning the frontier. In recent Battles we lost M-eq control of two moons and a planet, and some stations in Broca's Belt were abandoned. Mining equipment clings like dead spiders to the sides of asteroids.

My gaze moves effortlessly across distance and between scales. I can go anywhere that we have M-eq stations—and the Scatter is full of them. Some of our equipment was wrecked in the most recent Battle, of course. Yet, in turn, we've conquered some of their stations and adapted several of their ships. Their communications are substandard and they have people starving on three worlds because of predictions software errors. At least our infrastructures are still in place, and we are consolidating our gain.

In sum: on the brink of the latest Battle, we seem to be evenly matched with the enemy.

As I complete my scan I pick up a new battle cruiser, one of ours. It's zipping through Broca's Belt like a hornet on methedrine, bound for Losamo.

"That's enough," said Diego. "Your face looks okay."

I changed to Local Mode. There was a little jolt as my awareness of the Scatter retreated, and a second jolt when I turned to the mirrored column beside the table and checked myself out. With the M-ask melded to me, my skin was the same soft brown, my hair still black and straight; but my features were subtly different. I looked older—maybe as old as eighteen.

I smiled. I had to admit the M-ask was an improvement on nature.

"Look at me. I want to see your eyes."

Dutifully, I looked.

Diego scrutinized me like I was a zoo exhibit, consulted his Shade, and then nodded slowly.

"Good. Your visual cortex is well shielded."

"Is it?" I said, amused. *Shielded from what?* I wondered briefly, but didn't ask. Diego was liable to launch into a long and pedantic explanation about the hardware. But I'd been waiting long enough:

twenty months in this timespace, training, while the Project refined the M-ask. Enough already.

I stood up.

Diego had his head down and was muttering something to his Shade as he escorted me toward the door to the sunlit street. Nobody but Diego could see his Shade, so he looked weird. I gave an embarrassed little smile as we passed Cute Blond Guy's table. Cute Blond Guy stood up. Diego steered me away without really looking at Cute Blond Guy. I don't like being steered, and I resisted for just a second. In that time, Cute Blond Guy held out a sheet of paper to me.

I took it without thinking. He'd torn it out of his notebook. It was a sketch of my face. My old face. Before the M-ask.

"Hey!" cried Diego, snapping out of it. He lunged for Cute Blond Guy and missed.

Cute Blond Guy said, "Just so you remember who you used to be, before you started murdering millions of people in the name of commerce."

He dodged Diego again, darted out of the restaurant, and jumped on a bike. It was a kid's bike, small and maneuverable. It let him slither between two parked cars and then pedal madly against the traffic on Goffle Road before shooting across someone's lawn and disappearing behind a garage.

Diego hissed and muttered at his personal construct. I caught the phrases, "How'd *he* get through?" and "Get the bastard."

"I thought you said we were secure," I commented.

"We'll find him."

"You know him?" I said casually.

Diego gave a noncommital shrug. "Probably just some romantic loonybird from the Old Skool. Wants us to go back to shootouts and space jockeys. We do that and the opposition fries us out of the Scatter."

He glanced sidelong at me. He was worried I'd be influenced by the anti-M-ask faction, that this kind of personal contact with a protester would test my resolve.

I didn't say anything. *Let him sweat. Let them all sweat.*

I know what I am.

I was born a professional. My M-ask was built for me, and I was built to fight in M-space from the time I was conceived. I was younger than my opponent; in fact, I was the youngest ever to do Battle. Started when I was thirteen. Girls mature faster, and our brains adapt better to the new generation M-asks. Back in training, I'd left all the boys my age in the dust. By the time they had reached maturity, their M-asks would have become obsolete. And it's that little technological edge that keeps us ahead of the enemy.

See, warfare on an extraplanetary scale is a logistical nightmare. Most of the wars are about the same thing: who will control the M-eq. When you work across vast distances, if you want anything to happen in a coordinated way, you have to work outside the four dimensions that we humans intuitively understand. You have to access M-space, and that's what the M-eq is for. The M-eq is the equipment that uses M-space to groom timespace and make it behave well enough to take us to other planets or upstream/downstream in the same location. If you control the M-eq, you can do what you want in the galaxy.

The Project was always examining the best ways of integrating the M-eq. And they concluded that the best natural model of instantaneous and efficient coordination of multiple systems is the human body. Supercomputers couldn't cut it. The wet and salty human nervous system was an example of parallel processing extraordinaire.

To control the M-eq across timespace, our leaders knew they needed an executive system governable with the same speed and integration and feedback capabilities as the human body.

So they designed the M-ask, and the people who wore it.

Funnily enough, nobody anticipated what would happen next. Insurgents from the Scatter frontier discovered that they could take over the M-eq if they attacked the person whose bodymind was being used to run it. All they'd needed was a M-ask interface and an aggressor who could challenge the M-eq operative on a physical level.

That was how the Battles had gotten started. They'd evolved into a form of ritualized warfare, which meant there were rules that both sides had to follow.

I was just the latest model in a long line of M-eq-adapted humans charged with responsibility for protecting the Scatter from the insurgents. My opponent, Jarel (yes, I knew his name. We knew practically everything there was to know about each other, without having actually met), would also wear a M-ask, but the design would be inferior. In terms of response time and richness of perception, the enemy's M-asks couldn't compete. The insurgents had originated in a backwater of the M-stream, and their resources were limited. They usually had to copy our designs.

That didn't mean I could take victory for granted. Jarel was stronger, tougher, and faster on a physical level. And he was hungry. The enemy hadn't won control of the M-eq for the past four Battles. They needed to win this one, or be subsumed within our control of the Scatter. I knew that Jarel would stop at nothing. The insurgents had survived harsh conditions in the Scatter frontiers, and they were trained to fight like animals.

But me, I'd been genetically and developmentally primed for M-ask warfare. The M-ask allowed me to access large-scale data analysis on a subconscious level so that I could fight by intuition. And my brain—any human brain, in fact—could do what artificial intelligence had consistently failed to do: act on its thoughts in a coordinated way, and instantaneously. The integration of systems needed in M-warfare was already present in me, from the cortex right down through the brainstem and out into muscles, tendons, bone. Thanks to the intricate connections between the M-ask and our operational systems, every blow I struck on Jarel would hurt the enemy. Every blow he struck would hit not only me, but thousands or millions of people on my side, via his side's M-eq weaponry.

Some targets were vital. Some were equipment. Jarel and I could cripple each other's transport, communications, energy sources, you name it—all through direct attacks to the body.

He and I would fight the Battle.

Like the song said: *We are the champions*.

Except, we weren't like the champions of ancient Greece, who had fought each other so that the innocent need not die. We didn't fight *instead of* mass warfare. We *were* mass warfare.

Cute Blond Guy had been right, in a way: when the Battle began, I would be responsible for the lives of billions of people.

After failing to catch Cute Blond Guy, Diego consulted his Shade and then insisted on driving me home from Friendly's.

"I'll see you tomorrow at three fifteen," he said as the car pulled up outside my house. "We'll go over the rules formally. Stay in tonight. Get some sleep if you can."

He twitched violently and then scratched his neck to disguise the action. He claimed to be allergic to the soap they used in their clothes in 1994; maybe that was why he was always jumping like a cat with fleas. Or it could be that he had programmed his Shade to pinch him every time he was about to say something extemporaneous—something that would give him away as nonnative to 1994—which would be often. He talked openly to his Shade as he was walking down the street, even though this meant that 1994 people thought he had one of their mental diseases. He said there were some comforts he couldn't give up, even out in the field.

"You know, I'm a nervous wreck," he said as I was getting out of the car.

"Yeah?" I snapped. "And it would be *your butt* potentially getting kicked out there?"

I slammed the door before he could answer and ran up the lawn to the front door of the house. I let myself in.

My foster parents thought I was an Armenian refugee. I kept up a vague accent to support the lie. They were nice to me. Tracey, the mother, had two kids away at college. I guess she missed them. She kept Caffeine-Free Diet Pepsi in the fridge door, just for me. But I was so tense there that I always had to turn on the bathroom faucet before I could let myself pee.

I dropped my backpack in the hall.

"Hello?"

At first I thought no one was home. Salsa the cat took one look at me and hid under the sofa. This was not unusual. It saw the M-ask, even if the others didn't, and on the other side of the M-ask, it must have smelled M-space.

"Who was that guy?"

The voice belonged to Dave—that is, Mr. "Call Me Dave

Because I'm a Really Nice Guy" Siebel—my foster father. He was standing in the den looking through the blinds at Diego's Hyundai as it pulled away.

"New assistant track coach," I replied.

"Why's he driving you home?"

"We have a meet tomorrow. He wanted to go over some stuff."

Sniff!

Dave had a habit of sniffing his breath out through his nose when he was nervous or upset. Especially when he was angry. He made me think of a skinny little bull wanting to charge.

"I'm staying over at Karen's tomorrow night. Tracey said it was okay."

"Have you seen the remote control for the VCR?" he snapped. *Sniff!*

"Not since yesterday. Sorry." I went to my room and changed into sweats and running shoes. When I came out, Dave was on his hands and knees under the piano looking for the remote.

"Had it"—*sniff*—"last night . . . *NYPD Blue* . . . where?" he muttered. *Sniff!* "Oh, crapski . . ."

He only ever said "crapski" under extreme duress. Like the time Salsa threw up on his ski jacket.

"Are you okay, Dave?" I asked in my Armenian accent. Some part of me was hoping he'd say no. *No, I lost my job. No, actually, I'm thinking about having a sex change. No, I've decided to leave you all and move to Nepal.* It wasn't that I didn't like Dave or that I wanted something bad to happen to him. It was just that this place, these people, this life, were all so boring.

He straightened up and looked at me. I had my hand on the knob of the front door, wishing now that I hadn't asked the question.

"Well!" he exclaimed. "That is very nice of you to ask, Maja."

Sniff! "Actually, I have to give a big presentation at work tomorrow and it's making me a little . . . stressed out. Nothing for you to worry about." *Sniff!* "I took the afternoon off to prepare. I'll be fine."

He smiled without opening his lips.

I left him tearing the cushions off the sofa and sniffing.

"You think *you've* got a big day tomorrow," I muttered, shaking my head.

Once outside, I went straight into a working run.

Forgetting Dave was easy. He'd probably forget himself if you gave him half a chance. Forgetting the Battle that was to come wasn't so easy. This was my third Battle, but my first time fighting Jarel. I had home-court advantage because I had won the last Battle in 2112 on an orbital of Jain's World. Jarel would have to come to this timespace to fight me, but I had been here for months, acclimating myself to the conditions. When I needed to report for training, I M-folded myself to the simulations facilities, but the rest of the time I was a regular person, 1994-style.

Was Jarel here? Was he thinking about me? About what he was going to do to me?

Because I was thinking about him and it wasn't pretty. I pictured his face as I ran, and I saw myself flattening his nose, knocking out teeth with my fist. I hardened my abdomen, preparing for blows—or worse. Jarel had a powerful gut-wrench, and I'd seen him tie guys up like pretzels. I mustn't let him close with me.

All the while that I was thinking this, I put one foot in front of the other and ran.

Sense your bones, my trainer used to say. *Forget all that simulator crap. Kinesthetic perception is everything.*

I didn't want to get caught on the ground. I didn't want to

wrestle Jarel. I visualized myself going into a sprawl if he tried to shoot for my legs. *Hit hit hit,* I thought. And stuff like that.

I had watched realtime clips of my opponent on the M-ask. His targets had been mapped on his body like acupuncture points, transport meridiens gleaming like the armature of a sculpture. He moved nice. If you took off the M-asks and put Jarel and me in a ring or a cage and had us fight it out, I'd be meat. No doubt about it. The guy was bigger, stronger, and meaner, and judging from his pancratium fight profile, his pain threshold was way higher than mine.

My targets had not been painted on my body, but my opponent would know what each of my parts and systems corresponded to, in the M-ask. Nerves were communications, lymph was weapons transport, and blood was human lives. More specifically, each target, from giant M-eq generators to weapons silos a hundred light years away, had been mapped. My body and its correspondences had been plotted from the biggest institutions down to the last individual on the Scatter census. My elbows were plotted with schools, for example, and the Broca's Belt Mining Commission ran down the side of my right thigh in a thin line. The big arsenals were in my liver. Hospitals were clustered around my heart. The government, of course, had been mapped onto my brain tissue. They'd stay alive as long as I wasn't brain damaged.

Governments always knew how to save their own asses.

I started to run intervals. After a couple of miles, my left hamstring started to throb. I'd strained it three weeks ago while training in the simulator, and it still wasn't right. One of our M-eq power transfer stations was plotted there, and I hoped that Jarel wouldn't notice my weakness and capitalize on it.

I pulled up and walked home, trying not to limp in case anyone on Jarel's side was watching.

The next day was weird. I had a hard time concentrating in precalculus. I kept being tempted to switch my M-ask to Away Mode to see if anything major had changed in the Battle configuration. Every time I did this I got Diego in my auditory cortex telling me to let him worry about that stuff and pay attention to my own body.

But my body felt like it was going to jump out of itself. In driver's ed we were tested for night blindness and braking reaction time. I slowed my reactions deliberately, but I was still quicker than everybody in the class, including Derek the basketball star. As I walked down the hall clutching my books to my chest, I kept seeing people as targets. I had the urge to shoulder them out of the way, to headbutt them, to take their legs out from under them and kick them as they were lying on the floor.

I smiled more than usual to make up for it.

I was scared. I admit it. Anybody who isn't scared before a fight is just stupid.

After school I walked up to the construction site for the new industrial park. The top of the mountain had been shorn off by dynamite, and there were pits of tan earth in the process of being sculpted by bulldozers and excavators. It had been a year since the Project bought off the developers who owned this land, and it showed. Several of the big machines had been left parked as though their drivers had just gone on a coffee break, but scrub grass grew around their rusted blades and a sapling had sprouted from dirt collected in the back of a dump truck. Around the edges of the excavation stood a forest of maples and oaks, their leaves flaming bronze and crimson and their branches loud with migrating blackbirds. Squirrels sprang from tree to tree, getting ready for winter.

If I listened carefully, I could hear the marching band practicing on the football field.

It was 3:13. Diego was standing outside his car, putting mustard on a Sabrett hot dog.

"Is this a baseball game?" I said.

"Let's go over the map, wiseguy."

Dutifully I recited the Battleground boundaries: from the Kodak building, across the lily pond, to the housing development, across the back of McCoy Avenue to the woods behind the high school, down the hill to the Foodtown mini-mall, and back up through a maze of residential streets to the industrial park again. Most of the Battleground was wild: scrubland or undeveloped forest. But not all.

Diego used his Official Voice.

"The contest will take place within the above boundaries. Cross the perimeter and you automatically forfeit victory. Your onboard guidance will take care of orientation, so there's no reason for you to leave the perimeter unless you choose to do so."

"I'm not a coward," I said.

"I have to repeat these things," said Diego. "No weapons are allowed. Otherwise, you are permitted to use any and all resources you find within the perimeter, to any purpose you choose, provided that you don't violate the local timespace possibility parameters. Beyond that, I can only say the usual, which you already know by heart. War is war is war, yadda yadda, take no prisoners, poach no eggs, get your butt out in one piece. Make like Greyhound and leave the thinking to us."

"Me brawn, you brains," I said. "I am but here to serve. Are you going to eat that?"

He pushed the hot dog into my hand. "How's the hamstring?"

"Been better," I said with my mouth full. "But I ran on it yesterday. It'll hold."

"And of course, you'll have me in your ear the whole time."

I made a whirlybird gesture with my forefinger and swallowed pseudo-meat.

"Yippee."

Down in the excavation there was a rough pit that had been filled with sand by the Project. During the Battle it would be patrolled by Shades to keep the locals out. We could fight here under timespace protection, knowing we wouldn't be seen by the 1994 people. The rest of the area was more of a problem. Like, if we exchanged blows on the corner of Main Street we'd just be arrested.

The Battle would start here, and I wanted it to finish here. Cleanly.

Jarel was already in the pit, talking to his handlers. He was twitchy and pumped, just like I'd known he would be.

I started tuning out distractions. I ignored Diego's last-minute advice.

I'm going to rip your head off, I thought.

I thought: *Try to hurt me and I'll kill you.*

Everything but Jarel and me faded from my awareness. Diego and the other handlers M-folded to a remote timespace location. I knew I was ready because time was slowing down for me. Every eye blink stretched like a big gong counting time.

There was no referee. In the middle of the pit was a circle of darker sand. Once one of us stepped into it, the Battle was on. It wouldn't stop until a winner had been determined by the M-eq.

We both surged toward the dark sand. We clashed in the middle.

I had a lightning-fast left hand; that was common knowledge. I used the jab to keep him away from me, and then caught him with a right cross almost immediately. He took the shot pretty well, which was more than could have been said for my hand. Even given every genetic advantage, it was difficult to condition your hands to hit bone.

He winked at me. "I got a hard head," he said as I danced out of range.

But I wasn't fooled. He'd have a black eye; it was red and swelling already. Hah!

I angled off to the side to catch him with my round kick. People never think I'm in kicking range from this position, and Jarel was proving no exception. I caught him again and again before he changed his position, chipping away at that lead leg. I knew I'd hurt him even if he didn't let on. He was still holding back on me. He had the reach on me, and I was having to use every piece of footwork I knew to stay out of range of his punches. He attempted one shot and I evaded to the side, sending him careering off. He came up with a fistful of dirt, which he threw in my face as he shot for my lead leg again. The dirt didn't work—all that eye-shielding Diego had been talking about must have paid off. I kneed Jarel straight in the face. Missed his nose, unfortunately.

Now, that would have had an effect on the insurgents' power base. I split my awareness briefly to include Away Mode.

From the outside our ships look cool and smooth, running silent and lightless in moon orbit. The surface of Losamo is a wash of serene blues and greens, opalescent where the mountain ranges throw spikes of rare minerals toward the skies. The effects of our bombardment appear as white scratches on the colored planet. I don't know what this really means until I peel away another layer of the M-ask and look closely.

Great gouges have been carved in the fertile, inhabited regions of Losamo.

Refugees are piling into caterpillar-trucks by the thousands. Their Losamo-specific energy-skin, normally bright green, has been damaged by chemical agents and their hides now range in color from graphite gray to chalky white. They will not be able to survive long without working chloroplasts, and the assault has made sure no one for a thousand miles has those.

Our redevelopment teams will move in and reorganize the existing infrastructure to take it away from the enemy, but in the meantime most of these people will die.

I switched to Local Mode. I refused to let this get to me. I was here to do a job.

Diego weighed in with *"They're better off under us than under the enemy. Even if they don't know that."*

"Oh, save it, Diego," I muttered. "Any more Let's Save the Little People propaganda and I'm gonna be sick."

Jarel might have lost Losamo, but he feinted a left hook and then caught me with an uppercut to the gut. Involuntarily I said, "Ungh!" as the air went out of me, and he used the contact to try and wrap a guillotine around my neck. Now I was in trouble. I slithered out of the guillotine before he could crank it on tightly, but I knew it was only a matter of time before he caught me in some kind of lock. As long as we were in close proximity, the fight wasn't going my way.

I buried my fist repeatedly in his liver until he loosened his grip.

Tried to knee him in the groin but he blocked it with his thigh. He let me go fractionally and I spun and caught him with a back elbow across the same eye I'd already hit. He let go and I was away. But we'd reached the edge of the sand and I tripped and fell against the sharp edge of a bulldozer blade. The left leg again, dammit.

"Get out of there. You almost lost Broca's Belt and you've taken damage at the transfer station."

I broke into a run, leaping over heaps of plowed dirt, and sure enough, the twinge in my hamstring renewed itself at a higher pitch. I was bleeding now.

My trainer had always said never to be obsessive about hitting a particular target. Jarel's galactic map didn't really matter, she'd told me. *You have to beat the man,* she'd said. *There's a person inside that target map. Just as you are a person, even though you're wired for M-space. And don't you ever forget it, because that's how he'll be trying to beat you.*

I checked my Away Mode again. I'd blasted some low-grade storage facilities on Jarel's homeworld and there was a communication problem among his Broca ships.

I was thrilled.

"Take that, ya sonuvabitch," I muttered.

Yep, there's a lot to be said for space Battles. They don't affect the local environment, so they're green. They give both sides a chance to show off their hardware, which has had a trickle-down effect on the tek-literacy of the whole society that's been recognized since Sputnik. If you win: infinite glory. If you lose, your hardware goes up in a fiery explosion that makes a visible mark on the heavens. What could be better?

Well, let me tell you. Thanks to this very attitude, my predecessor Jack had had to be hospitalized with Post-Ironic Stress Syndrome (PISS). He'd wanted to shoot the big guns and fly fast ships without ever leaving the comfort of his La-Z-Boy, and he had been good at it. But then the latest M-ask design had come out, with its ultrafast feedback mechanism that meant not only did your every little action have a large-scale correspondence across space, but that you perceived these consequences. When Jack had worn the M-ask, he had actually experienced the obscenities of mass warfare. The simple fact that every blow he gave—or took—under the M-ask would result in thousands of deaths was enough to put Jack over the edge. The next thing the Project had known, Jack couldn't sleep, he'd broken out in hives, and he'd started complaining that the Project was insincere.

I mean, duh. The Project is run by our government, which means its Insincerity Quotient ranges from somewhere between Too Big and Astronomical, without getting into any heavy detail. Everyone knows this. Like, lose the hang-ups and move on already. Would you rather get taken over by barbarians like Jarel's people? We couldn't let just *anybody* run the M-eq. Galactic order would collapse.

Take M-space. Fold some dimensions up, do the *kalabi yau* boogie, and the next thing you know, you're making spacetime look like a bad-hair day. I could be sitting in American history and scoping out the forces of evil across the cosmos, and nobody but me would even know. I could live in 1994 and be a warrior across the Scatter a thousand years downtimestream, thanks to the M in M-ask.

That kind of power brings responsibility, and that's why we can't let the insurgents take over. So we have to fight. I guess that kind of superchunk paradox was just too much for the likes of Battlestar Jack.

Me, I just liked the physical side of hand-to-hand combat. I liked fighting; I'd been bred for it. And that's why I ended up in the Battle and Jack ended up in therapy for PISS.

I knew that M-ask warfare was the most efficient and most effective way to determine control of the galactic economy. Therefore, the war would be shorter and less damaging to all concerned. Knowing this, I accepted that there would be casualties and I could deal with it.

The Project had designed me. I'd been fortified with all the iron in irony. I was born tough.

So I ignored the damage, to me and to our people's lives. I limped through the woods and hid inside a hollow old tree that I knew. I watched Jarel walk right past me and carry on to the end of Page Drive. Then I followed him.

There are a lot of legends about past Battles. This particular Battleground was similar to two others from a similar time period and region. In one famous Battle, there was an unforeseen power outage halfway through, and our guy had been relying on a chainsaw he'd stolen from a garage. He'd tied the insurgents' warrior to a tree and prepared to literally rip him apart, when the power cut out. In total darkness, the insurgents' warrior managed to escape and kill our guy with a claw hammer.

After that, the rules changed and weapons were outlawed.

That was why I couldn't imagine what Jarel wanted in the hardware store. But that was where he went, straight after our first round of Battle. I knew he didn't have any money; it wasn't allowed. But in those days shoplifting was easy. So what was he after?

I had run a lot of scenarios through my mind. I knew how to

make pit traps and snares, and I could have tried to use tactics like those. There were various interesting ways to kill or disable somebody in 1994 suburbia that didn't involve "weapons" as such. I started to sift through these possible threats.

Jarel emerged empty-handed from the hardware store and then went to the drugstore. Came out pressing an ice pack to his eye.

This was getting boring.

I followed him all over the place. I paced the aisles of Foodtown, pretending to shop. I had to slip behind a stack of dog-food bags when he took an unexpected turn and almost saw me. I abandoned the shopping cart by the Entenmann's rack. Then I darted outside, past the dry cleaner's and post office and around to the loading bays at the back of Foodtown. I ended up scaling the rear facade of CVS and lying on the roof, my face resting on tar that was stained with pigeon droppings.

I didn't want to think what I looked like by then.

I crawled to the edge of the roof and peered over. I could see him leaving Foodtown carrying a couple of bags. No one tried to stop him. I wondered if he had mugged somebody for cash. . . .

As I watched, he got into an old station wagon, fiddled with something under the steering wheel, and pulled out of the parking lot. I felt outraged. He wasn't even native to this timespace, and he was in control already. And behaving criminally!

"I wish I'd thought of that," I said. "Is it legal to steal money and then hire locals to beat your opponent?"

"No," said Diego tartly. *"Pay attention—he's getting away."*

Actually, he was gone. Muttering four-letter words, I took a look at my left leg. Dried blood glued the fabric of my jeans to the wound, and I decided to leave it alone rather than risk opening it up again.

But it hurt, and the swelling would compromise my movement.

I switched to Away Mode.

The Broca power transfer station has taken severe damage. The M-eq there has been mangled and no M-folding exchanges can take place across Broca's Belt now. Repair bots have been diverted to patch things up, but that will take time.

Time. I didn't know where Jarel was now, only that he needed to stay within the perimeter or forfeit the Battle. So I made my way back to the industrial park and the sand pit.

He wasn't there.

I hadn't planned for this tactic. I wasn't sure what to do.

Diego presented his advice.

"Suggest you rest. Play possum and see if that draws him out."

It wasn't a bad idea. If Jarel was going to try a sneak attack, he would wait for me to fall asleep and then move in. I'd been trained to sleep only lightly and for brief periods. I would be ready for him.

The night was about half over and I was in a light doze when a sharp pain tore into my left side. I came awake instantly, my hand clutching at my side as I shot to my feet. I was already primed, and although I'd been startled I was ready to fight.

But there was no one there.

Not a sound.

Not a movement.

I pivoted in a circle, scanning my surroundings, but nothing stirred.

Waves of pain started to throb from my left side. It must have been a kick, but it hurt like no kick I'd ever received.

"Diego?"

Nothing.

My feet went out from under me and my open mouth hit the dirt. I thought I felt a tooth break. I rolled to try to get clearance, going into an open guard so that I could keep him away with my legs. Only one problem: he wasn't there.

I couldn't see him at all.

"Diego? Diego, what the—?"

No response. No sight of the enemy.

I got up. Paced the area. Picked up a stick and poked it into holes between the boulders. Banged it on the side of an excavator. Nothing.

Then my ears rang as something metallic hit me in the side of the neck. I staggered, managed to spin to confront him; but he wasn't there.

I tried to straighten up, but as soon as I did I started to retch. My stomach was empty, so I brought up only bile.

"Times like this are when I really need you to be there, Diego," I whispered. But the unnerving silence from the Project continued. I started to scramble away from the construction site, making for the woods. When I got under cover of the trees, I stopped and checked Away Mode.

Damage assessment:

The data-processing trees on Jain's World orbital have come under chemical attack. The biological computer farms have been obliterated.

A scan at the orbital level reveals the assailant powering down. It's a high-powered battle cruiser, one of the best ships in our fleet. Yes, that's right. Our *fleet.*

I changed to Local Mode.

I felt shaky and nauseous.

"Diego? Diego, what is going on? What's with the friendly fire?"

But his link was still dead.

How had Jarel attacked me without my even seeing him?

And if Jarel *had* attacked me, how come the source of the attack was registering as one of our own ships?

"Diego! Diego—something's going seriously wrong here."

Silence.

I thought: *I'm not old enough to drive a car, vote, or drink. But it's all up to me.*

I thought: *This bites.*

By morning it was raining, and I sheltered inside some giant sewer pipes that had been left aboveground, unused. According to my onboard, the Battle was still in effect, even though I couldn't contact Diego. Jarel had to be here somewhere, but I needed to keep a low profile if I didn't want to get in trouble for playing hooky from school.

My body slowly repaired the injuries, and robots worked frenetically in Broca's Belt.

I spent the day avoiding the locals. I couldn't go "home" for refreshments, but I did sneak into the kitchen of an unlocked house on Ryerson Avenue, where I filched bread and an orange before returning to the sand pit. Jarel never showed, so when it got dark I started to prowl. On Yawpo Avenue, near the Battleground border, I paused. A group of girls I knew from school were huddled together in the bus stop, laughing, their hair blowing in the stiff breeze. They were dressed in the uniform of hip-hop jeans and Doc Martens, multiple pierces, temporary tattoos. Their backpacks would be heavy with biology textbooks or whatever.

I thought how safe their lives were: parents getting divorced their biggest problem, or maybe bad skin. I had made sure not to become good friends with any of them. I went to the occasional party, I worked on the theater crew, I ran track. But I didn't get close to anybody.

That sucked. I would have liked to have had friends. But it wasn't possible, not for me.

They didn't know what I knew. About all of it. How fragile their world was. And people like Diego in charge of everything. Diego could only find his own butt by smell. It was worrying, it really was.

I don't know if I'm addicted to the rush, or what. I guess it's like, I know there's this one thing I can do really, really well. And I want to do it. The problem is, I'm only a weapon in somebody's hand. I'd like to be my own weapon, but that isn't the world I live in. That's like ancient Greece or something.

You can't just drop out of the Program. They don't take kindly to that. If I ditched Diego and stayed in deep cover, I'd be stuck here. Forever. No more M-folding. Just growing up in 1994, buried forever in history.

Once you know something, you can't pretend you don't know it. Once you've seen certain atrocities, those images can't be erased. I look at these girls and I don't know whether I despise them or envy them.

They belong here. I don't belong anywhere.

Then the bus came and the girls got on. The bus pulled away and I saw Jarel. He was standing in the darkness just on the edge of the streetlamp's pool of illumination. Watching me. Then he reached up and did something to his face. . . .

He was taking off the M-ask. He put it on the bench and backed away into the shadows outside the chiropractor's office.

He might as well have sent me a written invitation.

I edged forward.

The M-ask was sitting on the plastic seat under the bus shelter. Its nose lay in a shallow puddle of water where rain had found its way through a gouge in the shelter roof. Two messages had been scratched in the plexi of the shelter wall:

Ferris is a fag

and

Jenny loves Tom

The M-ask gleamed, and I felt the top of my head prickle softly.

I closed my eyes.

It had to be a trap.

I picked up the M-ask and went toward Jarel. There was a dignity about him that I couldn't quite place. He was supposed to be a primitive, but there was something pure about the way he moved.

Then he turned and in the light of the streetlamp I saw his face.

It was a ruin. M-erge agents swarmed over it, the primitive glue that bound his flesh to the M-ask. His eyes were filmed with vermillion. The insurgents had copied our early M-ask designs; thankfully I'd never had to wear one of those. I felt a weird mixture of triumph and pity.

He said, "You got me. Goods convoys disrupted, com patterns scrambled or broken. Climate on two worlds irreversibly changed. And I can't hear my advisor—how did you do that?"

I stared at him in disbelief. Then I opened my jacket, so he could see the bruises on my neck coming up purple. I couldn't figure out how he had managed to injure himself so badly, when I hadn't even been able to get near him all this time.

"I can't hear my advisor, either," I said slowly.

He took several ragged breaths as the implication of what I'd said sank into both of us.

"So there's a third party," Jarel said. "Something's hunting us."

We were both thinking fast now, racing each other to leap to conclusions.

"Whatever it is, it must be inside the M-cq," I said. "It's manipulating the M-ask system. That's why we can't see it."

"So it might not be localized here at all. It could be some kind of bug, operating all across the Scatter."

"I don't know. According to my M-ask, one of our most sophisticated ships attacked our own target. The worst damage from friendly fire I've ever seen."

"You're saying . . . that your injuries are a result of feedback? You're saying . . ."

"The M-ask isn't supposed to cut both ways," I said. "But that's what's happening. We're getting hurt because of events in M-timespace."

He thought about this. He nodded slowly. Then he said, "We could take off our M-asks. Both of us. Be real champions. Break the links. Fight with honor."

I snorted. "You'd like that, wouldn't you? You know I have a better M-ask than you do. Without M-asks, you'd be able to beat me easily. Then you could put on your own M-ask and declare victory."

He waved his hands in negation. "It's not just about us. These

M-asks are like executioners' hoods. They keep anyone from seeing us and holding us to account for what we're doing."

He sounded just like that Cute Blond Guy in Friendly's, with his accusations of mass murder.

I said, "This is war. You can't have a war without people getting killed."

"But it's not you or me who are getting killed, Maja. The M-asks will determine a winner before that can happen. And the M-eq in Broca's Belt will sign itself over to that side."

"Yeah, that's the system. We both agreed to it. Now you want to change it."

"I want to change it because if we don't, then this thing will use us to get to the M-eq."

"You don't know that."

"Let me put it to you like this," Jarel said. "As long as you remain M-asked, this bug, whatever it is, can get to the whole system through you. And the same thing with me. If we take the battle off-line, then it can attack us, but it can't destroy all of the Scatter through us."

"How do you know that?"

"Isn't it obvious?"

"No," I said.

Actually, I had to agree with what he was saying, in principle. But what if it was a trick?

"We have to work together, Maja."

I shook my head. I gave a belligerent *Sniff!* worthy of Dave. I said, "I have no way of knowing if this is for real, or just some stratagem you guys are using against me. So put your M-ask back on and let's do it."

"That's it?"

"That's it. End of conversation."

"You want to keep fighting?" he cried, incredulous.

"That's what I'm here to do. You putting your M-ask on or not?"

"No, I'm not. I think it's been corrupted."

I opened my mouth to tell him what I thought of that when I spotted somebody coming our way. Speak of the devil, it was Cute Blond Guy. He nodded at me and smiled as he approached the bus shelter.

Jarel quickly donned his M-ask, but just as it touched his face, he sucked in his breath with a shocked *hiss* and doubled over, staggering sideways until he sat down on the narrow metal bench.

I started to back away. I wasn't sure what was going down, but I didn't like it.

"Diego?" I tried again. Nothing.

Cute Blond Guy stopped just outside of my striking range. He looked easy, calm.

"Hi, Maja."

"I'm not talking to you," I blurted. "I don't do politics. Whatever you want to say, take it up with Diego and the Project."

"You don't know who I am."

"Why should I?"

He shook his head, looking at the ground and scuffing the sidewalk with the tip of his sneaker.

"Maja. I'm your predecessor. I'm Jack."

I took a step back.

"Did they tell you I cracked? Went soft?"

"No," I lied. "What do you want?"

"I want to talk to you about Medusa."

"Which?" I glanced at Jarel, who looked like he was suffering from an acute appendix attack. Jack ignored him.

"Don't play dumb. The thing that's been attacking you both. Medusa. It lives in M-space."

Jarel tugged the M-ask off again and leaned back against the Plexiglas, eyes closed, teeth chattering.

"This thing, Medusa," Jack began. "It doesn't even exist as a four-dimensional being. But when you cross into M-space, it can use you to act on its behalf. And it can use your M-ask against you, too. It can hurt you, destroy your targets, all without ever manifesting itself in any visible way."

"If you can't see it, how do you know what it is?" I said. I knew I sounded dumb; I never claimed to *understand* M-space. I just use it.

"Maja, Maja. It's very simple. The M-ask lets you use M-space. While you're in M-space, Medusa attacks you, and you think it's a strike from Jarel. So you strike back at Jarel, and he at you, until eventually the two of you either destroy each other—which is good for Medusa because it doesn't like either of you encroaching on its timespace—or you realize there is a third party involved. And when you realize there is a third party involved, and that the M-ask technology itself is to blame for both of your injuries, naturally you will remove the M-asks so as to prevent further bloodshed and horror. As Jarel has already done."

He grinned.

"Like this," he said.

And he looked at me. It was more of a stare, really—a corny, horror-movie stare. I wanted to say something cutting, but I couldn't speak, because a sudden, shooting pain had ripped up my left leg and into my pelvis. I felt myself gagging.

The M-eq has been compromised where the power transfer stations in Broca were damaged. They are sending out the wrong signals.

Details of the cities we have captured on Losamo appear in flashes. They are vaporizing under our own guns. A nursery school presided over by a young teacher; her face as she looks up and sees the missiles coming in . . .

The M-fold calculations have been corrupted.

Why was he doing this? What was it all about?

Jack was supposed to be on our side. . . .

I flashed a memory of Diego eyeing me over the ice-cream sundae. Saying, "Your visual cortex is well shielded."

Medusa. Greek mythology. A snake-haired woman who turns you to stone if you meet her gaze.

Losamo. Children, crushed like bugs. Green planet, clawed white with death.

I couldn't look, but I couldn't look away. My eyes were frozen open inside the M-ask.

Jack was still gazing at me. His dreadlocks seemed to move.

Snake hair.

"Jarel!" I screamed. "Don't look at him! It's in his eyes. He'll infect you!"

"Too late," Jack told me smugly. "I've already turned Jarel to stone—metaphorically speaking. I've fixed him in this timespace. He will never M-fold again. But you, Maja—your M-ask is a little more sophisticated. It's a generation better than the one that brought me into the fold. And I can use it."

"See, that's where you'd be wrong," I said shakily. "The M-ask is designed for me. You can't use it. No one else can. Only me."

"You haven't understood me. I'm not just Jack anymore. I'm

Medusa. And I'll be in you, too, just as soon as Medusa can convert you."

"I don't think so."

"Don't worry. It isn't painful. Not nearly as painful as what's happening to the people of Losamo, for example. And you'll see: M-space is best left to the Medusa. Humans don't belong there in any proprietary way. We're not designed for it. And like I told you: you're murdering people over commercial mining rights."

"No," I replied. "*You're* murdering them."

He smiled. "I was hoping we could do this the easy way, but if you want to do it the hard way, I can go there."

And now Cute Blond Guy was coming at me with snakes in his hair. As Dave would say, *Oh, crapski!*

"The Project doesn't understand, Maja. I tried to warn them. It was a waste of time. And then, when I saw Medusa for myself, I knew it didn't matter what the Project did. You'll see."

He was in my range. I kicked him across the thigh: one, two, three successive shots. Then, inexplicably, my left leg caved in and I staggered as though I'd been the one to take the blows.

Damage to Akaya Moon. Radiation shields in Broca 67 compromised.

I'd hit my own targets. Medusa was using me against myself.

Jack kept coming. Everything I did to hurt him only hurt my own side—until it was me rolling on the ground in a haze of pain. He moved in until he was sitting astride my chest with his hands around my throat.

I thrashed wildly, knowing I had a very short time before I lost consciousness. And if he applied pressure to my carotid artery, I'd be—

He let up the pressure just a little.

"No!" I coughed. "I don't want it! I won't!"

I heard his voice, close in my ear, loud above the sound of myself choking and gagging.

"Let Medusa in, Maja. Let it in, or I'll have to kill you. If you die with the M-ask on, all the systems under your care will suffer. Do you really want that?"

I saw my own ships, turning to fire on vital government targets, that is, my brain. I was running out of air.

I shook my head in the throttle of his grip.

"Look in my eyes. Let Medusa enter your M-ask."

Jack's eyes were hazel, which really meant they were pixillated with green, brown, yellow, and blue. Inside them, I could see the Scatter, all at once: all scales, all dimensions, all locations. It was like being conscious of every chemical reaction in my entire body at the same time. Knowing each axon as it fired. I felt skewered on this self-awareness as on a spear. My mind was pinned; it couldn't move.

Am I turning to stone?

I couldn't see Medusa. Its whole nature was inferential. I could only see its effects—but these were visible on almost every system, across power transfer stations and deep in the M-eq. Jack was right: in our efforts at mastering the timespace of the Scatter, we had tapped into something very, very strange.

Was it an alien? Was it a transcendent mathematical pattern? Was it something underlying the very basis of *us*—?

For that matter, was it God?

No way to know.

But I hoped it wasn't God, because I didn't like it much.

"Look deeper," Jack urged. "You're not letting it in. Let yourself become Medusa, and then you'll understand. . . ."

I was looking into Jack's eyes, but I was hearing Medusa's message:

You can have more. You can be more.

You can be more than you.

Surrender, and transcend . . .

It sounded nice. But I hadn't been trained to surrender. Even if it meant the demise of whole worlds.

I thrashed, bridged my body up, and attempted a reversal. My injuries had weakened me. The crippled power transfer station; the rubble of Losamo; the ruined computing trees . . . all of these told against me.

Jack laughed in my face.

"Stupid. You'll destroy yourself and all your kind. Such is human nature. Such is war."

I looked away from the violence of his eyes. Behind him, I saw Jarel move into range. I was fading from lack of oxygen, but the look on Jarel's face held my attention. It was not a nice look.

Then Jarel kicked Jack in the head from behind, and Jack toppled over like a sack of . . . sugar.

"You'll have to beat us both," Jarel said, and pounced on Jack.

He hurt Jack badly. Thanks to his inferior M-ask—and his superior pain tolerance—Jarel seemed to be able to punish Jack without suffering so much damage himself. Eventually, Jack must have taken one blow too many, because the Medusa M-folded him and his poisonous blond dreads into a different timespace.

Panting, Jarel and I regarded each other. And Diego was back in my ears.

Maja, are you okay? We've been having big problems.

I ignored him. I swallowed painfully.

"Thanks, Jarel," I croaked.

But he wasn't even looking at me.

"I'm frozen," he whispered. "I can't access Away Mode, and I can't M-fold. My M-ask is ruined. . . ."

Quit talking to him, Maja, Diego said. *The Battle is still on. Finish him off and we can all get out of here.*

I swatted at my ears, wishing I could shut Diego up.

"This timespace isn't so bad," I said to Jarel. "When you get used to it, you'll be okay. Like, try telling people you're Armenian."

He was inconsolable. "You don't get it. The Leader will punish me. This was our last chance to capture the M-eq. My people have been marginalized for too long. We can't recover from this. Now your government will monopolize the Scatter. I have failed."

Diego had parked his car in front of CVS and was walking up Yawpo toward us. I checked with my onboard and saw that the Battle was still in effect.

"Hey, I might be able to help you out there," I said. "You saved me from Medusa. The least I can do for you is—"

And I turned and broke away. I was only half a mile from the Battleground's boundary near Route 208. I started running across people's lawns.

Maja, no! Don't forfeit! We'll lose M-eq control! Maja!!

Diego ran back to his car and started it. He roared up Yawpo. He was going to cut me off if he could.

I had that bad leg, where what happened on Losamo would always be with me. I wasn't sure I could make it. I reached the edge of the woods. Route 208 wasn't far now.

It was dark, and my leg was killing me, but I wanted this. Not for the Project, not for the Scatter—for me. Because Jarel had saved me and—dumb as it might sound—there was still such a thing as honor. I had to believe that; I had to make it true.

I burst out of the woods just as Diego spun his car to a halt on the highway and came barreling toward me on an intercept course. I kept running, and when he charged me, I slammed my knee into his head.

It was too easy. He was out cold in the fallen leaves.

Lungs searing, I reached the highway and staggered across the invisible line. My M-ask went wild.

I switched to Away Mode. My forfeiture had been registered. The M-eq was already signing itself over to the insurgents.

Just like that, it was over.

There was no sign now of the Medusa. But then, that was the nature of the beast. It couldn't be seen. Jack wasn't defeated, and he'd be back. Or someone like him. Or something harder to name, or even perceive. If the Medusa lived in M-space, I had to be kidding myself to think I could M anymore. Every time I M-folded, I would be at risk.

I walked back along the shoulder to the edge of the woods and the place where Diego was just coming to. He was on his hands and knees, fingering his face like it was a porcelain sculpture. He didn't look too good.

For the first time I realized this was something I could do nothing about. By "this," I mean the situation. No matter what I did, here, today, the outcome would be the same. Diego, or someone like Diego, would carry on with the M-eq, the Scatter, and everything that the exploitation of M-timespace implied. Even if that meant the Project risked losing its agents to the Medusa. The M-ask technology was a one-way street.

I couldn't do anything to stop that. All I could do was make a decision for myself, about the way I wanted to live.

I loved fighting. I would not be rewarded for it, in this timespace. In fact, I would probably be reviled. And my unique M-ask abilities would not be understood, much less valued.

I might as well move to the Stone Age.

Diego was looking at me. He held his sleeve against his bleeding nose.

"Okay," he said thickly. "Party's over. You made your point. But it's only one Battle in the war. Time to go home."

I nodded.

"Okay."

Then I took off the M-ask and handed it to him.

Diego stared at me.

"Have you lost your mind?"

"I don't think so."

"Do you have any idea what your training *cost*? I ought to leave you here, teach you a lesson."

"Whatever," I said, trying to sound like I belonged in 1994. Diego looked at me for a beat, as if to give me a chance to change my mind. Then he M-folded, sneering.

I started to walk north along the side of the highway, against the traffic. Jarel was limping toward me. He offered his hand.

We shook.

"I guess we're both staying," he said.

"Until they come for us," I answered.

"You want to uh . . . hang out . . . sometime?"

I almost laughed at the idea, but checked myself. I said, "Does your face hurt?"

"Yeah, but it should be okay, once the M-ask agents disperse."

I winced. He still looked green, and there were irrigation canals dug in the flesh of his cheeks by migrating agents. He was no poster boy.

I dug a pen out of my jacket and wrote my phone number on his hand.

"I guess we could hang out," I said. "Fellow Armenians and stuff like that."

Jarel smiled.

After that I went "home."

For the first time ever, Salsa the cat rubbed against my legs.

I went into the kitchen and washed my hands. Tracey was at pottery class; she'd left a note and some pizza. As I was microwaving it, I heard the garage door open. Dave *(sniff!)* was home from the gym. I wondered whether he'd notice the limp. And the blood. The blood could be a problem.

There was a precalculus test tomorrow. I hadn't studied because I hadn't thought I'd still be here.

Full of surprises, that life.

I took my bottle of Caffeine-Free Diet Pepsi out of the fridge door. I ached all over. My face felt like a fried egg.

"Maja, you forgot to put the garbage out before you went to your track meet." Dave was climbing the stairs. "Now, I'm not making a big deal about it but that's"—*sniff*—"a really important job. We can't just let it pile up." *Sniff!*

I looked at my reflection in the shiny black surface of the family's fridge.

My old face was back. I even had a zit next to my nose.

I put the bottle to my lips. I'd just saved the world from M-self.

My old face and I smiled at each other.

TRICIA SULLIVAN was born in New Jersey in 1968 and studied in the pioneering Music Program Zero at Bard College. She later received a master's in education from Columbia University and taught in Manhattan and New Jersey before moving to the UK in 1995. Her first novel, *Lethe*, was published that year, and was followed by science fiction novels *Someone To Watch Over Me*, and the Arthur C. Clarke Award winner *Dreaming in Smoke*. She has also written fantasy as Valery Leith, including *The Company of Glass*, *The Riddled Night*, and *The Way of the Rose*. Her most recent novels are *Double Vision*, *Maul*, and *Sound Mind*

Her Web site is www.triciasullivan.co.uk.

AUTHOR'S NOTE

The idea behind this story was to take the concept of ancient Greek "champions" and stand it on its head. The irony is meant to lie in the fact that in the story the champions are not heroically risking their own lives to save others', but risking millions of lives in the name of more efficient warfare. Somewhere in the back of my head I guess I was thinking about PGMs, the technologization (that's probably not a real word) of warfare, and the tendency of the political leaders of our time to lead from the rear, safely.

I had two problems when I started writing. First, although I started out trying to write a far-future space story, I kept finding myself writing about ordinary suburban America—and in the past! My other problem was that my battle was going to happen between a girl and a guy. I can tell you from personal experience of reality-based martial arts that there are major problems for a girl coming up against a big, trained guy who's out to hurt her. I didn't want to resort to the Buffy-style kung fu fighting that we see way too much of in the movies. I wanted to give an accurate portrayal of a male versus female fight, but without my girl getting pulverized.

Luckily, this is a science fiction story, so I was able to fabricate the M-ask, which solves both of my problems and helps to give the story its focus.

INFESTATION

Garth Nix

They were the usual motley collection of freelance vampire hunters. Two men, wearing combinations of jungle camouflage and leather. Two women, one almost indistinguishable from the men though with a little more style in her leather armor accessories, and the other looking like she was about to assault the south face of a serious mountain. Only her mouth was visible, a small oval of flesh not covered by balaclava, mirror shades, climbing helmet, and hood.

They had the usual weapons: four or five short wooden stakes in belt loops; snap-holstered handguns of various calibers, all doubtless chambered with Wood-N-Death® low-velocity timber-tipped rounds; big silver-edged bowie or other hunting knife, worn on the hip or strapped to a boot; and crystal vials of holy water hung like small grenades on pocket loops.

Protection, likewise, tick the usual boxes. Leather neck and wrist guards; leather and woven-wire reinforced chaps and shoulder pauldrons over the camo; leather gloves with metal knuckle plates; army or climbing helmets.

And lots of crosses, oh yeah, particularly on the two men. Big silver crosses, little wooden crosses, medium-sized turned ivory crosses, hanging off of everything they could hang off.

In other words, all four of them were lumbering, bumbling mountains of stuff that meant that they would be easy meat for all but the newest and dumbest vampires.

They all looked at me as I walked up. I guess their first thought was to wonder what the hell I was doing there, in the advertised meeting place, outside a church at 4:30 P.M. on a winter's day while the last rays of the sun were supposedly making this consecrated ground a double no-go zone for vampires.

"You're in the wrong place, surfer boy," growled one of the men.

I was used to this reaction. I guess I don't look like a vampire hunter much anyway, and I particularly didn't look like one. I'd been on the beach that morning, not knowing where I might head to later, so I was still wearing a yellow Quiksilver T-shirt and what might be loosely described as old and faded blue board shorts, but "ragged" might be more accurate. I hadn't had shoes on, but I'd picked up a pair of sandals on the way. Tan Birkenstocks, very comfortable. I always prefer sandals to shoes. Old habits, I guess.

I don't look my age, either. I always looked young, and nothing's changed, though "boy" was a bit rough coming from anyone under forty-five, and the guy who'd spoken was probably closer to thirty. People older than that usually leave the vampire hunting to the government, or paid professionals.

"I'm in the right place," I said, matter-of-fact, not getting into any aggression or anything. I lifted my 1968-vintage vinyl Pan Am airline bag. "Got my stuff here. This is the meeting place for the vampire hunt?"

"Yes," said the mountain-climbing woman.

"Are you crazy?" asked the man who'd spoken to me first. "This isn't some kind of doper excursion. We're going up against a nest of vampires!"

I nodded and gave him a kind smile.

"I know. At least ten of them, I would say. I swung past and had a look around on the way here. At least, I did if you're talking about that condemned factory up on the river heights."

"What! But it's cordoned off—and the vamps'll be dug in till nightfall."

"I counted the patches of disturbed earth," I explained. "The cordon was off. I guess they don't bring it up to full power till the sun goes down. So, who are you guys?"

"Ten!" exclaimed the second man, not answering my question. "You're sure?"

"At least ten," I replied. "But only one Ancient. The others are all pretty new, judging from the spoil."

"You're making this up," said the first man. "There's maybe five, tops. They were seen together and tracked back. That's when the cordon was established this morning."

I shrugged and half unzipped my bag.

"I'm Jenny," said the mountain climber, belatedly answering my question. "The . . . the vampires got my sister, three years ago. When I heard about this infestation, I claimed the Relative's Right."

"I've got a twelve-month permit," said the second man. "Plan to turn professional. Oh yeah, my name's Karl."

"I'm Susan," said the second woman. "This is our third vampire hunt. Mike's and mine, I mean."

"She's my wife," said the belligerent Mike. "We've both got

twelve-month permits. You'd better be legal too, if you want to join us."

"I have a special license," I replied. The sun had disappeared behind the church tower, and the streetlights were flicking on. With the bag unzipped, I was ready for a surprise. Not that I thought one was about to happen. At least, not immediately. Unless I chose to spring one.

"You can call me J."

"Jay?" asked Susan.

"Close enough," I replied. "Does someone have a plan?"

"Yeah," said Mike. "We stick together. No hotdogging off, or chasing down wounded vamps or anything like that. We go in as a team, and we come out as a team."

"Interesting," I said. "Is there . . . more to it?"

Mike paused to fix me with what he obviously thought was his steely gaze. I met it, and after a few seconds he looked away. Maybe it's the combination of very pale blue eyes and dark skin, but not many people look at me directly for too long. It might just be the eyes. There've been quite a few cultures who think of very light blue eyes as the color of death. Perhaps that lingers, resonating in the subconscious even of modern folk.

"We go through the front door," he said. "We throw flares ahead of us. The vamps should all be digging out on the old factory floor; it's the only place where the earth is accessible. So we go down the fire stairs, throw a few more flares out the door, then go through and back up against the wall. We'll have a clear field of fire to take them down. They'll be groggy for a couple of hours yet, slow to move. But if one or two manage to close, we stake them."

"The young ones will be slow and dazed," I said. "But the

Ancient will be active soon after sundown, even if it stays where it is—and it's not dug in on the factory floor. It's in a humongous clay pot outside an office on the fourth floor."

"We take it first, then," said Mike. "Not that I'm sure I believe you."

"It's up to you," I said. I had my own ideas about dealing with the Ancient, but they would wait. No point upsetting Mike too early. "There's one more thing."

"What?" asked Karl.

"There's a fresh-made vampire around, from last night. It will still be able to pass as human for a few more days. It won't be dug in, and it may not even know it's infected."

"So?" asked Mike. "We kill everything in the infested area. That's all legal."

"How do you know this stuff?" asked Jenny.

"You're a professional, aren't you?" said Karl. "How long you been pro?"

"I'm not exactly a professional," I said. "But I've been hunting vampires for quite a while."

"Can't have been that long," said Mike. "Or you'd know better than to go after them in just a T-shirt. What've you got in that bag? Sawn-off shotgun?"

"Just a stake and a knife," I replied. "I'm a traditionalist. Shouldn't we be going?"

The sun was fully down, and I knew the Ancient, at least, would already be reaching up through the soil, its mildewed, mottled hands gripping the rim of the earthenware pot that had once held a palm or something equally impressive outside the factory manager's office.

"Truck's over there," said Mike, pointing to a flashy new silver pickup. "You can ride in the back, surfer boy."

"Fresh air's a wonderful thing."

As it turned out, Karl and Jenny wanted to sit in the back too. I sat on a toolbox that still had shrink-wrap around it, Jenny sat on a spare tire, and Karl stood looking over the cab, scanning the road, as if a vampire might suddenly jump out when we were stopped at the lights.

"Do you want a cross?" Jenny asked me after we'd gone a mile or so in silence. Unlike Mike and Karl, she wasn't festooned with them, but she had a couple around her neck. She started to take off a small wooden one, lifting it by the chain.

I shook my head and raised my T-shirt up under my arms, to show the scars. Jenny recoiled in horror and gasped, and Karl looked around, hand going for his .41 Glock. I couldn't tell whether that was jumpiness or good training. He didn't draw and shoot, which I guess meant good training.

I let the T-shirt fall, but it was up long enough for both of them to see the hackwork tracery of scars that made up a kind of T shape on my chest and stomach. But it wasn't a T. It was a tau cross, one of the oldest Christian symbols and still the one that vampires feared the most, though none but the most ancient knew why they fled from it.

"Is that . . . a cross?" asked Karl.

I nodded.

"That's so hardcore," said Karl. "Why didn't you just have it tattooed?"

"It probably wouldn't work so well," I said. "And I didn't have it done. It was done to me."

I didn't mention that there was an equivalent tracery of scars on my back as well. These two tau crosses, front and back, never faded, though my other scars always disappeared only a few days after they healed.

"Who would—" Jenny started to ask, but she was interrupted by Mike banging on the rear window of the cab—with the butt of his pistol, reconfirming my original assessment that he was the biggest danger to all of us. Except for the Ancient Vampire. I wasn't worried about the young ones. But I didn't know which Ancient it was, and that was cause for concern. If it had been encysted since the drop, it would be in the first flush of its full strength. I hoped it had been around for a long time, lying low and steadily degrading, only recently resuming its mission against humanity.

"We're there," said Karl, unnecessarily.

The cordon fence was fully established now. Sixteen feet high and lethally electrified, with old-fashioned limelights burning every ten feet along the fence, the sound of the hissing oxygen and hydrogen jets music to my ears. Vampires loathe limelight. Gaslight has a lesser effect, and electric light hardly bothers them at all. It's the intensity of the naked flame they fear.

The fire brigade was standing by because of the limelights, which though modernized were still occasionally prone to massive accidental combustion, and the local police department was there en masse to enforce the cordon. I saw the bright white bulk of the state Vampire Eradication Team's semi trailer parked off to one side. If we volunteers failed, they would go in, though given the derelict state of the building and the reasonable space between it and the nearest residential area, it was more likely they'd just get the Air Force to do a fuel-air explosion dump.

The VET personnel would be out and about already, making sure no vampires managed to get past the cordon. There would be crossbow snipers on the upper floors of the surrounding buildings, ready to shoot fire-hardened oak quarrels into vampire heads. It wasn't advertised by the ammo manufacturers, but a big old vampire could take forty or fifty Wood-N-Death® or equivalent rounds to the head and chest before going down. A good inch-diameter, yard-long quarrel or stake worked so much better.

There would be a VET quick-response team somewhere close as well, outfitted in the latest metal-mesh armor, carrying the automatic weapons the volunteers were not allowed to use—with good reason, given the frequency with which volunteer vampire hunters killed each other even when armed only with handguns, stakes, and knives.

I waved at the window of the three-story warehouse where I'd caught a glimpse of a crossbow sniper, earning a puzzled glance from Karl and Jenny, then jumped down. A police sergeant was already walking over to us, his long, harsh limelit shadow preceding him. Naturally, Mike intercepted him before he could choose whom he wanted to talk to.

"We're the volunteer team."

"I can see that," said the sergeant. "Who's the kid?"

He pointed at me. I frowned. The kid stuff was getting monotonous. I don't look that young. Twenty at least, I would have thought.

"He says his name's Jay. He's got a 'special license.' That's what he says."

"Let's see it then," said the sergeant, with a smile that suggested he was looking forward to arresting me and delivering a three-hour lecture. Or perhaps a beating with a piece of rubber pipe. It isn't always easy to decipher smiles.

"I'll take it from here, Sergeant," said an officer who came up from behind me, fast and smooth. He was in the new metal-mesh armor, like a wetsuit, with a webbing belt and harness over it, to hold stakes, knife, WP grenades (which actually were effective against the vamps, unlike the holy water ones), and a handgun. He had an H&K MP5-PW slung over his shoulder. "You go and check the cordon."

"But Lieutenant, don't you want me to take—"

"I said check the cordon."

The sergeant retreated, smile replaced by a scowl of frustration. The VET lieutenant ignored him.

"Licenses, please," he said. He didn't look at me, and unlike the others I didn't reach for the plasticated, hologrammed, data-chipped card that was the latest version of the volunteer-vampire-hunter license.

They held their licenses up and the reader that was somewhere in the lieutenant's helmet picked up the data, and his earpiece whispered whether they were valid or not. Since he was nodding, we all knew they were valid before he spoke.

"Okay, you're good to go whenever you want. Good luck."

"What about him?" asked Mike, gesturing at me with his thumb.

"Him too," said the lieutenant. He still didn't look at me. Some of the VET are funny like that. They seem to think I'm like an albatross or something. A sign of bad luck. I suppose it's because wherever the vampire infestations are really bad, I have a tendency to show up as well. "He's already been checked in. We'll open the gate in five, if that suits you."

"Sure," said Mike. He lumbered over to face me. "There's something funny going on here, and I don't like it. So you just stick to the plan, okay?"

"Actually, your plan sucks," I said calmly. "So I've decided to change it. You four should go down to the factory floor and take out the vampires there. I'll go up against the Ancient."

"Alone?" asked Jenny. "Shouldn't we stick together like Mike says?"

"Nope," I replied. "It'll be out and unbending itself now. You'll all be too slow."

"Call this sl—" Mike started to say, as he tried to poke me forcefully in the chest with his forefinger. But I was already standing behind him. I tapped him on the shoulder, and as he swung around, ran behind him again. We kept this up for a few turns before Karl stopped him.

"See what I mean? And an Ancient Vampire is faster than me."

That was blarney. Or at least I hoped it was. I'd met Ancient Vampires who were as quick as I was, but not actually faster. Sometimes I did wonder what would happen if one day I was a fraction slower and one finally got me for good and all. Some days, I kind of hoped that it would happen.

But not this day. I hadn't had to go up against any vampires or anything else for over a month. I'd been surfing for the last two weeks, hanging out on the beach, eating well, drinking a little wine, and even letting down my guard long enough to spend a couple of nights with a girl who surfed better than me and didn't mind having sex in total darkness with a guy who kept his T-shirt on and an old airline bag under the bed.

I was still feeling good from this little holiday, though I knew it would only ever be that. A few weeks snatched out of . . .

"Okay," panted Mike. He wasn't as stupid as I'd feared but he was a lot less fit than he looked. "You do your thing. We'll take the vampires on the factory floor."

"Good," I replied. "Presuming I survive, I'll come down and help you."

"What do . . . what do we do if we . . . if we're losing?" asked Jenny. She had her head well down, her chin almost tucked into her chest, and her body language screamed out that she was both scared and miserable. "I mean, if there are more vampires, or if the Ancient one—"

"We fight or we die," said Karl. "No one is allowed back out through the cordon until after dawn."

"Oh, I didn't . . . I mean I read the brochure—"

"You don't have to go in," I said. "You can wait out here."

"I . . . I think I will," she said, without looking at the others. "I just can't . . . Now I'm here, I just can't face it."

"Great!" muttered Mike. "One of us down already."

"She's too young," said Susan. I was surprised she'd speak up against Mike. I had her down as his personal doormat. "Don't give her a hard time, Mike."

"No time for anything," I said. "They're getting ready to power down the gate."

A cluster of regular police officers and VET agents were taking up positions around the gate in the cordon fence. We walked over, the others switching on helmet lights, drawing their handguns, and probably silently uttering last-minute prayers.

The sergeant who'd wanted to give me a hard time looked at Mike, who gave him the thumbs-up. A siren sounded a slow *whoop-whoop-whoop* as a segment of the cordon fence powered down, the indicators along the top rail fading from a warning red to a dull green.

"Go, go, go!" shouted Mike, and he jogged forward, with Susan and Karl at his heels. I followed a few meters behind, but not too far. That sergeant had the control box for the gate, and I didn't trust him not to close it on my back and power it up at the same time. I really didn't want to know what 6,600 volts at 500 milliamps would do to my unusual physiology—or to show anyone else what *didn't* happen, more to the point.

On the other hand, I didn't want to get ahead of Mike and company either, because I already know what being shot in the back by accident felt like, with lead and wooden bullets—not to mention ceramic-cased, tungsten-tipped penetrator rounds—and I didn't want to repeat the experience.

They rushed the front door, Mike kicking it in and bulling through. The wood was rotten and the top panel had already fallen off, so this was less of an achievement than it might have been.

Karl was quick with the flares, confirming his thorough training. Mike, on the other hand, just kept going, so the light was behind him as he opened the fire door to the left of the lobby.

Bad move. There was a vampire behind the door, and while it was no Ancient, it wasn't newly hatched either. It wrapped its arms around Mike, holding on with the filaments that lined its forelegs, though to an uneducated observer it just looked like a fairly slight, tattered-rag-wearing human bear-hugging him with rather longer than usual arms.

Mike screamed as the vampire started chewing on his helmet, ripping through the Kevlar layers like a buzzsaw through softwood, pausing only to spit out bits of the material. Old steel helmets are better than the modern variety, but we live in an age that values only the new.

Vamps like to get a good grip around their prey, particularly ones who carry weapons. There was nothing Mike could do, and as the vamp was already backing into the stairwell, only a second or two for someone else to do something.

The vampire fell to the ground, its forearm filaments coming loose with a sticky popping sound, though they probably hadn't penetrated Mike's heavy clothes. I pulled the splinter out of its head and put the stake of almost two-thousand-year-old timber back in the bag before the others got a proper look at the odd silver sheen that came from deep within the wood.

Karl dragged Mike back into the flare-light as Susan covered him. Both of them were pretty calm, I thought. At least they were still doing stuff, rather than freaking out.

"Oh man," said Karl. He'd sat Mike up, and then had to catch him again as he fell backward. Out in the light, I saw that I'd waited just that second too long, perhaps from some subconscious dislike of the man. The last few vampire bites had not been just of Mike's helmet.

"What . . . what do we do?" asked Susan. She turned to me, pointedly not looking at her dead husband.

"I'm sorry," I said. I really meant it, particularly since it was my slackness that had let the vamp finish him off. Mike was an idiot, but he didn't deserve to die, and I could have saved him. "But he's got to be dealt with the same way as the vampires now. Then you and Karl have to go down and clean out the rest. Otherwise they'll kill you too."

It usually helps to state the situation clearly. Stave off the shock with the need to do something life-saving. Adrenaline focuses the mind wonderfully.

Susan looked away for a couple of seconds. I thought she might vomit, but I'd underestimated her again. She turned back, and still holding her pistol in her right hand, reached into a thigh pocket and pulled out a Quick-Flame™.

"I should be the one to do it," she said. Karl stepped back as she thumbed the Quick-Flame™ and dropped it on the corpse. The little cube deliquesced into a jelly film that spread over the torso of what had once been a man. Then, as it splashed on the floor, it *woof*ed alight, burning blue.

Susan watched the fire. I couldn't see much of her face, but from what I could see, I thought she'd be okay for about an hour before the shock knocked her off her feet. Provided she got on with the job as soon as possible.

"You'd better get going," I said. "If this one was already up here, the others might be out and about. Don't get ahead of your flares."

"Right," muttered Karl. He took another flare from a belt pouch. "Ready, Susan?"

"Yes."

Karl tossed the flare down the stairs. They both waited to see the glow of its light come back up, then Karl edged in, working the angle, his pistol ready. He fired almost immediately, two double taps, followed by the sound of a vamp falling back down the stairs.

"Put two more in," I called out, but Karl was already firing again.

"And stake it before you go past!" I added as they both disappeared down the stair.

As soon as they were gone, I checked the smoldering remains of

Mike. Quick-Flame™ cubes are all very well, but they don't always burn everything, and if there's a critical mass of organic material left, then the vamp nanos can build a new one. A little, slow one, but little, slow ones can grow up. I doubted there'd been enough exchange of blood to get full infestation, but it's better to be sure, so I took out the splinter again and waved it over the fragments that were left.

The sound of rapid gunshots began to echo up from below as I took off my T-shirt and tucked it in the back of my board shorts. The tau cross on my chest was already glowing softly with a silver light, the smart matter under the scars energizing as it detected vamp activity close by. I couldn't see the one on my back, but it would be doing the same thing. Together they were supposed to generate a field that repulsed the vampires and slowed them down if they got close, but it really only worked on the original versions. The latter-day generations of vampires were such bad copies that a lot of the original tech built to deter them simply missed the mark. Fortunately, being bad copies, the newer vampires were weaker, slower, less intelligent, and untrained.

I took the main stairs up to the fourth floor. The Ancient Vampire would already know I was coming, so there was no point skulking up the elevator shaft or the outside drain. Like its broodmates, it had been bred to be a perfect soldier at various levels of conflict, from the nanonic frontline where it tried to replicate itself in its enemies to the gross physical contest of actually duking it out. Back in the old days it might have had some distance weapons as well, but if there was one thing we'd managed right in the original mission, it was taking out the vamp weapons caches and resupply nodes.

We did a lot of things right in the original mission. We succeeded rather too well, or at least so we thought at the time. If the victory hadn't been so much faster than anticipated, the boss would never have had those years to fall in love with humans and then work out his crazy scheme to become their living god.

Not so crazy, perhaps, since it kind of worked, even after I tried to do my duty and stop him. In a halfhearted way, I suppose, because he was team leader and all that. But he was going totally against regulations. I reported it and I got the order, and the rest, as they say, is history. . . .

Using the splinter always reminds me of him, and the old days. There's probably enough smart matter in the wood, encasing his DNA and his last download, to bring him back complete, if and when I ever finish this assignment and can signal for pickup. Though a court would probably confirm HQ's original order, and he'd be slowed into something close to a full stop anyway.

But my mission won't be over till the last vamp is burned to ash and this infested Earth can be truly proclaimed clean.

Which is likely to be a long, long time, and I reminded myself that daydreaming about the old days was not going to help take out the Ancient Vampire ahead of me, let alone the many more in the world beyond.

I took out the splinter and the silver knife and slung my Pan Am bag so it was comfortable, and got serious.

I heard the Ancient moving around as I stepped into what was once the outer office. The big pot was surrounded by soil and there were dirty footprints up the wall, but I didn't need to see them to know to look up. The vamps have a desire to dominate the high ground heavily programmed into them. They always go for the ceiling, up trees, up towers, up lampposts.

This one was spread-eagled on the ceiling, gripping with its foreleg and trailing leg filaments as well as the hooks on what humans thought were fingers and toes. It was pretty big as vamps go, perhaps nine feet long and weighing in at around two hundred pounds. The ultrathin waist gave away its insectoid heritage almost as much as a really close look at its mouth would. Not that you would want a really close look at a vamp's mouth.

It squealed when I came in and it caught the tau emissions. The squeal was basically an ultrasonic alarm oscillating through several wavelengths. The cops outside would hear it as an unearthly scream, when in fact it was more along the lines of a distress call and emergency rally beacon. If any of its brood survived down below, they'd drop whatever they might be doing—or chewing—and rush on up.

The squcal was standard operating procedure, straight out of the manual. It followed up with another orthodox move, dropping straight onto me. I flipped on my back and struck with the splinter, but the vamp managed to spin itself in midair and bounce off the wall, coming to a stop in the far corner.

It was fast, faster than any vamp I'd seen for a long time. I'd scratched it with the splinter, but no more than that. There was a line of silver across the dark red chitin of its chest, where the transferred smart matter was leaching the vampire's internal electrical potential to build a bomb, but it would take at least five seconds to do that, which was way too long.

I leapt and struck again and we conducted a kind of crazy ballet across the four walls, the ceiling, and the floor of the room. Anyone watching would have got motion sickness or eyeball fatigue, trying to catch blurs of movement.

At 2.350 seconds in, it got a forearm around my left elbow and gave it a good hard pull, dislocating my arm at the shoulder. I knew then it really was ancient and had retained the programming needed to fight me. My joints have always been a weak point.

It hurt. A lot. And it kept on hurting through several microseconds as the vamp tried to actually pull my arm off and at the same time twist itself around to start chewing on my leg.

The tau field was discouraging the vamp, making it dump some of its internal nanoware, so that blood started geysering out of pinholes all over its body, but this was more of a nuisance for me than any major hindrance to it.

In midsomersault, somewhere near the ceiling, with the thing trying to wrap itself around me, I dropped the silver knife. It wasn't a real weapon, not like the splinter. I kept it for sentimental reasons, as much as anything, though silver did have a deleterious effect on younger vamps. Since it was pure sentiment, I suppose I could have left it in the form of coins, but then I'd probably be forever dropping some in combat and having to waste time later picking them up. Besides, when silver was still the usual currency and they were still coins, I'd got drunk a few times and spent them, and it was way too big a hassle getting them back.

The vamp took the knife-dropping as more significant than it was, which was one of the reasons I'd let it go. In the old days, I would have held something serious in my left hand, like a deweaving wand, which the vampire probably thought the knife was—and it wanted to get it and use it on me. It partially let go of my arm as it tried to catch the weapon, and at that precise moment, second 2.355, I feinted with the splinter, slid it along the thing's attempted forearm block, and reversing my elbow joint, stuck it right in the forehead.

With the smart matter already at work from its previous scratch, internal explosion occurred immediately. I had shut my eyes in preparation, so I was only blown against the wall and not temporarily blinded as well.

I assessed the damage as I wearily got back up. My left arm was fully dislocated, with the tendons ripped away, so I couldn't put it back. It was going to have to hang for a day or two, hurting like crazy till it self-healed. Besides that, I had severe bruising to my lower back and ribs, which would also deliver some serious pain.

I hadn't been hurt as seriously by a vamp for a long, long time, so I spent a few minutes searching through the scraps of mostly disintegrated vampire to find a piece big enough to meaningfully scan. Once I got it back to the jumper, I'd be able to pick it apart on the atomic level to find the serial number on some of its defunct nanoware.

I put the scrap of what was probably skeleton in my flight bag, with the splinter and the silver knife, and wandered downstairs. I left it unzipped, because I hadn't heard any firing for a while, which meant either Susan and Karl had cleaned up, or the vamps had cleaned up Susan and Karl. But I put my T-shirt back on. No need to scare the locals. It was surprisingly clean, considering. My skin and hair shed vampire blood, so the rest of me looked quite respectable as well. Apart from the arm hanging down like an orangutan's, that is.

I'd calculated the odds at about five to two that Susan and Karl would win, so I was pleased to see them in the entrance lobby. They both jumped when I came down the stairs. I was ready to move if they shot at me, but they managed to control themselves.

"Did you get them all?" I asked. I didn't move any closer.

"Nine," said Karl. "Like you said. Nine holes in the ground, nine burned vampires."

"You didn't get bitten?"

"Does it look like we did?" asked Susan, with a shudder. She was clearly thinking about Mike.

"Vampires can infect with a small, tidy bite," I said. "Or even about half a cup of their saliva, via a kiss."

Susan did throw up then, which is what I wanted. She wouldn't have if she'd been bitten. I was also telling the truth. While they were designed to be soldiers, the vampires were also made to be guerilla fighters, working among the human population, infecting as many as possible in small, subtle ways. They only went for the big chow-down in full combat.

"What about you?" asked Karl. "You okay?"

"You mean this?" I asked, threshing my arm about like a tentacle, wincing as it made the pain ten times worse. "Dislocated. But I didn't get bitten."

Neither had Karl, I was now sure. Even newly infected humans have something about them that gives their condition away, and I can always pick it up.

"Which means we can go and sit by the fence and wait till morning," I said cheerily. "You've done well."

Karl nodded wearily and got his hand under Susan's elbow, lifting her up. She wiped her mouth and the two of them walked slowly to the door.

I let them go first, which was kind of mean, because the VET have been known to harbor trigger-happy snipers. But there was no sudden death from above, so we walked over to the fence and then the two of them flopped down on the ground, and Karl began to laugh hysterically.

I left them to it and wandered over to the gate.

"You can let me out now," I called to the sergeant. "My work here is almost done."

"No one comes out till after dawn," replied the guardian of the city.

"Except me," I agreed. "Check with Lieutenant Harman."

Which goes to show that I can read ID labels, even little ones on metal-mesh skinsuits.

The sergeant didn't need to check. Lieutenant Harman was already looming up behind him. They had a short but spirited conversation, the sergeant told Karl and Susan to stay where they were, which was still lying on the ground essentially in severe shock, and they powered down the gate for about thirty seconds and I came out.

Two medics came over to help me. Fortunately they were VET, not locals, so we didn't waste time arguing about me going to the hospital, getting lots of drugs injected, having scans, et cetera. They fixed me up with a collar and cuff sling so my arm wasn't dragging about the place, I said thank you, and they retired to their unmarked ambulance.

Then I wandered over to where Jenny was sitting on the far side of the silver truck, her back against the rear wheel. She'd taken off her helmet and balaclava, letting her bobbed brown hair spring back out into shape. She looked about eighteen, maybe even younger, maybe a little older. A pretty young woman, her face made no worse by evidence of tears, though she was very pale.

She jumped as I tapped a little rhythm on the side of the truck.

"Oh . . . I thought . . . aren't you meant to stay inside the . . . the cordon?"

I hunkered down next to her.

"Yeah, most of the time they enforce that, but it depends," I said. "How are you doing?"

"Me? I'm . . . I'm okay. So you got them?"

"We did," I confirmed. I didn't mention Mike. She didn't need to know that, not now.

"Good," she said. "I'm sorry . . . I thought I would be braver. Only, when the time came . . ."

"I understand," I said.

"I don't see how you can," she said. "I mean, you went in, and you said you fight vampires all the time. You must be incredibly brave."

"No," I replied. "Bravery is about overcoming fear, not about not having it. There's plenty I'm afraid of. Just not vampires."

"We fear the unknown," she said. "You must know a lot about vampires."

I nodded and moved my flight bag around to get more comfortable. It was still unzipped, but the sides were pushed together at the top.

"How to fight them, I mean," she added. "Since no one really knows anything else. That's the worst thing. When my sister was in-infected and then later, when she was . . . was killed, I really wanted to know, and there was no one to tell me anything."

"What did you want to know?" I asked. I've always been prone to show off to pretty girls. If it isn't surfing, it's secret knowledge. Though sharing the secret knowledge only occurred in special cases, when I knew it would go no further.

"Everything we don't know," sighed Jenny. "What are they, really? Why have they suddenly appeared all over the place in the last ten years, when we all thought they were just . . . just made up."

"They're killing machines," I explained. "Bioengineered self-replicating guerilla soldiers, dropped here kind of by mistake a long time ago. They've been in hiding mostly, waiting for a signal or other stimuli to activate. Certain frequencies of radio waves will do it, and the growth of cell phone use . . ."

"So what, vampires get irritated by cell phones?"

A smile started to curl up one side of her mouth. I smiled too, and kept talking.

"You see, way back when, there were these good aliens and these bad aliens, and there was a gigantic space battle—"

Jenny started laughing.

"Do you want me to do a personality test before I can hear the rest of the story?"

"I think you'd pass," I said. I had tried to make her laugh, even though it was kind of true about the aliens and the space battle. Only there were just bad aliens and even worse aliens, and the vampires had been dropped on Earth by mistake. They had been meant for a world where the nights were very long.

Jenny kept laughing and looked down, just for an instant. I moved at my highest speed—and she died laughing, the splinter working instantly on both human nervous system and the twenty-four-hours-old infestation of vampire nanoware.

We had lost the war, which was why I was there, cleaning up one of our mistakes. Why I would be on Earth for countless years to come.

I felt glad to have my straightforward purpose, my assigned

task. It is too easy to become involved with humans, to want more for them, to interfere with their lives. I didn't want to make the boss's mistake. I'm not human, and I don't want to become human or make them better people. I was just going to follow orders, keep cleaning out the infestation, and that was that.

The bite was low on Jenny's neck, almost at the shoulder. I showed it to the VET people and asked them to do the rest.

I didn't stay to watch. My arm hurt, and I could hear a girl laughing, somewhere deep within my head.

GARTH NIX was born in 1963 in Melbourne, Australia, and grew up in Canberra. When he turned nineteen, he left to drive around the UK in a beat-up Austin with a boot full of books and a Silver-Reed typewriter. Despite a wheel literally falling off the car, he survived to return to Australia and study at the University of Canberra. He has since worked in a bookshop, as a book publicist, a publisher's sales representative, an editor, a literary agent, and a public relations and marketing consultant. He was also a part-time soldier in the Australian Army Reserve, but now writes full-time.

His first story was published in 1984 and was followed by novels *The Ragwitch*, *Sabriel*, *Shade's Children*, *Lirael*, *Abhorsen*, the six-book YA fantasy series The Seventh Tower, and most recently, the seven-book Keys to the Kingdom series. He lives in Sydney with his wife and their two children.

His Web site is www.garthnix.com.

AUTHOR'S NOTE

I tend to write short stories when I should be working on a novel. "Infestation" was written when I was supposed to be checking page proofs of my novel *Sir Thursday*, so I guess this story can also be classified as the product of an avoidance technique. At least it is a more productive technique than making a cup of tea or reading the newspaper, two activities that often occur when I am supposed to be working on a book.

The image of the out-of-place surfer dude vampire hunter came first with this story. He was all alone, without any context, and the rest came into focus around him as I worked out who (and what) he actually was. Because I wanted to write a story specifically for this collection, it had to be SF, not fantasy (though it could have gone down that road). As Jonathan Strahan was reminding me to hurry up with it, the various elements that were floating around in my head went into a kind of pressure cooker. I had the ingredients, the customer was demanding science fiction, and I just had to cook it right.

As befits the pressure-cooker analogy, I wrote the first draft of the story very quickly, in just a couple of days. Then I spent rather more time spread over several months fine-tuning it and ended up (as I usually do) delivering the final version later rather than sooner.

It's not the first "vampires as aliens" story, nor is it the first story to depict major religious figures as interfering aliens, but while it is not particularly original in its big ideas, I hope the smaller ideas and details, the mood, and the style will all make it work for the reader.

PINOCCHIO

Walter Jon Williams

Errol has the kind of eagerness that you only see when someone can't wait to tell you the bad news. I can see this even though his hologram, appearing in the corner of my room, is a quarter real size.

"Have you seen Kimmie's flash?" he asks. "It's all about you. And it's, uh—well, you should look at it."

I'm changing clothes and sort of distracted.

"What does she say?" I ask. Because I figure it's going to be, Oh, Sanson didn't pay enough attention to me at the dance, or something.

"She says that you took money for wearing the Silverback body," Errol says. "She says you're a sellout."

Which stops me dead, right in the middle of putting on my new shorts.

"Well," I say as I hop on one foot. "That's interesting."

I can tell that Errol is very eager to know whether Kimmie's little factoid is true.

"Should I get the Pack together?" he asks.

I stop hopping and put my foot on the floor. My shorts hang abandoned around one ankle.

"Maybe," I said, and then decide against it. "No. We're meeting tomorrow anyway."

"You sure?"

"Yeah." Because right now I want a little time to myself.

I've got to think.

THINGS TO DO IF YOU'RE A GORILLA

- Make a drum out of a hollow log.
- Look under the log for tasty grubs and eat them.
- Pound the drum while your friends do a joyful thumping dance.
- Play poker.
- Make a hut out of branches and native grasses. Demolish it. Repeat.
- Groom your steady.
- Learn sign language. (It's traditional.)
- Do exhibition ballroom dancing.
- Go to the woods with your friends. Lie in a pile in the sun. Repeat.
- Intimidate your friends who are gibbons or chimps.
- Attend a costume party wearing eighteenth-century French court dress.

- Race up and down the exteriors of tall buildings. Extra points for carrying an attractive blonde on your shoulder, but in that case beware of biplanes.

- Join a league and play gorillaball. (Rules follow.)

I pull on my shorts and knuckle-walk over to my comm corner. My rig is an eight-year-old San Simeon, assembled during the fortnight or so when Peru was the place to go for things electronic—it's old, but it's all I need considering that I hardly ever flashcast from my room anyway. I mostly use it for school, and sometimes for editing flashcast material when I'm tired of wearing my headset.

I squat down on a little stool—being gorilloid, I don't sit like normal people—and then turn on the cameras so I can record myself watching Kimmie's broadcast.

I don't think about the cameras much. I'm used to them. I scratch myself as I tell the San Simeon to find Kimmie's flash and show it to me.

Kimmie looks good. She's traded in the gorilloid form for an appealing human body, all big eyes and freckles and sunbleached hair. She's never been blonde before. The hair is in braids.

She seems completely wholesome, like someone in a milk ad. You'd never know that sometime in the last ten days she came out of a vat.

I watch and listen while my former girlfriend tells the world I'm slime. Vacant, useless, greedy slime.

"He's a lot angrier than people think," Kimmie says. "He always hides that."

Unlike someone, I think, who isn't hiding her anger *at all*.

For a while this doesn't much bother me. Kimmie's body is new and it's like being attacked by a clueless stranger. But then I start seeing things I recognize—the expressions on her face, the way she phrases her words, the body language—and the horror begins to sink in.

It's Kimmie. It's the girl I love. And she hates me now, and she'll be telling the whole world why.

Kimmie lists several more of my deficiencies, then gets to the issue I've been dreading.

"There was a point where I realized I couldn't trust him anymore. He was taking money for the things he used to do for fun. That's when I stopped being in love."

No, I think, you've got the sequence wrong. Because it was when you started pulling away that I got insecure, and in order to restore the kind of intimacy we'd had, I started telling you the things I should have kept to myself.

THINGS TO DO WHEN YOU'VE JUST BEEN DUMPED

- Lie in bed and stare at the ceiling.
- Feel as if your heart has been ripped out of your chest by a giant claw.
- Find the big picture of her you kept by your bed and rip it into bits.
- Wonder why she hates you now.
- Beat your chest.
- Try to put the picture back together with tape. Fail.
- Cry.

- Beat your chest.
- Run up into the hills and demolish a tree with your bare hands.
- Watch her flashcast again and again.

When I watch Kimmie's flashcast for the third or fourth time I notice her braids.

Braids. She's never worn braids before. So I watch the image carefully and I see that the braids are woven with some kind of fluorescent thread that glows very subtly through the cooler colors, violet, blue, and green.

And then I notice that there's something going on with her eyes. I thought they were blue at first, but now I realize that the borders of her irises are shifting, and they're shifting through the same spectrum as the threads in her hair.

I had been paying so much attention to what she was saying that I hadn't been looking at the *image*.

Image, I think. Now I understand what she's trying to do.

I was wrong about her all along.

I call my parents. My mom is 140 years old, and my dad is 87, so even though they don't look much older than me, they have a hard time remembering what it was like to be young. But they're smart—Mom is a professor of Interdisciplinary Studies at the College of Mystery, and Dad is vice president of marketing for Hanan—and they're both good at strategy.

My dad advises me not to try responding to Kimmie directly. "You're a lot more famous than she is," he points out. "If you get involved in a he-said-she-said situation, you're both legitimizing her arguments and putting her on an equal plane with yourself. It's what she wants, so don't play her game."

"I never liked Kimmie," my mom begins.

Hearing my mom speak of Kimmie in that tone makes me want to jump to Kimmie's defense. But that would be idiotic so I don't say anything.

Mom thinks for a moment. "What you should do is be nice to her," she said. "Saint Paul said that doing good for your enemy is like pouring hot coals on her head."

"A *saint* said that?"

My mom smiled. "He was a pretty angry saint."

The more I thought about Mom's idea, the more I liked it.

I decided to order up a bucket of hot coals.

I became famous more or less by accident. Forming a flashpack was one of the things my friends and I decided to do when we were thirteen, for no more reason than we were looking for something to do and the technology was just sitting there waiting for us to use it. And, of course, everyone and his brother (and his uncles and aunts) were flashcasting, too. Our first flashcasts were about as amateurish and useless as you would expect. But we got better, and after a while the public, which is to say millions of my peers, began to respond.

What the public responded to was me, which I didn't understand and still don't. I would have thought that if people liked anyone, it would have been Ludmila or Tony—Ludmila was much more glamorous, and Tony had led a much more interesting life. But no—I became the star and they didn't.

The others in the pack either accepted the situation or faded away. I think I'm still friends with the ones who left, but I don't see them very often. Being famous has a way of taking you away from one world and putting you in another.

In flashcast after flashcast it turned out that I was good at only one thing, which was explaining to other people what it's like to be me. In our world, where there are very few young people, that turns out to be an important skill.

Kids are pretty thin on the ground. I have a parent who's over a hundred and who looks maybe twenty-five, and who is essentially immortal. If something happens to the body she's in, she'll be reloaded from one of dozens of backups stored on Earth or in space. She won't die as long as our civilization survives.

Neither will anyone else. That doesn't leave a lot of room on Earth for children.

In order to have me, my parents had to pay a hefty tax, in order to pay for the resources I'd be consuming as I grew up, and then demonstrate that they had the financial wherewithal to support me until I could earn my own living. Financial resources like that take decades to build. That's why my parents couldn't have children when they were younger.

So by the time they had me, my parents had pretty well forgotten what it was like to be young. My friends' parents weren't young either. We were a very few kids trapped in a world of the very old. I regularly hear from kids who are the only person in their town under the age of sixty.

Sometimes it's good to know that you aren't the only kid out there. Sometimes we have to have help to remind us who we are. Sometimes it's good to have someone to aid you with all the rituals of growing up, the problems of dealing with friends and rivals, the difficulties of courtship, the decisions of what body to wear and what shoes to wear with it. It's good to have a friend you can count on.

Well, boys and girls, that friend is me.

Q: Do we really have to play gorillaball *naked*?
A: We tried it in darling little blue velvet suits with knickers, but the lacy cuffs got all spoiled.

Next day, the pack meets so that we can practice gorillaball. It's a game that we—mostly me—invented, so now we're sort of obliged to play it.

Our team is called the Stars. Because, let's face it, we are.

We practice in the hills up above Oakland, natural gorilla country. The air is heavy with the scents of the genetically modified tropical blossoms that stabilize the hillsides. We crash through bushes, smash into each other with big meaty thuds, rollick up and down trees, and scamper over the occasional building that finds itself in the way. The birds are stunned into a terrified silence. It's a good practice and we end up with our fur covered with dust and debris.

For a while I forget about Kimmie.

We've got grain cameras floating in the air the whole time and everything is uploaded, available for anyone interested in the gorillaball experience. Shawn will edit the thing tomorrow and make a more or less coherent story out of it. We keep uploading as all fifteen of us pile onto the roof of a tram and head back to our clubhouse, waving to people on the street and hanging over the edge of the tram roof to make faces at the passengers.

Our pack headquarters is in the Samaritain, which is a hotel and which gives us the suite free, because the owners of the apartment like the publicity we bring them. We jump off the tram and bound over the pointed iron fence into the pool area, where we splash around until we get the dust out of our fur, and then we lie in the sun and groom each other till we're dry.

You don't want to smell wet gorilla fur if you don't have to. That's one reason for the grooming. The other is social. We're a pack, after all, and packs do things together.

The grain cameras are still floating around us, maybe a hundred of them, each the size of a grain of rice. No single camera delivers an acceptable image, but once the images are enhanced and jigsawed together by a computer, you have a comprehensive picture. We're still flashcasting, and for some reason the world is still interested. The splice on my optic nerve tells me that a couple hundred thousand people are watching us as we comb through one another's hair.

Mostly I groom Lisa. I don't know her as well as I know the others, because she's a year younger and new to the pack. She's a member because her older cousin Anatole has been part of the group from the beginning, and he made a special request. He's the brash, self-confident one . . . and Lisa's not. That's about all I know about her, aside from the rumor that she's supposed to be some kind of genius with electronics—even more so than the rest of us, I mean. So I figure it's time I get to know her better.

As I comb through the fur on her shoulders, I ask her about what she's studying.

"Lots of things," she says. "But I'm really getting interested in cultural hermeneutics."

Which produced a pause in the conversation, as you might imagine. I imagined tens of thousands of simultaneous calls on online dictionaries demanding a definition of *hermeneutics*.

"So, what makes that interesting for you?" I say.

"It tells you who created a thing," Lisa says, "and why, and what tools were used, and how it relates to other things that were created. And—" She flapped her hands. "You know, I'm not saying this well."

"Give an example," I urge, because I figured my audience was getting lost.

"Well, look at the headplay *Mooncakes*. It helps to know that it's a rewrite of an earlier work called *The Prodigal*, and that in the original the character of Doctor Yau was a parody of a politician of that period named Coswell. And that the character of Hollyhock has to do with a fad of that time called mindslipping, where people deliberately inserted a shunt between the right and left sides of their brain, and programmed it to randomly shift dominance from one to the other."

"So," I say, "that's why half the time she's talking like a machine, and the rest of the time her dialogue sounds like some kind of poetry."

"Right," Lisa says. "But people had given up mindslipping by the time *Mooncakes* was released, so much of the audience wouldn't understand the character of Hollyhock at all. So instead of Hollyhock being a comment on a contemporary phenomenon, she was just played for laughs in the remake. And though the Doctor Yau character was more or less the same as the original, the references to Coswell are lost."

"Maybe I'll download it and viddie it again with all that in mind."

"I wouldn't bother." She shrugs. "I didn't think it was that good the first time." She looks up at me. "I'd better fix the hair on your head," she says. "If it dries that way, you'll look like Vashti the Dwad for the rest of the day."

She crouches behind me and begins to comb my hair. "So it's flashplays you're interested in?" I ask.

"Not usually. Hermeneutics can analyze any artifact—a book, a video, a building. Any cultural phenomenon. The idea is that you start with the phenomenon and work backward to try to figure out the people and the culture that produced it."

I looked at her. "You could analyze *me*," I said.

"I could," she said. "But why? You're one of the most analyzed phenomena in the world. Anything I could say has already been said."

"I hope not."

She lowered her eyes. "You know what I mean."

"Yeah. I know. But people say things anyway, even if they're not new."

I shake myself and roll onto my feet and knuckles. I take a breath. What I say now is crucial.

"So, has anyone seen Kimmie's flashcast?" I ask.

Just about everyone raises their hands. Lisa didn't, I notice.

"Let's watch it together," I say. I look at Lisa and wink at her. "See if she has anything new to say."

We roll into the clubhouse. The furniture creaks under our huge gorilla bodies.

People put on headsets or visors or pull their video capes from out of their pockets, and I tell video walls and the holographic projectors to turn on, and then I look up Kimmie's flashcast and play it. Suddenly Kimmie is everywhere in the room, her image repeated on practically every surface. It's overwhelming.

My breath catches in my throat. I've watched the flash enough times so that I think I've immunized myself, but apparently I'm wrong. A horrible sense of dread seeps into my veins.

So we watch the flash. There's a lot of groaning and laughter as Kimmie offers her revelations. I begin to feel the dread fade. This is a lot better than watching it alone.

By the end people get raucous, and Kimmie's final statements are drowned out by denunciations.

"Hey," I say. "Let's not get angry! This is still someone I have feelings about." I give what I hope is a wise nod. "I know what we should do."

We should pour a bucket of coals on Kimmie's head.

"We should all send a message to Kimmie telling her that we love her," I say, "and that we understand her problems." I picture Kimmie's message buffer filling with millions of messages from my audience.

"And while you're at it," I say with a wink, "tell her that you really like that thing she did with her eyes."

If you're not gorilla, you're just vanilla.

After we'd sent our messages to Kimmie, I ask if anyone has any questions. I'm kind of nervous so I roll to my left, end the roll on my feet, and then roll back to my right.

Simple gymnastics are one of the great things about being a gorilla. I'm going to miss that when I'm back in a standard human body.

Cody raises a hand. "Were you really mad at Albert that time?" she asks.

Everybody sort of laughs.

"No," I say. "I was amused. Kimmie was kind of mad at him, though, so maybe she thought I was mad at him, too."

Take that.

I do some somersaults on the Samaritain's deep pile carpets. "Anything else?" I ask.

"Okay," Errol says. "Everyone wants to know if you really took money for wearing the gorilla body."

"I'm not going to answer that right away," I say. I roll to my left, then to my right. It's important that I get this right.

"What I want to do is ask another question," I say. "Now, Errol, you've got your visor on, right?"

"Sure."

"And what brand is your visor?"

He blinked. "Esquiline," he says.

"You like it? You think it's a good visor?"

He shrugs his huge ape shoulders. "I guess," he says.

"What if I offered you money for wearing the visor? Would you take it?"

Errol looks at me. "But I'm *already* wearing it," he says.

"So, what if I offered to pay you for what you're already wearing? Would you take the money?"

He raises his shaggy eyebrows. "All I have to do is wear it?"

"Right."

"I guess I'd take the money, yeah. If that's all there was to it."

"Okay." I look up into the corner of the room where we've got a camera, and with my visor I tell the camera to zoom in on my face so that I can look right at my audience of millions.

"What would *you* do?" I ask.

• • •

"You've had an eight percent drop in your audience in the last six weeks," my father says.

I put down my forkful of chicken in Hunan sauce.

"It's a blip," I tell him. "It's the part of the Demographic that wasn't interested in being a gorilla."

"The gorilla thing was a mistake," my father says.

Wearily, I agree that the gorilla thing was a misstep.

Wearily, I eat my Hunan chicken.

"The problem is that there aren't any great clothes to wear with a gorilla body," my dad says. "No designer's dressing for the Silverback. Baggy shorts and floppy tees, that's all you had to work with. No wonder you couldn't make it cool."

I wish I could get out of the gorilla body. But I can't, not till after the last gorillaball game.

What happened was that DNAble had sent a vice president to show me their new body lines. "The Silverback just isn't moving like we thought it would," she said. She looked at me. "It's got a lot of unexplored potential. It just needs somebody like you to show everyone how much fun it could be."

I knew right away why the Silverback hadn't become popular, reasons totally separate from the issue of how you fashionably clothe a hairy gorilla. If you want to be an ape, you'd pick a gibbon or a siamang or an orangutan, because those are the ones that can zoom hand-over-hand through the trees. Our pack had already been orangutans, and it was *great*.

By comparison, gorillas just sort of sit there.

But I needed to start something new. My audience was starting to get bored with my current round of parties and clubs and clothes.

"I'll think about it," I said. Already the first thoughts of gorilla-ball were stirring in my subconscious.

The flattery worked—*Only you can save us, Sanson!*

The VP looked at me again. "I'm authorized to offer you inducements," she said. "If there's a big uptick in gorilla body sales, we can arrange for a bonus."

I didn't answer right away.

But what really happened wasn't quite what I told the pack by the pool. Real life is more complicated than you can express on video.

"Want some more fish?" I ask my dad.

"Thanks."

My dad's body is tall and wiry and at home he dresses in khakis, very immaculate, as if at any moment he might be called upon to sell something and need to look his best. He's cooked this whole Chinese meal, with sticky rice in lotus leaves and a steamed fish and Hunan chicken and orange peel beef, and since my mom is delivering a lecture series in Milan, there's only the two of us to eat it. Huge platters of food cover the antique oak table between us.

Fortunately the gorilla body needs a lot of feeding.

"We've got to figure out a way to grow the Demographic," my dad says.

"The Demographic" is what my dad, the marketing whiz, calls my audience. Every product, according to him, has a "demographic" that forms its natural consumers, and his job is to alert that demographic to the existence and alleged superiority of the product.

By "product," he means me.

My dad's audience has to be alerted by stealth. Nobody has to look at advertisements if they don't want to. In my Media and

Society classes, I learned that broadcast media used to be full of adverts, but they're not anymore because people can download their entertainment from other sources. You see holograms and posters in stores and public places, but every other form of advertising has to be sneaky. It has to disguise itself as something else.

My dad is a specialist in that kind of advertising.

If you're my age, you grow up suspicious. When you see something new, you wonder if it's genuine or a camouflaged advertisement for something else.

That's why Kimmie's revelation could be trouble for me. If I turn out to be nothing but an advertisement for DNAble, then the Demographic might never trust me again.

The numbers are important because they can turn into money. Even though my flashcasts are given away free, I get paid for an occasional fashion shoot, or an interview, or for appearing on broadcast video. *Darby's Train* and *Let's Watch Wang* may be silly comedies, but they pay their guest stars very well.

Fortunately I don't have to do any acting on these programs. I appear as myself. I walk on and all this insane comedy happens around me and in the third act I deliver a few pearls of wisdom that solve the star's problem.

Which means I'll be starting my adult life with a nice little nest egg. I won't be rich, but I'll be ahead of the average twenty-year-old.

"So how do we grow the Demographic?" I ask my dad.

"A new love interest always produces a bounce."

"So do babies," I say, "but I'm not going to start one now."

He grins. "Okay. The Demographic is growing older. You need to give them a more mature product. More mature clothing choices, more mature music . . ."

I want to tell him that my tastes are my tastes, and they've done pretty well for me so far.

Eight percent.

I've got to do *something*, I think.

We all know how lucky we are. There aren't any wars anymore. There's no permanent death. Nobody has to get old if they don't want to. There's no poverty, except for a few people who deliberately go off to live without material possessions and eat weeds, and they don't count. There are diseases, but even if one of them kills you, they'll bring you back.

Our elders have solved all the big problems. The only things left for us to care about are fashion, celebrity, and consumerism.

And the pursuit of knowledge, if that's the sort of thing that appeals to you. The problem being that you'll have to do a few hundred years of catching up before the elders will pay you any attention.

We can change bodies if we like. You lie down in a pool of shallow warm water that's thick with tiny little microscopic nanobots, and the bots swim into your body and swarm right to your brain, where they record everything—every thought, every memory, every reflex, everything that makes up your self and soul. And then all this information is transferred into another body that's been built to your own specifications by *another* few billion nanobots, and once a lot of safety checks are made, you bound out of bed happy in your new body, and your old body is disassembled and the ingredients recycled.

Unless you want something unusual, the basic procedure costs less than a bicycle. Bicycles have moving mechanical parts that have to be assembled by hand or by a machine. The nanobots do everything automatically and are powered by, basically, sugar.

Our custom brains are smart. We don't have to deal with stupid people or the messes they cause. We *do* have to cope with a bunch of hypercritical geniuses nitpicking us to death, but at least that's better than having a bunch of morons with guns *shooting* at us, which is what people in history seemed to have to deal with all the time.

Within certain limits our bodies look like whatever we want. Everyone is beautiful, everyone is healthy, everyone is intelligent. That's the *norm.*

But where, you might wonder, does that leave *you*? Who are *you*, exactly?

What I mean is, how do you find out that you're *you* and not one of a bunch of equally talented, equally attractive, equally artificial *them*s?

How do you find out that you're a person, and not some kind of incredibly sophisticated biological robot?

You find out by exploring different options, and by encountering challenges and overcoming them. Or *not* overcoming them, as the case may be.

You learn who you are by making friends, because one way of finding out who you are is by figuring out who your friends think you are.

Your friends can be the kind you meet in the flesh. If you live in the Bay Area, like me, there are eight or nine thousand people under the age of twenty, so odds are you'll find some that are compatible.

You can make the kind of friends you only meet electronically, through shared interests or just by hanging around in electric forums.

Or you can work out who you are by watching someone else grow up and struggle with the same problems.

If you're my age or a little younger, odds are that someone else would be me.

I check out the messages that have been flooding in since the last flashcast. The artificial intelligence in my comm unit has already sorted them into broad categories:

- I'd take the money.
- I wouldn't take the money.
- I wouldn't take the money, and if you did, you're evil.
- I hate Kimmie.
- I hate you.
- Gorillas are lame.
- I'm a reporter and I'd like an interview.
- I built the hut, so now what?
- I'd really like a date, and here's my video and contact information.

Some of those last videos are very stimulating.

Stimulating or not, they all get a polite but negative response. Meeting girls is not a problem for me.

And in any case, I can't get Kimmie out of my head.

The messages from reporters I file till later. All they want to talk about is Kimmie anyway.

I pick a representative sample of the rest of the messages and make a flashcast of them. I give some a personal reply. The whole point of flashcasts is that they create a community between the subject and the viewer, and so even the ones who don't like me get their say, and sometimes I'll respond with something like, "Well if *that's* the reason you hate me, you'll probably like Joss Mackenzie, go check out his flashes, I think he's still a snake," or "Sounds like you and the girl in the previous message should be friends."

When they hate me, I don't hate them back. Not publicly, anyway. That's not who I am.

(Publicly.)

After the flashcast, I take one of my classes. I'm sixteen and should finish college in a year and a half. I don't personally attend class very often, because then the class fills up with people who want to watch me instead of the teacher, so instead I use a headset to project myself into a virtual class.

The class is Media and Society, and the professor is Dr. Granger, who I don't like. He's got a young, seamless face and wavy gray hair like sculpted concrete, and he paces up and down and gestures like a ham actor as he orates for his audience.

That's not why I don't like him, though that's probably bad enough. When he found out I was taking his class, he opened up the flashcast to anyone, not just those who had signed up for his class. He knows this is his chance to be famous, and he's not about to miss it. If he realizes how pathetic it is that he, a man in his nineties, is leaching off the fame of his sixteen-year-old student, he has shown no sign of it.

"The chief characteristic of modern media," Granger says, "is the existence of near-instantaneous feedback." He's dressed very stylishly today, with a charcoal-gray turtleneck and a blazer and a white silk scarf that he's somehow forgotten to take off when he entered the lecture hall, and that ripples when he walks. Awareness of a worldwide audience has upgraded his wardrobe.

"The reaction of the audience can be viewed by the performers immediately after the performance—sometimes during it. So while performers have always taken their audience into account—always judged their performance and its effects with regard to the public—there is now a special urgency involved. A worldwide consensus on a given performance can be reached before the performance is even over."

I know what the consensus on Dr. Granger's performance is. The Demographic despises him. I wonder if he knows it.

"For those the audience chooses to condemn," he says, "the penalty is oblivion. For those to whom the audience grants its favor, instant fame is possible. But continuing fame depends on continuing positive feedback. Performers have to take their audience into account every minute, and the good ones, like all good performers, anticipate what their audience wants and find a way to give it to them. But now more than ever a performer has to be careful not to alienate their core demographic."

There's the damn Demographic again, I think.

He turns to me. "Sanson," he says, "do you keep your audience in mind when you're making a flashcast?"

He's always using me in class as an example, another reason I don't like him.

At the moment, however, I purely *hate* him, because he's asked one of those questions for which there's no good answer. If I say I worry about what the audience thinks, then I'm not my own person. But if I say that I don't care what the audience thinks, the Demographic will get mad at me for saying that they don't matter.

"I'm not a performer," I say. "I'm not any kind of actor at all. I just *do* stuff."

"But still you present programs with yourself as the focus," Granger says. "You perform in that sense. So I wonder if you concern yourself with what your audience is going to say after each flashcast."

I feel a little flutter of unease.

"I respect their opinions," I say. "But that still comes afterward. We can all have a big discussion later on, but when something's going on, the only people I'm interacting with is my pack."

Dr. Granger gives me a big smile. "Aren't you worried about losing your audience?"

Eight percent, I think.

Let me tell you what it's like. When I was eight my parents took me on a vacation to the Middle East, and we went to the Dead Sea and I took a swim. The water is so dense with salt that it holds you up, and you just lie there with the hot sun shining down on you in the warm water, as if it were the most comfortable mattress in the world, and you know that no matter what happens, you'll never drown.

That what it's like to have the Demographic on your side. There's this outpouring of interest and friendship and love, and they respond to everything you do. There's a whole community there to help you. Anytime you want a friend, a friend is there. If you want information, someone will give it to you. If anyone offers you disrespect, you don't have to respond—the Demographic leads the charge on your behalf, and you can stay above the fight.

You just float there, in that warm salt water, with the sun

shining down, and you'll never drown as long as the Demographic is behind you.

Am I worried about losing that?

I'd be crazy not to.

"It's like any other kind of friendship," I tell Dr. Granger. "There's feedback there, too. But if friends respect each other, they won't tell each other what to do."

Doctor Granger gives a nod.

"You'd better hope they're your friends, then, hadn't you?"

I think of Kimmie and feel a knife of terror slice into me.

She stopped loving me. What happens if everyone else stops loving me, too?

I do some other work and then catch Kimmie's next flash, in which she goes shopping with a couple of her friends. She's wearing big hoop earrings and a wraparound spider-silk skirt, sandals, and a loose-fitting cotton tank with flowery embroidery.

Next, I think, she'll be wearing a headscarf.

She's still wearing the color threads in her hair, the ones that match the color shifts going on in her eyes. It's a subtle style, and not the sort of thing people would notice at once. I'd only spotted it because I viewed her flash more than once.

Once I viddied it, though, I recognized it as a statement as clear as a tattoo. Her flashes weren't just a kind of personal electronic diary she was sharing with whoever chose to view them; she had greater ambitions.

Picking such a subtle style meant that she hoped people would notice, only not right away. She was hoping that the whole hair-eyes thing would start small and snowball and become a craze, and that before a few weeks were out, hundreds of thousands and maybe millions of kids would have their hair and eyes in synch.

And after that, after she'd set a major trend, Kimmie was hoping those millions of kids would turn to her for the latest in style, that they would watch her breathlessly for clues as to what to wear, or what music to listen to, or who to be.

That was why I'd suggested that my viewers send Kimmie a note telling her they liked what she'd done with her eyes. It was my way of telling her, *Hey, Kimmie, you're busted.*

It was my way of saying that I know she's trying to be *me.*

I watch as Kimmie walks through shops and looks at clothes and laughs with her friends. She's bouncy and sort of flirting with the cameras.

I feel sick as I remember how she used to flirt with me. She never loved me, I think. She just wanted to be around someone who could teach her to be famous.

"Sanson would have liked this," she says, holding up a flirty top. Then she shrugged and put it back on the rack.

Her friends giggle. "That style's so over," she says.

Given up on subtlety, have you? I think.

Kimmie nods. "I saw Sanson's mother wearing something like this, once, except it was blue."

"Leave my mother out of it," I tell the video.

She touches her friend's arm. "Sanson and his mother are so cute together," she says. "They're really close. He takes her advice on everything."

I snarl and throw a pillow at the holographic image. Lasers burn Kimmie's image across the crumpled pillowcase.

If there's one thing the Demographic isn't going to want to hear, it's that I depend on the advice of a 140-year-old parent.

Kimmie has declared war. And I don't know how I'm going to fight back—as my dad said, I can't respond directly without giving her more credence than she deserves.

And besides, what am I going to say? That I hate my mother?

I don't need a bucket of hot coals. I need a cannon.

Next day we have the semifinals in our gorillaball league. We chose a field half a kilometer long, with a three-story municipal office building in the middle, plus a row of stores and two groves of pine trees. The six goals were in hard-to-reach places that would involve a lot of climbing.

The Samurai arrive with angry designs shaved into their fur, arrows and snakes and snarling animals—I wish I'd thought of that, actually. Shaved into each of their backs are the words WE LOVE KIMMIE.

They've got a lot of nerve, considering that they're only playing gorillaball in the first place because they're in *my* Demographic.

Before the game starts, the Samurai get in a circle and start chanting, *"Sanson is a sellout!"*

It goes on for what seems like hours while we stand around and can't think of any way to respond. Eventually Errol starts shouting *"Play or forfeit!"* and the rest of us pick up the chant, but it's far too late. Our fighting spirit has already drained into the dirt, and we look like a gang of lames to our worldwide audience.

The Samurai stomp us. They've practiced a lot, and they have some moves we haven't encountered, and they play rough. The final score is 16–5, a complete rout, and by the end we're dusty and bruised and angry. I'm limping because a couple of the Samurai body-checked me off a building and I didn't catch myself in time. We leave with the *Sanson is a sellout* chant echoing in our ears.

And I'm *still* stuck in the gorilla body till the league finals, which are next week.

I decide it's all Kimmie's fault.

There's a lot of silence in the pool area after the game. I shave an area of my calf and slap on an analgesic patch. Hardly anyone is watching anymore, so I ask everyone to turn off their cameras, and we groom each other listlessly.

When I ask Lisa into my office, I run all the detectors that are supposed to make certain that no one is eavesdropping. I don't want anyone to know what I'm planning.

"Kimmie's attacking me in her flashcasts," I say. "And I can't respond to what she's doing, because that would give her more credit than she deserves."

"Okay," Lisa says. "I can see that." She sits on one of the three-legged stools and rubs a bruised shoulder. "All you have to do is wait, though, because sooner or later she's going to make a mistake."

"No," I say. "I want to be able to respond—but I don't want anyone to know it's me."

She looks uneasy. "You want me to make a flashcast attacking her?"

"No," I say. "I don't want anyone in the pack to do it, because then it'll look like I'm just telling them what to say."

Lisa is relieved.

"I want to do it myself," I say.

She stares at me. Though our bodies are hulking gorilloids, our faces are a lot more human, so that there's room for brains behind the forehead and so that people can understand us when we talk, but that also means that we have a nearly full range of human expression. I look at Lisa and I know that she's looking at me with calculation.

"I want to create a false identity," I say. "I want to be somebody else when I start talking about Kimmie."

Lisa considers this. "What exactly do you want to do?"

"I want to create an artificial personality, one who makes flashcasts of his own. Maybe he could be based on Mars or somewhere even farther out." I grin at her. "Anatole says you're good at this kind of thing."

"Maybe I am," Lisa says, "but nothing I do is going to be foolproof."

"Lots of people make anonymous flashcasts."

Lisa looks dubious. "I don't think very many of them are as famous as you are."

"I won't do it for very long."

"All right," she says. She still seems doubtful. "If anyone really *wants* to find out, they will."

"Let's do it," I say.

"Let me look into a few things first," she says. "Before I start, I want to make sure I'm not going to make a mistake and wreck things."

I agree. I like the fact that she's being careful.

I start making plans for what I want to say.

"You've lost another fifteen percent of your audience," my dad says.

Tonight's meal is Italian. There's stuffed tomatoes, herring artichokes, squid salad, ravioli stuffed with pheasant, braised beef in the Genoese style, and a ricotta pie. And again it's all for the two of us because my mom's giving a talk in Peru.

"I know," I say.

"You're a trend spotter," he tells me. "What trends look good?"

"I've been looking around. But with everything else I'm doing . . ."

"How about the whole neo-barbarian thing?"

"No legs," I say, my mouth full of squid. I swallow. "Besides, after being a gorilla, I don't ever want to have to deal with fur coats ever again."

"You need to find some coincidence of fashion and culture—video or music." He waves a ravioli on his fork as he repeats his mantra. "No modern cultural phenomenon ever lasted unless there were great clothes that went with it."

"I know," I say.

"And a new dance style always helps."

"I know."

I know. I know more than he does. I'm the one who's a slave to the Demographic, not him.

So I start casting about for trends. I stay up nights listening to music from all points of the solar system, and looking at the flashcasts of obscure designers. For a while I think about getting a second pair of arms, like some of the asteroid miners, but then I realize how much I'm longing to inhabit a basic human body again.

I keep looking. Put *this* style with *this* music with *this* dance. I've done it before. How hard can it be?

It's hard. Especially because I hear in my head what the Demographic is going to say about it. *You want me to wear* those *heels?* Or, *These people are singing in* Albanian! Or, *Hell, I'd rather be a gorilla.*

But in the meantime we have to deal with the last gorillaball event, the Samurai versus the Night People, the other Bay Area team that survived the semifinals. I've viddied their games and I don't think they stand a chance.

I appear in person to award the league trophy, which is a huge, fierce gorilla head chomping with its fangs on a ball. Since I don't want to go alone, I bring the whole pack.

"Hey, a question," I say to the Samurai captain at the coin toss. "If you like Kimmie so much, how come you haven't gone blond?"

He doesn't have an answer for that but wins the toss anyway.

I watch with the pack as the Samurai begin one of their patented jackhammer attacks and commence their long afternoon's humiliation of the Night People. The score is 4–1 when I look at Deva and give her the nod.

She quietly leaves, and takes the league trophy with her, out of range of anyone's cameras.

After the Samurai finish, they find that the trophy has been replaced by a piece of paper pinned down by a large pinecone. The rest of us are in our vehicles. (I have a new but deliberately down-market Scion. I'm not legally allowed to drive it, but I can always program it for a destination and let the onboard navigator take over.)

"Hey!" the captain says. "Where's the trophy?"

"It's gone for a walk," I say, "but it left behind a clue as to its current location."

What I'd written on the paper was this:

There once were gorillas of note
But overly tempted to gloat.
They played ball without peer
Till a brave Mutineer
Carried them off on his boat.

HOW TO FIND THE LEAGUE TROPHY

- Scratch your heads in puzzlement until someone watching the flashcast sends you a message informing you that Errol's mother owns a boat called *Mutineer*.
- Troop down to the marina in Alameda, and then stand around like a bunch of apes until you finally notice that the boat is flying flag signals.
- Decode the flags and follow directions across the Bay to Sausalito.
- Spend the next several hours tramping back and forth across the Bay, knowing all the while that millions of people are watching your purgatory in realtime, and that Sanson and his pack are in their clubhouse rolling on the floor with laughter.
- Finally find the trophy in a pine tree on the field where the Samurai had beaten the Stars, and realize that the pinecone was a clue that you were too dense to get.
- Limp off into darkness and obscurity, knowing that millions of people are laughing at you, and will laugh for years to come.

After we stopped flashcasting, Lisa came over to me and said in a low voice, "You know that thing you asked me to do?"

"Yeah?"

"I've done it."

I take her into my office and she gives me the codes. "All you need to do is decide what your avatar is going to look like," she says.

"Magnetic," I answer.

That's how the Duck Monkey begins. A Martian, the Duck Monkey gazes down from the sky and looks at the cultural scene on Earth with mixed amusement and scorn.

The Duck Monkey examines all of Kimmie's flashcasts. He mocks her fashions and shows ridiculous people in history who have worn similar clothing. He points out similarities between her flashes and mine, and suggests that she's nothing but an imitator. He closely examines her ideas and expressions and provides links to the originators of those ideas and expressions. He makes fun of her friends. He points out that it's tacky to use information I gave her in private.

No one could survive such scrutiny with her dignity intact. Not Kimmie, not me, not anyone.

Nor does the Duck Monkey stop with Kimmie. I don't want him to be a one-note critic, or the electronic equivalent of an obsessed stalker. The Duck Monkey also hates the singer Alma Chen and the actor Ahmose. He likes the band Peninsular & Orient, and because I want him to be different from me, I have him like al-Amin even though I personally think he's pompous. The Duck Monkey likes classical music, to which I'm mostly indifferent, and praises a number of virtuosi. (I look up their reviews to make sure that what I'm saying is plausible to someone who actually knows that scene.)

Other than Kimmie, I never attack anyone who isn't big enough to take the hit. Ahmose has millions of fans—why should he care what the Duck Monkey thinks?

He does, though. He makes a few vicious remarks about the Duck Monkey in an interview and gives my Martian avatar instant credibility. The Duck Monkey's numbers jump.

A pro like Ahmose, you'd think he'd know better.

I really love being the Duck Monkey. I can say anything I want and not have to worry about the Demographic. I can be as sarcastic as I like, and if I love something, I can say so without having to worry about whether my opinion is sufficiently fashionable.

But in the meantime, I also have to be me. And that isn't nearly as much fun.

My new human body isn't beautiful. Beauty isn't interesting when anyone can be beautiful. People my age have grown up around physical beauty, and we instinctively distrust it. Besides, I've been beautiful in the past, and I don't like the way it makes people look at me.

What I want instead of beauty is *sincerity.* I want to blink my dewy eyes at the camera and have the Demographic believe everything that comes out of my mouth.

At first I plan on straw hair and blue eyes and then I realize everyone's going to think I'm imitating Kimmie. So my next body has olive skin and a sensitive mouth and soulful brown eyes, and that's the face I see in the mirror as soon as I climb out of the vat.

I look at myself carefully. Hey, *I'd* believe me.

I give the rest of the pack a few days to choose and settle into their new bodies, and then we have a Style Day. I'm always getting sent stuff—clothes, shoes, hats, accessories—by designers who hope I'll popularize it for them. There's quite a backlog after our two months as gorillas, so we unpack it all by the pool, and model things for each other. We flashcast it all live, and the Demographic send in their comments and instantly rate each item.

There's nothing very exciting. The designers seem to be going through a dull patch.

Wakaba makes a nice cream-colored shirt that fits me, with a standing collar that brushes my ears. It's got French cuffs, so I can use a pair of chunky lapis cuff links that I've had around for months. I find a thin black tie with a gold stripe, by Madagascar, and tie it around the standing collar with a simple four-in-hand knot. Then I find a navy blue silk jacket designed by Desi, with braided lapels and a single vent.

No need to bother with a mirror. I just check out the feed from the others' headsets.

I mostly like what I see. The style is kind of severe, but its very plainness invites the use of jewelry. And the look is mature. I remember that Dad wants me to find an older look.

"You look like a schoolboy from Bombay," Anatole says, which deflates me a little.

"Wait a minute," said Lisa. "I know what he needs."

Lisa has acquired the body of a Taiwanese basketball player, tall and rangy, with almond eyes and long black hair. She walks to one of the white metal poolside tables, rummages around the packages for a moment, then returns with a pair of sunglasses. I can feel the warmth of her breath on my cheek as she perches the shades on my nose.

"Ooh, nice," says Deva. I check her video feed. The shades are gold-rimmed wraparounds with deep jade-green lenses, and they've got camera pickups for flashcasting. Wearing them I viddie like a cross between the Bombay schoolboy and a dapper young gangster.

"Now you look like a vicious lawyer," Lisa says. I sneak a look at the online poll and 70 percent of the Demographic approve the look, with a furious 25 percent hating it. And even the 25 percent *care.*

"I like this look," I say. "We should become the Pack of Vicious Lawyers."

I sense a certain resistance in a few of the pack members, but after all I'm the star—so we all adopt the style, or something similar, and for the next several days the Pack of Vicious Lawyers crosses the Bay Bridge to a series of clubs in San Francisco. (As a loyal citizen of the East Bay, I refuse to call it "the City" like the natives do.) We invade clubs en masse, listen to bands like Sylvan Slide and the Birth of China, and are invited into the VIP rooms by management eager for the free publicity. I meet and chat with famous people like the artist Saionji—who invites us all to his opening—and the producer Jane Chapman, who asks the name of my agent.

Considering that none of us can even drink legally, this isn't bad at all.

I regain a third of the audience lost during the gorilla fiasco, but then the numbers begin to slide again. People have seen me go to clubs before.

I know the Pack of Vicious Lawyers is only a transitional phase. It's too mature a style for all the Demographic—a fourteen-year-old couldn't pull off the Vicious Lawyer look. And there's nothing in the package but clothing and style—the Vicious Lawyers don't *do* anything; they just stand around in groups and look intimidating. I hope it will last till I can find the new style that will bring the Demographic screaming back into my camp.

I start to sweat. I want all the love back. I'm knocking myself out looking for the next trend—and of course I'm going to college and being the Duck Monkey as well. Time is running out, and so, for that matter, is my audience.

And then I think I find it. The music is from Turkmenistan, coincidentally where my mother gave a lecture series a few years ago, and is called Mukam. It's descended from a traditional form that goes back for centuries, but everyone in Southwest Asia has been trading licks and musical styles for ages now, so in addition to using the flute and the two-string lute native to the area, the Turkmen imported the double-ended *dhol* drum from the Punjab along with modern electric instruments and insanely rigorous vocal styles from places like Tuva and Mongolia. The musical forms are incredibly complex, but the *dhol* drives the music forward and makes it compulsively danceable, at least if you can dance to 5/4 time or the even more complex polyrhythms native to the area.

And the clothing from the region is terrific. Baggy tops and drawers, riding boots of leather or felt, and long fur-trimmed lambskin coats. Some of the coats have lace and trim and frogging that would do credit to a nineteenth-century drum major, and others are ornamented with wild, colorful felt applique.

The only element I don't care for is the huge fur hats the size of beachballs, which make people look like giant dandelions. I reckon we can do without the headwear.

The Turkmen style had everything. Music, movement, fashion. It had all that was needed for it to become a major trend, everything except exposure.

Exposure I could provide.

I call a meeting of the pack and specify that no cameras are to be worn. I draw the blinds on the clubhouse and play the music and show videos of the clothing.

"That's great," Anatole says. "But how are we supposed to dance to any of this?"

"People have been dancing to this music for hundreds of years," I point out.

Errol just gives me a blank stare. *"How?"*

I don't have an answer for that one. "Let's look at the videos again," I suggest.

The videos don't help— they're all of professional dancers who are infinitely more skilled than we are. They even look good in those huge fur hats.

Lisa approaches me later, after we break up in confusion. She is still very shy and doesn't like talking in front of the whole pack, but I guess she's comfortable with just me.

It's those trustworthy brown eyes, I decide.

"We could do research on the dancing," she says.

"Yes," I say. "But we don't want to do old stuff."

"It doesn't have to be new," she says. "It just has to be *new to your audience*."

I look at her for a moment. "You're right."

Lisa goes into the computer archives and digs up information about the sort of dances they were doing in Central Asia clubs about forty years ago. I find old instructional videos. Most of us aren't very good at it, but Lisa turned out to be a natural.

I'm the star and I get to pick my partners, so I dance with Lisa for most of the afternoon and get her to tutor me. I ask her why she's so good at it.

"It's just a matter of counting. For most dances, all you have to do is count to four. For the waltz, you count to three. And for this . . . well, the left side of your brain counts to eight while the right side counts to five."

"Right."

But everybody's smart these days, and after a few more afternoons of practice, I get so I'm good at counting exactly that way.

Autumn comes on, wet and chill. My mother leaves for Mars, where she'll teach for a semester, leaving me with Dad and tons of fresh-cooked gourmet food, which, no longer being a gorilla, I cannot eat nearly fast enough.

We all get good at dancing like Turkmen. Clothing appears at the clubhouse. We listen to hours of music and pick our favorites for our debut, which we decide is going to be at the Cryptic Club down in the Castro—the management is happy to comp us for a night and play our music in exchange for all the free publicity.

I don't let anyone take video of any of our practice sessions. Not only because we don't all look particularly expert, but because I don't want any pictures getting out into the world. Nobody's going to know about the Turkmen style till I spring it on the world Saturday night.

We make appointments to get hair extensions. I've decided that long, wild hair is going to be part of the look.

I'm on top of the world. I'm having enormous fun being the Duck Monkey. Kimmie's audience has stabilized at about a quarter the size of mine and isn't getting any larger. I know that I'm about to popularize a style that will sweep the world and bring the Demographic back.

And I'm seeing a lot of Lisa. She isn't part of the pack because she wants to be around me or to be famous, but because her cousin Anatole had talked her into it. That makes her different from the others. Lisa has friends outside the pack who she spends time with. She has a mind that analyzes and categorizes everything that goes on around her, including me. Sometimes I think she looks on me as just another artifact to be studied.

But sometimes when she looks at me it isn't analytical. I'm not analyzing her, either. I like the way she dances, the way she feels in my arms, her scent. Sometimes I want to lean over and kiss her, just to see what might happen.

I begin to think about that. I don't hurt so much anymore when I think about Kimmie. I think maybe Lisa's a part of that.

But Lisa and I are doomed. The Demographic would hate her—she isn't their style at all. They want me to go with strong, outgoing personalities who also happen to be really beautiful. If I start seeing Lisa, my numbers would start to slide.

And she'd get a ton of hate mail. I don't know whether she could cope with that. So for all sorts of reasons I don't kiss her.

But still I enjoy thinking about it.

The catastrophe happens on a Friday evening, the night before we're due to premiere our new style at the Cryptic. Tonight the pack is at Errol's place up in Berkeley, looking at music videos the Demographic sent us. We listen and watch and give our verdicts, and the Demographic watches us and responds to what we're saying.

We're watching Fidel Nuñez lament the state of his *corazon* when I get a message on my headset from Deva. *Check Kimmie's new flash. Don't say anything.*

I look at Kimmie's flash through the splice on my optic nerve, and I feel like someone's just slammed me in the head with a crowbar.

Kimmie and her pack—there are only seven of them—are flashing live from a club I recognize, Toad Hall on Treasure Island, and they're wearing long fur-trimmed Turkmen coats and baggy pants and tall riding boots. They carry horse whips, and they're dancing to Mukam using the same steps that we've planned to use. They have a different playlist than the one we've built, but it has a lot of the same songs.

I sit in Errol's media room and watch my whole next phase crumble into dust. If I show up tomorrow night at the Cryptic, everyone will think I'm imitating Kimmie. I can't even prove the idea originated with me because I'd been so strict about not recording anything.

My head swims and I feel as if I'm going to faint. Then I realize that for some time I'd completely forgot to breathe. I take in some air, but it doesn't make me feel any better.

Fidel Nuñez finishes his song. There's silence, and I realize that the rest of the pack have been watching Kimmie's flash, too.

"What do we think?" Errol asks. His tone is anxious.

There's more silence.

"I think it's *boring*," I say. I stand up and I reel because I'm still light-headed. "I think we need to get *moving*."

There is a certain amount of halfhearted approval, but mostly I think the pack are as stunned as I am.

I look at the pack and wonder which one of them told Kimmie about the Turkmen style.

One of my friends has betrayed me.

"Spending a Friday night looking at videos?" I ask. "How pathetic is *that*?"

"Yeah!" Anatole says. "Let's get out of here!"

We go outside and the cool night air sings through my veins. There's a heavy dew on the grass and mist drifting amid the trees. I turn back and see Errol's house, with its red tile roof curving up at the corners like a Chinese temple, and the trellises carrying twining roses and ivy up the sides of the house, and the tall elm trees in the front and back.

"You know," I say, "this place would be great for gorillaball."

Errol looks at the house. "I'm glad you didn't say that back when—"

"Let's play now!"

Errol turns to me. "But we're not—we're—"

"I *know* we're not gorillas," I say. "But that's no reason we can't play gorillaball. Let's have the first gorillaball game without gorillas!"

Errol's horrified, but I insist. Errol's parents, who actually own the house, aren't home tonight, so they can't say no. I captain one team, and Errol captains the other. We choose up sides, all except for Amy and Lisa.

"I'm not playing," Lisa says. "This is just crazy."

Amy agrees.

"You can referee, then," I say.

We set up one ladder in the front and another out back. We put one goal in a tree in the front, another in a tree in the back. I win the toss and elect to receive.

The ball comes soaring over the house and Sanjay catches it. He goes for the ladder and I lunge for a trellis. Errol and his team are scrambling up the other side.

Sanjay reaches the roof, but already two of Errol's teammates are on him. He passes the ball to me and I charge. I knock Michiko sprawling onto the roof tiles and then I hit Shawn hard under the breastbone, and he grabs me to keep from falling. So now we both fall, sliding down the tiles that are slippery with dew. As Shawn goes off the roof he makes a grab at the gutter, something he could have done easily as an ape, but he misses. I get the gutter myself and swing into a rosebush just as I hear Shawn's femur snap.

Thorns tear at my skin and my clothes. I drag myself free and run for the elm tree that overhangs the street. I grab the goalkeeper's foot and yank him out of the tree, then climb up myself and slam the ball into the bucket we've put in a crotch of the tree.

"Goal!" I yell.

The others are clustered around Shawn. I'm limping slightly as I join them. Blood thunders in my veins. *Which one of you ratted us out to Kimmie?* I think.

Errol turns to me.

"Shawn's smashed his leg up bad. Game's over."

"No," I say. "You're down one player, so we'll give up one to keep it fair." I turn to Sanjay. "You can take Shawn to the hospital. The rest of us can keep playing."

Lisa looks at me. "I'm going, too. This is insane."

I look at her in surprise. It's practically the first thing she's said in public.

"Go if you want," I say. "The rest of us are playing gorillaball."

And that's what the rest of us do. No more bones are broken, but that's only because we're lucky. By the end of the night I'm bruised and cut and bleeding, with sprained fingers and a swollen knee. The others look equally bad. I've scored seven points.

The trick, I decide, is not to care. If you don't care who you hit and who you walk over, you can score a lot of points in this world. You could be like Kimmie.

We should have fought the Samurai *tonight*, I think. We'd have crushed them.

The ratings are great. Many more people watch us live than

watch Kimmie. And when I edit the raw flash into a coherent, ninety-minute experience the next day, the number of downloads is as good as anything I've done.

Gorillaball leagues start forming again, only without the gorillas. People are inspired by the madness of it.

I'm back on top.

But only for a short ride. I have to cancel the Cryptic appearance, and after the gorillaball blip, my numbers resume their slide. And word gets out about Kimmie's new style, so her numbers start to soar.

She's riding the trend that should have been mine.

We trade in the Vicious Lawyer look for Byronics. It's one of the styles I'd considered, then rejected in favor of the Turkmen look. Byronics is all velvet suits and lace and hose with clocks and beads and braid and rickrack. It's the sort of thing that the part of the Demographic who enjoyed being gorillas would hate.

The true weakness, though, is that Byronic music is boring. They're supposed to be sensitive poets, but all they really do is whine. *I'm young in an old world.*

Yeah, tell us something new.

My numbers continue to sicken. I try not to think about the fact that I'm losing thousands of friends every day. I try not to want their love, but I do.

The crowning insult comes when Dr. Granger gives me a B in my Media and Society class. He decided that my understanding of the media scene was "insufficiently informed."

I complain and flash the complaint. It gets me a lot of sympathetic messages, and a notice from Dr. Granger that he's decided, after all, to fail me.

The swine. It's a piece of petty malice beyond anything even the Duck Monkey has ever done.

He must have read what the Demographic was saying about him.

I have nothing to lose. I make another flashcast, this time telling the world what a pathetic old geezer Granger is, sucking up to me as long as he thought he could vamp a piece of my fame. For a moment, my downloads blip upward again, then start to slide.

It's then that the management of the Samaritain decides to repossess our clubhouse. I'm passé, and they don't want anyone connecting their expensive hotel with passé.

I'm told that they've decided to repaint and redecorate the suite, and that we should get our stuff out.

"So you're getting rid of the furniture and the carpet and everything?" I ask.

They assure me that this is the case.

I call a pack meeting—the pack is down to eleven now—and we rendezvous at the Samaritain for one last live flashparty. The hypocrisy and opportunism of the Samaritain's management have got me in a rage. I show up with buckets of paint and brushes and knives and crowbars.

"Since the Samaritain's going to redecorate," I announce, "I think we should help them. They don't want any of this stuff anymore."

Most of the paint ends up on the walls, though a lot gets ground into the plush carpet. We smash the furniture and cut up the pillows. Foam padding falls like snow. We rip out paneling with crowbars. We tip the couch in the pool, and then skim the paintings onto the water. We're in our Byronic finery as we do this, and all our clothes are ruined.

We leave the Samaritain singing and head to my place.

After the cameras are turned off, we groom each other as if we were still gorillas. I sit at the foot of my bed as Lisa sits behind me and tries to comb the paint out of my hair.

I check the ratings and announce that they're stellar. Anatole gives a little cheer.

"They're only watching to see you fall apart," Lisa says.

I give her an annoyed look over my shoulder. *What's wrong with that?* I want to say.

If the audience wants me to fall apart, I'll fall apart. If they want me to cut off my hand, I'll cut it off and flashcast the bleeding stump.

Anything to get the love back.

"Maybe you should decompress," she says. "Just be a regular boy for a while."

"Don't know how," I say. Which happens to be true.

"You could learn."

"Who wants to be normal anyway?" Anatole asks. I agree, and that torpedoes the subject.

We talk about other things for a while, and then Lisa bends over me and murmurs in my ear. "You know that project we're working on? Some people are getting very interested in it. I've been able to hold them off by routing everything through the moons of Saturn, but it's not going to last."

"Okay," I say.

"You've got to stop it," she says.

Errol is looking at us strangely. Maybe Lisa whispering in my ear made him think we might be an item.

"Soon," I promise.

But I'm lying. The Duck Monkey is my only consolation. By now he's become the whole dark Mr. Hyde of me. The Duck Monkey doesn't have to worry about the Demographic or my pack or anyone. He can just be himself. He eviscerates everything he looks at, Kimmie in particular. There's a whole subculture now who view Kimmie's flashcasts, then check the Duck Monkey to see what he says about her.

The pack descends on the opening of Saionji, the artist who'd foolishly invited us to his opening. We're in our wrecked Byronic outfits, shabby and torn and splattered with paint, a complete contrast to Saionji's art, which is delicate and fluttery and imbued with chiming musical tones. Saionji is polite but a little distant, knowing he's being upstaged. But I have some intelligent things to say about his pieces—I've done research—and he warms up.

Over the buffet I meet Dolores Swan. She's petite and coffee-skinned and wears a short skirt and a metallic halter. She's got deep shadows in the hollows of her collarbones, which oddly enough I find the most attractive thing about her. I'm vaguely aware of her as a model/actress/flashcaster/whatever, and even more vaguely know that she was last employed as the host of a chat show that lasted maybe five weeks. We make polite sounds at each other, and then I'm off with the pack to ruin the tone of a long series of clubs.

It's a week later that Jill Lee dies playing gorillaball in a human body. Even though they return her to life from a backup, there's a big media flap about whether I'm a good example for youth. I point out in interviews that I never told Jill Lee or anybody else to play gorillaball without a gorilla body. I point out that she was dead for what, sixteen hours? Not a tragedy on the order of the *Titanic.*

The consensus of the media chatheads is that I'm not repentant enough.

That wrangle hasn't even died away when the Duck Monkey is unmasked—by that cheeseball Ahmose, of all people, who paid a group of electronic detectives to dig out my identity. Ahmose is *shocked* that a celebrity with such a wholesome image would say such bad things about him. Kimmie tells the world she's so terribly, terribly hurt, and she cries in front of her worldwide audience and scores about a million sympathy points. I'm besieged by more interviewers. I answer through the Duck Monkey.

While I am flattered that some people claim that I am Sanson, I am in fact a completely separate person, one that just happens to live in Sanson's head.

The chatheads agree that I'm insufficiently apologetic. My ratings jump for the sky, however, when the Duck Monkey takes a scalpel to Kimmie's interview with the Mad Jumpers, the number one band from Turkmenistan. I mean, when you're doing an interview, you're supposed to talk about something other than *yourself*.

The Duck Monkey thing is at its height when Dolores Swan drives up in her vintage red Hunhao convertible, the one with the license plate that reads TRY ME, and invites me to elbow my way through the mass of flashcasters and personality journalists camped out in front of my house and drive away to her bungalow in Marin.

Next morning, I've got a new girlfriend who's forty years older than me.

THINGS TO DO WHEN YOU'RE CRACKING UP

- Fly to Palau for a romantic honeymoon with your girlfriend.
- Have a drunken fight the first night so she runs off to Manila with a sports fisherman named Sandy.

- Throw up in the lobby fountain.
- Console yourself with a French tourist called Françoise, who looks fifteen but who turns out to be older than your mother.
- Have Dolores catch you and Françoise in the bed that she (Dolores) is paying for, so there's a huge scene.
- Make up with Dolores and announce to the world you're inseparable.
- Throw up in the swimming pool.
- Record everything and broadcast live to your world-wide audience of millions.
- Repeat, with variations.
- Repeat.
- Repeat.
- Repeat.
- Repeat.

The ratings are *great.*

By the time I make it back to the East Bay, there is no longer any debate about whether I'm a bad influence on youth.

A consensus on that issue has pretty much been reached.

The thing with Dolores is over. She gets enough of a bounce off our relationship to get a new job with the Fame Network as an interviewer and fashion reporter. When I last see her she is on her way to Mali.

After the suborbital lands in the Bay and taxis to shore, I walk to the terminal through a corridor lined with posters for KimmieWear. Her clothing line, now available worldwide. Even *I* never managed that.

I wonder if Kimmie has ripped out all the parts of me that had talent and taken them all for herself.

My dad takes me in and makes three pizzas. He doesn't reproach me for running off because, face it, my ratings are as good as they ever were. He talks about his new viral marketing campaign, which sounds just like the last forty years of his viral marketing campaigns.

I've got a whole new Demographic now. Hardly any of my old audience watches me anymore.

The new viewers are older. My dad wanted me to find a more mature audience, but I'm not sure he had in mind my present assembly of celebrity junkies, scandal watchers, sadists, and comedians. The latter, by the way, have been mining my life for their routines.

Q: What's the good news about Dolores breaking up with Sanson?

A: She'll never accuse him of stealing the best years of her life.

Q: What's another good thing?

A: She'll never complain he was using her. She was using him.

Oh yeah, that's funny all right.

Dad offers ideas for growing my Demographic, like I need another legion of perverts in my life.

I get a good night's sleep. My current wardrobe of tropical wear is unsuitable for a Bay Area spring, and I can't stand the sight of any of my old clothes, so I go shopping for replacements. I buy the most anonymous-looking stuff available. Everywhere I go, there are holograms of Kimmie laughing and pirouetting in her Turkmen coats.

I remember that laugh, that pirouette, from the Style Days our pack used to have.

The day wears on. I'm bored. I call the members of the pack. It's been three months since I flew off with Dolores, and they've all drifted away. They're all in school, for one thing—the spring semester that I blew off.

I wonder whether, if I called a meeting, anyone would show up.

I leave messages with people who would once have taken my call no matter what they were doing. I talk briefly to Errol and Jeet, who promise to get together later. I call Lisa and am surprised when she answers.

"What are you doing?" I ask. "Want to come over?"

She hesitates. "I'm doing a project." I'm about to apologize for bothering her when she says, "Can you come here?"

I program my Scion for Lisa's address. As I drive over, I think about how Lisa's the only person I knew who didn't want something from me—attention, a piece of my fame, an audience, a boost in their ratings. Even my dad seems to want me around only to test his marketing theories.

I think about how she had danced so expertly in my arms. I think about how I hadn't kissed her because I'd thought the Demographic wouldn't approve.

I don't care what the current Demographic thinks at all. They're all creeps.

Lisa's sharing an apartment in Berkeley with a girlfriend, and when I come in she's sitting cross-legged in the front room, with different video capes around her, all showing different flow charts and graphs and strange, intricate foreign script.

"What's up?" I ask.

"Fifteenth-century Persian manuscripts. I'm trying to work back from illumination styles to a vision of manuscript workshops."

"Ah."

I find a part of the floor that isn't being used yet, and sit.

"So," I say, "you were right."

"About what?" Lisa's frowning at one of her flow charts.

"About my audience watching only to see me fall apart."

She looks up. "I probably should have phrased that more tactfully."

I shrug. "I think you voiced the essence of the situation. You should see the kind of messages I get now."

Once I felt this whole swell of love from my audience. Now it's sarcasm and brutality. Invitations to drunken parties, offers of sex or drugs, suggestions for ways I could injure myself.

"The thing is," she says, "it's a feedback loop you've got going with your audience. They reinforce everything you do."

Positive feedback loops, I remember from my classes, are how addictive drugs work.

"You think I'll succeed in kicking the habit?" I ask.

Lisa's expression is serious. "Do you really want to become a real boy?"

I think about it.

"No," I say. "I don't. But I can't think of anything else to do. Where can I go in flashcasting once I've mastered the art of being a laughingstock?"

She doesn't have an answer for that, and goes back to her work. There is a long silence.

"Can I kiss you?" I ask.

"No," she says, without looking up.

"Does that mean No, or does that mean Not Yet?"

She looks up and frowns. "I'm not sure."

"Tell me about your work," I say.

So I learn all about the hermeneutics of Persian manuscripts. It's interesting, and I love the intricate, complex Arabic calligraphy, whole words and phrases worked into a single labyrinthine design. There are charming little illustrations, too, of people hunting or fighting or being in love with each other.

Lisa offers me a glass of tea. We talk about other subjects till it's time for me to go.

I think about those Persian designs all the way home. I think about how you could base a whole style on it. I can see the clothes in my head. I wonder what kind of music would go with it.

When I get home, I hear my dad in his office talking to some of his colleagues. I go into my room and watch other people's flashcasts. They're all inane.

The Duck Monkey could rip them to shreds, but they don't seem worth the bother.

It's a strange thing, but the Duck Monkey's ratings have held steady, fed by a stream of celebrity gossip from Dolores and her friends. The Duck Monkey has a completely different demographic from my own audience. They're smarter and funnier, and they're not trying to get me to kill myself in some horribly public way.

It's like the Duck Monkey is some kind of viral marketing campaign for something else. A new Sanson, perhaps, one who comes swinging back into the world with a style based on Persian manuscripts.

Or maybe the Sanson who's a real boy.

I lie on my bed and think about Lisa and the Duck Monkey and

Arab calligraphy. I wonder if I can live without the love of all those people who made up my Demographic for all those years.

I decide I'll try to get the love of just one person, and if necessary go on from there.

I send a message to Lisa to tell her I'd like to see her again.

ALTER JON WILLIAMS was born in 1953 in Minnesota. He tended the University of New Mexico and received his bachelor of arts in 1975. He lives in rural New Mexico.

Williams first started writing in the early 1980s, publishing a series of naval adventures under the name Jon Williams. His first science fiction novel, *Ambassador of Progress*, appeared in 1984 and was followed by fifteen more, most notably *Hardwired*, *Aristoi*, *Metropolitan* and sequel *City on Fire*, and his Praxis trilogy. Upcoming is a new novel, *Implied Spaces*.

A prolific short story writer, Williams published his first story, "Side Effects," in 1985, and it was followed by a string of stories that were nominated for major awards, including "Dinosaurs," "Surfacing," "Wall, Stone, Craft," "Lethe," and Nebula Award winner "Daddy's World." A number of these are collected in *Facets*.

His Web site is www.walterjonwilliams.net.

AUTHOR'S NOTE

For me, stories hardly ever spring out of the blue. They accumulate, layer by layer, like sediment stored up by the sea, until such time as I have enough material to create a whole story.

"Pinocchio" began some years ago, when I saw a television documentary on former child stars, all of whom would seemingly have gnawed off their right arms if only it would have made them celebrities again. It was saddening, and a little bit sickening, to see forty-year-old mature men talking with such hunger and desperation about their glory days, when they were thirteen.

This set off a train of thought about celebrity in general. It seems to me that celebrity rewards you for all the wrong things—not for being a good person, but for playing a good person on television. Celebrity makes no moral distinctions, and sees no difference between saving the lives of African children or smashing someone over the head with a telephone—both are of equal use for a couple minutes worth of exposure on *Entertainment Tonight.*

I combined these thoughts with ideas about the instantaneous feedback that is such a part of twenty-first-century media, and rather slowly produced this story of a boy who became famous because he was unstudied and natural, and who fell from public grace when he began to understand too well the machine that was driving his fame.

ACKNOWLEDGMENTS

Editing an anthology can either be a lonely solo effort, or it can take a community. The community that made *The Starry Rift* possible was large and varied, and I'd like to thank them all. First, and foremost, my three partners in crime, Charles N. Brown, Jack Dann, and Justin Ackroyd. During the nearly two-year-long gestation of this book, they were always there, always willing to help when it was needed most. Next would come Russell B. Farr, who stepped in toward the end and helped bring the ship home, and Ellen Datlow, who was always ready and willing to help whenever it was needed. To that number I'd add each and every one of the contributors to the book, each of whom labored mightily, produced wonderful work, and often were patient beyond any reasonable measure. I'm incredibly grateful to all of them. I'd also very much like to thank Ken Macleod for his understanding; Kelly Link for persisting; and Gavin Grant, Garth Nix, Robin Pen, Gordon Van Gelder, Terry Dowling, and everyone else I discussed *The Starry Rift* with as I reached the finish line.

There are four other people who deserve special thanks here. My editor, the incredible Sharyn November, has been a joy and a delight to work with at every stage—supportive, understanding, and completely committed to this project; *The Starry Rift* wouldn't exist without her. I'd also, as always, like to thank my partner, Marianne, and my two girls, Jessica and Sophie. They understood when I had to not be around every now and then to get things finished, and made every single other day a joy and a delight. Thank you.

which have been published in Australia and the United States. These include various "year's best" annuals, *The "Locus" Awards* (with Charles N. Brown), and *The New Space Opera* (with Gardner Dozois). As a book editor, he has also edited *The Jack Vance Treasury* and *Ascendancies: The Best of Bruce Sterling*. In 1999 Jonathan founded The Coode Street Press, which published the one-shot review zine *The Coode Street Review of Science Fiction* and copublished Terry Dowling's *Antique Futures*. The Coode Street Press is currently inactive.

Jonathan married former *Locus* Managing Editor Marianne Jablon in 1999, and they live in Perth, Western Australia, with their two daughters, Jessica and Sophie.

ABOUT THE EDITOR

JONATHAN STRAHAN is an editor, anthologist, and critic. He was born in Belfast, Northern Ireland, in 1964, and moved to Perth, Western Australia, in 1968. He graduated from the University of Western Australia with a bachelor of arts in 1986. In 1990 he cofounded a small press journal, *Eidolon,* and worked on it as coeditor and copublisher until 1999. He was also copublisher of Eidolon Books.

In 1997 Jonathan started work for *Locus: The Newspaper of the Science Fiction Field* as an assistant editor. He wrote a regular reviewer column for the magazine until March 1998 and has been the magazine's Reviews Editor since January 2002. His reviews and criticism have also appeared in *Eidolon*, *Eidolon: SF Online*, *Ticonderoga Online*, and *Foundation*. Jonathan has won the William J. Atheling Jr. Award for Criticism and Review and the Australian National Science Fiction Ditmar Award.

As a freelance editor, Jonathan has edited or coedited more than a dozen reprint anthologies and three original anthologies,